A NOVEL

NEW YORK TIMES BESTSELLING AUTHOR
KARINA HALLE

First edition published by
Metal Blonde Books April 2017

ISBN-13: 978-1545101964
ISBN-10: 1545101965

Publisher's Note: This is a work of fiction. Names, characters, places, and incidents either are the product of the author's imagination or are used fictitiously. Any resemblance to actual events, locales, or persons, living or dead, is entirely coincidental.

Copyright © 2017 by Karina Halle
Paperback Edition

All rights reserved, including the right to reproduce this book or portions thereof in any form whatsoever.

Cover design by Hang Le Designs
Edited by Laura Helseth
Formatting by Champagne Formats

Metal Blonde Books
P.O. Box 845
Point Roberts, WA
98281 USA

Manufactured in the USA

For more information about the series and author visit:
www.authorkarinahalle.com

Also by Karina Halle

The Experiment in Terror Series

Darkhouse (EIT #1)
Red Fox (EIT #2)
The Benson (EIT #2.5)
Dead Sky Morning (EIT #3)
Lying Season (EIT #4)
On Demon Wings (EIT #5)
Old Blood (EIT #5.5)
The Dex-Files (EIT #5.7)
Into the Hollow (EIT #6)
And With Madness Comes the Light (EIT #6.5)
Come Alive (EIT #7)
Ashes to Ashes (EIT #8)
Dust to Dust (EIT #9)

Novels by Karina Halle

The Devil's Duology
Sins and Needles (The Artists Trilogy #1)
On Every Street (An Artists Trilogy Novella #0.5)
Shooting Scars (The Artists Trilogy #2)
Bold Tricks (The Artists Trilogy #3)

Donners of the Dead

Dirty Angels

Dirty Deeds

Dirty Promises

Love, in English

Love, in Spanish

Where Sea Meets Sky (from Atria Books)

Racing the Sun (from Atria Books)

The Pact

The Offer

The Play

Winter Wishes

The Lie

The Debt

Smut

Veiled

Heat Wave

Black Hearts

Dirty Souls

Before I Ever Met You

For Scott – You're the truest gentleman I know.
I'm all in, baby

PROLOGUE

Will
Two years ago

"You know, I hate to be optimistic about things, but I really think thirty-nine might just be my best year ever," I call out to Sasha after I spit the toothpaste into the sink. "I know I say that every year, it's just that every year keeps getting sweeter."

I expect to hear some sort of murmur from the bedroom, usually in a tone of voice that indicates she's rolling her eyes. But there's silence.

I try and ignore it, watching the water roll down the drain of the shiny black sink, but she's been strange all day. Usually my wife goes all out on my birthdays, starting with breakfast in bed, followed by a blowjob, followed by brunch out with mutual friends, and then topped off with dinner at one of LA's hotspots.

But while the water drains, my mind goes with it. I have to remind myself that it's been a few years now since I've had a birthday like that. Not that I'm one to ever make a big deal about it, it's just that Sasha always had. For the last year of my thirties, I guess I expected something.

And today, well we did go out for brunch with Ted, who happened to be in town, and Jeremy and Megan. And we did just come back from dinner at Mr. Chow, only it wasn't the intimate dinner I'd assumed. I appreciated my friends being there, but what I really wanted was some alone time with Sasha to try and get our marriage back on track.

But on the Uber ride back to our rancher house in the hills of Los Feliz, she barely said two words to me. Just reconfirmed our address with the driver and then the two of us sat side-by-side in silence, like strangers, in the back of a Honda Civic with half-filled bottled water and a few packets of gum.

It was strange, to feel so utterly disconnected from someone you've spent the last fifteen years with. The darkness of the car combined with the lights on Santa Monica Blvd created a distorting effect, amplifying the distance between us.

And now that distance is still here. It's in the house with us, growing thicker, bigger, by the second. She keeps feeding it.

I sigh, staring at myself in the bathroom mirror. A few grey hairs at my temple. Probably some more at the back of my head. Otherwise my hair is looking pretty good, dark, almost black, thick and not going anywhere, at least for the time being.

I run my hand over my jaw, wiping away any last vestiges of toothpaste, flex my arms and abs, making sure the body I work so hard for is still behaving. I don't look any older, save for a few lines by my eyes brought on by the California sunshine and my ever-present tan. I don't feel any older, either. And yet there's something inside of me that feels weathered and aged, cracking at the edges. Whatever it is feels irreparable, and has been for a long time.

It's getting harder to ignore, just like the distance between us.

And yet, every year we go on, because facing the truth can be the hardest thing to do.

"Sasha?" I call out.

Nothing.

A touch of fear prickles the back of my neck.

I step out into the bedroom. The lights are all off.

And there is Sasha, standing out on the terrace, staring at the lights of the city below, the curtains billowing behind her in a rare breeze.

"Hey," I say as I step out beside her, the tiles feeling cool against my feet. There's a strange clarity to the air that's a bit off-putting. I swear I smell the ocean instead of exhaust and smog. It's like the city has disappeared for a moment.

"What are you doing?" I ask her, leaning on the railing, turning my head to face her.

She's staring straight ahead, her nightgown shimmering against her dark skin. I want to reach out and push her hair behind her ears, the color now muted in the dim light, but I don't. It doesn't feel right.

Nothing about this feels right.

Is this what our marriage has become? When touching each other feels like an effort? When birthdays are no longer celebrated? When the most we talk is during the day, when we're working together at the office?

It wasn't what I signed up for fifteen years ago.

But whoever imagines things will end up like this?

The skin beneath her eyes shines with dampness. Oh

shit. She's been crying. Sasha doesn't cry, ever.

My heart immediately hardens with fear.

"Hey," I say softly to her. "Are you okay? What's wrong?"

She wipes at her cheeks and mutters a swear word to herself before facing me. She doesn't say anything for a moment, just rubs her lips together. I find myself staring into the eyes of the girl that I married, back when we were young and stupid in love. But it was wonderful, being that dumb in love. It was the kind of dumb where you took all the chances, made all the risks, just to share your heart with someone else.

And then something lifts from her eyes and that girl is gone. She's back to being a stranger again.

"Will," she says. Her voice is so low it's barely audible. "I didn't want to tell you on your birthday . . ."

Oh god. Oh my god. She's dying. She's sick, there's something wrong with her.

It takes everything in me to try and keep my breath steady. My hands grip the railing. "What?"

She sucks in a sharp breath.

"I'm pregnant," she says through a burst of air.

I stare at her blankly. The words do not compute.

"I don't . . . what?"

She nods slowly, her eyes flashing with something I can't read.

I'm just confused. It doesn't make any sense. At all.

"How could you be pregnant?" I ask her. "The doctors said, well, the chances of that happening are one in a thousand."

I'm not sure how I'm feeling right now, I might be teetering on the point of elation. I got my vasectomy four years ago because Sasha didn't want children, and to be honest, I didn't either. But now, I feel like that ground that we laid those plans on is starting to shift and shake. If I'm a father . . .

"Will," she says forcefully, bringing my attention back to her, and now I recognize what's in her eyes.

Pity.

Guilt.

Guilt.

Oh fuck.

I am a stupid, stupid man.

I can't speak. I can only stare at her, her shadowed guilty face and the city of angels behind her.

"I'm so sorry," she says quietly. "I didn't plan on this happening."

I open my mouth. Close my mouth. Anger builds from somewhere dormant inside me, creeping into my hands until I can't grip the railing any tighter.

"I didn't want to hurt you. I was going to tell you, I swear. It just . . ."

"Who is he?" I manage to say, my voice laced with razors.

"You don't know him."

"*Who is he?*"

"Will, please, it doesn't matter."

"Like fuck it doesn't matter!" I erupt. "Tell me who he is, the father of your child! Tell me, so I can beat the ever living shit out of him!"

"Will, be reasonable."

"Reasonable?!" I yell, my face going red, every part of me growing hotter and hotter, and I'm ready to rip this railing right off the balcony. "You're my fucking wife. You've been cheating on me. You fucking lied to me!"

"I never lied, I—"

I shove my finger in her face, aware that I'm spitting on her as I speak. "You told me you didn't want children. I know that's your right and I went along with it to please you, and I know it's your right to change your mind, but that child should be mine!"

"I didn't lie!" she yells back, as lights flick on from our neighbor's house and I know they can hear everything. I don't fucking care. Let them all hear. "I just didn't want kids with *you*."

I know she regrets it the moment she says it. But it doesn't matter.

Everything comes to a stop. I can't even feel my heart beating in my chest. It's like I'm being submerged in concrete and it's rising, rising fast.

"I'm sorry," she says quickly, rubbing her slender hands down her face. "I didn't mean it like that, it's just I, I thought I knew what I wanted. And I know you hate me right now and I'm sorry. I never wanted to hurt you, Will. You're such a good man, such a good husband."

I burst out laughing. It feels like acid in my mouth.

"Such a good husband that you have to go fuck the first man you see?"

She looks reprimanded. I go on. "How long has this been going on for? Tell me. Be honest now, completely honest, it's the fucking least you could do."

"A few months," she says quietly, looking away.

"And you're already pregnant."

She nods. "Will. I'm so sorry. It wasn't planned."

"You can be as sorry as you want, Sasha. It doesn't change a thing." I shake my head, trying to pretend this is all a nightmare. But it's not. It's reality. And if I'm honest with myself, it was a long time coming, even if I didn't see it happening this way.

Fuck. This is killing me.

"Does he know?" I whisper.

"Yes," she says. "I told him yesterday. I didn't want to tell you until tomorrow."

"Well happy fucking birthday to me."

"I'm so sorry."

I turn away from her, walking back into the bedroom. "Please stop saying that."

"But I am."

"And I don't fucking care," I sneer, whipping around to face her as she stands in the doorway. "I can't believe you would do this to me."

"You had to know."

"*What*?"

"What I mean is, things haven't been right between us for some time, and I know you know this. It takes two to tango."

I blink at her, utterly baffled. "Fuck you."

"I'm not saying it's your fault, I'm just saying . . ."

"And I'm saying fuck you," I tell her. "There's a thing called communication."

"Yeah there is, and you didn't use it much either."

I throw my hands up, so ready to put my fucking fist in the wall. "I'm not sleeping here tonight. I'm not sleeping here any other night." I give her my hardest glance, hoping she might turn to stone. "This is on you, Sasha. Maybe we could have communicated better, maybe I could have tried harder, but this is on you, okay? You fucked around. You got pregnant." Another wave of rage rolls through me. "Jesus. You're going to have someone else's child!"

I press my knuckles into my forehead, pinching my eyes shut. "I did all of this for you, all of this for you! Moved here when I didn't want to. I was happy in Vancouver. I bought this house when I would have been happy with our last condo. I got a fucking vasectomy because you didn't want children. I did it all for you. Gave you every part of me these last fifteen years. And look where it's got me."

She's not saying anything. I suppose it's a blessing. It's better than her just apologizing again.

"Fifteen years," I go on bitterly. "I loved you for fifteen years. And yeah, maybe the last few we failed a bit. We lost the way. But you either grow together or apart."

"And we grew apart," she finishes, her eyes shining in the dark. "And there is no going back."

I stare at her, my whole world crashing around me. Then I head to the dresser, grabbing some things and shoving them in an overnight bag.

She watches silently as I pack. It matches her silence from earlier today. All this time, all while people were wishing me a happy thirty-ninth birthday, she was carrying her lover's baby inside her, counting down until when she could tell me.

God fucking damn.

When I'm done packing and scoop up my work bag and laptop, I give her one last glance. "I'll be at a hotel. I'll get a lawyer in the morning. I assume you've already planned for this and are using Martina."

She doesn't say anything. Figures she'd swipe our lawyer first.

Then I head out the door. I know that when the time comes for me to return she won't be there.

But she will be at work. Monday to Friday. Like clockwork.

The thought nearly chokes me on the spot.

When Sasha joined Mad Men Studios as general manager of the LA office, I never imagined it would backfire on me. I never thought I'd get divorced. Never thought we would be anything other than a married couple working together.

Now I'm not only losing her, my wife, I might be losing my very job.

Happy birthday, *fucker*.

CHAPTER ONE

Jackie

ARE THERE EVER "FIRSTS" THAT AREN'T absolutely awkward and nerve-wracking?

There's the first day at school (pee your pants, have the kids call you "Jackie Pee Pee" for the rest of the year).

There's the first kiss (teeth clacking, not enough lip, zero tongue control).

There's the first time you have sex (not enough lube, over in one minute).

There's the first time you get drunk (vomit in someone's shoes, wake up in a neighbor's water fountain).

And then, of course, the first day at a new job.

In particular, your first day at a new job that could provide a fantastic opportunity for you and change your whole entire life.

That kind of a *first day at a new job*.

And to say that I'm a nervous wreck is a ridiculous understatement.

I stare at myself in the bathroom mirror and take a deep breath in through my nose, out through my mouth, like they try and teach you during yoga, only I've never taken a yoga class in my entire twenty-five years. I'm starting to think that maybe I should, if it can help prevent me from hyperventilating.

"You've got this Jackie. Breathe," I tell my reflection, hoping no one can hear me. It's a full house these days.

At least I look the part. I didn't have a lot of money to spend on office clothes, and while I know that the company is pretty casual, I wanted to make a good first impression. I'm going into the job with an uphill battle already.

Luckily, Forever 21 and H&M are life-savers for the financially challenged, even though I have to go up a few sizes to accommodate my size-10 curves. I borrowed my mother's car, took it downtown, and braved Vancouver's busy Robson Street and mall, searching for enough outfits to last me the first week.

For today's first impression I wiggled myself into a grey pencil skirt and a blue and white pinstriped dress shirt, paired with grey kitten heels. The skirt shows off my ass and hips in a good way, nipping in at the waist (though Spanx would be nice), the shirt somehow manages to keep my boobs streamlined and under control. To complete the outfit my mom gave me her Louis Vuitton Neverfull bag to use, since my only handbag is a denim piece of shit from Old Navy I snagged on sale years ago.

I decided to keep it simple with my face: tinted moisturizer, used the only tube of tinted lip balm I own, and loads of mascara that highlights my eyes. My hair, on the other hand, is a hopeless case. Long and blah-brown, I haven't had the time (nor money, nor expertise) to get it cut or colored in a long time, so I just pull it back into a bun. My mother has been dying to get me into a salon ever since I moved back home two weeks ago, but it's been low on my priority list.

Though now, I can kind of see her point. I sigh, wishing I had lip liner to define my lips underneath the balm, and decide I look good enough. Pretty and polished, but not enough to turn heads or seem like I'm trying too hard. Anyway, I'm sure the moment I step into that office it won't really matter what the hell I look like. I imagine everyone has heard that I'm the boss's estranged daughter.

Yeah. My first day at work and it's for my father's film company. Which isn't a bad thing per se, just that the circumstances that brought me here have been difficult, to say the least. It's been a hell of a month. Actually, the last few years have been hell. The only saving grace in my life has been my seven-year-old son, Tyson, who has somehow braved the worst with me and turned out to be the most mild-mannered and intelligent little boy.

Me, on the other hand, I feel like a complete mess. One moment I'm struggling to make ends meet up in buttfuck nowhere in the northeast corner of British Columbia, Ty's deadbeat dad Jeff turning to a life of crime and leaving me to work two jobs to support us. The next moment Jeff's being hauled off to prison and I'm packing up my supremely shitty life and heading back south to the city with my tail between my legs. I'm just lucky that my parents took us in, and even more lucky that my father found a job opportunity for me. They might be family, but our relationship has been nothing but distant and strained for almost a decade.

Of course I'm not working directly for my father. He already has an executive assistant, Patty Le, who has worked with him for a long time. My position is as executive assistant to his business partner, William McAlister.

Honestly, I have no idea what to expect, all I know is I'm organized and a quick learner, and if I do a good job I might have a bright future there, providing my boss isn't a hard-ass, which I don't think he is. I remember Mr. McAlister from a long time ago, back when I was a teenager. Other than having a mild crush on him because he reminded me of some of my favorite actors (Gregory Peck, Montgomery Clift, Cary Grant), he was just my father's friend and business partner, and would sometimes visit with his gorgeous wife for dinner. He was always exceedingly nice, funny, and very charming.

To be honest, I could use a lot of nice in my life right now.

"Mom," Ty calls out softly from behind me.

I turn around and see him standing in the doorframe of the bathroom, wringing his hands together anxiously, his brow furrowed with worry.

My heart squeezes at the sight. He's been so resilient with the move and all the changes, but I know it's been really hard on him, and the fact that I'm leaving him to go to work only makes it more difficult.

"Yes Ty?"

"Do you have to go?"

Ugh. My heart is melting all over the place.

I go over to him and drop to my knees, pulling him into a tight hug. "You know I do," I say into his hair before pulling back. I put my hands on his shoulders. "It will be just like before, but better. Because this time I won't be working so long or so often. I'm off at five. And you have Grandma to take care of you. Didn't you want to spend some time with the horses?"

He tries to give me a small smile but fails. "I'm scared of them."

I sigh, brushing his hair off his face. "You know, when I was your age I was scared of them too. They were so big and I was so small. Smaller than you. But you know, your grandmother is a really good teacher. It's what she does best. She taught me not to be afraid and, in time, the horses became my friends." I pause, whispering. "And you know what? If you're really good, she might teach you about the special magic."

"Magic?" he asks suspiciously, getting to that age now that magic is questionable.

"That's right. She taught me all about it. This magic let me control the horse, so it would listen to me. Not only did the horse become my friend, but I had all this power and the horse would do whatever I said. Magic."

Ty's nose scrunches up as he thinks it over. The fact is, I'm not really lying. My mother was a member of the Canadian Equestrian Team before I was born, competing numerous times at the Pan American Games, so I was raised into the world of horses. In fact, we're standing in the house I grew up in, located right in the rural, horse-friendly suburb of Southlands in Vancouver. My mother still runs the equestrian center on the property, mainly boarding other people's horses, but she still gives lessons a few times a week, along with the occasional workshop. Riders come from all over the country to train their show jumpers with Diane Phillips.

But while I was more gung ho about them, and even had my own pony growing up, Ty's never really been around them. I moved up with him and Jeff to Fort St. John for Jeff's work when Ty was just a baby. We never visited my parents. They only came up twice, both times for his birthday. Jeff didn't like it much when I talked to my family, let alone saw them, and I was the idiot who listened to him for far too long.

"What if I come with you to work?" Ty asks hopefully. "I would rather see the dinosaurs than the horses."

I get to my feet and ruffle his hair lightly. "You know Grandpa's company just draws the dinosaurs, right? There aren't actually any dinosaurs there. In fact, I'm pretty sure if I brought you to work you would be bored out of your mind. A bunch of people sitting in cubicles and staring at their computers all day."

He shrugs just as I hear my mother calling from the kitchen. "Jackie-O, you're going to be late."

Shit. I eye the clock on the wall. I should have left five minutes ago to catch the bus on time.

I grab Ty's hand and scoop up my mother's LV, putting it on my shoulder. "Come on, come say bye to me with Grandma."

We leave the room and head down the hall to the kitchen. While I'm getting back on my feet and living with my parents for the time being, I've scored the downstairs suite in the house, which used to be guest room. Ty is upstairs in my old room, which I think he likes because it gives him more privacy than the couch he used to sleep on in our old trailer.

My mother is filling up a glass of water from the sink when we walk in.

"Well you look nice," she says to me but her eyes don't reflect the smile. It's been a bit of a learning curve this last bit, trying to get to know each other all over again. Then there's the fact that I think she's waiting for me to lose my mind at any moment. I guess I don't blame her. I've been through a lot and, frankly, I'm not sure how I'm managing it so well.

I attempt to do a quick curtsey in jest but then realize

my pencil skirt doesn't bend that way. "Thank you. Let's just see if I can get through the day without spilling something on my blouse."

She grins at Ty. "You excited for your first riding lesson today?"

He stares at her, suddenly shy, and wraps his arms around my leg.

"He's excited," I tell her, prying his arms off me. "He just doesn't know it yet. I told him that you might teach him about the magic."

"Magic?" she asks, and then reads the pleading look on my face. "Oh, of course. Horse magic. Here," she says, snapping up the keys to her SUV from the counter and coming over to place them in my hand. "Take my car. You've missed the bus already. I don't know why you thought you should take it to begin with. You know transit is a nightmare going from here to downtown."

Because I already feel like a freeloader, I think to myself, but manage to give her a grateful smile, taking the keys.

Meanwhile she scoops up Ty into her arms and he looks so uncomfortable I almost laugh. I can only hope he survives the day. He starts his new school next week; we moved just as the schools were going on spring break, so until then my mom has her hands full.

"All right, I'm going," I tell them, kissing Ty on the head and giving my mom an awkward wave.

"Good luck," she says. "But you won't need it. You know everyone at Mad Men is pretty amazing."

Actually I don't know it, but I'm about to find out.

The drive from this area of Southlands, which is across from the airport, all the way to downtown Vancouver shouldn't take more than thirty minutes most days, but of course today there's bumper to bumper traffic on Granville

Street and I don't know the city well enough anymore to try any shortcuts. By the time I pull up to Mad Men Studios, and then circle the block a few times trying to find the right parking garage, I'm already ten minutes late.

Just fucking great. It takes everything in me not to have a panic attack right there in the garage, and through some hasty breathing exercises I make my way down the street to the building. At least it's not raining, though the grey clouds seem threatening.

The Mad Men Studios I remember growing up, back when it was Phillips Films before my father partnered with Mr. McAlister, was this damp warehouse in East Vancouver, a dangerous part of town even back then. I know they've moved buildings once or twice since, but I'm totally not prepared to see this.

Mad Men Studios seems to take up the entire block, housed inside a red brick building with iron details. Everything about it screams fresh, hip, and new, fitting right in with the surroundings in Yaletown, the yuppie part of downtown. The rent here has to be astronomical, which is another indicator of how well my father must be doing.

I know it sounds totally nuts to not know these things about your own father and his business, but since I was eighteen I've pretty much been cut off from this world. The only reason I know a little bit about the company is because I researched it once I realized he was giving me a job.

I hate that part, the fact that I've been granted this job with no interview, like I'm a charity case. Don't get me wrong, I'll do whatever I can to provide a better life for myself and Ty, it's just my pride is stubborn—dangerously stubborn at times—and I would much rather earn it than be given it. But beggars can't be choosers, and a month ago I was begging to start my life over again.

And I'm sure most people in my position wouldn't sweat it if they were ten minutes late on their first day. After all, what's my father going to do, fire me? But if anything that fact makes me want to prove myself even more. The last thing I want is for the rest of the employees to think I've been given anything.

I walk through the glass doors and into the reception area, quickly taking in the room. Movie posters adorn the brick walls in thick gold frames, while black couches and chairs sit atop a white sheepskin rug.

The space is empty except for the receptionist who is in the middle of a call, talking into a wireless headset. She's young, Asian, and teeny-tiny with square-frame glasses, talking in a clipped voice. I can't tell if she's utterly bored or just trying not to expend any excess energy.

Finally, she glances up at me and her expression changes. She comes alive. "You must be Jackie."

I smile, relieved to find her friendly. "I am. I'm so sorry I'm late. Traffic was horrible and I missed the bus and . . ."

She shrugs. "Eh, doesn't make a difference to me. I'm not your boss. And I doubt Will would care either. In fact . . ." she leans back in her chair and peers through an archway that leads into the rest of the open office, a mild murmur and clattering of keyboards wafting out, "I don't even think he's here yet. So you're good." She looks me over. "You might want to button up your top though."

I glance down and see the top buttons of my blouse have already busted open. My face goes red as I quickly do it up. "Shit. This is what I get for buying this at Forever 21."

"Hey, I'm twenty-one myself and half their clothes are too slutty for me. Those buttons never had a chance. Buttoning them up goes against their destiny. Here." She pulls something out of her desk drawer and holds it out of me. It's a safety pin. "Remember, in case of emergency, break the glass and ask for Tiffany. Whatever you need, I've got."

I give her a grateful smile as I pin my shirt back together. I don't trust the slut buttons. "I can see why my father hired you."

"He hired me because I lied on my resume," she says bluntly. "They found out pretty fast that my miraculous skills in Excel and PowerPoint were all bullshit. But then I just worked extra hard with the Tiffany charm and made up for it. There's no way in hell I'm going back into that job market out there." She jerks her thumb toward the window, as if the vile job market is lurking at the door.

I'm already enamored by her honesty. "How long have you been working here?"

"About five months," she says. "But everyone in the office is kind of new these days. Including Will, as you know."

I'm not sure I want to admit to Tiffany how little I know, but she seems to read it on my face. "Will controlled the LA office, right," she says. "They deal mainly with visual effects. We used to do that too, though now we're doing the animation side of things. But he moved back here last month, so even he's a bit of a noob. As in newbie. As in the same as you and me."

"Why did he move back?"

"He went through a divorce. His ex-wife is the general manager down there."

"Ex-wife?"

Tiffany gives me an odd look and shoves her glasses up the bridge of her nose. "How much did your father tell you about the job?"

"To be honest, not that much. He just knew I needed work and said Mr. McAlister needed an executive assistant." I pause. "The last few years I've been up north, and I haven't really kept in the know about my father's company. Or really anything."

"Mr. McAlister," she says with an impish smile. "That's cute."

I let out a soft laugh. "I remember him from when I was teenager. That's all he was to me. My dad's friend. A younger friend, much younger than my dad, but even so, when I was fifteen anyone above twenty was super old. He was probably thirty at the time? So yeah. An ancient old man to teenage Jackie."

Tiffany raises her eyebrow. "Well I'm guessing he was married back then too. All I know is he split from his wife a year or two ago and tried to tough it out, but I guess it was too hard. I can't blame him. They've got a staff of like a hundred and fifty in the LA office, but when you're working next to your ex all day that's got to be rough."

"How many work here?"

"About fifty. But we're growing each day. The dinosaur movies, you know, DinoWars, are a real hit right now, so as long as Warner Brothers keeps doing deals with us, we'll keep expanding. Maybe get some new clients. Hence all the new hires, some of which I still don't know their names. Whatever. But I'll know yours. Otherwise Ted will kill me."

Ted's my father. Will and Ted, the CEOs of Mad Men Studios, coined because apparently the two of them are mad when they're together. Least that's what the company bio said. In reality, I think that means they drink a lot in each other's presence.

"He'd probably kill me for being late if he were here," I point out. One good thing about today is that my father is away on business, so I don't have to deal with the awkwardness of being around him on my first day of work.

"He probably won't be here all week, so you're golden," Tiffany says. "He travels so much now that Will's here. Heading down to LA all the time."

I have to admit, it's a bit weird to be around someone who knows more about your father in the last five months than you have in the last twenty-five years. I better start getting my shit together before people catch on that my father and I aren't exactly close.

She glances at her computer. "Hmmm. I guess I should call Alyssa and tell her you're here."

"Who is Alyssa?"

"She's the office manager. She'll be training you, I think."

"I thought my father, Ted's assistant, Patty, was doing that."

"She's with your father traveling. It's for the best anyway, Patty takes everything too seriously. Alyssa is a lot more fun—she knows everything and will tell you everything. Especially when she has a few drinks in her. Not that we drink at work." And at that Tiffany cups her hands around a mug of coffee (at least I think it's coffee, though now I'm suspicious) and takes a sip before placing it back down. The mug says something about Muggles, and I automatically know I'm dealing with a Harry Potter fan, which makes me like her even more. I swear those books got me and Ty through some pretty lonely nights up north.

Lonely, and scary. I shudder at the thought.

"You all right?" Tiffany asks, peering at me. "I suppose if I was the kind of receptionist I pride myself on being, I would have offered you tea or coffee or water by now."

"No, it's fine," I say quickly. "Thank you."

She studies me for a moment more and then hits a few keys on the computer. "Alyssa," she says into the headset.

"Your nine o' clock is here to be initiated into the program." She looks to me. "She'll be right out."

"Program?" I repeat.

"Joking," Tiffany says brightly.

A curvy blonde woman in skinny jeans, t-shirt, and blazer appears in the doorway, a notepad in hand. She eyes me through her blunt-cut bangs and extends her hand.

"Hi Jackie, nice to finally meet you. I'm Alyssa," she says, taking my hand into hers and giving it a quick shake. "Are you excited? Nervous?"

"Both?"

"Don't worry, you'll fit right in here, I promise." She looks at Tiffany. "You've been nice to her, right?"

Tiffany just rolls her eyes. "Yes master."

Alyssa grins at me, showing off a gap in her white teeth that reminds me of Ty. "I get to boss her around, it's the best part of the job."

"Ha ha," Tiffany says before she answers a call. "Good morning, Mad Men Studios, how may I direct your call?"

"Shall we start with the tour?" Alyssa asks, gesturing toward the rest of the office. "Come on."

I follow her out through the doorway and into a large rectangular space with high ceilings and exposed beams. Along the edge of half the room are classic offices, glass exteriors with wood doors, plus blinds for privacy. Across from a few of the offices are desks and a few cubicles. In the middle of the room are what look like long, white picnic tables, with a few monitors and people sitting in front of them. In the corner of the room are couches, coffee tables, and chairs, like some hip café. More people are strewn across them, some talking but most listening to their headphones and furiously typing on their laptops.

It takes me a moment to realize where I am, that this

is my father's company. Who the hell knew he would create something so fresh and urban? Though there are some classic features, this place definitely has a trendy slant with the iron details, the brick work, and the communal work benches.

"This is the belly of the beast," Alyssa says proudly, "where all the administrative, communications, finance, and executives work." She points across the room where a glass door leads down a hall. "Down there is where the so-called magic happens, where the animators work. I'll show you that later, but I don't think you'll have much to do with them. So what do you think? I'm the office manager in case you didn't know, so I pride myself on first impressions of this place."

"It's pretty cool," I tell her, looking around. A few people look up at me but quickly go back to work. "Everyone looks so young."

"Median age is twenty-nine," she says. "Your father is the oldest, which makes sense since he started the company. The LA office is a bit older, which is probably why he's started traveling down there more often. I think he feels like a grandpa here."

"Well he *is* a grandpa," I tell her.

"Oh that's right," she says, giving me a sheepish smile and briefly putting her hand on my arm. "I'm sorry, I forgot. He's been excited to have you and your son back home. You have a little boy, right?"

"Yeah. Tyson."

"How old is he?"

"Turned seven in November," I tell her, waiting for the inevitable *but you look so young, you must have been a baby when you had him*, etc.

To Alyssa's credit she doesn't say that. "A Scorpio. He

must be a feisty one."

"Actually he's pretty quiet. Just likes to read. And he's currently obsessed with dinosaurs, so he's a bit jealous that I'm working here now. He knows Grandpa is in charge of all the dinosaur cartoon movies."

"Shhh," Alyssa says sharply, putting her finger to her lips. "You call them cartoons and you immediately get tossed out the door by the artists. Animation. Always animation."

I raise my brow. "Even if it's not animated?"

"Yes. Just to be safe. The artists are touchy."

"Good to know. So how does the table set-up work here? Where do I work?"

"Oh, well," she says, gesturing to picnic tables. "A lot of people don't have permanent desks or offices. They just work wherever they want."

I frown, not too thrilled about it. "Where do they keep their stuff?"

"They have lockers in the back, and under the table there's a drawer for stuff they need on hand. We just like to keep it flexible. But you have a desk right across from Will's office. This way."

I sigh with relief, following her along the row of offices, doors all closed. I read the names: Alyssa Martin, Darlene Birch, Bob Cantu. "This is your father's," Alyssa says, gesturing to a large one in the corner that says *Ted Phillips, President*, on a gold plate on the door, then the office right next to it that says *William McAlister, Vice President*. "And this is obviously Will's. They like to both be tucked away in the corner and away from the riff-raff."

"I'm guessing my father is the one calling them riff-raff?"

"You got that right." She turns around and splays her

palms out to the cubicle across from the offices, split into two with a partition between. "This is your desk. Patty is on the other side."

It's a nice sized desk, wrap around style with lots of room for folders and files, with both a MacBook and a desktop Mac as well. The partition between Patty and I is frosted, so it provides a bit of privacy too and I won't have to feel like someone is breathing down my neck.

I've just put my bag on the desk and am about to ask Alyssa where the restrooms are, when she puts one hand on her hip and says in a coy voice, "And here comes the man of the hour himself. Late as usual."

I look over to see a tall, broad-shouldered man stride into the office, briefcase in one hand, and leashes attached to two dogs in the other.

The dogs take me by surprise.

As does the man's hulking silhouette.

Alyssa goes on, whispering to me, "There's no excuse for him being late though, he lives just around the corner. You should see his place. Heard it costs three million. Wait, I forgot to check, you're okay with dogs right?" she asks me quickly.

"Huh? Dogs? Yeah," I say absently, unable to take my eyes off him—my boss—as he approaches, walking toward us with the two dogs, one a small Pitbull type, the other a scruffy thing. Both extremely cute.

I don't really get a good look at him until he's just a few feet away. A few feet away, stopped, and staring at me with a wry grin on his face.

Holy shit. Is this really Mr. McAlister?

The Mr. McAlister I remember from when I was a teenager was tall, dark, and handsome, his voice and furrowed brow reminding me of Gregory Peck. A total old-fashioned movie star. Now he's all those things magnified. Age has made him one hell of a sexy beast dressed in a sharp navy blue suit, his dogs now sitting politely beside him.

"You couldn't possibly be Jackie," he says to me, looking me up and down with the kind of wonderment that nearly brings heat to my cheeks. His voice is stronger than I remembered, shoots some kind of electricity through me. It's as deep as sin, smooth as scotch, the kind of voice that should do voiceovers for car commercials.

"That's me," I manage to say, straightening my back and trying to look professional, even though this whole exchange is unraveling me for some weird reason.

"You were just a kid when I saw you last," he says smoothly. "You look like your mother now. Thank god because I couldn't stomach someone else looking like your father. Getting a bit sick of his mug already."

Alyssa breaks out into a nervous hyena-like laugh. I frown at her, wondering what her deal is.

"So," he goes on, ignoring her, that distinctive voice drawing my attention immediately back to him, and he stares at me for a moment. I can't help but stare right back, marveling at the color of his eyes, green-blue, like a lagoon, the bare masculinity of his wide jaw covered with a five o' clock shadow, the dark swoop of thick black hair off his forehead.

How the hell am I supposed to work with a man—*for* a man—who looks like he could be the next James Bond?

It could be worse than having daily eye candy, I quickly remind myself. When I worked at Safeway, my manager had ear and nose hair you could braid.

"Sorry I'm late," he says, glancing down at the dogs. "They tie me up most mornings. This is Sprocket," he looks at the scruffy one, then to the Pitbull. "And this is Joan of Bark."

I can't help but laugh. "Joan of Bark?"

"We call her Joanie for short. I don't always bring them in, but the dog-walker cancelled today. God, I hope you're a dog person," he says, running his long, tanned fingers over his stubble as he seems to ponder the consequences.

"And what if I wasn't?"

He grins at me, a smile that lights up the space around him. "I'm sure Joanie would make you a believer. Maybe not Sprocket though. He can be a little dick." He looks to Alyssa. "Are you done giving her the tour?"

"We were just getting started," she says.

"Good, give me a bit to get ready," he tells her before he winks at me. "See you later, kid."

He takes the dogs into his office and shuts the door.

I look at Alyssa. Did my new boss just call me *kid*?

But she's got a silly smile on her face, her cheeks pink. "So that's Will. You're a lucky girl you know, he's probably the best person to work for here." Her voice is rich with some sort of nuance I can't place. She pauses. "I mean, your dad is really nice too, don't get me wrong. I've been working for him for almost five years now and—"

I raise my palm and nod. "It's okay. It's my dad. You're not going to hear me signing his praises, believe me."

"Right, well I guess it's good you're helping Will then." She leans in close. "You know he's recently divorced," she whispers. "Poor guy. I'm still in contact with his ex, Sasha, pretty much every day. She's the general manager at the LA office. She's nice and all, but I've heard things . . ."

I just nod, not sure at first what she wants me to say, and then remember Tiffany's warning about her being a gossip. "The last I saw Mr. McAlister, he was with Mrs.

McAlister," I tell her, finding it neutral enough.

She laughs softly, eyes dancing. "You call him Mr. McAlister. That's funny. Anyway, let's get going."

She picks up her notepad and starts walking toward the sleek white picnic tables in the middle of the room.

I look behind me at the closed door to Mr. McAlister's office, catching him just as he's done opening his blinds and turning around, saying something to his dogs as they come running over.

Jeez. I've talked to him for a few seconds and I'm already a smitten kitten. I take a moment to admire his back side, before hurrying after Alyssa to continue the rest of the tour.

CHAPTER TWO

Will

D## AMN.

I was not prepared for that.

Not the fact that Elsi, my dog-walker, cancelled, because she's done that at least twice now; usually on Monday mornings when I know she goes dancing Sunday nights. I should probably get another dog-walker, but I'm new to the city and she was recommended by someone in my building. Someone that doesn't have a dog, mind you, so maybe that should have been my first warning.

Besides, it's not a bother to have the pups at work, since Ted kept yammering on and on about the Vancouver office being dog-friendly, hip, and whatever the fuck, as if I would really care, as if it would make the whole move any better.

No. What I wasn't prepared for was the fact that Ted's daughter, Jackie, is no longer the petulant teen with big eyes and a bad attitude. That's what I remember her as, and I have to be honest, I never gave her much thought beyond that. Why would I?

But now... *now*...

She does look like her mother, that wasn't a lie. Her mother is a beautiful lady. I guess I just wasn't prepared to see how absolutely stunning their daughter turned out to be. Those big eyes are still the same, but her lips are fuller, as is every other part of her in ways that are *entirely* inappropriate for me to think about.

I guess I was still expecting that teenager with her dyed jet-black hair and nose ring to be my assistant. My mind just latched onto the girl that I remembered, the one who seemed bored out of her mind every time Sasha and I were over for dinner. She couldn't wait to leave the table so she could hang out with who knows who. I know she gave Ted an ulcer most days.

That girl is gone. Jackie Phillips is one absolutely gorgeous woman, looking as lost and adrift as I did my first day here. As I'm sure I still look sometimes.

Luckily, I'm pretty good at pushing beautiful woman out of my head, even ones I'm supposed to work with every day. Couldn't Ted have hired some long-lost aunt of his instead?

I sit back in my chair and look at Joanie and Sprocket, who have flopped down in the dog bed I have by the couch. I know they're pleased to be spending the day with me again, but if they get to be a pain in the ass, at least now I can get Jackie to take them for a walk.

I've only been back in Vancouver for about a month, but I don't feel close to having settled in, and it's kind of strange to have an assistant. In the LA office, Sasha and I shared Megan, who was the office manager, but I still did most things on my own. Booking travel arrangements, filing expense reports—the no-brainer stuff that I could easily do myself.

The moment I came up here though, Ted was insistent that I get an executive assistant of my own. I don't know if it's because the workload up here is heavier, especially with the animation side of things really taking off, or he just wants me to be comfortable. I suspect it's a little of both. Ted is still handling me with kid gloves, as if the divorce has rendered me fragile and completely incompetent.

I'm definitely not fragile. Incompetent is something that remains to be seen. Sasha officially moved out of our house two years ago to be with Ansel, but the divorce was messy and only final four months ago. I tried to stick it out in LA, tried to show her that what she did to me didn't destroy me, that I could be the bigger person here, but...sometimes you know when to pack up and leave.

My alarm beeps, reminding me of a conference call with Ted. Again, it's strange to do these things in reverse. It used to be me down in LA, calling him up here.

But Ted is Ted, and always gets right to the point with these calls. Half an hour later, after Ted has assured me that everything is on track, he asks, "So how is she doing?"

"I assume you mean your daughter."

"How does she look? Is she presentable?"

I smile into the phone. "She's more than presentable, Ted. You never told me she'd grown up to be quite the beautiful young lady."

"Easy now, Will. Don't be getting any wrong ideas."

"Don't worry, I'm not. I'm just saying, she looks...very sweet. I'll be meeting with her in a bit to go over everything, and I'll have more of an idea then." I pause. "Are you sure I need an assistant?"

"Who the hell is going to tie your shoes?"

"Right. But I did just fine in LA without one."

"Because you had Sasha."

I can't help the bitter laugh. "Sasha only looked out for number one. And that was the company."

Ted gives a long sigh. "Look, you know Jackie and I aren't exactly close. To be honest, I'm not even sure how to talk to her anymore. When she was up north... well, I'm overjoyed she's back here. Diane is too, but I don't know what to expect. I just know that she needs this job and you could use the help, and why not help the two most important people to me?"

"Sentimental? At this hour of the morning?"

"I haven't had my medication yet," he says dryly. "Don't get used to it. I better go, we have another meeting here with the new VFX production coordinator. You know, you have a nice crew down here. How did you manage to leave them?"

"I wonder that myself."

"It was your choice, Will."

I exhale slowly through my nose. "Yes. It was."

"No regrets?"

"We'll see."

I'm about to hang up when I hear him say, "Take it easy on my girl. She's had it rough lately."

"I promise not to ride her too hard." I smirk.

"*Will...*"

"Ted."

He sighs and hangs up.

I wait a few moments, getting my bearings, before I stand up and head to the door, the dogs watching my every move. I open the door and poke my head out.

The office is bustling, though not as frantically as one would think. That's the difference I've found so far between the animators here and the visual effects crew in LA. The animators are lazy as fuck, half of them looking stoned at all hours of the day. They get the work done, but not as quick as I, or Warner Brothers, would like, and unfortunately I'm the one who hears about it.

Jackie is sitting across from me at her desk, her side to me, frowning at the desktop computer and repeatedly clicking on the mouse.

"Never used a Mac before?" I ask her, leaning against the doorway.

She looks over at me, her lips twisting together sheepishly. "How can you tell?"

"Just a guess. How was the tour? Alyssa being good to you?"

She nods. "It was informative."

"Did she tell you the astrological signs of everyone, their salary, and how much they weigh?"

She smiles, close-lipped. Damn. Her cheeks are something else. "Pretty much. She may have told me how often they use the bathroom too."

I stare at her for a moment.

"I'm so sorry," she says quickly, going a shade of red. "I should probably avoid toilet humor first day on the job. I keep forgetting you're my boss."

"If it makes you feel better, I keep forgetting you're my assistant."

I meant it as a joke but I can see the lines appearing on her smooth forehead. What Ted said runs through my mind. The last thing I want is for her to feel insecure here.

"Well," I go on quickly, "since you've had the grand tour, how about we go over the job. I have to admit, I'm not used to having an assistant so I'm not really sure if I'm doing the right thing or not . . . what that even is. So, with that in mind, how about I get you up to speed . . . while we walk the dogs."

Her eyes brighten. "Sure. Whatever you like." She gets up and I glance down at her shoes, grey kitten heels that only add an inch to her height, making her five-four at most.

"Are you going to be okay to walk in those?" Granted, Sasha used to wear ones that would put her at six-two—my height—with complete ease. She would have slept in them if she could have. All the better for jabbing me in the middle of the night, preferably near the heart.

She shrugs. "I'm more at home in a pair of boots, but I can handle it." While she grabs her jacket, I get the dogs on their leashes, making sure I grab an umbrella from reception on the way out.

Tiffany, the receptionist, gives me one of her patented withering looks as I do so, and I open the door for Jackie as we step out onto the street.

"What was with that look?" Jackie asks me as I hand her Sprocket's leash. She takes it without second thought. Good girl.

"She finds it amusing that I grab an umbrella every time I step outside."

She glances up at the sky, wrinkles her nose. "It could rain at any minute."

"She would give me the look even if it were a torrential downpour. A true Vancouverite doesn't use an umbrella. They're like ducks. The water just rolls right off them."

"But you used to live here," she says to me as we start walking down the street, Sprocket pulling her slightly ahead of me and Joanie. "Right?"

"Technically I was born on Vancouver Island, grew up in Victoria," I tell her, realizing that just because she's Ted's daughter doesn't mean she knows jack shit about me. That's probably for the best. "But being in LA changes you. Did you know that back when The X-Files were filmed here, David Duchovny made production pack up and move to LA because of the rain? After eight seasons he just couldn't handle it. Honestly, now that I've lived in LA, I don't blame him. It's nice to know what you're going to get every day."

"Well I think it's pretty obvious what we get every day here," she says, stopping as Sprocket sniffs along a bike rack. "Rain."

"Look at us," I tell her, feeling strangely pleased. "We're standing here, talking about the weather. It's like we never left Vancouver to begin with."

She gives me a small smile and looks off. I probably sound like a tool.

"Anyway," I continue smoothly, "I have to say I prefer the sunshine to the doom and gloom."

"So why did you move?"

I eye her carefully. Surely Alyssa told her, probably along with my social insurance number.

But she's staring at me with an open expression, sucking her lower lip in such a manner that a thread of heat works its way into my chest. I wish she wouldn't do that, and yet I can't seem to look away.

I clear my throat. "Sasha and I, I'm not sure if you remember her, we got divorced. I tried to tough it out but, you know we worked together and it was either she went or I went. And she wasn't going anywhere."

She nods. "So you're not really here by choice."

"No," I say slowly, pulling Joanie's head away from a pile of shit on the sidewalk. "It was my choice. Not necessarily one I wanted to make . . ."

Fuck. What am I doing? This sort of personal business probably shouldn't be discussed with my assistant. What we should be discussing is just what the hell she's supposed to do for me.

I can think of a few things.

The thought flashes across my mind and I wince internally, hating myself for thinking it. It's wrong, wrong, wrong.

I need to behave.

Luckily I have the gentleman thing down pat.

I clear my throat again. She probably thinks I've got a cold at this point.

"So, I think the best place for us to start is to find out what your father told you about the job. What you know about Mad Men Studios. What we do."

She tucks a strand of loose hair behind her ear, and I didn't realize until now that my fingers were itching to do it for her. "Well, honestly, I don't know much. My father and I weren't exactly close over the last seven years or so. When I moved up north, I, uh . . .it's complicated."

I can see that it is. And the last thing I want to do is pry.

"That's fine, you don't have to explain. Let me just start from the top then. As you know, I joined your father about ten years ago. Before that he had Phillips Films. When I came on board it turned into Mad Men Studios. Because I had a background in animation, or at least a pipe dream." Her eyes spark at this but I keep going, least I dwell too much on said pipe dream. "Sasha, my ex, she's American and it was her idea to expand down in LA. She became the general manager there. Fast forward over the next ten years and we decide to make the Vancouver office the animation one, LA concentrating on visual effects. That's why there's some growing pains over here right now. A lot of turnover as we change."

"And that's where I come in," she says. Her eyes look impossibly bright in this dull, grey light. "I'm here to help with your growing pains."

"Right. Well the truth is, it's been a bit of an adjustment for me here. The office runs a lot differently from the LA one."

"Bunch of stoners?"

I grin at her. "You've got that right. But that's on par with animation."

"And you used to do animation?" She pauses, a devilish look coming over her. "I called them cartoons earlier and I thought Alyssa was going to have my head."

Now I'm laughing. "Oh god. Yeah. Cartoons. They won't let you forget that one. But honestly, it's sometimes what I think of them. I quit drawing back in my early twenties. Went to Vancouver Film School, but just didn't have what it took. So I stuck to being a production assistant and it's eventually where I met your father, on set."

She watches me carefully, like she's inspecting every line on my face. It's almost unnerving. "How old are you?"

"How old are you?" I fire back. Can't help myself.

"I'm twenty-five."

"I am *not* twenty-five."

She stares at me expectantly.

"Forty-one," I tell her, and I immediately hate how old I sound. Honestly, I know forty-one isn't old at all and I have to say I've never felt old, except when I'm playing ice hockey these days on the pick-up team.

"That's a good age," she says. "Gregory Peck was forty-one when he made *On the Beach*."

I cock my brow. This one is full of surprises. "Kid, I'm not sure if I should be flattered that you've compared me to Mr. Peck, or concerned considering that's one of the most depressing and scary films you'll ever see."

"How about you don't call me kid. It's just Jackie."

"All right, Just Jackie."

If she was annoyed at all about the kid comment, it's melted away into something softer. "I'll keep calling you Mr. McAlister . . ."

I shrug, pretending not to care. "Fine with me kid, it gives me an air of authority that's sorely needed around here."

She sighs and starts walking off with Sprocket. I pull on Joanie's leash and hurry up alongside her, waiting at the light to cross the street.

It's then that I notice the top button on her blouse has popped open, showcasing some gorgeous cleavage. Fuck. Her skin looks like cream.

She looks up at me and I avert my eyes just in the nick of time.

"I guess I shouldn't complain," she says.

"About what?" *Don't look down her shirt, Will. Don't be that boss.*

"I'll take whatever name I can get. I've been just *mom* for so long. Not that I'm complaining at all, but it just feels like I'm two people. There's mom. Or *Ty's mother*. And then there's Jackie. Or Just Jackie, or kid, or whatever else people want to call me. It's just weird to be split like that sometimes." She pauses giving me a quick smile. "I'm sorry, I shouldn't be unloading this on you."

Are you kidding me? I think. I want nothing more than for her to keep talking about herself. Unload all of it.

"Don't worry about it," I tell her as we start crossing the busy street, navigating around the pedestrians. "The more I know about you, the better we'll work together. We're a team, you got that? You're a fish out of water, so am I. That's probably why your father put us together. We'll both figure it out at the same time."

She starts laughing, so fucking adorable.

"What?" I ask.

"Nothing. It's just I was reminded of the first day of school, you know, or camp, where you get assigned a buddy."

"That can work," I tell her, coming to a stop by a bush that I know Joanie and Sprocket love to spend hours sniffing. It's the dog equivalent of the water cooler.

I hold out my hand. "Buddies?"

She chews on her pink lower lip for a second, almost shyly, before sticking her hand out. "Buddies."

I grasp her hand, giving it a good shake, knowing I should let go sooner rather than later. But, no, of course I'm holding on a bit longer than I should.

"Just don't forget I can fire you," I quickly add, letting go of her hand.

"I'll try not to," she says, flashing those dimples my way again.

I wait until she's turned and walking away with Sprocket before I breathe in deep through my nose and try to compose myself.

Having an assistant might be a lot harder than I thought.

CHAPTER THREE

Jackie

"Well, well, well," Tiffany says to me as I shrug on my jacket, about to leave the office.

"What?" I ask, looking myself over. It's been a long-ass, busy day. I wouldn't be surprised if I had coffee all over me or put my jacket on inside out.

"You survived your first week at work," she says. "That's no small feat."

"Do I get a medal?"

"You get a pat on the back. That's the best I can do."

"Hell, I'll take it."

Somehow the week flew by. Maybe it's because Mr. McAlister—I mean Will—is still reluctant to hand work off to me so I've got a pretty easy gig so far, or maybe it's because everyone here has been really nice and welcoming, but Friday got here before I knew it.

Of course, it doesn't really feel like a Friday to me.

Probably because Mr. . . . *Will*, is coming over for

dinner tonight.

I'm waiting for Tiffany to say something about it. Maybe she doesn't know. It's better that way. Obviously there's nothing abnormal about Will having dinner at his business partner's house—from what mom said, it used to be quite the regular thing—but it feels weird now that I'm his executive assistant. I mean normally your boss doesn't come over for dinner after the first week of work.

Naturally, I'm nervous. My interactions with Will this week have been sporadic, usually him emailing me about something, though sometimes he'll hover around my desk uncertainly, like he wants to ask me to do something but isn't sure what. But with my dad being away all week, I have no idea what our dynamic is going to be like when we're all together in the same room.

I'm about to tell Tiffany to have a good weekend and head out the door to catch my bus, when Alyssa comes scurrying into the reception area.

"Jackie," she says in a hush, her eyes dancing, her low-cut shirt showing off ample amounts of boob. "You didn't tell me that Mr. Hung was coming over to your house for dinner."

"What?" Tiffany exclaims, staring at me accusingly.

"Mr. Hung?" I repeat.

They exchange a knowing look. "Yes," Alyssa says. "One of our many nicknames for him. Along with Mr. Right."

I blink at her.

"The two are related," Tiffany says matter-of-factly, flashing a fake smile at Bob Cantu, the head accountant, as he walks past and out the door.

Alyssa places a hand on my arm and leans in conspiratorially. "Don't tell me you haven't noticed he hangs to the right."

I don't have to ask her to clarify what and who we're talking about. My cheeks flame and I look away. Because, yes, I have noticed. I noticed it at the end of the first day, and I've noticed it every time I've seen him since. Will doesn't even wear tight pants, it's just—that dick print of his is always there. It doesn't help that he's apparently hung like a horse, so if your eyes ever travel south of his belt, it's all you can focus on. It's like staring at the sun though. If you stare too long, you will get burned.

I glance at her. "Is it wrong that I want to order him some briefs just so I can get some work done?"

The two of them erupt into laughter, giggling like schoolgirls.

"In time you'll welcome the distraction," Alyssa says, wiping a tear away. "Especially on the really boring days. Though it's extra frustrating when you're single."

"I'm not even single and I still find it frustrating," Tiffany says with a dreamy look in her eyes. "I love my boyfriend, but damn. That man is packing a lot of heat. If you know what I mean."

"Yeah we know what you mean," I tell her. Then I shake my head, trying to get back on track. "It doesn't matter. He's my boss. I can't talk about him this way, and I definitely can't think about him this way."

"Why not?" Alyssa says with a shrug. "I'm sure he says the same about us."

"He thinks we have penises?" Tiffany asks, taking a sip out of a *Stranger Things* mug.

Alyssa and I give her a dry look in unison. "No," I tell her and then look to Alyssa. "And I highly doubt that. Will is nothing if not professional."

And charming. And easy to talk to. And ridiculously handsome.

"You're right," she says after a beat. She sighs. "He's too . . . I don't know. Old school for that."

"He's totally old school," Tiffany interjects. "Like those classic movie stars. Or George Clooney."

"Back when men knew how to dress, how to act, and how to treat a lady," Alyssa adds.

"Bet he's wild in the bedroom though," Tiffany says with a faraway look in her eyes. I can practically see her glasses getting steamy. "He cleans up good. He probably gets dirty just as well."

"Oh god yes. I bet that dick never goes to waste."

"You guys," I say quickly, raising my palm. "Please. You're not his EA. I am. And I have to have dinner with him *and* my parents tonight, so all talk about his dick needs to stop ASAP."

"You girls seem up to no good," Will says from the doorway.

All three of us yelp and jump, turning to see him staring at us with a bemused look on his face.

Oh my god. Oh my god. Please don't let him have heard what I just said. Please Lord All Mighty!

"We're always up to no good," Tiffany says dryly without missing a beat. "It wouldn't be a very fun office otherwise."

Will grabs his umbrella from the stand and points it at me. "Keep in mind that Just Jackie is mine. I will not have her corrupted."

I know he's just being glib, but holy hell. Just Jackie is mine? That does something to me, something entirely inappropriate. Especially after what we were just discussing. An image of him shedding his suit, getting wild, rough, and dirty enters my mind for long enough to make me blush even more.

And now he's smiling at me, white teeth against tanned skin, that sexy jaw and stubble, and I can't think of a single good thing to say in response.

Luckily Alyssa keeps talking. "No promises," She says in a teasing voice, making gaga eyes at him.

"Right," he says. He heads toward the door. "I'll see you ladies on Monday." Then he glances over his shoulder at me. "And I'll see you in a few hours, kid."

Then he's gone, off strolling down the street.

I can't even be annoyed at the *kid* thing. I look at the girls with wide eyes.

"Please tell me he didn't hear any of that. *Any* of it."

Alyssa shrugs. "Well, even if he did you weren't the one saying anything bad. And I'm pretty sure he knows by now how Tiffany and I feel."

"It's his fault for not wearing underwear," Tiffany says, starting to shut things down at her computer.

"This is so wrong," I tell them, heading toward the door. "Any other office and the two of you would be slapped with sexual harassment suits."

"If he's doing the slapping with his penis, I honestly don't care," Tiffany says.

"Okay, that's it. I'm going to leave on that note. See you on Monday," I tell them, needing to get out of there before it gets worse. Will was right, they will corrupt me and I'm easily corruptible.

The truth is, I've been fighting all week not to think about Will that way. In any way, really, other than my boss. It's even been hard to forget that he's the man who came to visit during the holidays with his wife. Every time I think about the dinner tonight, my mind is brought back to those times.

It's kind of amazing how the span of one week has

shifted things. How a person can exist in your past and your future as two separate people. I feel like there's the Will I knew when I was younger, my father's friend, someone I never much thought about. The Will that I know now, older, dashing, somehow even more handsome, is someone else entirely.

I try and push that all aside and out of my brain as I walk up to Granville St. to catch my bus. Vancouver isn't a huge city, maybe a million or so people in the greater area, but compared to where I was before, a town of less than 20,000, it feels like New York to me. There's this hustle and flow here, all these people, so many of them my age, trying to make it. Rent is astronomically high, the job market is competitive, and yet every single day people are stubbornly trying to live their dream. The ambition is contagious.

There already seems to be a change within me, at least on a superficial level. I'm feeling reenergized. April is approaching, spring is in the air and in my step, and I'm starting to feel like anything is possible. There's hope where there wasn't hope before.

It's a nice feeling, even if it's a foreign one. Sometimes hope is like wearing someone else's coat. You know it can shield and protect you, just as it did them, but it still doesn't feel right. You're just not used to it.

Being up north whittled my life down to just one thing: Tyson. I did everything I could to ensure there was enough food on the table, that the rent was paid, that he was happy. Did everything I could to protect him from the horrors that surrounded us.

I did everything I could until I couldn't anymore.

And when that day happened, we got out of there.

It still feels like yesterday, because it practically was yesterday.

Less than a month ago I was calling 911, my blood dripping onto the phone.

Don't focus on the past, I remind myself while I get in line with the rest of the commuters at the bus stop. Now that I've done one week at the new job, survived the commute, survived the awkwardness and pitfalls that come with the territory, I'm starting to feel more free. I try not to berate myself for not doing it earlier, although that guilt remains.

By the time I get back home—yes, I'm finally calling it home, even if it's just temporary—an hour of commuting and switching buses has gone by and Tyson is running toward me with open arms across the broad sweep of immaculate grass that makes up the front lawn.

"Mummy!" he cries out, a big goofy smile on his face, his bowl-haircut flapping as he runs. I feel every single worry melt away as I scoop him up in my arms, even though it takes a little more effort than normal. I swear he's gained a few pounds this week, and it's his grandma's baking to blame.

"Hey Ty-Ty, how was your day?" I ask him.

"Grandma showed me how to use her magic. Now it's my magic," he says excitedly, his blue eyes dancing.

"Is that so?"

"Today Tyson met Taffy," my mother says to me as she steps out of the front door. I don't know how she manages to always look so immaculate, whether in the kitchen or flying over fences on a horse. While I got the short curvy body from some long lost relative (and a love of all things beer, let's not kid ourselves), she's tall, skinny elegance. Right now she's in her jodhpurs, ankle riding boots, a green dress shirt and a cream scarf around her neck. Grace Kelly reincarnated.

"He even sat on him briefly," she adds, a satisfied smile to her lips. Back when I was a child, I learned on a Welsh pony called Silkie. She was my very own, until I outgrew her. Silkie passed a long time ago, as did my old thoroughbred Ruger, and now my family only has two, my mother's old warmblood Duke that nearly took her to the Olympics, and her younger horse, Jeopardy. The rest of the horses at our twelve-stall stable are boarders, and one of them happens to be an Icelandic Horse, which is just small enough for Ty to feel comfortable around.

"That's amazing," I tell Ty, setting him down on the ground. "See, it's not so bad to live here, when you get to use your magic on ponies."

He still doesn't look all that convinced but at least he grabs my hand as I walk to the house. "I still wish they were dinosaurs. I tried the magic to turn Taffy into a *Styracosaurus*, but it didn't work."

"Well I'm glad it didn't work, Ty," I say. "Could you imagine all the damage he would do?"

"Yes! It would be *so* cool."

"Thanks for taking care of him," I tell my mom as I pass her in the doorway. "Next week when he's in school he won't be in your hair as much."

"Are you kidding?" she says, and standing this close to her I'm suddenly hit with that sad realization that she's getting older. I guess that is what happens when you don't see your parents for a while. "I'd keep him at home if I could. I have a lot of missed time to make up for with my little man."

I give her a faint smile. Can't help the pang of guilt over that.

My mother picks up on it and pinches my cheek like she used to. Chipmunk cheeks, as she once called them, only now I seem to have grown into them a bit. "I'm just so glad you're both here, honey," she says warmly. "How does it feel to have finished your first week at work?"

I nearly roll my eyes. "It doesn't feel like I'm done, considering my boss is coming over for dinner."

"Right, your boss," she says as we step inside, heading toward the kitchen. "It's kind of strange to hear you talk about Will that way."

"Honestly, it's been kind of weird."

"But everything has been working out, right?"

"Well, yeah. Of course. He's . . . nice."

Nice. I need to try harder.

My mother is watching me with discerning eyes. "He is very nice. You don't remember him much from when you were younger, do you?"

"Not really. And it's probably for the best. I have to keep reminding myself as it is that I'm working for Dad now in a roundabout way. Speaking of, where is he?"

"Your father just got in. Taking a shower."

"I think I'll do the same. You'll keep an eye on Tyson?"

"Of course."

Earlier on my mother had said the dinner was at seven thirty, which gives me just over an hour to get ready. Even so, I'm taking my time, not wanting to rush. In fact, I wish I had brought a bottle of wine to my room, it would really help with my nerves.

I'm not sure if I'm nervous that my boss is coming over, if it's because it's the first real family dinner since I've been here, or a combination of the two. I feel like I have to impress not only Will but my parents too. Thank god the only person who doesn't expect anything different from me is Tyson. He's always on my side.

Until he grows up to be a resentful teenager, but until

that happens, he's definitely my biggest fan.

I decide to make a bit of an effort. I blow dry my hair, so it's this shiny sheen of light bronze, then do what I can with the little makeup I have. I should probably raid my mother's bathroom for some contouring powder or something, but that reminds me too much of being a kid. Hell, every moment that I'm here reminds of being a kid.

My wardrobe is another challenge. I've worn every single work outfit I've got, and the rest of my shit is barely suited for anything other than running around at home after a seven-year old. The only thing I can salvage is the grey pencil skirt I wore on the first day, which desperately needs a wash since a few drops of spilled coffee made their way to the hem, and a simple black tank top.

I eye myself in the mirror, front, back, and side, sucking in my stomach and trying to make myself look as streamlined as possible. *Abs in, abs in*, I tell myself, like it's a mantra. Thankfully I should be sitting behind the table for most of this.

Unless my parents seat me next to Will.

Oh god, I hope not.

I don't know why the idea is freaking me out so much. But it is.

I take a deep breath in and out, make another mental note to take up yoga, and decide to ask my mother if she has a necklace or earrings or something that I can borrow to liven this outfit up. I step out into the hall and immediately hear Will's rich, deep voice sounding from the living room.

Ah, shit. How is he here already?

Then I hear my father's laugh.

Hell. This is going to be a fucking trip.

I take another deep breath and make my way down

the hall. With its floor to ceiling windows overlooking the pasture and riding ring, warm décor, and gas fireplace, the living room is one of my favorites, a place where I used to spend a lot of time drinking Dr. Pepper, doing my nails, and staring out the window at the horses.

Only now I'm staring stupidly at Will as he sits in the leather arm chair, leaning forward as he talks to my father, elbows on his thighs.

For the first time this week he's not wearing a suit. And for the first time I'm realizing how fucking fit he is. It was always a given that he was in shape, what with his slim hips, his firm ass (not that I've been staring), and broad-shoulders. But now in an olive silk short-sleeved shirt, I can actually see the ropey muscle of his tanned forearms, the hard width of his biceps.

Wow.

I keep my mouth clamped together to prevent any drool from escaping and look to my father. That oughta set me right.

My father looks so old next to Will, especially with his shock of white hair and black framed glasses. Then again, he's always had this Leslie Neilson thing going on. Both of them have a few fingers of scotch in their crystal highball glasses. A couple of Mad Men indeed.

"Jackie-O," my father says loudly. He's probably been at the scotch since he got on his plane this afternoon. "I was just talking to Will boy over here about you. I asked if it was time to get you a raise already."

"And?" I ask, folding my arms across my chest.

"He says you're on the right track," my father says. "Would you like a drink?"

I probably should say no but I don't. "Sure," I say, heading toward the decanter on the bar car.

"Here, you sit," Will says, getting to his feet. "I'll get it."

Before I can protest he's pouring me a glass. And I'm staring at his ass.

"Well, well, well," my father says. "And the boss is getting the employee a drink. Come on, Will, it should be the other way around. You've got her now, use her."

I give Dad a wry look. Will just raises his brow at him before he passes me the glass, our fingers brushing against each other for a second. Any longer and I probably would have melted.

"Cheers to you, kid," he says, raising his own glass at me, his eyes looking right into mine. "Sorry. Just Jackie."

"Thank you, Mr. McAlister," I say deliberately.

"Mr. McAlister," my father says with a laugh. "Boy, doesn't that make you feel old?"

"Yes, it does," Will muses.

"Oh come on," I tease as I sip the scotch. "How can anyone feel old when you're next to my father. He's ancient."

"That's enough out of you," my father admonishes me. "I've been away all week, and it feels like the world has crumbled without me here to keep you all in line."

"Where's your boy?" Will asks me, ignoring him. "Tyson, right?"

I look over my shoulder to the kitchen where my mother is calmly getting everything ready. He's not there, which means he's probably in his room.

"He's hiding," I tell him. "He gets shy around people he doesn't know."

"Hell, the kid is still shy around me and I'm his grandfather."

"Dad," I say, warning him.

"I'm sure it will take him awhile to get used to things," Will says smoothly. "But kids are resilient."

Ty definitely is. But even so, he's been through a lot. The other day he asked when Jeff was coming down to live with us. It tore me up inside to remind him it was just the two of us from now on, and Jeff was going to be gone for a long time.

God, I hope so, I think to myself, scared for one deep second at the idea of Jeff somehow showing up at our door one day.

"You okay?" Will asks, his voice low as he stares at me.

I look at him, blinking a few times. "What? Oh. Yes. Just, uh . . .thought of something."

He stares at me for a moment, his eyes searching my face. I paste on a smile. "I should probably go check on him. Dinner will be ready soon, and for all I know he's sitting around in his underwear."

I quickly place the scotch on the coffee table and head upstairs. I can't help but feel relieved the moment I'm alone in the hallway. Something about having both my father and Will here makes me feel like I'm on display, ripe for judging. I've had more than enough judgment in my life.

Tyson's door is closed, so I take a moment to get my emotions under control before I knock. He's so astute at picking up on them, and the last thing I want is for him to be freaked out. In fact, if he doesn't want to have dinner with us, I don't see a good reason for making him.

I knock softly. "Ty-Ty? Can I come in?"

"Yeah."

I open the door and see him sitting on the floor flipping through one of his favorite dinosaur books. He's probably read it a million times by now, can name you every single dinosaur that's in there. I pretty much know their names too, which would help at work if Will ever gave me anything that remotely pertained to the projects Mad Men

Studios is helming.

"What are you doing?" I ask.

"Reading," he says, not looking up at me.

"You know it's almost dinner time."

He pauses mid-page flip. "Yeah. Who is the man again? He sounds like Batman."

I can't help but laugh. "Well if you come down and meet him, maybe you'll find out he *is* Batman."

He gives me a suspicious look, wrinkling up his nose. "Batman would never just tell you he's Batman."

"Unless he trusts you and you ask nicely." He's not sure about that. "Look, I don't really want to have dinner with them either," I admit. "But he's Grandpa's friend. And my boss."

"Batman is your boss?"

"Yes. Maybe. We haven't figured out if he's Batman yet, remember?"

"Right." But I can tell he's a little more intrigued at the possibility that I might be working for Batman. I can only hope Will plays along with it.

"So do you want to come down?"

"Why don't you want to have dinner?"

I sigh. "I mean, I do want to. It's just . . .you know, I'm tired too. I had a long day at work, I wasn't off riding Snickers and using magic."

"Taffy. The pony was called Taffy."

"But," I remind him, "sometimes we do things we don't feel like doing because it will make other people happy. This will make your grandma and grandpa very happy."

"And Batman?"

"Sure." I don't think Will necessarily minds me being here, if anything I suspect it amuses him. Come to think about it, I'm pretty sure all I've been doing this week is amusing him in some way. He probably still thinks of me as a sulky teenager.

"So is his name Bruce Wayne?"

"We call him Will."

"A fake name," he says, tapping his fingers against his chin as he thinks.

I jerk my head toward the door. "Come on. We'll go down together."

Luckily he looks fairly presentable in jeans and a yellow polo shirt. Even though I rarely bought clothes for myself over the last few years, I always made a point to make sure Ty dressed well. Whatever he wanted, I did what I could to make sure he had it, one way or another. It's just that Ty isn't one to want for much, let alone ask for it. And the thing he does want—a good father—is something I can't provide for him.

"You look sad," he says to me as he gets to his feet.

I didn't even realize my eyes were watering. "I'm not, just tired."

I can tell he doesn't believe me.

I take his hand and we head out into the hall.

Dad and Will are still in the living room, my mother now setting the dining room table.

"Right on time," she says to us, placing a roast on the center of the table. Man, she went all out. When I was younger roasts were for very special occasions. I guess the second coming of Jackie Phillips is a good enough excuse.

Will and my father get up, finishing their glasses of scotch before coming over. Tyson holds my hand tighter.

"You excited for dinner, Tyson?" my dad asks, smiling at him. "Or are you more excited about dessert?"

Ty doesn't say anything, just leans into me a little more.

"Ty," I tell him, gesturing to Will. "This is my boss, Batman."

Will breaks into a devastating smile. I swear I grip Ty's hand tighter, as if to ground me. Will's smile should be made illegal. Or at least taken with caution. *Warning: may make you weak at the knees. Do not look at smile if operating heavy machinery.*

"Well, you know the first rule of Batman is that you never talk about Batman," Will says. He crouches down so he's at Ty's level, and I can't help but marvel at the hard muscles of his back. "But I can tell you're the type of guy who can keep a secret."

Ty nods slowly.

"Atta boy," Will says, patting him lightly on the arm and straightening up to look me in the eye. "Cute kid you got there, Just Jackie."

"Thank you Mr. McAlister." My lips twist into a smirk.

"Dinner is getting cold," my father says, even though you can plainly see the steam rising up from the dishes.

I'm about to ask them where we should sit when Ty makes the decision for us. He heads straight over to his chair and pats the empty one beside him. "Mom, you're sitting here."

"As you wish," I tell him, happily taking my place.

But that means Will is beside me at the head of the table.

I have to take extra care not to accidently play footsies with him.

Dinner ends up a lot less awkward than I had anticipated. It might be because my father and Will are loose with scotch, it could be because my mother and I have had nearly a whole bottle of red wine. Either way, it's working.

Until Dad and Will start talking about work.

Something to do with problems with the lead animator at our office.

"Must you two talk about this during dinner?" my mother scolds them.

"As you can see, dear," my father says lazily, gesturing to his empty plate that he practically licked clean, "I've eaten my dinner like a good boy."

"Well, I'm sure Will didn't come here to talk about work."

"Phfff," my father says. "Work is all Will and I talk about." Then my father looks to me. "And now we have another employee of Mad Men Studios at the table. What say you, Jackie. What do you have to say?"

I exchange a glance with my mom before nibbling on a carrot, fully aware that everyone is staring at me. "I, uh . . ."

"Ted, come on," Will says. "Give the kid a break. She's only been working a week. Let her have her weekend. It doesn't help that her boss is here."

My father makes a grumbling sound then looks to my mother. "Where's the pie?"

"Grandpa Ted," Ty says loudly, surprising everyone since he's been silent the entire meal.

"Yes, my boy?" my father asks him, adjusting his glasses.

It's not your glasses that are the problem, it's the scotch, I think to myself.

"I really like dinosaurs, as you know."

My father grins at him. "I do know. I also hear you're an expert."

"Yeah, well," Ty says, wobbling his head from side to side. "I saw this thing on TV today for the World of Science and they said they have dinosaurs and I was wondering if you could take me."

This is the first I'm hearing of it. "What thing?" I ask him.

"I dunno," he says with a shrug, shoving his vegetables to the corner of the plate. "After I was with Taffy I was watching TV. Grandma Diane let me. And I saw a commercial and it said it was here in Vancouver. A whole dinosaur exhibit."

Oh. "Well, I'll take you honey, you know I'm up for that," I tell him.

He sucks on his teeth, looking down.

Fuck. This is definitely one of those cases where he doesn't want his mom to take him, he wants a man. A dad. Someone who will appreciate the fine art of the prehistoric kind.

"I'd love to take you," my father says. "But my week is pretty busy."

"What about tomorrow? It's Saturday. You don't work Saturdays."

My father sighs and I can tell it pains him. He glances at me briefly before looking back to Ty. "Maybe next week, okay? I've got a lot of work to do this weekend."

I'm wondering if that's true. My father is fifty-seven. He shouldn't be working this much.

Ty goes back to looking crestfallen.

Will clears his throat. "I know you didn't ask me, Ty," he says, folding his hands in front of him. "But I would love to go."

Everyone looks at Will in surprise.

"Really?" Ty asks quietly. Because he can't believe Batman would volunteer for this.

And neither can I.

"Absolutely. We'll go tomorrow. Make a whole day of it." Will shoots me wink. "Just Jackie, you can come too."

"Oh, well thank you." I'm amazed Will is putting himself out there like this. Does he not realize how absolutely insane it will be on a Saturday? Does he not realize he's going to be dragging a kid around? And me. Whom he considers a kid.

"Mommy doesn't like dinosaurs," Ty admits.

"Is that so?" Will asks.

"That is not true," I say, strangely defensive as I stab a piece of broccoli with my fork. "I'm a big fan. I know almost as much about them as Ty does."

"You know, Ty," Will says to him, "when I was your age I went to Science World all the time."

"Did your father take you?"

Loaded question. Everyone seems to stiffen.

Will just gives him an easy smile. "No. My father died when I was young. I went with my Uncle Pete. We had a great time. I haven't been back since, but I can tell you're going to love it."

"How young were you when he died?" Ty asks, obviously fixated on this now. To be honest, I'm curious too, though I don't want Will to be put on the spot.

"Ty, it's personal," I chide him softly.

"No, no," Will says to me with warm eyes. "It's quite alright." He looks at Ty. "I was five years old. I grew up on Vancouver Island, in a small town called Tofino. Lot's of surfing. Big waves. It's very wild, very beautiful."

"How did he die?"

"Ty," my mother warns.

Will goes on. "He had an accident. So my mother raised me."

"Is she still alive?"

"Yes she is," he says. "She and her new husband run a campground. She loves it. Maybe you'll get to visit one day."

Ty looks at me with big eyes. "Can we go camping?"

"Finish your dinner and then we'll talk about it," I tell him, giving Will a look. If he's been amused by me all week, I'm certainly amused by him right now.

After dinner, the desert comes out—homemade cherry pie—and then the adults retire to the living room for their digestifs. Even though my mother insisted I drink with them, I honestly just want to call it a night.

When I'm done saying goodnight, I head up the stairs and down the hall toward Ty's room, where he's probably reading his dinosaur book again, since he made a beeline for it the moment he was excused from the table.

"Jackie," I hear Will's deep voice from behind me.

I pause and turn around to see him at the top of the stairs.

"Hey," he says, keep his voice low. "I hope I'm not stepping on anyone's toes." I shake my head, walking closer to him. The hall is dimly lit and his face is half-shadowed, the strong lines of his cheekbones and jaw highlighted.

I stop in front of him and have to crane my head back slightly. He's almost a full foot taller than me, and right now he somehow seems even taller.

He licks his lips and I can't help but watch his tongue. "I understand if it's completely inappropriate for me to take Tyson. I just . . .felt for him, that's all."

Oh my god.

My heart is doing a backward summersault.

Even his own grandfather doesn't seem to feel for him, though I know that thought isn't exactly fair.

"That's fine," I manage to say, clearing my throat. "Thank you. I was just worried you didn't mean it. He's had so many heartbreaks lately . . ."

"I mean everything I say," he says to me, his voice

sliding over my skin. "Always. If you don't know that already, you'll know it soon."

I swallow hard. It feels so different, being with him alone in this hallway, him without his suit, without the office lights, without a million people around us. He seems so much older somehow, not in age, but just . . . such a man. His large, focused presence around me like this nearly tips me off balance.

"Well, again, thank you," I tell him, making myself feel awkward. "You really don't mind if I tag along?"

"As long as you don't mind having spent Friday night and Saturday with your boss," he says, a sly grin spreading across his face, "then I insist."

Boss.
He's your boss.
Don't forget it.
Your father's business partner and friend.
Don't forget that either.

I nod. "Great. What time?"

"Eleven too early for you?"

"Not at all," I say.

"Good. I'll swing by here, pick you guys up."

Is this really happening?

He pats me on the arm, gives me another wink that makes me weak at the knees. "I'll see you tomorrow, kid."

I watch as his tall, muscled frame saunters down the hall, disappearing down the stairs.

Then I lean against the wall, trying to regain my breath.

CHAPTER FOUR

Will

WHAT AM I DOING?
I honestly think I must be losing my goddamn mind.

Not only was it pushy and presumptuous to volunteer to take Jackie's son to Science World, it was completely rude of me. I made Ted to look like a total asshole and a deadbeat grandfather by stepping in like that.

I just couldn't help myself. I saw how destroyed that little boy was from something so simple. I should have just kicked Ted under the table, but instead I opened my big fat mouth, and next thing I know I'm signing up to take a kid I don't know to a museum of science.

And I can't forget his mother, either.

In other words, my employee.

My assistant.

Just Jackie.

No. Try as I might, I definitely can't forget her.

Thankfully, Ted was okay with it all. More than okay.

As he walked me out to my car later, frogs chirping from a nearby ditch, he thanked me.

"You don't mind?" I'd asked.

"Where there's a Will, there's a way," he said, a phrase people used to throw my way a lot. "I know what you're doing."

"You do?"

"Yeah. You want to make Jackie feel comfortable and settle in here. I haven't been around all week, so I'm no help. I really appreciate it."

But even with Ted's approval, I'm still a bit anxious as I drive down the country lanes of Southlands, glancing at the large, sprawling properties with their big houses, barns, and riding arenas. The perfect slice of rural suburbia in the city, as groomed and idyllic as they come.

I find myself thinking about Jackie, wondering about her life up north. She grew up here in this affluent neighborhood, went to a good high school, had a successful father and mother who made names for themselves while giving her everything that she could want.

And yet the Jackie that I'm slowly getting to know doesn't seem to remember that she came from all this. As gorgeous as she is, she looks foreign in these surroundings, from her unease to the clothes she wears. Not that there's anything wrong with what she puts on—she could make a potato sack look like couture if she wanted—but it's cheap stuff. I'm pretty sure that Diane has offered a few times to take her shopping, but for whatever reason Jackie has turned it down. Hell, she's taking the bus most days when I know Diane would let her borrow their car, if not get her one.

Jackie's stubborn, I'll give her that. And a go-getter, eager to prove herself. All week while I've struggled to give her stuff to do—delegating isn't my strong suit—she's been asking for more to work on. She wants to be involved, earn her way. She wants her job to be legitimate, not just something her father has given to her.

I pull into their long circular driveway and park, heading up the stairs to the front door.

Before I even get a chance to knock, it opens.

"Watch it," Jackie cries out just as Tyson bursts through the door, past me and down the steps, running toward my car.

"He's eager," I say, turning to her.

And fuck me.

There, she's standing in front of me looking impossibly radiant. Instead of work clothes, she's in light skinny jeans that hug onto every curve of her thick thighs, the slope of her hips. Up top she's in a long-sleeved billowy red top with just enough cleavage. Her hair is pulled back in a loose braid, showcasing her face that's completely makeup free and tempting beyond sin.

Wholesome. Dangerously wholesome.

Stop staring. Stop staring, now.

Say something.

"I hope you realize what you've done," she says to me with a smirk before I can even open my mouth, closing the door behind her and taking a step toward me. I should probably turn and head back down the steps or at least get out of her way, but I hold my ground.

"What did I do?"

"You've agreed to take this dinosaur-crazy young boy to the World of Science, and his grandmother gave him extra sugary cereal this morning."

"Uh oh," I say, raising my brows. "I guess I should probably ditch all the candy I have in my car. And my pockets."

Her lips twist. "You have candy in your pockets and car? You know, people warn children about men like you."

"They're for me," I tell her.

"And maybe me?" she asks.

Jesus. Is she . . .flirting?

Then she walks past me to the driveway where Tyson is running around in circles, making what I assume are dinosaur sounds.

"This is yours?" she asks, pointing to my car.

"I hope so."

"It's nice."

It is a nice car. A brand-new Mercedes E-class coupe. Dark grey.

"Bought it the day I moved back," I tell her. "Has that new car smell."

"Even with the dogs?"

"Actually, I have one of those special covers that goes in there. They love it. I removed it for Tyson, though."

"How thoughtful."

"I wanna sit in the front!"

"No way," she tells him. "You know kids have to sit in the back. It's the law." She peers in the back of the car. "I should probably get his booster seat, though he's going to hate it."

"Oh mom!" he cries out, obviously embarrassed. "I don't want to."

"Hey look Ty," I tell him. "How about I sit in your booster seat and you drive? I've always wanted to sit in one, they look so darn cool."

"What are you doing?" she whispers to me.

I grin at her. "Actually, I have no idea."

"I can't drive," Ty says, looking at me like I'm a total idiot. "I'm only seven years old you know."

"You can't? But your mother told me you have your driver's license."

He's looking at Jackie with shock. I have to bite my lip to keep from laughing.

"Why would you tell him that?" he asks her.

She rolls her eyes. "I'll be right back," she says and then runs back into the house. I can't help but watch as she goes, that ass of hers looking incredible.

I then pick that moment to bring my gaze to the window to see Diane watching me.

I give her a wave, pretending I wasn't checking out her daughter's ass, and then promptly turn around to talk to Ty.

"Sorry Ty," I say to him. "I don't know where I got that idea from. You just seem so old."

He frowns at me. "You're old."

"Older than a *Parasaurolophus*?"

"What do you know about *Parasaurolophus*?" He says this as if I just conjured one in the front yard.

"I know they're my favorite. Don't forget I'm the one in charge of the dinosaur movies you love so much."

"So is Grandpa Ted, but he doesn't talk to me much about it."

"Because Grandpa Ted is boring, kid," I tell him. Ted is going to murder me over that one.

"I've got it, sorry," Jackie says, coming out with a plush booster seat and looking flustered.

"Not a problem."

"Batman says Grandpa Ted is boring," Ty says. "He also knows what a *Parasaurolophus* is."

Jackie tries to look annoyed but she's smiling. "I'm not surprised at any of those things. He is Batman after all."

It's not long before Ty is sitting reluctantly in the

booster seat and we're driving back toward downtown.

At first I think that Jackie and I won't have much to talk about and the drive could be a bit awkward, but Ty doesn't seem to stop for air. I guess admitting I know something about dinosaurs kind of opened the gates, and now he's finally found a kindred spirit to speak to.

And speak he does. By the time we get to the silver sphere of Science World (now called Telus World of Science, but nostalgia hangs onto the old name), Tyson has gone over his list of his favorite dinosaurs about five times. And he likes a lot of them. And apparently the ones I like aren't that cool, *Parasaurolophus* included.

To be honest, I'm already dinosaured out, but it's just the beginning.

The building is all encased in a sphere, like a smaller version of the ball at Epcot, and it's an absolute madhouse. Children running everywhere. Tyson suddenly becomes shy, holding onto Jackie as we walk through the exhibits, until he finally comes to the dinosaur one. Half the area has life-sized (and disturbingly life-like) replicas, and the other half has an interactive play zone full of who the hell knows what.

While Ty zooms around the play zone, jetting from one thing to the other, I stand back with Jackie by the tail of a *Stegosaurus*, watching him.

"Thank you again," she says, almost shyly this time.

"It's not a problem. I hope he's having a good time." I put my hands in the pockets of my dark jeans, feeling slightly awkward, like I'm about to say the wrong thing and I'm not sure what that is.

But of course I know. It's anything that would make me out to look like a fool. I have some mystique as her boss—it would serve me well to keep it.

"He's having the best time," she says, glancing up at me for a moment. "He woke up early this morning, so excited. I haven't seen him like that in a long time."

"Well I'm glad I could help. When does he start school again?"

"Monday. Remember, I'm taking him in before work. I'm worried for him, though. I wish he didn't have to start so close to the end of the school year, but I wasn't about to mess up his education."

"He seems like a bright kid."

"He is. Very. He's just shy. You know. Has trouble making friends. He's in his head a lot. Then again so am I, so I guess he takes after me."

I can't help but watch her face, every movement and tick as she stares after her son. Something inside me swells for a moment, a dangerous feeling. And yet I can't tear my eyes away.

I clear my throat. "Did he have friends in Fort St. John?"

"One," she says softly, still not meeting my eyes. All the better for me to watch her. "Simon. Lived next door. His mother, Kim, she took care of both of them all the time. Simon was older, had a learning disability, but it didn't matter to Tyson. I'm not sure they even talked much, but they got along. Liked each other's company."

"Communicated in other ways."

"Yeah. I guess."

"You were working?"

Now she looks at me, briefly, before her attention goes back to Tyson. "I thought you've seen my resume. Not that there was much to put on it."

"Ted said you were working two jobs."

"Yeah, well. Someone had to."

"What about your ex?"

She swallows. "He had a good job. For a few years. It's why we moved up there, you know. Lots of money in the oil and gas industry. That's all there is there. I wouldn't have moved otherwise, believe me, but Jeff really made me believe we'd be a family and that I wouldn't have to work and he'd take care of us. But then Jeff lost his job and . . . he never really recovered. I took care of Ty on my own. Sometimes Jeff would sleep there, at our house, well, mobile home. Sometimes he wouldn't. I'd feed him, if he was behaving. He'd always have a promise, that he had some job lined up. Later I found out what he meant . . ."

Damn. That's far too much for a girl her age to be dealing with. "If you don't mind me asking . . . why didn't Ted, your parents, help?"

"They tried," she says. "They wanted to, of course they did. But we'd had a big fight when I moved. They thought I wasn't thinking, I was making a mistake. They were right of course. And then Jeff made me cut them off." She licks her lips, looking incredibly small next to me. "Of course, I thought about contacting them sometimes. But I didn't want to seem . . . like I was using them. You know, only talking to them because I wanted money. And Jeff, I knew it would be trouble if he found out. Anyway, I provided. I did it on my own. I gave Ty everything he could want."

"You did good," I tell her. "Jackie, that boy is here and he's bright and he's funny and he's healthy and it's all because of you."

She looks away, raising up her chin. "I'm not sure if I can deal being this . . . sentimental with you."

Ouch. "Why not?"

"You're my boss."

"And what did I say the first day of work? The more we

know about each other, the better. Besides, what did you say again? We're assigned buddies now? And as your buddy, it's my job to tell you you're doing fucking great." She looks away. "It's okay to take a compliment, Jackie. It's okay to be proud."

She still doesn't look convinced.

"Hey, sometimes life throws us a curve ball. It doesn't go the way we planned. All that matters is how we handle it and the person we become on the other side. You're here now, you're on your way. There's no use dwelling on the things you could have changed. Believe me. Too much reflection on all the could-haves and should-haves will only hold you in your past."

"And what about you?" she asks after a minute.

"What about me?"

"What can you tell me about you?"

I purse my lips. "What do you want to know?"

She glances up at me, watches my face for a moment. "You seem like a natural with Ty. You never had kids? Never wanted to?"

I try not to let anything show on my face. The sore spot she's unknowingly poking. "No, I never had kids. It was . . . complicated."

"What does that mean?"

I exhale through my nose, looking away from her and concentrating on the shadow room in the distance, a place where a camera records your shadow on the wall. I remember that place so well from when I was a kid.

"Hey, do you remember coming here when you were young?" I ask her suddenly.

"What? Kind of . . . ?"

Without thinking, I grab her hand and lead her over to Ty, who is playing some dino-guessing game. "Hey Ty-Rex, come here." I hold out my hand for him.

He looks at me unsurely until Jackie gives him a slight nod.

I have to ignore the fact that her small, soft hand feels unbelievably right in mine. Then I take Ty's and lead them over to the shadow room.

"What is it?" Ty asks.

"You'll see," I tell him as we enter a long space and stop in front of a plain white wall, facing it along with a bunch of other children.

I raise my arms so I'm lifting both their hands in to the air and hold the pose.

"What are we doing?" Ty asks.

"Just wait," I tell him. "Lights are going to come on behind us in ten seconds and it's going to capture our shadows on the wall."

"Capture our shadows?" Ty sounds scared. I hold his hand tighter. Somehow it makes me hold Jackie's tighter too.

"You'll be safe. Get ready."

A burst of white light flashes from behind us and, just as I remember it, the wall glows green with the frozen shadow of the three of us caught on the wall.

"Wow!" Ty cries out, running over to it and running his hand over the outline. "It has my shadow." He turns to look at us. "Can I get it back?"

I chuckle. "You'll get it back when it fades. Watch."

Slowly the shadow and the green around it starts to fade back to white, as if nothing happened.

And it makes me realize I'm still holding Jackie's hand.

"Sorry," I apologize quickly, dropping it.

"That's okay," she says, her voice sounding strangely high-pitched. "It's uh, been a long time since I've done this.

That. The shadow thing."

"I wanna do it again! I'm going to be a velociraptor this time."

"You've created a monster," she tells me under her breath as we exit the room, watching as Tyson stays behind and strikes his best raptor movements.

"You never know, with the VFX studio in LA, he might have a bright future as a stop-motion actor. You know, Andy Serkis works constantly."

"That would be his dream. Pretending to be things for a living," she pauses, glancing me over. "You're not off the hook, you know."

"For what?"

"For avoiding my last question."

So the shadow room didn't distract her.

I sigh. "All right. Was it the question about kids? Fine. Here we go, since I said we should be open with each other and apparently I have to follow my own bullshit." I pause. "I didn't think I wanted them. And Sasha definitely didn't. She never wavered. So eventually I got a vasectomy."

"Oh. Well, that's pretty common."

"It is. Until she got pregnant."

"It failed?"

I give her a steady look. "No."

She blinks at me as the truth hits her. "Oh," she says, hand at her chest. "Shit."

"Yeah. Oh shit. She was cheating on me and got herself knocked up. But surprise, surprise, she wanted his baby. Just not mine."

Her brows knit together as she tries to think of the right thing to say.

"It's okay," I tell her quickly. "It's done. It happened. I'm over it."

"I just can't believe that. What a bitch."

My hackles go up at that one. "She wasn't a bitch. Don't get me wrong, she was really shitty to do that to me. I mean, really shitty. But I was married to her for fifteen years before it blew up in my face. I know she wasn't trying to hurt me. She was just . . . careless. Selfish. Scared."

"And a bitch," Jackie says. "Sorry, not sorry. But she could have, you know, not had an affair."

I shrug. "Yeah, well. She did. There was a lot she shouldn't have done. But she fell out of love with me. Honestly, I saw it coming. I was falling out of love with her too. I just believed, stupidly, that we could work through it. Find our way back. You know, that romantic idea of getting through the rough patch of the marriage. She just . . .took the easy way out. Had her cake on the side. Anyway, it's old news."

"Not really, since you literally just moved here."

"Yeah, well I guess because I was attached to the idea of working through our marriage, I thought working through the office situation would pay off. It didn't. In fact, it was Sasha that asked me to move."

"She did?" Jackie asks incredulously. "Why? She should move, she fucked up. Don't you have authority over her?"

I'm smiling, just a bit, at how worked up she's getting. "I was trying to prove that she can fuck around on me but not make me give up my job or affect that part of my life. So I stuck it out at that office far longer than I should have. It got on her nerves. Our divorce took such a long time, because of the business, that when she offered me the condo we bought here back in the day, among other stuff, I took it." I shake my head, still not able to believe it sometimes. "If I didn't take it, I would have made both our lives miserable. I didn't want to be that guy. I mean, I had been for over a year, working with her side-by-side, trying to prove something, but you got to know when to stop."

"Wow," she says softly, her eyes tender as she stares at me. "I'm so sorry. I honestly had no idea."

"Well, that's comforting to know I'm not the talk of the office. But, yes, it's been an adjustment."

"Fuck," she swears, biting on her lip for a second. "If I'd known all you'd been through, I think I would have worked harder this week."

"Kid, you've been working hard enough. You're spending your weekend with the boss. How about that for going above and beyond?"

"Believe it or not, this is a better weekend than what I had planned. Which was just sitting around at home. My home which isn't really my home. God, it's weird to be back with my parents. They've been great and all but it's . . . it's weird. Strained. Awkward."

I nod. "Seven years is a lot of time to be apart. I'm sure you'll get back into the swing of things soon. Go back to the way things were."

"But I'm no longer the girl I was at eighteen. Not even close. I was bad news. A mess. And now, well I guess I'm still a mess. I just can't wait till I make enough to move out and get a place of my own. Though with the rent in this city, I have no idea when that will happen."

"Just take it one step at a time. That's all I'm doing."

"And you seem to know what you're doing."

"At least I have you convinced."

At that, Tyson comes running out of the room. "Did you see all the shadows? Did you? Bam, bam, bam! It captured all of them and then gave them all back."

"That's great Ty," she says. "Are you ready for lunch?"

"No!" he yells, laughing, and then runs back to the

dinosaur area, running his hands over the giant replicas when the signs clearly say not to touch.

"Oh, Jesus," Jackie says under her breath, giving me an apologetic glance before running after him. "Tyson Phillips, don't touch those!"

I watch for a moment as she runs him down, unable to keep from smiling. There's some part of me, deep inside, maybe stemming from the primal caveman days, that wants me to take care of both of them. To provide for them. To protect them. It's honestly unlike anything I've felt before.

But I know it's not a smart feeling to have. Not in this situation we're in. Not when she's Ted's daughter, my employee, and sixteen years younger.

Still, I hold on to that urge for a moment, reveling in it, before I push it away.

I join Jackie and Ty.

We eat shitty cafeteria-style food.

Walk around the water of False Creek for a bit, watching the water taxis and seagulls, before it starts to rain.

Then I drive the two of them back home.

It's almost bittersweet to be alone again.

CHAPTER FIVE

Jackie

MONDAY MORNING.
It's raining. Pouring, actually.
It's cold.

I want nothing more than stay snuggled in bed, warm under the covers.

When the alarm goes off, I want to murder it.

I've never been a fan of Mondays.

I mean, that goes without saying.

Anyone who says they love Mondays is a big, fat liar.

But this Monday marks the start of my second week at work. It also marks the day that Ty starts school. So whether I like Mondays or not, I'm getting out of bed, ready to face the day.

Ty is going to be a bit of a handful today. He's always been a mama's boy and it's no wonder that he's been extra attached to me lately. Luckily I cleared it with Will last week to come in an hour later to work so I could take him in on his first day. Originally my mother was going to do it, but Ty's been extra clingy and emotional and I know he needs me there.

I can't help but feel that it had something to do with our Science World visit the other day. Ty's always been shy, especially around adults, but I really saw him open up with Will. Not that I'm too surprised—Will has this way about him that puts anyone at ease—but it was a shock to see nonetheless.

It's obvious that Ty is missing a father figure and needs one badly. I was hoping that my own father would be more involved, but I don't blame him either way. He is busy, I see that firsthand, especially now that I'm working at the company. I know all he has to deal with, plus there's the fact that Ty and my father don't have a relationship yet. They will though, I have no doubt. My father is a difficult man sometimes but I know he cares a lot about Ty.

But after the outing with Will, I think it made Ty realize how much he needs a man around. Hell. It made me realize how nice that would be. But after everything I've gone through, I know I'm not ready, and it's something I need to push out of my head. I like Will as a person and as my boss, and yes, he's hot as hell. Yet I know it's asking for trouble for me to get attached to him in any way whatsoever. The outing on Saturday was just him being nice and I appreciate it more than anything.

I get dressed, not surprised that my clothes don't look as good as they did after a wash. That's what I get for buying a $20 skirt. Still, I slip on a black blazer, a white dress shirt, and that grey skirt again, and pull my hair back into the bun. I add what makeup I have and decide I look good enough. Besides, the first week is already over. The pressure is off. Things should get easier.

But easy or not, it's Ty that breaks my heart. The poor

boy is practically crying as he gets in the back of my mom's SUV as we take him to the school, which is a ten-minute drive away, the very same elementary school that I went to as a kid.

My mother and I try and tell him stories about the things I remembered while going there, but the school looks totally different now, larger and more immaculate. Thankfully our meeting with the principle goes well—he's jovial and kind and not at all like the principle I used to have, who always looked like he'd been drinking—and he personally escorts Ty to his classroom. I wave goodbye to him and promise to see him later after Grandma picks him up.

"We really oughta get you a car, eh?" she says to me as she drives downtown. I insisted on taking a bus but my mother rarely takes no for an answer.

"I'll buy my own when I can afford it," I tell her.

"Jackie. Please," she says and the tone of her voice makes me look at her. Her brow is furrowed, creating lines that even Botox can't tame. "Sweetie, you have to let us take care of you. You did a great job when you were up north, but now you're here and we're your parents. We want to spoil you. We want to spoil Ty. So let us."

"You've done enough by getting me this job," I tell her. "I know Will doesn't really need an assistant."

"Yes, he does," she says. "He's just as stubborn as you are. He had a process down in LA, he had it all worked out with Sasha. But those days are over. Now he's up here and dealing with new things in a new city in a new office. You're a great help to him, even if he doesn't know it yet." She looks me over. "Just a small car, a little cheap hatchback. We'll get a lease and you can take it over when you're able to."

"We'll see," I tell her.

"And how about a new wardrobe, hairstyle, makeup?"

"Mom."

"You know you look so beautiful regardless, but I just think it will give you more confidence."

I cross my arms and look out the window as rain pelts down. "I have confidence."

"You're going to have to find a man someday."

"Oh my god, can we not talk about this?"

"Fine. But—"

"No buts. No buts at all."

We're silent for the rest of the drive, though I surprise us both when she drops me off by leaning in and giving her a hug. I know she's trying, I just have to stop being stubborn at some point.

When I get inside the office I find someone else, I think a temp, at reception.

"Where's Tiffany?" I ask her.

"Oh, they're all in a meeting. In the boardroom."

Well, shit. I had no idea that being late would mean I'd miss out, if I was even supposed to be in the meeting to begin with.

I look in the office. It's half-empty. The blinds in the boardroom are drawn and I can make out a row of people sitting in there.

"They do this every other Monday morning," the temp says to me.

"Do you know if I'm supposed to go in?"

She shrugs.

Great. I head over to my desk and put my bag away, hovering around it, unsure of what to do. No one is in their office, which means most people are at that meeting. Which means I have no idea if I should go over there and knock on the door and interrupt it or just stay put. If I'm not supposed to go into the meeting and I do, that would be super embarrassing.

I decide to stay put. Start organizing things around my desk. Check my emails. See one from Will sent this morning. Like, two minutes ago.

It says: Are you at your desk yet?

I smile to myself and look over at the boardroom, the door still closed.

I type back: Just got in now. I didn't know there was a meeting. Should I go in there?

I press send and then wait, watching the room. A few minutes pass and I get a reply.

Oh hell no. Stay where you are. Save yourself. These meetings are a waste of time. The only thing I've learned is that Bob Cantu smells like blue cheese and dinosaurs just aren't sexy enough.

I laugh quietly and send: Sounds like fun. Want me to come rescue you?

I honestly don't know if that's pushing it a bit. I mean, he probably doesn't want to be rescued, nor need to be.

But he sends back: Yes! Three minutes. Come knock on the door with some sort of emergency. Make something up and you need to talk to me privately.

Grinning, I type: Okay.

I get up, look around, and then slowly work my way past the picnic tables to the boardroom, standing outside the door for a bit until I think it's been three minutes.

I knock and then open the door, poking my head in.

Tiffany, Alyssa, Patty, my father, Casey the communications guy, Bob Cantu who smells like cheese, a few other people, and Will all sit around a large table, staring at me with interest.

Will is already slipping his phone away, trying to hide his grin.

"Jackie," my father says. "Nice of you to drop in. Come sit and we'll get you up to speed."

Nice try.

"I, uh, need to talk to Will alone. Will, there's some sort of . . . emergency."

Good one, Jackie.

"What kind of emergency?" my father asks.

"Uh, with his travel plans? I booked him a flight and I think I did something wrong because he's on the no fly list as a terrorist." Everyone gasps, looking shocked. I went too far. I smile. "They said it will be resolved once they speak to him."

Will gets up, embarrassed. "Well, I better go deal with this."

He gives me a loaded look as he goes past me and I shut the door.

He waits until we're both in his office to say, "That was the best you could come up with? You accidentally have me as a known terrorist?"

I shrug, palms out. "I don't know. Everyone was staring at me. I panicked. I didn't know what kind of emergency you should have."

He sits down at his desk and rolls up the pristine white sleeves of his dress shirt, showcasing his tanned forearms. "You could have just said I had an important call."

"But then I probably would have been roped into that meeting."

"Every man for themselves around here, kid."

"You're right, Mr. McAlister."

"Even after this weekend, that's what I am to you," he says playfully.

"Even after that, you're still calling me the kid," I point out.

Then I notice on the corner of his desk he has a charcoal pencil sticking out of a shut pad of sketching paper. "Are you drawing again?" I ask him, though I honestly don't know that he ever stopped. He'd just mentioned his animation goals and I figured it was something that was put to the side when he took on the company.

He glances at the pad of paper, folding his hands in front of him. "Maybe."

I bite my lip for a moment. "Can I see it?"

He cocks his head, studying me. "What are you going to do for me?"

"What?" I blink at him, wide-eyed.

A small smile appears on his lips. "If I show you this, you have to show me something of yours."

Holy hell. Did this conversation take a turn for something sexual?

This is so, so wrong.

And yet I want it to keep going. See how wrong we can make it.

"You mean like flash you some leg?"

Will bursts out laughing and I immediately feel flush with embarrassment. "No," he says, hand over his mouth. "Well, I mean, if you're offering. But no, Ted wouldn't let me hear the end of that. I just meant you have to give me something of yours. Like, what do you like to do? What are your hidden talents?"

I wish my cheeks would stop burning. I try and cover it up by putting one hand on my hip and taking a sassy stance. "What if showing off my leg is my talent?"

He blinks at me in surprise and now I think I've taken it too far again.

"Are you talking about doing the can can in front of me? Because I completely agree that it's a fair trade."

I almost bite the bullet. I almost go for it. Of course I can't do the can can in this skirt, and I can't do it in general (my legs aren't all that bendy, another reason to take up yoga).

I sigh, trying to think of something.

To be honest, I feel like I lost those passionate parts of myself a long time ago. There was always horses, of course, until I grew out of them. Then later, when I was a teen, I was really obsessed with classic films and then that lead me into screenwriting. I never officially studied it, but when I was pregnant I read every book I could and wrote a few scripts of my own. They never went anywhere of course, I didn't share them with a soul. But it was therapy. In a way it was how I dealt with being pregnant at eighteen, by a guy I never could manage to keep. I threw myself into it, and even thought about applying for school for it.

But we know the rest . . .

Dreams were put on hold. Tucked away. My world became about Ty. And then it became about surviving.

"Look," Will says softly, bringing my attention back to him. "I was just joking. I'll show you if you want."

I stare at him a moment, studying the sharp cleft in his jaw, the slant of his dark brows, his eyes as they take me in, warm and steady and never wavering, and in that moment I am lost. I don't know if I want to be found.

But I'm being dramatic. Over romantic. Foolish.

He's a man with a pretty face, and in the end, he's just my boss.

My boss that everyone thinks is on the terror watch list now.

I nod. "Maybe some other time," I tell him. "Maybe

when I have something to trade. You know, I used to dabble in screenwriting, back when I was pregnant with Ty but I wouldn't even know where to begin now." He watches me for a moment and I can tell he has a million more questions. But then concedes, leaning back in his chair.

"By the way," I add, "am I normally supposed to be in those meetings?"

He shrugs. "Probably. We have a buddy system set up after all."

I give him a withering glance before I walk out the door. "Let me know if you have work for me this week. Real work."

Then I sit down at my desk and prepare for the week.

I can feel his eyes on me the whole time.

CHAPTER SIX

Jackie

"Cheers," Alyssa says, raising her glass of prosecco toward me. "Here's to surviving your first month at Mad Men Studios."

I lift my glass and gently clink it against hers before taking a sip, the bubbles tickling my nose. I probably shouldn't be drinking during my lunch hour but it seemed like a good enough occasion. Besides, it's a Thursday and I've noticed most people have started treating Thursdays like Fridays at work. At least on the administrative side. Even though I've been working there a month now, I still don't know what happens down the animation hall. What I do know is that those animators work long ass hours. Some even sleep there overnight. Considering the young age of our office, I wouldn't be surprised if they all slept with each other.

"Cheers to that," I tell her.

"And so how are things? What's your one-month recap?" she asks. "Be honest with me. You know I won't tell a soul."

Yeah right. I give her a wry smile. "Things are fine."

"Just fine?"

I shrug and start flipping through the menu again, even though I'd already placed my order for a goat cheese salad. "It's great, actually. But I mean, I think any job would be great after where I used to work."

"And where was that?"

She's asking innocently, and it reminds me that over the last month the only person I've been open and forthcoming with has been Will. I'm starting to think my boss knows far more about me than he should. Definitely not everything, but the more I'm around him, the more I just find myself talking about everything, even the ugly things.

"Oh, well," I say, trying to figure out the right way to phrase it. "You know, in Fort St. John, there's not a lot of glamorous jobs. I never went to university or anything so I just did what I could. Worked as a cashier at Safeway during the day and a few nights a week I bartended."

"Two jobs?"

I nod, taking another sip. "Jeff, my ex, he wasn't around much."

"Right," she says slowly, getting it. "He was stepping out?"

"God, who knows. Who cares." Thank god I had the presence of mind to never stop using condoms with him after Ty was born, who knows what I could have got. "Anyway," I say, wanting to change the subject. "The job is going great. And Will is finally giving me enough work to keep me busy. I swear, it's like pulling teeth with that man."

She tilts her head slightly, eying me through her lashes.

"What?" I ask, not liking this sly gaze.

"I never noticed when you stopped calling him Mr. McAlister."

"Huh. I guess I never noticed either. I do still sometimes, just to piss him off."

"He likes you," she says.

My heart jumps in my chest. I swallow, wondering, hoping, wishing . . . "It's Will. He likes everyone."

"That's true," she says. "I just mean, it's good. You make a good team, that's all. Like Patty and your father. You might just end up working for Will for another ten years."

"Oh god, I hope not," I blurt out.

"Why not?"

How do I explain to Alyssa that every single day I see Will, I find myself getting more wrapped up in his world and everything about him? It's getting to the point where I can barely concentrate. Other than Science World, I haven't seen him outside of work—he's been flying a lot to Sydney, Australia, to a studio there that they want to take over—but even, so I'm unable to ignore the feeling that comes over me when I hear his voice, see his face, get a whiff of his woodsy smell, like moss and cedar on a spring day.

It's a crush is what it is. A total overblown schoolgirl crush.

I've just never crushed this hard on anyone, even in high school when I had posters of Zac Ephron on my wall and drew doodle hearts in my diary. And maybe pornographic pictures of me and Zac together.

To be honest, it's almost painful. Almost. As long as I just keep living in this fantasy bubble I'll be all right. More than all right. My fantasy bubble keeps me happy.

In my fantasy bubble, I'm not his assistant. I'm just some woman he meets at a bar. A woman he ravages in the alley behind it after a few drinks. I imagine how it feels to kiss him, to have his large hands on my skin, what it's like to have the weight of his sculpted body on top of me. He's a big boy—I want to feel how big he is in every single way.

"Jackie?"

I blink. My cheeks burn. "Sorry, what?"

Alyssa narrows her eyes at me. "How come you can't see yourself at Mad Men in ten years?"

"Oh," I say, taking a large gulp of champagne, "that. I totally see myself staying there. The animation side is kind of fascinating, I just wish I knew more about it. Maybe even get into development? I know that's not what we do right now, but down the line, something with scripts. I just don't think I'd be Will's assistant. Maybe I'll have my own assistant."

And I'm not lying either. I could totally see myself staying within the company. I just don't want to tell her that the thought of working for Will for ten more years with this unrequited crush would be like the world's longest case of blue balls (or the lady equivalent, in this case).

"I suppose you're right. I just don't know where to go up from office manager. My accounting skills are pretty weak, but at least in that department you can go somewhere."

"What about the communications department?" Which at this moment pretty much just consists of Casey Templeton, a bearded hipster in his early thirties who won't stop hitting on me.

"Maybe," she says. "You know Casey has a crush on you."

"I was just thinking about how obvious that is."

"You going to go for him?"

I give her a look. "Hell no."

"He's cute."

"Cute? Maybe. But he's smug beyond reproach. And I work with him. There are rules. You don't sleep with the people you work with."

"You know there aren't any official rules at the office, don't you?"

The way she's saying it makes me pause. "I didn't say there were . . . why, have you . . . you and Casey?"

She laughs, shaking her head. "I'm pretty sure Casey hates me. He sure doesn't give me the same treatment he gives you."

"Meaning making lewd comments when I use the copy machine?"

"He's harmless. Threaten him with a sexual harassment suit and he'll stop."

"I'm sure that will go over well."

"So are you dating anyone?"

I'm thankful the waiter comes by with our food, interrupting that question for a moment.

"No," I tell her in between mouthfuls of salad, trying in vain not to get the dressing all over my new shirt. Even though I've had two paychecks already, I've been saving up instead of spending my money. But my mother went and got me a $500 gift card to Banana Republic, practically forcing me to upgrade my wardrobe. Unfortunately, $500 at BR doesn't get you very much, unless you have an eye for the sales rack like I do.

As for getting me a car, she's still working on it.

"No one at all?" she presses.

"I've been in Vancouver for like, six weeks."

"But you're pretty."

"Thanks," I mumble.

"Then again, Vancouver is notorious for being a dating nightmare."

"Luckily I don't have any interest in dating anyone"

"Really?" she says this like I've personally insulted her.

I shrug. "I work and then I go home and be a mom and that's my life and for now I'm totally cool with it. I don't need a man coming in and messing all of that up."

"Well, what if you just had a man to mess you up a few nights a week. Try a dating app."

"Yeah, take him back to my parent's place, that will be totally sexy. Besides, the moment most men find out I'm a mother, they look the other way. Something about being used goods."

"Oh give me a break."

"It's true. Guys my age don't want the baggage of a child. Believe me. Guys my age want to find that right girl to screw for a while and then maybe get married and then maybe have children with."

"So you just sped up the process."

I give her a wry look and point my fork at her. "No. I appreciate your concern but it just doesn't work that way."

"Concern for your vagina," she says.

"My vagina can handle it. It's a camel."

"When's the last time you had sex?"

"I don't think we know each other well enough to have this conversation."

She rolls her eyes. "Mine was last week."

"Really?"

"Just because I'm single doesn't mean I can't have fun. Do you know how many of the dating apps I belong to?" She reaches into her purse and pulls out her phone, pushing it toward me and scrolling to a screen that's all Tinder and Bumble and who else knows what. "Eventually you find a guy that knows what he's doing, even if just for a night."

"Well, no offense at all, but that's just not my style..." I pause, feeling the fear rising up inside me. "I'm not ready."

She frowns and then a wash of realization comes over her, softening her delicate features. "Oh. I see. You're still hung up on your ex."

Hung up is one way to put it. The truth is, I'm desperately trying to forget that Jeff ever existed. But even though the marks have faded, I still remember who he was and what he did. What could have happened if I didn't call the police. It's something I can't talk about, to anyone really, let alone Alyssa. I'm not ready in so many ways.

"It was complicated," I admit. "I am moving on but it's going to take some time."

"I get that," she says, a wistful look on her face. "I think it's probably the same for Will too."

I straighten up. "Why Will?"

"Because of his divorce. That can't be easy to get over. Have you seen his ex-wife? Holy moly. Legs up to her chin, I swear. At least he's here so he can make a fresh start, but I have yet to hear of him dating anyone."

I can't ignore the hot coal of jealousy in my stomach. "Why would you hear about that anyway? Isn't his private life private?"

She smirks at me. "Tiffany is pretty observant. And I'm pretty sure you would have said something."

"Why would I have said anything?"

"Because you're his assistant. The closest person in the office to him now, aside from your father. And he's rarely here."

"I don't pay much attention to Will's private life," I tell her. "If he goes on dates or has a girlfriend, I wouldn't know about it."

"I think you would," she says thoughtfully. "I think

you'd be making reservations at fancy restaurants. God, can you imagine the girl who gets to date him?"

I would rather not.

"With that condo and his money and his looks and that dick . . . it would be a real Cinderella story. And he's definitely Prince Charming. Prince Charming with a big fucking dick."

I nearly choke on my food. "He is charming, I'll give him that," I say nonchalantly, trying to ignore the heat on my cheeks. God damn it, twice already I'm blushing during this lunch.

She studies me for a moment. I wonder if she buys the act.

"Well, if I do happen to run into anyone nice, you should really let me set you up."

"I'll think about it," I tell her, even though I won't.

When we get back to the office we're running a bit late. Luckily no one notices except Tiffany, and that girl honestly doesn't care about much except for books, BBC shows, and a weird fascination with WWE. The three of us have talked about starting a monthly book club, but with Tiffany's attachment to YA fantasy, Alyssa's love of all things smut, and my tendency to read either historical romances or biographies, we have yet to agree on anything.

Still, it's a nice thought. I'm grateful to go out for lunch with them sometimes. So far they're the only friends I have in this city. Everyone else I knew from high school has moved on to other things, and I burned a lot of bridges back in my wild-child days.

I'm a bit buzzed when I get back to my desk, which is nice. I've barely had time to sort through a few emails when I feel someone hovering above my desk. I look back to see Casey peering over my shoulder.

"Do you mind?" I ask him, unable to keep the annoyance out of my voice.

Casey grins at me. As I admitted to Alyssa, he's a cute guy. Beard is a little scruffier than I would like—bordering on hobo chic—and there's something in his ice blue eyes that I don't quite trust. But he's funny. Most of the time. I try not to laugh though because it only eggs him on.

"What are you doing this weekend?" he asks me.

Oh, lord.

"Why?"

He shrugs. "Thought maybe you wanted to get a drink."

"Are you asking me on a date, Casey?"

"Me? Nah. Just as friends."

I eye him suspiciously. "Earlier today you told me I had an ass made for belt marks."

"I say that to all my friends."

"Right. Well, I'm busy."

I turn around and go back to my emails. There's one from Will, sent while I was out, needing another flight to Sydney booked soon.

But then Casey is leaning right over me, his mouth far too close to my ear.

"Come on," he says quietly. "You should get to know me outside of work. I'm not who you think I am."

"Can I help you with something, Casey?" Will's booming voice crackles behind us.

Casey straightens up and I twist in my chair to look at Will as he stands by his door. He's staring right at Casey, and for the first time since I started working here he's not smiling. All of Will's usual charm and ease is gone. In his sleek black suit he's absolutely formidable looking, his brow lowered, eyes focused and cold.

Jesus. I don't know who *this* guy is but I can tell you don't want to cross him.

"No, just talking to Jackie here," Casey says and I swear I hear his voice waver. He's afraid of him.

"Well Jackie is my assistant, not yours."

"It was personal," Casey explains, folding his arms. But against him, Will looks like a damn linebacker.

"Then it can wait until after business hours," Will says then flicks his cold eyes over to me. "Jackie, can I speak to you for a second? In private?"

He turns and heads into his office.

I avoid Casey's eyes as I get up and follow him, my heart starting to race. I feel like I just did something horrible and I don't know what. Is it that Casey was asking me out? Is it the drinks at lunch? Oh my god, am I somehow being fired?

"Close the door," he says to me in a clipped voice as he sits down at his desk.

I do so with shaking hands and slowly turn to face him.

"Mr. McAlister . . ." I say, prepared to grovel.

He gives me a sharp look. "Why are you calling me that?"

"I don't know. I feel like I'm about to be fired?"

"Fired?" he says, his forehead creasing. "Ah, shit. Sorry. No, no I'm not firing you. Why would I do a thing like that? Come, sit down."

I reluctantly take the seat across from him, hands folded in my lap.

"It's been a month since you started working, I just wanted to do a bit of an evaluation with you. Your father's idea, really."

"Oh. Okay."

My heart slows a bit.

"Was he hitting on you?"

"Who? Casey?"

Will just stares at me. "You looked uncomfortable."

"I was uncomfortable," I admit. "I mean, you know, I get that's how he is."

"No one here should make you uncomfortable." His look and his voice are so hard, it makes me sit up a little straighter.

"It's okay," I say quickly, not wanting him to make a big deal out of nothing. "He was asking me on a date. I think."

"I see."

"I told him no, of course."

"Good."

Good?

"He's not really my type," I explain. "I know what guys to stay away from and he seems like one of them." I swear Will looks impressed. "And I would never mix business with pleasure. Not that there would be any pleasure with him. I mean, I should probably just stop talking. But you know what I'm saying."

"You don't date within the company. That's smart."

"Right. I mean you would know from personal experience, right?"

"Yes, I do," he says, looking down at something at his desk. The he shakes his head. "Frankly, I think Casey is a slime-ball. I've wanted to fire him a few times since I've been here, but your father thinks he does great work, so for now he's not going anywhere. But if he says anything else to you, does anything to make you feel uncomfortable, he's out of here. Got it?"

"Got it," I tell him with a nod, my heart feeling all warm and gooey at his protectiveness.

"You're very valuable to me, kid," he says gravely, his voice going low as he glances over at me. "You're a great asset to me. To the team. I don't want to lose you."

"I promise, I'm not going anywhere."

"Good." He takes in a deep breath through his nose and seems to relax before my eyes. The smile returns. God, he is so fucking pretty, it's not fair. "So, now that that's out of the way, how have you been enjoying it here?"

"I love it," I tell him, a standard response.

"It hasn't been strange working for your father?"

"You're my boss. That's how I see it. Besides, Dad is hardly here."

"That's true. So, do you have any complaints? Or suggestions? Anything I can improve on?"

I smirk at him. "You're asking if I have any complaints against you, my boss?"

He nods, earnest. "Yeah."

"I'm not sure you get how this works," I tell him. "You're supposed to have complaints and suggestions for me. It's not the other way around."

"We're a team, kid."

"Not when you call me kid."

"We're a team, Just Jackie."

"Marginally better," I mutter under my breath.

"Look, I want you to be happy. I'm happy. Well . . . happier than I've been in a long time."

"I am happy," I tell him, but the words feel ghostly. Transparent. And I know from the way that Will is staring at me, intensity flaring in his lagoon blue eyes, that he can see right through it.

I have to look away, concentrating on a water ring that's formed on the cherry wood desk.

"Jackie," he says softly, and lets my name dance in the

room. He clears his throat, taps his fingers against the desk. I can't help but let my eyes be drawn to his ring finger, where any sign of a wedding ring has faded away.

He doesn't finish his sentence though. Finally I look up at him expectantly.

"Never mind," he says. "I just want you to be happy here, at the very least."

"I am happy here," I tell him. "Honestly."

He nods again, rubbing his lips together. A strange silence settles over us. I'm not sure if I should leave or not, but I know I'd rather be in here with him.

"I have a present for you," he says suddenly, reaching into his desk drawer and pulling out an envelope. "A thank you for a good first month."

"What? Really?" Part of me wants to bashfully wave the present away but the other part is both flattered and curious.

He holds it out for me, but when I reach for it he snatches it away. "There's a catch though."

"What's the catch?"

"I'm the catch."

My eyes widen. He gives me back the envelope.

I have no idea what he's talking about, but he is a fucking catch so there's no argument there. I open it and take out three tickets to a Canucks game, Vancouver's NHL team.

"Hockey?"

"Playoffs start tomorrow night against San Jose," he says. "You can't get better seats than those. Right up against the glass. I was thinking you could bring Tyson. If he wants to. Shit, I don't know if he likes hockey. Or if you do. Fuck. Don't feel you have to use them."

He starts to take them away, his hand closing over

mine and holding it there tight. Something so simple as the heat of his palm pressing into my skin ignites something inside me, a tiny flame I've tried so hard to put out.

I stare into his eyes, lost in them, and the whole office disappears. There are no framed movie posters on the walls, no desk, no computer, no bookshelves full of binders and DVDs, no couch, no houseplants I suspect are fake. There's nothing except his eyes and my eyes, his hand and my hand.

God help me.

I'm done for with this man.

Stop this right now, I tell myself.

It kills me to pull my hand back, to edge back in my chair, to move away. To break it all and bring reality back.

Somehow I find my voice. "I would love to go. And I would love it if you came too. And I know Ty would feel the same way."

He holds my eyes for a few more beats and I'm captive and I'm scared because he's looking at me in a way that I've only dreamed of and I don't dare fall for it, fall for him, fall for anything.

And then he nods, looks down at the envelope. "Well great." He gives it back to me. "It should be a fun experience at any rate, even if they lose. Which they probably will because we're going." He shoots me a grin.

"I'm sure it'll be fun," I say dumbly.

"Game starts at seven, but I like to go early. I'll call Diane and see if she'll bring Tyson here right after school."

It's so bizarre—and yet so right—how Will has access to my family like this, that he can handle all the plans, even those that involve my son, and I don't have to do it all alone.

"Don't worry," he says, "we can play hooky together."

In that whiskey-rich voice of his, playing hooky sounds kinky as hell.

"Get off together at four," he adds.

Oh, lord. He's making it worse. A dull ache throbs between my legs.

I swallow. "Sounds good."

If he only knew how damn good it sounds.

CHAPTER SEVEN

Will

"YOU ASSHOLE," MY FRIEND EMMETT TELLS ME over the phone.

I chuckle to myself. "Next game, I promise it will be you and Ted."

"Promises, promises," he says. "Does Ted know you're taking his daughter and grandchild instead of me and him?"

"He bailed weeks ago," I tell him.

"That doesn't answer my question. Does he know you're taking his daughter instead?"

I anxiously rub at the scruff on my chin. "Well, no. I don't think he'd care much though. Why would he?"

"Because, man, it's . . . well, it's an overly generous thing for a boss to do for his employee."

"It's like a bonus, Emmett. Shit like this happens all the time, especially for employees who deserve it. And Jackie, well, she's been through a lot. She deserves it. In LA I often took the receptionist, Luciana, to dinner."

"I'm sure Sasha was with you though."

"She was . . . so what?"

"I just think a hockey game is above and beyond. Especially ringside seats during the playoffs which you were supposed to give to your buddy Emmett!"

"Next game, I promise."

He grumbles. "Next game. It's the Canucks. They'll lose. There won't be a next game. They'll be out of the playoffs in no time."

"If that's the case, I'll take you to a Lions game."

"Canadian football? Give me a break. I'd rather go watch Disney on Ice."

"That can be arranged."

"Right. You'd probably bring her kid along too."

"I'm going to hang up now."

"Call me when you have good news, okay?"

I hang up the phone and lean back in my chair. Emmett is actually taking it pretty well, considering I said I would take him to the first game of the playoffs. Tickets are expensive and rare and I lucked out. Money talks, but so does knowing the right people.

Unfortunately for him, I had a last minute change of heart. Ted bailed on the game last week, saying he had a function to go to instead, so I immediately thought of Jackie and Tyson. I know going to a game with your boss isn't exactly normal, but neither is going to Science World. Luckily, Jackie wanted to go.

And luckily Emmett is an understanding guy, if not a bit nosy. He's one of the very few people I didn't lose touch with when I moved to LA. Of course I kept in touch with the office here, but other than that, everyone I had known, either through school or the film industry, those ties fizzled.

And even though I'm not one to talk about my problems, Emmett was more than supportive during the divorce, sometimes more so than Ted. I consider Ted to be one of my best friends, but what happened with Sasha and I was a little complicated. As much as Ted took my side throughout everything, Sasha still worked for him so he had to be as fair to the both of us as possible. Talk about being put in the middle.

That all said, I haven't mentioned to Ted that I'm taking Jackie. I suppose I should. I pick up my cell and eye the time. Right about now.

I get up and gather my leather briefcase and grab my trench coat. Though May is just around the corner, the April weather has been merciless this year. Even the city's famed cherry blossoms didn't last very long before the downpours washed the petals away.

Jackie is at her desk, furiously clicking away at what I assume is my expense report for the month.

"Almost ready?" I ask her.

She looks up at me in surprise, her big blue eyes reaching straight into me.

"Oh my god, is it already four?"

I nod. "I need to talk to your father for a moment but I'll meet you at reception."

She nods. "Okay." And goes back to work, though I can feel her eyes on me as I knock on Ted's door.

"Come in," he says.

I open the door and step inside. His assistant Patty is sitting across from him with a notepad and pen, tapping it. She gives me a discerning look. I'm not sure the woman likes me.

"Sorry, am I interrupting something?" I ask.

"Not really. What is it?" he asks, barely looking up

from the folder he's flipping through.

"I'm heading out. The Canucks game."

"The one you're taking my daughter to."

"You know?"

Now he gives me a wry stare over his glasses. "Come on, Will. Diane might be my wife but she still talks to me. Sometimes I even listen. Said she that you're taking Jackie and Ty to the game tonight."

"Is that a problem?"

"Not at all," he says, then eyes Patty. "You're just putting me to shame here. What if Patty starts expecting hockey games and Science World too?"

Patty doesn't say anything but I can tell that's the last thing that she wants.

"Well, we're off now," I tell him. "Have a good weekend, Ted."

"Take care of my daughter, Will," he says, flashing me a smile. But I don't miss the hint of warning in his tone. That he might not trust my intentions.

Honestly, I don't trust my intentions either.

I try not to think about it.

I leave his office, noting that Jackie's desk is already empty, and head to reception.

There I find Diane and Ty and Jackie. And Tiffany, watching us all with tepid amusement.

"Ready to go?" I ask.

Jackie nods. Ty sinks into her side, back to being his shy self.

Diane smiles broadly. "This is so nice of you Will."

"Think nothing of it," I tell her. "Next time I'd be happy to take you and Ted, if you can ever tear him away from his desk."

"That will be the day," she says then gives everyone a

wave. "I'm going to go shopping since I'm already here. Holt Renfrew has been teasing me for weeks with their spring sale. See you all after the game."

With Diane gone, I look to Tiffany. "If anyone calls—"

"Tell them you're at a hockey game?"

"No, smarty pants," I say to her. "Just patch it through to voicemail. I'll deal with it on Monday."

She nods and looks at Jackie. "You know when I did one month here, all I got was a coupon to Subway."

"You make it sound like prison," I tell her, opening the door for Jackie and Ty.

"I call it as I see it," she says, and then goes back to reading the giant hardback fantasy novel on her desk.

"Hopefully the rain holds off," I say glancing up at the sky. "Do you both mind coming over to the apartment? I'd like to change if possible."

"Sure," Jackie says as I start leading the way down the street.

"Oh wait, is Ty good with dogs?" I ask.

"What? Dogs!" Ty pipes up. I guess that answers that.

Jackie grins at me. "As long as you don't promise to get him one, I think we'll be okay."

"I am stepping on your toes a bit, aren't I?"

She stares up at me, sweetness in her beautiful eyes. "You've been nothing but wonderful, Will." Then she smiles, looking away, almost embarrassed. "You're definitely in the running for the best boss of the year award, that's for sure."

"Oooh. And what do I get if I win?"

Fuck. Please say it's you.

"I'll think of something."

I wish I could have heard something flirty or sexual in her tone but I don't. Wishful thinking. As always.

My apartment isn't far from the office, about a ten-minute walk. A bit of rain has started to pick up just as we round the entrance. Normally I go in another way—the complex takes up an entire block of Richards Street—but the main entrance is impressive.

"Oh my god," Jackie says as we stare at the tall iron gates between the Mediterranean style buildings, gargoyles overhead. "You live at The Grace?"

"You've heard of it?"

"I just remember this building when I was young. I thought it was the prettiest one in the whole city."

"That's what Sasha and I thought too," I tell her. "This here was the original building—townhouses—and they added on the residential tower in 2007. We had the good sense to snap it up then. Rented it out until a few months ago. I have to say, I'm glad we didn't sell it. I'd be homeless."

"I'm sure you would have figured something out," she says to me. "Jeez, look at the tile work." Her eyes wander all over the terracotta tiles, the elaborate chandeliers that hang above us in the outdoor archway, the plethora of plants in giant glazed pots, the fountains. Ty has taken a fascination with the gargoyles and statues. It's a little slice of Italy in this rainy Canadian city.

I lead them both through the courtyard and past the townhouses, toward the high-rise section of the property, getting them in the elevator and pressing the button for the twenty-fifth floor.

"We're going way up," Ty says excitedly.

"I can't imagine what it would cost to live here," Jackie says. "Even a simple one-bedroom apartment in Vancouver costs at least half a million dollars."

"At least."

My apartment takes up half of the twenty-fifth floor,

and my only complaint is that it faces east instead of west. That said, I still get stunning sunsets from the terrace if I lean over the railing.

I place my finger on the print reading scanner at the door, which I knew would make Ty whisper, "So cool!" and then lead them inside.

I have to admit, the condo is a bit much for just me, and it took a few weeks for it to really feel like home, but I'm slowly getting used to it. I haven't taken for granted how extravagant it is.

It also reminds me that aside from my dog-walker, I haven't had a woman up here since I've moved in.

"Holy shit," Jackie exclaims as we step inside.

"Mom, don't swear," Ty chides her just as Joan of Bark and Sprocket come running out from the guest bedroom where they usually sleep.

Both of them are overjoyed to see me, which is one of the best parts of owning a dog. Unconditional love and enthusiasm, even when you don't deserve it.

Ty squeals playfully as Joanie comes over to lick his hands, then his arms, then tries to slurp up his face.

"Joanie, have some respect," I tell her, pulling back on her collar just as Sprocket shoves his nose in, showering Ty with an equal amount of love and slobber.

"Joanie," Ty says, giggling.

"Joan of Bark is her full name," I explain. "And this is Sprocket."

Both of the dogs want to love up all over Ty, but eventually they move onto Jackie, who crouches down to get the most of their attention.

I grin as Joanie licks up the side of her face, Jackie's nose scrunching adorably at the ambush.

"She likes you as much as I do," I tell her.

Jackie opens her eyes, looks right at me, and something I can't read passes over her. I was joking, obviously, (right?) but for a moment I swear that maybe she likes the idea of me licking her all over.

Fucking hell. Get a hold of yourself.

I clear my throat.

"I'm going to give you guys a quick tour and then I'll have to take them down to the courtyard for a walk before they piss all over the place."

She straightens up and walks over to me with Ty, the dogs sniffing at the backs of their legs.

"This really is . . . stunning," she says softly, eyes wide and taking it all in.

"Two bedroom, two baths, and an office," I tell her proudly. "Limestone flooring, geothermal heating. And the best views in the city." I gesture to an open kitchen of rich cherry cabinetry and marble, an immaculate living room with gas fireplace that separates it and the dining area, floor to ceiling windows that lead to a large terrace.

Ty immediately makes a beeline for the doors, but Jackie instinctively holds him back. The balcony has high enough railings, but if she thinks he's the type to climb over them, then he'd probably best avoid the area.

I take the two of them down the hall, dogs in tow, showing off the rest of the place, the views of the North Shore mountains, shrouded in cloud, to the north, False Creek to the south. Jackie doesn't let go of Ty. "This place is too white and pristine," she explains. "No way I'm letting his sticky fingers get everywhere."

"Don't let this place fool you. Sometimes I prefer it when things are a little dirty."

Did I mean that as innuendo?

Yeah. I did.

And from the raise of her expressive brows, she knows it.

I probably should cover it up and mention something about how you can't really have a pristine place when you've got two smelly dogs but I let the comment sit.

When the tour is over I tell them to help themselves to whatever they want in the kitchen while I quickly take the dogs down to the courtyard and back. Then I head to my bedroom to shuck off the suit and slip on something hockey appropriate. I don't have a Canucks jersey, but I do have a vintage ringer t-shirt of theirs with the old logo. It's a bit on the small size but it will do. I then slip on a Canucks baseball cap, worn jeans that can handle beer being spilled on them, and grey skate shoes.

I step out of the bedroom to see the two of them sitting at the bar at the kitchen island, a glass of water in Ty's hands.

"Please tell me this doesn't look ridiculous," I say. "I feel like I'm eighteen."

But from the way Jackie's eyes are roaming all over me, I know she likes what she sees.

I raise my arms out to the side, my shirt riding up my stomach. "Too small, right?" I ask, and now I'm deliberately teasing her. Because fuck it, I've been hitting the gym in my building extra hard most mornings, coupling that with hour-long bike rides around Stanley Park. I know my abs look good. Maybe not eighteen-year old good, but fucking fantastic nonetheless.

"You look fine," she says after a moment, biting her lip and looking away.

I'm pretty sure that expression says I look better than fine.

God, I want to see that expression more.

A lot more.

"I like your hat," Ty says, pointing at it.

I tug down at the brim. "Do you? Well I'll tell you what, Ty-Rex, how about we get you your own at the game."

"Really?"

"Absolutely."

"Will," Jackie says.

"What?" I glance at the clock on the stove. "We should get going if we want to get something to eat. What do you guys think, eat something at the game? Nachos, hot dogs, whatever you like."

Now Ty is really excited. The poor kid is probably forced to eat healthy meals at home, courtesy of Diane.

We get in the elevator and on the ride down I catch Jackie eyeing me.

I glance down at her and grin. "What is it?"

"Just never seen you so dressed down before. I thought maybe you slept in a suit."

Actually, I sleep completely naked. The words are on the tip of my tongue but I manage to hold them back. Once again, it's getting difficult to remember that I'm her boss, and even though this is outside of the office, I have to be really careful with how I act and what I say. She may like my abs but that doesn't mean much.

And it shouldn't mean much, I remind myself. *For fuck's sake, she's Ted's daughter. She's got a kid. She's got enough on her plate. She doesn't need some old man like you lusting over her.*

And yet I am lusting after her. Even standing next to her, catching a whiff of her coconut shampoo, seems unbearable half the time. If I was being really honest with myself, I'd know that I'm doing all these things for her because I like her. I like Ty a lot too. But when it comes to Jackie . . .

at this point I want any excuse to spend time around her.

I'm not sure where I think this could even go.

You're on thin ice, Will.

At least my inner warnings are hockey-themed.

Roger Arena is closer to the office than it is to my place, but it's an exciting walk on game day regardless. The streets are absolutely packed with drunk fans in Canucks attire, the lucky ones heading to the stadium, the rest of them heading to the bars. Being in LA, and having no desire to cheer on the Kings, I have to say I missed the crazy enthusiasm of this hockey town, especially during the playoffs, even if most fans are of the fair-weather variety.

"This your first hockey game, Ty?" I ask him as we wait in line to be scanned by security.

He nods, big eyes, overwhelmed with it all as he grabs his mother's hand tighter.

"Actually," Jackie says to me, "he's played hockey a few times. Until he outgrew his skates. It snows a hell of a lot up north, and sometimes there's nothing but ice for miles."

"Is that so? I know it doesn't snow in Vancouver most winters, but have you thought about putting him on a team? Might be good for his confidence."

"We'll see," she says. "Depends what Ty wants."

Inside the arena it's even more chaotic, but we manage to get to the merchandise store to get Ty a hat before making our way to our seats, all the way down at the glass beside the Shark's penalty box. With a bit of time to spare before the game, I tell them to stay put as I go and get their food from the vendors. I know I could have afforded the club seats or boxes at the very top, but there's almost no point in coming to a game unless you're right there in the action. Even the nosebleed seats here have more authenticity and enthusiasm than the boxes full of execs and suits.

Not knowing what they want, I get a tray of two beers, orange juice, pizza, nachos, and hot dogs. With Ty sitting between us, he ends up holding the tray as we feast. It's messy as hell but it's fun. I just wish when Jackie ended up getting mustard on the tip of her nose I could have reached over and kissed it off. It's probably a good thing her son is between us.

The game gets off to the usual dismal start for the Canucks, but it doesn't make the game any less exciting. Ty seems enthralled by it all, face pressed against the glass as the puck shoots back and forth down the ring, the players whizzing past.

"I want to be a hockey player when I grow up," he says as Jackie yanks him back to his seat moments before a Shark's player gets slammed into the boards.

Jackie gives me a dry look as if to say, *thanks for putting the hockey idea into his head.*

I shrug, delighting in it.

When the first period is over, Jackie heads up to the use the washroom while Ty and I stay put. "You're crazy," I tell her as she passes in front of me, and it takes all my strength not to grab her ass. "The woman's restroom will have lines out the door."

"I'll get a beer for the wait," she says happily, heading up the stairs between the rows.

"Counterproductive," I call after her.

I look back to the rink and the Zamboni machine doing a quick sweep. Ty's eyes are focused on the big screens at the top showing replays of the first period, including when two of the players got into the usual hockey brawl. Gloves came off, helmets came off, and the Canucks player who started the fight ended up bloodied up with a broken nose and who knows what else, though it always looks far worse than it is.

"Is he going to be okay?" Ty asks in a quiet voice.

"The player?"

He nods, giving me a wary look, brows draw together. It takes me a moment to realize I probably should have checked on him during the game. I forget that the fights can look pretty scary to someone who isn't used to them.

"He's going to be fine," I tell him. "It always looks worse than it is. He'll be out later skating, you'll see."

"But he was bleeding all over his face."

"The blood washes away Ty-Rex. It's part of his job."

He wriggles his lips, thinking that over, and I glance up at the screen making sure the fight scene is over.

Then Ty says, "Mom's face used to look like that."

And everything inside me runs cold.

I turn to look at him. "What did you say?"

"My mom," he says, looking at his drink. "Her face was all bloody like that. But she was crying. She wasn't like this guy."

I can barely find the words. I can only pray that Ty is talking about something else, something I can understand.

"Your mom got in a fight? With another lady?"

He shakes his head. "No. With Dad."

My chest squeezes together, like there's a vice around my heart. "Your father hit her?"

He nods.

Holy fuck.

"When? When did he do this?"

"Before we moved."

"Jesus," I whisper. "Did he hit you too?"

He shakes his head. "No," he says in a small voice. "He yelled at me but he never hurt me. Just mom."

"When . . ." I lick my lips, my mouth feeling full of

sawdust. Raw anger is building from within. "I mean . . . god, I'm sorry Ty. You should have never seen that. He should have never done that."

"He did it before," he says, looking at me with big eyes. "It wasn't as much blood but I saw that too. He pushed her down, kicked her. But then he left. He always left."

"How long ago was that?" I whisper.

"I don't know. Last year."

God. I don't know what to say. There's too much to say. Fuck.

"I had no idea. She never said anything to me," I say stupidly, because I'm an idiot. Why would Jackie tell me that? I'm just her boss, I'm barely even her friend. "Does your grandfather know?"

He shrugs. "I don't know. She doesn't talk about it."

"But you do."

"Only to you," he says, now looking worried. "Please don't tell her I told. She might get mad."

"I promise," I tell him, my heart shattering inside. "Just promise me that you'll talk to me about it, whenever you feel like it. Don't hold it inside, okay? Talk to your mom about it too."

"She doesn't like when I mention Dad. She says it's her fault he's in jail now."

Fucking hell. "Ty, listen to me," I say, putting my hand on his shoulder. "It's not your mother's fault, no matter what she says."

"I know," he says. "Dad hurt her and she didn't want him to hurt her anymore. I still miss having a dad. I hope when he gets out of jail he'll move back down here and be nice to her."

Hell no. If her ex dared to show up in this city I would personally remove his head with my bare hands.

I sigh and lean back into the seat, trying to come to grips with everything Ty just told me. It explains so much. The look I've seen in Jackie's eyes, this haunted quality that comes over them when she thinks I'm not looking at her. And let's face it, I am always looking at her.

God. The worst part is, I know exactly what they've both gone through. When I was younger, before my father died in a drinking and driving accident (his fault), he used to beat the absolute shit out of me. He did it to my mother too, I was sure of it, but I seemed to be his number one target.

I used to hate feeling this way, but when he died, even though I was so young, I remember being glad. Glad that the terror and fear were removed from my house.

I've had thirty-six years to deal with it. I started acting out in high school because of some of the shit I repressed, and my mother and I ended up going to counseling together. It did wonders, even though I still have the occasional nightmare. You never really recover, you just learn to live with it.

But Jackie . . . this *just* happened to her. She was all alone up north, cut off from her family by an abuser. Shit. No wonder Ted and Diane were so concerned, especially when now I realize her ex was probably cutting them out on purpose. Typical bastard, making sure that he was the only one around for Jackie. Even if he only beat her up twice, twice is two times too many and I am sure he would have been emotionally abusive to her as well.

Thank god she had the sense to get out when she did.

"Are you mad?" Ty asks me quietly.

"Mad?" I say, leaning close to him and looking him in the eyes. "Hey, no. I'm not mad. Not at all. I just feel sorry for you and your mother, for having to go through all that.

I know it couldn't have been easy to see that. But you must know that you're both safe here, you got that?"

"Because you're here? And you're big and strong like the hockey players and you'll protect us?"

Another crack forms along my heart. Shit, this kid is getting to me.

"I'm a friend. Of your grandpa, of Jackie, of you. I will do whatever I can to protect you, to make sure you'll all safe and happy. You got that? And I know your mother and grandparents will do the same. Okay? Nothing like that will ever happen to either of you again."

"Or you'll turn into Batman?"

I give him a sad smile. "Yes. I'll turn into Batman. Believe me, it sounds cool, but you don't want to see it."

He eyes go up over my shoulder and I know Jackie is approaching. I briefly press my finger against my lips and he nods in agreement.

"You were right," Jackie says as she squeezes past me. "That line was a nightmare and I'm going to have to go again after I finish this. I got you one because I want you to feel my pain."

She hands me a beer as she sits down, flashing me a smile.

I grasp the cup, feeling myself break for her all over again. Just her smile disarms me. She's so incredible, beautiful and strong. Stronger than I could have imagined.

I know I'm gaping at her. She doesn't say anything, just meets my eyes.

I know, I think to myself, wishing she could read me. *I know and it's okay.*

I've got you.

I want to protect her.

I want her under my arm, under my wing.

And I don't ever want to let her go.

"Did you get me anything?" Ty asks.

It takes her a moment to break our gaze.

"Of course," she says, reaching into her back pocket and pulling out a packet of pretzels, handing it to him.

He tears into it eagerly, munching away as the second period starts and players take to the ice.

Luckily there aren't any other fights on the ice, because if there were I'd be tempted to take Ty and Jackie out of there, and eventually, as the game goes into overtime, the Canucks end up winning.

But as we stand outside among the cheering crowds, waiting for Diane to pick Jackie and Ty up and take them back home, I feel a strange sense of bereavement that I won't see Jackie until Monday, and when I do we'll be back to work, back to being boss and employee.

This is starting to become a problem.

And what a beautiful problem to have.

CHAPTER EIGHT

Jackie

DO YOU EVER HAVE ONE OF THOSE DAYS WHERE you can't stop smiling?

We'll I've had that.

For a week now.

It's that fucking bad.

The moment that Will, Ty, and I left the office and walked the few blocks to his apartment, like a family, is the moment a ray of sunshine hit me in the chest, eradicating the gloom. That hockey game changed everything and I don't even know why.

Everything that Will has been doing for Ty and me has been so sweet and thoughtful, I could so easily chalk it up to him being a good man and having a big heart. Even after all he's been through with his divorce, the man gives without thinking.

And yet some silly, hopeful part of me is starting to wish that maybe it's not so cut and dry. Maybe Will does think of me as nothing more than his assistant, the daughter of his best friend. Maybe he just wants to help out, to make me feel at home and welcome.

Maybe he's just lonely himself and wants the company, though I can't imagine there aren't any women in this city throwing themselves at him. I mean he's stupidly good-looking, fit as fuck, and rich as hell in a city where there are barely any eligible bachelors. He wouldn't last a minute.

But somewhere inside me, deep in that part of your heart that churns out the butterflies and the fantasies, somewhere in there I'm hoping that there's something more to this.

That maybe, just maybe, Will likes me as much as I like him.

And by like, I mean, wanting to screw his brains out.

Because honestly that's all I've been able to think about.

Screwing him.

Fucking him.

Anything with him.

It all started when I caught a glimpse of him changing at his apartment. I was looking for the washroom, and as I passed by his bedroom I noticed he only closed his door halfway.

I also noticed him standing there, totally naked.

I was right. He does not wear underwear.

And I sincerely hope he never does.

I caught him from the side view. He's totally tanned all over, almost golden, with a firm, strong ass, big thighs and a flat stomach.

And one hell of a huge dick. Of course. That was never a surprise, given that Alyssa and Tiffany have bets going at how many inches it is, but even though I just caught a glance of it before he could catch me looking, it was enough to ruin me for every other man.

And ruined I am. My attraction to Will has been building since I started working for him, there is no doubt about that. The fantasies I've started to have are dirty enough to make Samantha Jones on *Sex and the City* blush. But there was always a hint of the unknown. I had to imagine the images, conjure them up. I'm usually just seeing Will dressed in one of his impeccably tailored suits.

Now that I know what he looks like naked—*naked!*—something I never thought I'd see, it's impossible to wipe it from my brain. Every time I look at him, talk to him, even write an email to him, I keep seeing him, nude and gorgeous.

I keep thinking about what it would be like to be nude with him.

Would he be soft and tender?

Rough and hard?

What would it be like for him to push into me—aside from probably hurting a bit. How would it feel to have his heavy weight on top of me, making me feel so feminine and small, his strong, thick muscles against my soft skin?

Then I catch myself because these thoughts are going to go nowhere.

I haven't been with a man since Jeff, and even then it was at least a year ago, sex I had only because I was fighting so hard for the three of us to become a family. Because I didn't want Ty to lose his father, because I would do anything for us to overcome it all.

Little good that did me.

I sigh, my face resting in my hand, tapping my pen against the corner of the desk.

It's Thursday. I've had shit-all to do since my father and Will have been on conference calls all morning. I'm counting down the minutes to my lunch break.

Patty pokes her head over the partition, glaring down at me.

"Do you mind? I'm trying to read," she says, eying my pen.

I give her an apologetic smile and stop, though the moment she sits back down, I roll my eyes. I know Patty has this loyalty and affiliation to my father since she's worked for him for so long, so it probably rubs her the wrong way that I'm here. I think she feels threatened because I'm family and I could take her job away. Little does she know that I'd never work for my father like that. Granted, working for Will has become so distracting lately, but even so I still love my job.

It's five to noon and I'm slowly getting ready, pondering where I should go eat lunch, when Will emerges from Dad's office looking stressed and worse for wear.

"What are you doing?" he asks me, leaning against my desk.

"About to go for lunch," I tell him. "How was it in there?"

"Before Sasha and I started fighting? It was fine," he says wryly.

"Eep."

"Yeah. Anyway, it's over. Did you want to get lunch? My treat."

Try and act calm and nonchalant.

Except I'm already grinning.

"You're the boss," I tell him.

"I like it when you say that," he says, heading into his office.

I bite down on my smile and stand up, grabbing my purse, and notice Patty staring at me with disdain. She's probably jealous. Or disapproving. I ignore her and wait for Will outside his office until he's grabbing his laptop bag.

"Are we coming back?" I ask him.

"You can, if you want," he says with a smirk, closing his door behind him.

I look back at my desk, unsure if he's joking or not. Thankfully I have everything I need in my purse if he's serious.

We leave the office, Tiffany giving me a suspicious look over her glasses as we go, and all I can do is shrug. As we head down the street, Will leading the way, I ask, "So where are we going for lunch?"

He glances at me over his shoulder. "We're heading to my place first."

Oh? I want to ask what for but I don't dare. Instead I move my little legs to keep up with his long strides, and marvel at the looks of the people that pass him by on the street. Even though Will is terribly easy-going, his presence is commanding. It makes people look at him and take notice, doesn't matter if you're a man or woman, the heads swivel. He's just so much man, something missing in a city full of men in skinny jeans.

We get to his building, The Grace, and it's just as beautiful as I remembered from last week. Then I was sort of in a daze, so I make a point to take in the different gargoyles perched along the terracotta-tiled townhouses, the detail that went into the statues and water fountains. It's an oasis of privilege and calm in the middle of the city.

I have to admit though, I'm a bit nervous when I get into the elevator with him. I shouldn't be but I am, and it's all because of the damn fantasies in my head. It starts freaking me out a little as the elevator rises up, the mere smell of him, herbal and woodsy, like moss in the sun, invading my nose. What happens if I just reach out and grab him? If I kiss him? I could just kiss him and ruin everything.

I'm almost having a panic attack, as if my body could act without being told, and let out a huge sigh of relief when we get to his floor.

Once we're inside his stunning apartment though, he doesn't waste a lot of time. He leashes the dogs once they've come bounding over and have licked and sniffed and wagged their hearts out, and then we're back in the elevator, heading all the way to the parking garage.

"Are we taking the dogs to lunch?" I ask as we walk toward his sleek Mercedes.

"I was wondering when you'd start questioning this," he says, grinning at me as he unlocks the door.

"I pride myself on being adaptable," I tell him. "It's one of my key characteristics listed on my resume."

"Is that so?" he asks, getting the dogs in the back and gesturing for me to get in the front. "You'll have to run the rest by me, I've forgotten."

"Well," I say after I've buckled up and he's bringing the car on to Richards Street, and then taking a right on Davie. "Aside from adaptable, I'm also responsible, honest, hard-working, and detail-oriented."

"Except one of those is a lie," he says.

I glare at him. "What?"

He drapes his hand over the steering wheel and gives me a grin that I feel in every part of my body. "You're not that hard-working if you're here with me right now."

I narrow my eyes. "May I remind you that I'm *your* assistant and my job is entirely dependent on the work that *you* give me."

"So if I ask you to spend the rest of the afternoon with

me and give the middle finger to work, that's on me, not you?"

"You got it."

"I can take responsibility," he says with a nod. "Though that's listed on your resume too."

I watch him for a few moments. Just take him all in, no shame. His large hand on the wheel, the glint of his silver Rolex just as the sun pokes out from behind a cloud, the dark hair on his arm, the silver cufflink on his dress shirt, the tailored edge of his slate grey suit. He's got a scar below his thumb, something light that doesn't tan like the rest of his skin.

I start wondering about his scar, wondering where he got it. Accident with a letter opener? An oyster shucker? A paper cut gone wild?

And then I'm quickly reminded that as much time as we spend together, I don't know everything about him. He's talked about Sasha a few times, thankfully he never sounded like he was pining for her, or even hurt. He's talked about the film business, the old days of being a production assistant, when he first met my father. He's even touched on his drawings a bit.

But as for his teenage years, his childhood, I know nothing except his father died when he was five and he was raised by a single mother, just like Ty is.

That shames me a bit. That I've been so blinded by his money and worldliness that I've forgotten he may have had a harder upbringing than I gave him credit for.

I'm sure people look at me and assume because I went to a nice high school, lived in a big house, was raised by loving and successful parents—was pretty much born with the proverbial spoon in my mouth—that I wouldn't know what hard work is, that I've had it easy.

They'd be wrong. And I might be very wrong about Will.

"Have you been to Cypress Mountain?" he asks, after we've spent at least ten minutes in the car trying to get out of downtown, sitting in comfortable silence.

"Not since I was young. I used to love their toboggan run."

"Thought maybe if the clouds part for a bit, it could be worth the view. Plus, the dogs need to really get out there and be in the wilderness for a change. These city parks aren't cutting it."

"Did you go for hikes with them in LA?"

"Actually I only adopted them from the rescue when I got here."

I twist in my seat to look back at the smiling Pitbull Joan and the scruffy terrier mutt Sprocket, their tongues hanging out of their mouths, all too happy to be on an adventure. "You've only had them since, what, February? They're so good with you."

"They're good dogs, Jackie," he says with a smile. "You ever follow that account on Twitter? We Rate Dogs? Anyway, inside joke. Yeah, they're good dogs. And they were a bonded pair. When I went to the rescue, they said they came together and I said the more the merrier."

"So you didn't have dogs in LA?"

He shakes his head. "Sasha didn't want them."

"Well what the fuck else didn't Sasha want?"

"Aside from me?" He says though I can tell he's a bit uncomfortable at my outburst.

"Sorry. Just getting mad on your behalf."

"I'm flattered."

"I'm glad you rescued them though."

"Me too. I just knew I'd be a bit lonely here. They've

really helped. I needed the company, they needed the company. Everyone should rescue a dog, in my opinion. I think in the end they always end up rescuing you."

Now is the perfect time to ask him something I really don't want to ask him, and which I'm really afraid of the answer.

I swallow. "So have you been dating anyone?"

He gives me look, frowning. "Dating?"

I shrug, looking out the window at the tall trees as we cruise into Stanley Park. "Yeah. Have you gone on dates since the divorce?" I pause. "Or is that too personal?"

"It's personal," he says. "But I don't mind telling you. In LA I dated a few women, friends of friends. But, I don't know. After a few dates, what was the point really?"

"Right," I nod. "You're not ready to move on."

"I *have* moved on," he says emphatically. "That's not the issue. I'm just . . . extremely picky and selective who I spend my time with. I don't have time for games. For the bullshit. I know what I want when I see it and if I can, I'll go for it."

Sadly, that could explain why he hasn't gone for me, because he doesn't want me. And why should he? I have to get this god damn crush under control. And I especially have to stop picturing him naked. Like, right now. When he's right beside me in this small car and my gaze keep being drawn to his pants.

"Where there's a will there's a way," I find myself saying.

Will laughs. "Your father teach you that one?"

"He did. Well, just so you know, if you do meet the one, you won't have any problems snatching her up."

He watches me for a moment, his blue green eyes searching my face. "Why?"

"I'm sure it's entirely inappropriate for me to say, but

you're quite the catch."

His face slowly breaks into a grin, his forehead lined in surprise. "Am I?"

"You are."

"Who says?"

"Tiffany and Alyssa."

"Not Patty?"

I laugh. "Oh hell no. The only thing she's sexually attracted to are Excel spreadsheets."

"The bane of your existence."

"That's right."

"And what about you?"

I glance at him warily. "What about me?"

"Do you think I'm a catch?"

He's grinning at me in a cocky way that makes me realize this is all fun and games to him, but even so I have to tread carefully.

"I think you're going to make some woman very happy one day."

He stares at me for a beat, nodding. "Very diplomatic. You're picking up the business pretty quick."

"I have a good teacher," I remind him.

It takes quite the drive to get to the top of Cypress Mountain: over the Lions Gate Bridge, across the Upper Levels Highway, and then up the steep and switchback-riddled road to the ski lifts.

But the view is spectacular, the clouds lifting just for us it seems, and once we're at the top I even manage to hike a good ten minutes before my shoes start killing me. Thank god I wore my ballet flats today.

After we get back in the car, the dogs happy, we head down the mountain and toward Horseshoe Bay where we finally stop for lunch at Trolls. We sit on the patio and eat fish n' chips as we watch the ferries leaving the harbor, the mountains rising from the ocean like monoliths. At one point a rainbow comes out, spanning from side of the bay to the other.

I end up having two Caesar drinks at lunch while Will promises me he can make me his own version one day that blows every bartender's Caesar out of the water. I want to hold him to that. In fact, I'm close to asking him to make me one back at his place, but I have enough decency to keep my words in my mouth.

I am, however, tipsy enough to forget about going back to work. And it's just as well. We get back into the Mercedes and Will takes the long way back to downtown, cruising along Marine drive, past the billion-dollar seaside homes overlooking English Bay, the glass towers of downtown Vancouver in the distance.

It's magical, for lack of a better word. With the window rolled down and the soft, briny spring breeze coming in and rustling my hair, one arm outside and feeling the air, Roy Orbison playing on the stereo, I feel like I'm in another world. In a movie. In a place where it's just me and Will and the sun glinting off the water. I feel . . .at peace. And I realize it's been a long time since I've felt that.

So by the time we get back to his apartment and get the dogs back, I'm not disappointed in the least when he says to me, "I don't want to go back to the office. Want to catch a water taxi to Granville Island? Get a drink and some sushi?"

Even though we literally ate an hour ago, I can't find anything to say no to. Any extra time with Will is pretty much heaven to me.

We hop on the little water taxi heading across the stretch of False Creek toward Granville Island (which isn't really an island) and I think about Ty and how much he'd like to be with us doing this. Then I realize that this is the first time I've actually been alone with Will outside of the office without my son. As much as I know Ty likes his company and vice versa, it's refreshing to be with Will like this and not have to be Ty's mom. I can just be me.

And after we find a sushi place and I've had a few tiny cups of hot sake with Will, I forget that I even work for him. I'm not even Will's assistant. I'm . . . Just Jackie.

We sit side by the side at the bar overlooking the sushi chefs doing their chopping and folding, and start daring each other to eat whatever the other person orders for them. The sushi chefs are having an absolute ball with this.

I have to admit, I used to be an adventurous eater when I was young but I lost that palette when I moved, so when Will makes me eat an octopus roll stuffed with fish eggs, I'm nearly sick. Still, I manage to get it down, though it takes a few more cups of sake to do the trick. I try to get Will back with an eel roll but he seems to really enjoy it and instead orders two. Bastard.

I'm pleasantly drunk and my stomach is bursting when Will leans in close to me, his elbows on the bar, palming a cup of green tea. From the look in his eyes, I know he's going to say something serious.

"Listen, Jackie," he says to me, his voice low. "There's something I've been meaning to ask you."

Oh god. I know that he's not going to fire me, but even so my heart is starting to beat fast again.

He glances at me through dark lashes. So fucking pretty. So not fair.

"And I realize this is entirely inappropriate and I apologize in advance for it."

Oh my god. Now my heart is beating fast for different

reasons. I can barely breathe.

"It's not my place at all," he continues. "Especially as we don't know each other that well, and that I'm your boss first and foremost."

First and foremost.

My heart sinks.

"But aside from being your boss, I like to think of you as a . . . friend."

Good lord, just stick the knife in further. Where is he going with all this?

"In fact you're one of my few friends here, aside from Ted and my friend Emmett."

Great. So I'm his friend along with my dad. Without breaking his gaze, I raise my sake to my lips and knock back the rest of it, not even wincing as it burns hot.

"The point is . . . I care about you. A lot."

Oh?

He exhales through his nose. "More than you probably think. Maybe more than a boss should care about their employee."

Now I'm just staring at him, waiting for whatever it is.

And he knows I'm waiting. He nods. Says, "Sorry. I'll just say it." He licks his lips and bites down on his bottom one for a moment. Naturally my eyes fix there, wondering what would happen if I kissed him now. Those same scary elevator thoughts.

"I was talking to Ty while you went to the restrooms at the game," he says.

I straighten up. "And?"

"He was watching the screen, the playbacks of the first period. He was upset about the fight."

Oh shit. "He was?"

I knew the moment I saw the fight broke out between

the two players that it could be a trigger for Ty. Hell, it was almost a trigger for me. I knew what one of those punches felt like. But I watched him closely. Ty seemed to be okay with it. But of course that doesn't mean anything.

God, I'm a terrible mother.

"Jackie," Will says, reaching over and lifting up my chin with his fingers so I'm looking at him. "It's okay. He wasn't traumatized. He explained why he was upset."

Fuck. So he knows.

"He, uh . . . what did he tell you?"

He stares at me with such tenderness that it rattles me more than the conversation. "He told me what your ex did to you. Said it happened twice. Says he never hurt him. Says that you put him in jail."

I pull my face away and bury it in my hands, trying to breathe.

"Jackie," Will whispers, his warm hand pressing on my back. "It's okay. I told Ty I wouldn't tell you, but you know I had to. He needs to talk to someone. You need to talk to someone. Do your parents even know?"

I shake my head, unable to speak.

This isn't happening.

I'm so fucking embarrassed.

This will forever change the way that Will thinks of me. He's going to think I'm a bad mother for sticking around with Jeff. He's going to think I'm an idiot for going up north with him. He's going to think I'm damaged goods, if he never thought that before.

"Is that why you brought me here?" I ask, my voice muffled in my hands.

"No. Not at all. I just wanted to be with you." His hand goes up my back to my hair, cupping the back of my head. Oh god. It feels so good I might just cry.

"I'm going to tell you what I told Ty," he goes on softly, leaning in close so that his lips are at my ear, his breathe warm. So warm. "And that's if you ever need someone to talk to, you can talk to me. I understand not wanting to tell Ted and Diane. I get it. And I get not wanting to tell anyone aside from the police. But this is something you can't keep bottled up. And neither can Ty. He wanted to talk, Jackie. He's open to it. He needs help dealing with it just as you do."

"You don't know what you're talking about," I tell him, abruptly getting off my stool and stumbling out of the dark restaurant.

Outside it's raining again and I walk under the awning and around the corner, holding back the tears until I can't anymore.

They pour out of me in one loud sob and I cover my mouth with my hand, biting down on it, trying to keep quiet, to compose myself.

And then Will is there, my purse and blazer in hand. He sets it down on the ground next to me and pulls me into his arms.

I'm too weak to fight it. I'm too tired to pretend I'm all right. I've been pretending for too long, even fooling myself most days. Thinking I can just forget it and move past it. But the effort might slowly be killing me.

"Jackie," Will says, holding me tight in his arm, his chin resting on the top of my head. "It's okay. It's okay. Let it out."

And I do. I press my face into his hard chest and I cry and I cry, getting his shirt soaked with my tears.

He just holds me. He barely says a word. Just keeps me tight to him, containing me even when I feel so uncontained.

But as I cry, the feelings don't subside. Not in the least.

"I feel so ashamed," I sob into him, unable to keep it inside.

"Why?" he whispers.

I pull my head back enough to look up at him. I know I look like hell with a snotty nose, red eyes, cheeks wet with tears, but I don't care.

"Because I let it happen."

He frowns, his eyes going hard, like emeralds dug from the earth. "You didn't let it happen. You did nothing wrong Jackie. Nothing."

I try to swallow, the guilt overwhelming me. "But I chose him. I knew he was bad news and I chose him. I was so . . . stupid. In love. I thought that once he was around Ty, he'd change."

"You were eighteen. You were young."

"I wasn't thinking."

"Yes you were, you were thinking of Ty. You wanted him to have a father, to have a family."

I shake my head because it doesn't matter what I wanted. What matters is what happened. "I should have stayed in Vancouver with my parents. I shouldn't have gone. My life would be totally different."

"Different doesn't mean right."

"It does when I could have avoided being a fucking punching bag!" I yell. "It would have saved me from working two jobs, trying to keep the heat on in the winter, trying to give Ty what he needed, trying to believe that maybe we'd be a family. And Jeff, he'd always tell me that he was getting better. He'd tell me he loved me and Ty, and then he'd disappear. Dealing drugs. Stealing. I spent so many nights afraid and alone because I knew what he was like when he was high and desperate. I never said no to him, do you understand? I could never say no."

Will's jaw tightens, his eyes glittering intensely. He swallows, his Adam's apple bobbing. He understands completely.

"I did everything wrong," I go on. "Everything. I tried my best and it was just . . . bullshit."

"Was it just twice that he hit you?" Will's voice has a knife's edge.

I nod, another tear rolling down onto his shirt. "The first time was around Christmas. My parents had called my neighbor trying to reach me. I tried to call them back but they didn't answer. Jeff searched my phone, saw the call. Pushed me to the floor. Kicked me in the stomach. In front of Ty. He was drunk and who knows what. He left and then I didn't see him for three weeks."

"Jesus Jackie."

"The other time was the end of February. He'd been gone for a week, off on a bender. He came home in the middle of the night. Yelling. Trashing the place." I close my eyes, everything flooding back. I can even smell him.

"You don't have to explain," he says.

"It's okay. It's okay. You were right. I need to talk to someone about it. Say it out loud." I take in a shaking breathe and I realize he's still holding onto me just as tight, our bodies pressed against each other. He's immovable and therefore I'm immovable. "He was freaking out. I don't know why. I didn't understand him. I don't think he understood. But Ty was sleeping on the couch so I told Jeff to shut up. I told Ty to get in my room."

I can see it all. Ty's frightened face. Jeff's horrible silhouette in the darkness.

I go on, quietly. "Jeff reached for Ty and I didn't know if he was going to hurt him or what. Maybe nothing. But I didn't want him touching him. So I pushed Jeff back, told him to get out or I'd call the police. Well that did it. He punched me in the face. I went flying back against the wall, but I didn't fall. I started looking around for a weapon. Saw the ceramic teapot I left out on the coffee table. He saw it at the same time. Before I could get it, he grabbed it. Bashed it across my face. Thank god he was off-balance, he wasn't able to do as much damage. Then punched me again. I thought he'd broken my whole face. My brain. I don't remember much after that. I started screaming for help and that's when Jeff disappeared. I remember picking up the phone and calling the police. I remember Ty crying. And that was it."

Will is silent, breathing heavily. His hands grasp the back of my shirt, balling them up.

"The cops came. I don't remember it all, but I do remember telling them it was Jeff and that he'd done it before and that he was probably dealing drugs too or something. They said they had enough to put him away. And I'm so, so ashamed to admit it but for a moment I thought I made a mistake. Because I didn't want Ty to lose his father. As stupid as that sounds."

"You made the right choice," he whispers. "You made the only choice."

"I know. I know that now. But . . . I can't get over it. I can't . . . I feel so guilty, you know, just guilty that my choices got us in that mess. I can't shake it."

"Listen to me," Will says, pulling back and holding me by the shoulders, peering into my eyes with limitless concern. "What you told me, you need to tell someone else. A professional. You need to tell your parents too. You need the right help, for both you and Ty, and with it you'll do more than shake it. Jackie, you're the strongest woman that

I know. Raising Ty like that, doing everything you could for him. I am just . . . I am in total awe of you. And I know you'll be able to come out of this even stronger."

"My parents will hate me," I whisper, looking away.

"They won't. I promise you they won't. They love you."

"They'll judge me for not leaving him sooner. People always judge the mother."

His eyes glint sharply as his grip on my shoulders grows tighter. "Jackie. You went through a horrible traumatic event that no one should ever experience. Whether people are in your shoes or they have no idea at all what it's like, no one has the right to judge you. No one. You got out when you reached your breaking point. It's different for everyone. You put Jeff in jail. You protected your son when I know it couldn't have been easy. Anyone who dares to judge you and your life and how you handled yourself in the face of such horror is pure garbage. A sorry excuse for a person. Plain and simple. There are some people out there who never get out. Who always stay with the abuser. They shouldn't be judged either. The only fucking thing they need is compassion. Something this world has been lacking for a while."

I nod slowly, trying to take it all in even though it's hard, even though I'm stubborn and want to hang onto the guilt. I have to admit, he is making me feel a little better. Actually, it feels like a giant weight has lifted off of me. It's not entirely gone—Will is right, I have to go to a therapist to really work through it—but it's been lifted. There's a glow of catharsis inside me, like someone letting fresh air into my soul.

But I'm also drained.

Emptied.

Utterly exhausted.

I stare down at his soggy shirt. "I'm sorry I ruined your shirt."

"I don't care in the slightest."

I stare up at him, worried. "I hope this doesn't change the way you think of me."

He cocks his head. "Why does it matter what I think?"

I breathe in deeply through my nose, summoning my courage. "Because, just like you, you're one of my only friends too. So it matters. It matters a lot."

His mouth quirks up into a brief smile. "But the way I think about you has changed."

"Oh." I knew it.

He cups my face with his large hand, its warmth pressed against my skin, causing shivers to descend down my back. His eyes search mine, deeper and deeper. "I'm now realizing exactly how incredible you are. Jackie, you are an amazing human being. I'm even more enamored with you than I was before, and that's saying a lot."

Enamored?

Holy fuck. I don't think anyone has ever said anything like that to me before. In fact I know they haven't. If he didn't have one hand behind my back, holding me in place, I'm pretty sure I'd be falling to my knees.

I don't know how long we stand like that outside the sushi restaurant as the rain pounds around us, but eventually we realize we have places to go and roles to assume.

And me, now I'm left feeling shy. Overwhelmed by Will's affection and unsure how to process it. What we just shared was not an employer concerned about an employee. But was it more than just a friend being concerned for a friend?

I don't know. I guess at the moment it doesn't really

matter. What does matter is that Will is someone I can count on. Someone I can talk to. Someone to lean on.

Only time will tell if it will ever become anything more.

CHAPTER NINE

Will

"Are we done talking about business now?" Ted asks me, leaning back in his chair and tilting his head back to catch the sun's rays. "Because I could really get to the drinking part of this meeting."

Considering Ted's had two martinis already, I'm sure the drinking part has already started.

It's Friday afternoon, mid-May, and the city is finally getting the sunshine it deserves. Ted and I just had a two-hour lunch with the Warner Brothers executives who flew into town to check on how DinoWars was going.

The meeting went well. They're happy, everything is on schedule, which means we're happy.

Add in the fact that the weather is good and we're on the patio at Carderos in Coal Harbor, watching the seaplanes take off and sailboats coming in to their slips, and things really couldn't be better.

Well. I guess that's not quite true.

They could be better—a lot better—and it's something I don't dare dwell on sitting across from Jackie's father.

The truth is, I'm heading down a slippery slope and the incline gets steeper with each passing day.

The last time I fell head over heels obsessed with someone was with Sasha. Back when I was in my twenties. And that was just a fraction of what I've been feeling lately.

After she confided in me at the sushi restaurant, I've felt a bond with her unlike any other before. I can't explain it. I just feel that she gave me a part of her that she never gives anyone and it's up to me to protect it, keep it close to my heart and keep it safe. It's not that she gave me a piece of her own heart, it's more like she gave me a fragment of her soul. A part that burdens her and this somehow lightens that weight.

Maybe I'm looking too much into it because I want to. But I know something about her that not many people know. Perhaps if I had never brought it up, if Ty never said anything, she would have never discussed it with me. I love to think that in time I could become close enough to her that she would open up naturally. But that could just be wishful thinking.

In fact, I'm not so delusional to think I'm powered by anything other than wishful thinking. I know that she probably doesn't look at me other than her dad's friend, her boss, and now, just a regular friend. I know it. But it doesn't make what I feel go away.

And it doesn't make me understand what I'm feeling any easier. There's still so much about her that I don't know—her hopes, her dreams, her fears—but I'm determined to do whatever I can to learn more.

I'm fucking obsessed with her.

Plain and simple.

"So Jackie is working out pretty well," Ted says to me, pulling off an olive from the garnish with his teeth.

"She's terrific," I tell him.

"Think she's due for a raise at six months?"

"I think she's due for a raise now. You do want her moving out, don't you?"

He chuckles. "Actually, I think Diane loves that she's back at home. And she adores Ty. They've both given her a new lease on life. You know for a while there she was even losing interest in the horses. She was just . . . depressed. And it wasn't the weather. Ever since Jackie and Ty came back, she's . . . glowing." He sprawls back in his chair. "Just like this gorgeous weather. Hot damn."

"I'm sure Jackie wants a place of her own."

He shrugs. "Maybe. It's not like she's seeing anyone. Thank god. I hate to say it, but my daughter has horrible taste in men."

I watch Ted carefully. He's too glib about it, which means I doubt Jackie told him what really happened up north, though I know she will when she's ready. At least she's booked her first appointment for a therapist next week.

"Plenty of nice guys in the city. I'm sure she'll see someone eventually," I tell him. "She's a beautiful woman."

"You've said that a few times to me, Will," Ted says, looking at me over his glasses.

I raise my palms as a mea culpa. "I call them as I see them."

"And what about you?"

"What about me?"

"You're not dating anyone. This worries me. I am nonplussed."

"I've never seen you plussed, Teddy."

"That's true. Still, you need to get back in the game, Will. I know what Sasha did to you was the pits but you can't stay a bachelor forever. You at least need to get your knob polished."

"Are you sure you need another drink?" I ask him. "You're cruder than normal after a few martinis. Maybe it's heat stroke."

He grins at me devilishly and snaps his fingers for the waitress. "More. Just bring us more," he says to her, then looks back to me. "How about I set you up with someone?"

"How about no?"

"She's beautiful. Maybe not as young as my daughter . . ."

"Careful, Ted," I warn him, starting to feel uneasy.

"I'm just saying. She's up your alley. Thirty-five, blonde, big rack, legs to the sky. Works in development at Omni."

"Another film person? You know how small the world is."

"Look, you don't have to date her. You can just screw her."

"What's her name?"

"Mona."

"Mona?"

"Maybe it was Moana."

"Ted, I'm not interested."

"Look, the film gala is tomorrow night, you need a date."

"I thought you were my date."

"I'm flying to LA in the morning."

"Diane can be my date."

"Diane has grabby hands and I know she likes you in a tux, so no way."

"I'll take Jackie."

"You will not," he says, sitting up straight.

I shrug. "Why not?"

He thinks that over, pursing his lips in a comical manner. "I don't know. I guess why not?" Then he gives me the stink-eye. "But I don't like how you're trying to get out of this relationship set-up thing."

"I thought it was just a knob-polishing screw."

"Whatever it is, I'm going to call Moana, Mona, at some point, and I'm going to get her on a date with you and that's all there is to it. Please Will, I will sleep easier at night, and you know all my success rides on how much sleep I get."

"I'll think about it. Okay?"

Luckily the waitress comes by with our drinks, so Ted is happily distracted once again. I'm off the hook on with this set-up.

And I get to ask Jackie to go to a gala with me.

Where there's a will there's a way.

I am completely overstepping my boundaries here.

After the meeting/drinking session with Ted (and the excess alcohol plus rare good weather may factor in here), I call Diane and ask if she'll look after Ty tomorrow night. Then I fill her in and ask for Jackie's dress and shoe size.

Diane is practically squealing over the fact that I'll be inviting her daughter to the gala. It's a nice change of pace from Ted, who was more or less indifferent. She keeps saying how good it will be for Jackie to get out and have a real man on her arm, even though I know she doesn't mean it in any way other than platonic, friend of the family. That sort of thing.

At least, that's what I assume Diane means and I'm not going to fuck it all up by asking.

I have to admit, it puts the pressure on me. I know I don't have to do much to appear better than that fucking monster ex of hers, Jeff, but even so, I have to do things exactly right, behave exactly right.

Not that I haven't been on my best behavior so far, but I feel like it's coming to a close. I fear that the longer I'm around Jackie, the more likely I'll be unable to control myself.

Which is something entirely new to me. I've always been in control, always had a handle on most situations, but the last few years have really thrown me for a loop. First there was Sasha, pulling the rug out from under me in the most humiliating way, now there's Jackie, who is seeping under my skin, right into my veins, like some sort of drug. She's invading my thoughts, my dreams, everything, until I find myself thinking of her, even craving her, more than anything else in my life.

Here's hoping I manage to keep it together.

The next day at work I get there early, before even Tiffany arrives. I like the office at this time of day and make a mental note to try and do this more often. There's no one here except for a few animators down the hall. You'll occasionally see them heading into the breakroom for coffee, looking sleepy as hell after pulling all-nighters, but that's about it.

I place a note on Jackie's desk asking her to see me in my office. Then I go into my office and hang up the dress behind the door, still in the garment bag, then slide the shoebox underneath my desk.

Then I sit and wait for the office to get busy and for

Jackie to come in, hoping Diane never mentioned anything to her.

Okay, I admit it's a bit presumptuous, completely bold, and maybe even a bit creepy, that I've picked out a dress and shoes for her and she doesn't even know about this event, but what I've learned about Jackie is that if you give her an inch, she'll take a mile. Her stubbornness is legendary, as is her pride, and if she thinks at all that she'll be a bother, she won't go for it. If I had asked her, the first thing she'd say is that she doesn't have a dress, and then if I offered to get her a dress, she'd flat-out turn me down, saying she didn't deserve one, etc., etc.

So, I figure this bypasses all the stress. It's done. And Diane agreed that it was the best route because it's one less decision for Jackie to have to make.

I just hope that Jackie feels the same way. If she doesn't, this could backfire in a major way.

It's nine a.m. on the dot when Jackie knocks at my door. She certainly wasted no time.

"Come in," I call to her.

The door opens and she stands in the doorway.

"You wanted to see me?" she asks.

Even though I call her in to my office often, she always has this guilty look on her face, like she's done something wrong and is about to get fired. Regardless, the sight of her works on me better than a cup of coffee. She warms me up from the inside out.

"We need to talk," I tell her, trying not to gawk at her as usual. Her tits look spectacular in her shirt. "Close the door."

A flash of fear goes through her gorgeous blues.

I decide to let her squirm for a bit.

"Listen, I have something important I have to run

by you and hope you'll make this process as painless as possible."

I watch as she swallows, her fingers fiddling with the hem of her shirt. "Okay."

"Tonight is the Vancouver Film Industry annual gala that your father usually attends, but this year I'm going. It's at the Hotel Vancouver. And I need a date. I think that date should be you."

Her eyes go wider. I didn't think that was possible.

"Um . . . I don't . . . your date?"

I nod, not breaking eye contact with her. "Purely professional, of course."

She licks her lips, and I can't tell if she's relieved or not. "Of course. But . . . I wouldn't know anyone. And I've never been to a gala. And I don't have a dress or shoes, and I would need to ask my mom to watch Ty, and I don't want to add to all the shit I'm piling on her. I'm sorry . . . I'm sure you can find someone else."

Ouch. I hope her resolve to give up this easily isn't something I should take personally.

"There is no one else," I tell her. "Only you, Just Jackie."

She stares at me, her features softening.

I clear my throat. "Besides, all the arrangements have been made. Your mother has agreed to watch Ty-Rex. I've got a dress for you right there," I nod at the door and then pull out the shoebox from Christian Louboutin, "and your Cinderella shoes right here."

"Uh," she says, staring at the garment bag and then the shoebox and then back to the bag again.

"As for your hair and makeup, I think you look beautiful just as you are, but I know you're going to say something about how you don't have the makeup or time to get your hair done or something like that. So I bypassed that as well. You have an appointment in my apartment at five-thirty. A Glamsquad girl is coming by to do your hair and makeup. Whatever you want."

She's blinking at me, utterly baffled. "I don't know what to say."

"You don't need to say anything."

Her head shakes as she reaches up and takes the garment bag off the hook, peering at the label. "Dolce and Gabbana?"

I shrug. "Your mom gave me your size. I told the salespeople at Holts that you have a body like Marilyn Monroe. They said this should fit and flatter you. I believe them. Besides, you can't go wrong with black."

"I'm a size 10," she tells me, looking almost embarrassed. "On my good days. No way would a designer accommodate my size and have it look right."

"I bet it looks just fine."

"Will," she says, licking those lips again. She has to stop that. "I really appreciate you taking the reins like this but . . . this is like a borderline alpha male thing to do. This is like a Christian Grey thing to do."

I raise my brow. "And that's bad?"

She opens her mouth to speak but I go on, "Jackie, I've been around the block a few times now, and know how things work. I told you that when I see what I want, I go for it. And I want you to accompany me to the gala tonight."

Her brows knit together in frustration. "But . . . why *me*?"

"Because it will be fun." I edge the box toward her with my elbow. "Tell me you like the shoes."

"Will," she says again, not moving. "I can still say no to all of this."

"You can. But I know you won't."

"Oh do you?"

I grin. "Go ahead and prove me wrong." I pause. "On second thought, don't. You're stubborn enough to do it."

And she seems to think about that. Fuck. I hope I didn't speak too soon. I'm coming on strong and from a place that she can't figure out. I'm still her boss, and so far that's all I've been. This is edging it to another level. I might just scare her away.

But she's edging closer to the desk and the shoe box.

She glances me as if to ask "is this okay?" and then takes the lid off the box.

She gasps. They aren't glass slippers, but they are high heels made of teal suede with gold spikes, the classic red sole on the bottom looking slick as nail polish. I know many women in the LA office splurged on Louboutins so I figured I couldn't go wrong, providing Jackie even knows who the designer is. But from the shocked look on her face, I think she does.

"I was looking at the five-inch heels," I explain, "but decided I didn't want to push my luck. These are three and a half inches, should be just fine for you to walk in."

Jackie is turning them over in her hands, marveling at them. "You shouldn't have. You really shouldn't have." Her face grows serious, a line appearing between her brows. "These shoes are almost a thousand dollars. That dress has to be about the same."

"More like three thousand."

She closes her eyes, raises her brows and shakes her head. "Will. I can't let you just buy me this stuff."

"Why not? It's coming out of your paycheck."

Her mouth drops and I let out a laugh. "Relax. Let me do it. You deserve it."

"But—"

"You deserve it Jackie. Now do you want me to keep your stuff in here?"

She nods, still obviously overwhelmed.

"Hey," I tell her softly, leaning across the desk. "This is supposed to be a fun thing, right? A gala. Don't worry so much about it." I pause. "As your boss, that's an order. Got it?"

"Am I getting paid for it?" she asks with a small smile.

"Don't push your luck, kid. Now get back to work."

She rolls her eyes and then leaves me alone in my office, smiling to myself.

CHAPTER TEN

Jackie

HOLY SHIT.
That's all that keeps going through my head.
Holy shit, holy shit, holy shit.
Followed by, *is this a dream?*
And *what the hell is going on?*

I spend the majority of the morning attempting to work and not getting anywhere, because all I can do is think about Will and what he just did for me.

I need a second opinion.

I need to talk to someone who isn't Will.

And fast.

At lunchtime I show up at Alyssa's office, poking my head in.

"Hey, do you want to do drinks? I mean lunch? Now?"

Alyssa is already getting up, grabbing her purse. "You said the magic words."

Minutes later we're sitting on the patio at the Yaletown Brewing Company and I'm slamming back my amber ale like there's no tomorrow.

Alyssa watches me keenly as the glass empties. "So, want to tell me what's going on?"

"What makes you think there's anything going on?" I ask her, wiping my lips.

She ticks off her fingers, her jeweled nails catching the sunshine. "For one, you never ask me out for lunch, I'm always bugging you. For two, you've been a space cadet all morning. For three, you finished that beer in literally five seconds."

"I need another one too," I mutter, looking for the waiter.

"So spill," she says. "What has you all flustered like a dog in heat?"

"A dog in heat?"

She shrugs with one shoulder. "First thing that popped in my head."

"I don't know," I tell her, studying her face. Her eyes are wide and inquisitive and I know she has a penchant for gossip, but I'm hoping she can keep this all a secret. "I just have something on my mind and I want to talk about it. But I need it to stay between you and me."

"You got it."

"I'm serious."

"So am I," she says, brushing her bangs off her face, even though they just fall right back in her eyes. "You tell me not to tell a soul and I won't. I'm good for promises, trust me."

I exhale forcefully. "Okay. So, there's a gala tonight."

She nods. "Yup. The industry gala. Hotel Vancouver."

"You're going?"

"No. But I've been. I went with Ted one year when Diane couldn't go."

"Oh," I say, feeling slightly deflated. "So it's totally normal for someone from work to go with one of the higher ups?"

"I wouldn't say it's a regular thing," she says. "Why, are you going?"

I nod. "With Will. I'm not sure I have much of a choice."

She lets out a low whistle. "He asked you?"

"Yeah. Well. No. He told me I'm going with him."

"And you have a problem with that? Because if you have a problem with that, I will certainly take that problem off your hands." She rests her chin on her hand and stares off with a dreamy expression on her face. "He is going to look so beautiful in a tux."

Damn. I hadn't even thought about that. Another reason why tonight is going to be a night to remember.

"The thing is," I tell her carefully, "it's not that I don't want to go, it's just that I'm surprised he asked me."

"Why?" she asks after a few beats, her attention coming back to me as whatever daydream she had in her head shuts down. "You're his assistant. You guys are together all the time."

"At work."

"Outside of work too," she says. "I notice when he takes you out for lunch. I notice a lot of things."

"Like what?" I ask, leaning forward in my seat.

Her bright pink lips quirk up into a wry smile. "Well, you certainly seem interested."

"I'm not. Never mind."

"Mmmhmm," she says, sipping her Caesar. "So that's what you wanted to talk to me about? That he's bringing you to the gala?"

"I just wanted to know if it was normal."

"It's normal. Will bringing *you* to the gala is the most normal thing I've ever heard. What are you going to wear?"

"That's the thing, he bought me a dress already. And shoes. And he's got some hair and makeup people coming to his apartment after work to doll me up."

Her eyes bug out. "Say what?"

"That's weird, right?"

"That depends," she says slowly. "He actually bought you everything?"

"Yeah. Without me knowing. He asked my mother to take care of Ty and then got my dress and shoe size."

She makes an O with her mouth. "That is . . . forward."

"Right?"

Now she's grinning.

"What?" I ask.

"You're fucking lucky," she says. "That's what."

"But what do you think it means? Anything?"

She seems to think that over. "I don't know Will enough to tell you. But it does make sense with all I've noticed."

Now I have to know.

"Tell me."

"Well, some people are obvious. Take Casey for example. Though I've noticed he's bugging you less, maybe because you give the guy nothing. But he's out there. Will is a subtle man."

"Until he isn't."

"Apparently." She pauses. "Will gives you the eyes, you know."

"What eyes? The rolling of the eyes?"

"No, he gives those to Tiffany. You know, *the* eyes. He stares at you. I'm not sure if you notice."

"Well obviously I don't. How does he stare at me?"

"It's hard to describe. But it's definitely not how Ted stares at Patty. It's like a mix of total adoration and need. Like when you've been wanting something for so long and you finally get it and you don't know how you got to be so lucky or what to do next. Does that make sense?"

I swallow. My heart has been beating louder and louder with each passing second. "Are you sure that can't be attributed to me being an amazing assistant and him realizing how badly he's needed one?"

"No," she says, grinning. "Because then lust wouldn't come into the equation."

Lust? I'm dumbfounded. And there's a whole pack of butterflies being held back at the gates, waiting to swarm my stomach.

"He doesn't stare at me with lust . . ." I say, praying she's about to say something that proves me wrong.

She cocks her head. "You know, when you said you weren't looking to date or get involved with anyone, you weren't kidding. You don't even see the signs when they're in front of you."

Oh god. Oh, I fucking *hate* how giddy this is making me feel. It takes all my strength to push it all down, to try and keep my heart rate steady, to keep the smile off my face. But I'm smiling inside. A big fat grin.

"You said the signs were subtle," I remind her.

"They are. Will is restrained, but sometimes I catch this burning look in his eyes, like he's never wanted something so badly in his life."

I shake my head. "You must be mistaken."

"I don't think so. I'm pretty good at picking up on vibes. You, on the other hand, are not."

"Because he's my boss."

"So?"

"So!" I exclaim. "So everything. I can't think of my boss that way."

"But you do."

"Do not."

Now she's rolling her eyes. "Jackie, it's okay. You know how we all feel about Will. You can't possibly tell me you don't find him attractive, you've said so much on more than one occasion."

"Being attracted is one thing . . . I'm not thinking about dating my boss."

"Who said anything about dating?"

"You just did."

"You don't have to get into a relationship with him. Hell, I wouldn't. He probably has enough baggage because of Sasha. But there's nothing wrong with having some action on the side."

"Again, Alyssa, he is my boss. And my father's business partner. And best friend. And, like, sixteen years older than me. And, I mean, even just one of those things should be enough to hold up a big 'hell no' sign. You don't mix business with pleasure, you don't mix pleasure with any of those things. Nothing good could come out of it, believe me. It would jeopardize my job, my relationship with my father, my relationship with Will . . ."

"So, what? You're just going to go on this date with him tonight and nothing is going to happen? Jackie, he bought you a dress, shoes. You're fucking Cinderella for crying out loud." She pauses, staring at me with determination, like I'm an endless challenge. "The man knows what he wants and he wants you. So let him have you."

I twist in my seat, looking around wildly for the waiter again and flag him down. I put in an order for another beer, while Alyssa throws in the towel and gets herself another drink too, as well as an order of nachos for us to pick at.

Honestly, I don't feel like eating at all now. I'm a whirlwind of nerves, all twisting up inside me. Lust. I'd never seen Will stare at me with lust.

Or maybe I have. Maybe when he's staring at me so intensely that it nearly knocks me off balance, when he gives me a look that takes my breath away. I've just been training myself to not read into anything, to not look for any signs.

Fuck. What if Alyssa is right?

What if Will is attracted to me?

What if he wants me?

What then?

"Maybe I shouldn't go tonight," I tell her quietly.

"Why?" she exclaims, looking horrified. "Why would you do that to him?"

"Well, it's not like he asked me."

"Jackie, listen. Will might be giving you the eyes and he most likely thinks of you more than just an assistant. Maybe just his assistant he wants to bone, that wouldn't be a stretch. But we both know he's not the type to try anything with you. Got it? You have all your excuses and he has a million more. You're *his* assistant, you're the daughter of *his* friend. He's not going to risk anything unless you let him. He's a gentleman, remember? Cary Grant wouldn't just go feeling some girl up."

"I'm pretty sure Cary Grant was gay."

"Whatever. The point is, he was a gentleman. An old-school man of class and manners, just like Will. They don't come around very often. You have nothing to worry about. You're in control here. You want him? Then you should know that you can probably have him."

"Probably?"

She sucks back her cocktail through a straw and then shrugs. "I could be wrong about everything."

I shake my head at her and finish the rest of my beer.

"Ready to go?" Will asks me.

I literally jump a mile in my chair. I turn and look at him, hoping my heart doesn't burst out of my chest.

He's standing beside my desk, shoe box under one arm, the garment bag draped over his shoulder. I can't even imagine how good he's going to look in a tux when he looks this stunning in a simple grey linen suit.

And then he smiles.

And I smile back.

It's always been impossible not to.

I manage to pull myself away from his gaze and look at the clock. A few minutes before four.

"I figured we might as well leave early," he explains. "That way we don't have to rush. Maybe even get a bite to eat, order in. There will be finger food at the event, but that's never enough to fill you up, especially with all the free-flowing champagne."

"Okay," I tell him, feeling nearly dizzy at it all. I'm leaving the safety and security of the office and heading off for a strange new world.

"Have fun," Alyssa says to me as she walks past us, giving me a wink as she goes. I quickly look to Will to see if he noticed, but he's just staring at me.

Don't read too much into it, I remind myself.

But, god, how can I not? Ever since lunch it's all I've been thinking about, dreaming about.

And I can't pretend I'm not scared.

I'm full of pins and needles as I follow Will's tall, broad-shouldered frame out of the office, my dress draped over his back, my shoes under his arm. All for me, all this for me.

Normally it's extremely easy to converse with Will, but as we head down Richards Street toward his place, I'm finding the words hard to come by. Will talks, as usual. He touches on the wonderful weather, about team-building events for the office, about plans for the summer. He asks me if I like sailing and my mind is so frazzled I don't even question why he's asking me (I've actually never been), nor do I ask if he has a boat (pretty sure he doesn't but you never know).

My case of nerves gets even worse as we head up to his apartment. The elevator just sings with sexual tension and I'm so focused of every single breath he takes, how close his body is to mine, the amount of times his eyes glide over me.

"Want a drink?" he asks me after we've stepped into his apartment, Sprocket and Joanie dancing around us excitedly.

"Yes, please," I tell him, hoping I don't sound as desperate as I feel. "Anything will do."

He brings a bottle of white wine out of the fridge and pours me a glass.

"What about you?" I ask him.

"I'll make myself an old-fashioned when I get back up. I just want to take the dogs out for a moment."

An old-fashioned. Figures.

The moment he leaves the apartment with his rescue pups in tow, I let out a sigh of relief. It's like I've been holding my breath this whole entire day.

I drink half the glass, waiting for it to wash over my nerves, then start examining the dress and shoes.

I kick off my flats and carefully slip the Louboutins on, praying that they fit.

They do. They're a bit snug, and the back of the heel digs in a little bit, but at least they won't slip off or cause too much pain, and I can walk in them—which is a bonus. Maybe not very well—I wobble a bit going from one end of the apartment to the other, and the bottoms are slippery on the white tile floor—but it will do for a night.

Plus, they're gorgeous as hell—who cares what they feel like. I never in a million years dreamed I'd get to wear shoes like this, shoes I'd only ogled while I flipped through all those fashion and beauty mags during downtime at my old job.

That's already feeling like a second life. I can't forget what Jeff did or the life I struggled to have, but during these last few weeks especially, I feel like I've been reborn. And tonight, tonight feels like the beginning of the fairy-tale.

I can't even tell myself not to get my hopes up. There's no point. I can only swim in this feeling, swim until I'm drowning in it.

I sit back into his couch and lift my legs up in the air, staring at the shoes with glee. So fucking pretty.

The front door opens, making me sit straight up, legs pressed together.

Will peers around the corner at me. "What are you doing?"

Joanie and Sprocket come running over, distracting me for a second.

"Trying on the shoes," I tell him.

He hangs up their leashes and then proceeds to take off his blazer so he's just in a white shirt and tie. One of my favorite looks on him. I have had many fantasies of undoing that tie and slowly unbuttoning his shirt, or just watching him do it himself.

"How do they feel? Do they fit?" he asks, striding over to me. He holds out his hand for me and then pulls me up to my feet. I wobble for a moment, leaning forward so I'm right up against him.

We're close. So close. And I'm frozen. A statue that's hiding a wildly beating heart. I keep my eyes focused downward on the tops of my shoes, staring at the sight of them across from his almond-toed dress shoes. "They feel good," I manage to say, aware that he's still holding onto my hand, my breath hitching in my throat.

"You won't fall over if I let go?" he asks.

Don't let go, I think, bringing my gaze up to look him in his eyes.

He swallows thickly as he stares down at me. I can feel the color of his eyes in my bones. Rich green-blue. Like an emerald at dusk, a tropical lagoon in the early morning. A lush pool shaded by palm trees.

How easy it would be to kiss him. To reach up and grab the back of his head, feel his thick hair in my hands. Bring his mouth to mine. Sink in the warmth of his mouth. God, I bet he's a fantastic kisser. Soft at first, then rougher as he gets going.

I close my eyes, breaking the spell, a spell that needed to be broken. I swear my head was moving up toward his, like a magnet, and I might have done something really stupid.

"I hope you'll be able to dance in them," he says to me, voice low, stepping back an inch and letting go of my hand. I already feel a rush of cold air in the space between us. But I need it, it braces me, bringing me back to reality.

Only this reality right now could go in any direction.

"I'll manage," I tell him. "Wait, what kind of dancing?"

He walks over to the bar-cart in the corner and starts making himself a drink, while Sprocket and Joanie fight over a spot to sit on the dog bed by the window. "Oh, it's tradition to do some line-dancing just before the awards are given out. Don't worry though, you'll pick it up right away."

"Are you serious?"

He covers his mouth with his glass but his eyes are dancing. "Of course."

"You dick," I tell him. "You should know better than to joke about something like that."

"You do know how to slow dance, right?" he asks, going back to mixing his drink and smiling impishly.

"That I can handle." I sigh, trying to get the jitters out of me and eye the dress. "I suppose I should go try this on just in case it doesn't fit."

"Then you'd have to go naked. A real shame."

I glance at him and he doesn't seem even the least apologetic about that comment. Okay. Good to know that as we go into the night, the cards are slowly being laid on the table.

I busy myself by grabbing the dress and then step into the guest bedroom to try it on.

It's sparsely decorated; just a bed, a dresser, and more dog beds in the corner absolutely covered in their hair, as well as a hamper stuffed with their toys. I smile at the sight, thinking of Will coming here after work. Relaxing on his sofa with a drink, perhaps throwing the toys around for Sprocket and Joanie.

I wonder if he gets lonely. He never talks much about Sasha, but I wonder if he ever looks back with regret. If he misses having her around.

The thoughts pinch my heart with jealousy so I push them out of the way and get started on the dress.

I only glanced at the tag earlier, so other than the brand and the fact that it's black, I don't know what it looks like. I fear it's either too revealing or two dowdy.

But when I pull it out of the bag, it's neither.

In a way, it's just a simple black cocktail dress, but it's also one of the sexiest dresses I've ever seen. It's fitted, made of a jersey-crepe material with off the shoulder sleeves, a ruched bodice, and fluted hem that must reach my shins. The material is sturdy and stretchy and I think I can get away without a bra for once.

I strip down to nothing and then slip it on. It's a bit of a struggle—a size ten in Dolce and Gabbana is more like an eight—but I still manage to zip it up.

I turn and look in the full-length mirror propped against the wall.

Holy crap.

I don't even have my proper hair and makeup done, and I already look like someone else.

Someone beautiful.

Someone better.

The dress is extremely flattering. The ruching around the stomach hides all my fluffy bits, nipping in at the waist, accentuating the curve of my ass, while the sweetheart neckline shows off the girls, pushing them up and together. I slip my new heels back on and I look like a million dollars. Cinderella eat your heart out.

"How is it?" Will asks from outside the door.

"Great!" I answer.

"Can I see?"

"Well I don't have my hair and makeup done yet."

"That doesn't matter."

I take in a deep breath and open the door.

Will is standing in the middle of the living room, his drink in hand.

The moment he sees me his gaze goes from shocked to something more . . . primal.

I have to admit, as on-the-spot as I feel right now, I'm absolutely enjoying his eyes on me, the expression on his face. Maybe Alyssa was right. He looks like he's wanted me for ages and finally has me. Or maybe that's what I'm feeling right now. Either way, I never want him to stop looking at me like that.

I stop a few feet away and playfully push my hips out to the side. "So what do you think?"

It takes him a moment to tear his eyes off my chest and bring them to my face. "What?" He sounds dumbfounded.

"You better not be calling me kid tonight," I joke, my skin starting to heat up, "because I think I look like the opposite of that."

He shakes his head, licking his lips as he looks me over again. "No," he says hoarsely. "I'll call you Dream Girl. Because that's what you are to me."

Dream Girl.

Damn.

We stare at each other for a few moments as the air around us seems to crackle with life, brewing up all those unsaid words and stolen glances. Everything is rising to the surface now, everything, and I'm not sure how I'm going to survive the night. I'm not even sure how I'll survive this moment, standing in his apartment while the space between us hums with want and need and a million beautiful things.

And yet it's not too late to pull it all back. We haven't

crossed any line. Glances can be misinterpreted, words can be explained away. He may have just called me his dream girl and I might be clinging to that like a life raft, but nothing can stop us from going back to normal. Back to boss and employee. Like nothing has happened.

Because nothing has happened.

God, how badly I want that to change.

Will clears his throat, stands up a bit straighter. "Need help getting out of that?"

I raise my brow, trying not to smile. "Getting out of it? No, I think I'll keep it on. Especially if hair and makeup people are coming, it's easier if I'm already dressed."

He looks me over and brings out his phone. "You don't even need them, you know that. You should go just like this."

"I appreciate it. But I've never had my hair and makeup done before. It will be fun."

"All right. Well, I'll order in some food. How about sushi?"

"As long as you don't make me eat octopus and fish eggs again, that sounds great."

He grins at me and makes a phone call.

Soon the sushi is delivered.

Soon after that the makeup and hair girl, Theresa, shows up—young, pretty, and bubbly—armed with an arsenal of beauty kits. And, like most women do when they meet Will, she can't help but ogle him either.

While I sit outside on the terrace, enjoying the breeze from twenty-five stories up, sipping wine, she talks to me about this and that. She was actually going to the film gala too until her date, her ex, messed things up. She tells me all about him, this actor, and how toxic their relationship was and how she still wants him back after everything he did to her. The guy sounds like a real cad, but not even close to someone like Jeff.

"How long have you been with your man?" she asks as she slicks red liquid lipstick on me.

I give her a look since I'm unable to speak when she's doing my lips.

"Oh, he's not . . . you're not together?" she asks, glancing inside the apartment where I'm sure Will is putting on his tuxedo.

"No," I say when she's finished. "He's my boss. We're just going together to the event."

"Oh," she says. "Then can I say, *damn*. You've got a pretty sweet job having to look at him all day. He is fucking gorgeous. You don't see men like him anymore, especially not in this city."

"I know," I tell her, unable to keep from smiling. "Not just that, but he's pretty amazing too. I have a son and he's so good with him."

Theresa gets the same dreamy eyes that Alyssa had at lunch. I'm starting to wonder if that's how I look most of the time.

"Well if you don't mind me saying, the two of you would make a stunning couple. You've got such wonderful skin, I barely had to put any foundation on you. You're just glowing."

The funny thing is, I feel like I'm glowing. Inside and out.

And every time I think of Will, that glow intensifies.

It's starting to blind me.

Luckily it doesn't take long for Theresa to do her job, putting false eye lashes on my eyes and then pilling my hair up into a soft up-do. The only thing missing from the whole thing are earrings—Will hadn't thought of jewelry—but Theresa fishes out a pair of faux diamond studs from her bag of tricks and insists I keep them.

"They'll bring you good luck," she tells me with a wink, and I don't have to guess what she means by that.

When she's finished and heads out, Will is in his bedroom.

"Almost ready to go?" I hear Will ask.

I spin around to see Will, who's come out of his bedroom dressed in his tux, and my jaw is on the motherfucking floor.

And actually, so is his. He stops in his tracks and he gawks at me just as I do the same.

"You look beautiful," he says to me, his voice low and soft as it sweeps over me.

"So do you," I blurt out, unable to help myself.

Because he does.

His hair is off his face, black as sin with just a sprinkling of salt at his temples, showcasing every gorgeous angle of his face, from the arch of his dark brows, to his cheekbones, to his sharp jawline and wide strong jaw. He hasn't shaved, so there's just a hint of sexy stubble, roughing up the elegance of the black tuxedo.

He really is James Bond. Batman. He's everything sexy and mysterious wrapped up into one. And at this moment, he's no longer my boss. He's just Will McAlister, my date for the evening.

"I feel like I should call you Mr. McAlister," I admit as I slowly walk over to him.

"I'll keep on calling you Dream Girl," he says, trying to straighten his bowtie. "Tell me it's not crooked."

"It's not," I tell him. "And I think you should wear a tux to work now."

"Only if you'll wear that," he says, and I feel the heat of

his gaze as it burns over my breasts. "Though I can promise I'll get even less work done around you. Someone should have warned me how hazardous it is to have my dream girl as my assistant."

I blush, even though I hate that we're talking about work again and our roles, as much as the line is blurring between them. For a night I just want to pretend that he really is my Prince Charming and there's a chance I might not come home from this ball.

"Shall we?" he asks, flashing me a smile that I feel *everywhere*.

"We shall."

CHAPTER ELEVEN

Jackie

There are a lot of firsts for tonight.

First time in designer clothing.

First time getting my hair and makeup professionally done.

First time in the Hotel Vancouver.

First time at a gala.

First time I've truly felt like a princess.

Because how can you feel anything but magical when you're dressed to the nines and your hand is grasping Will McAlister's strong bicep as you climb up the marble staircase of the hotel toward the ballroom. I think it would be impossible.

The ballroom is already packed, even though Will had insisted we were early. Waiters in fancy suits prowl the venue, armed with drinks and appies. Even though I'm still full from our sushi earlier, my eyes are bigger than my stomach and I can't help but try every single item that comes by our way.

"I like this," Will says, eyeing me and the fact that I have a glass of champagne in one hand and a small paper plate piled high with finger food in the other.

"What?" I ask through a mouthful of sweet potato tartlet.

"You shoving food in your face," he says. "It's very becoming."

"Shut up," I tell him, trying not to spit out food as I'm talking.

"I'm serious," he says. "Sasha never ate. Says it kept her thin, but I think it just kept her mean. You can't be happy if you're hangry all the time." I nod, trying to swallow. "It's nice to be with a woman who knows what she wants and goes for it."

His words sink like stones.

Nice to be with a woman?

I'm the woman?

"What?" he asks. He's peering at me inquisitively.

I shake my head. "Just trying to figure out what spices they used in this."

Smooth, Jackie.

"I guess you're a pretty good cook," he says, taking a glass of champagne for himself off a passing tray.

"What makes you say that?"

He cocks his head. "You care too much about your son to have ordered him in takeout every day when you were up north. I bet you cooked for him as much as you could."

He's actually right. Sometimes the budget and my schedule didn't allow it and I had to do the Kraft Dinners and Hamburger Helpers. It comes with the territory of being a single mom trying to make ends meet. You have to put something on the table. But when I had the extra money and time, I always tried to make sure Ty had a healthy meal.

"I did," I tell him. "Can't say I'm any good at it though. He barely ate it half the time. But mention the word McDonalds and his face lights up like Christmas."

"I can be like that if I'm hungover," he says. "Nothing sets me right like a Sausage and Egg McMuffin, extra hash browns, a big thing of Diet Coke."

I laugh. "I'm sure the Diet Coke makes a big difference. Funny, I can't imagine you being hungover."

"Ask me about that tomorrow," he says, downing the rest of his champagne. "I can do a good breakfast though."

"That's not all that hard," I tell him. "Crack some eggs, fry up some bacon. Boom. Everyone's fucking Jamie Oliver."

"Well, maybe you can make me dinner sometime," he says to me, his voice taking on this silken quality that feels like stepping into a warm bath.

"Oh yeah?" I ask him, hoping my voice isn't as shaky as I feel. "And what do I get in return?"

"A good breakfast." And for a moment I don't think he's joking. His expression is asking something of me, something I might be too blind, too scared to give.

"You're starting to sound like you're flirting with me," I tell him, my tone slightly warning, though I don't mean it to be.

He keeps staring at me and he doesn't even flinch at what I just said. I think that scares me most of all. That maybe this isn't in my head. That I'm someone that he really wants.

I remember what Alyssa said. It's all in my hands. He's not going to do anything, not going to try anything, until he knows for sure it's something I want. There's too much for him to lose, there's too much at stake. An employee can get reprimanded for hitting on her boss, but if it's the other way around the boss could get slapped with a sexual harassment suit, or worse.

These looks, these words, this is the most I'm going to get out of him.

Unless I tell him otherwise.

Suddenly my bravery slinks away. I need liquid courage. Or more food. Stat.

I focus my attention on my plate and tentatively bite into a goat cheese and almond stuffed date. My eyes close at the taste. It's delicious.

When I open my eyes, Will is staring at me with wild wonder. "What?" I ask, thinking I might have goat cheese on my face.

His head shakes slightly though his eyes are still trained on me. "Nothing," he says softly. He swallows, his nostrils flaring slightly.

Then his attention is elsewhere, searching the room. "I think I need another glass of something," he says, his voice low.

He grabs my hand, holding tight, and pulls me along through the crowd.

As we go, people seem to part for him. Men and women glance at him appreciatively as we pass. I know Will isn't all that well-known in the city, though perhaps he is when it comes to his own industry, but I don't know how you can't stare at this man, especially in a tux. He has a way of turning heads, whether he wants to or not.

How could Sasha even cheat on him? I mean, I'm not a fool to think that good looks equal a happy marriage or even a nice personality, but Will is the total package. His looks, his body, his dick, plus the fact that he's funny, sweet, kind, generous. He's everything any woman could ever want.

And fuck, do I ever want him.

Want, need, desire, lust after.

I'm not sure how much more I can take.

But then the evening goes on and more drinks are had, as well as more delightful canapes, and then the slow dancing starts.

We're standing in the corner of the room after we were just in a long conversation with some film executives and we're both a little tipsy.

"Maybe I'm Amazed" by Paul McCartney starts to play, one of my favorite songs ever.

Will offers his hand to me. "You owe me a dance," he says, his voice strangely quiet.

I nod, putting my hand in his as he leads me to the dancefloor.

He takes complete control. One hand firm at the small of my back, another hand gripping mine. I'm pressed up against him, tight. His eyes are locked on mine, their grip just as strong as his hands around me.

It's hard to breathe. Not because my boobs are squished up against his hard abs and chest. Because the warmth of him wraps around me, lowering my inhibitions. The champagne swirls inside my head and everything else heats up my heart. His smell, sweet and spicy and woodsy, like walking through a mossy forest under a full moon, fills me from head to toe.

I close my eyes, sinking into him. This feels right. So incredibly right. To sway back and forth in his arms. To do anything in his arms. I want his arms to become my home, the place I go to when I need everything I never knew I could have.

Then he seems to stiffen against me, his posture

growing rigid, with space growing between us. I look up at him and see his attention is elsewhere, something going on behind his eyes.

"What are you thinking about?" I ask him.

A few beats pass while Paul McCartney sings on.

"Baseball," Will says hoarsely, not looking down at me.

Baseball?

"Why are you thinking about baseball?"

Hockey would make more sense.

He clears his throat. "Because I don't dare think about you."

His glances down at me, his eyes holding mine and it takes me a long moment to realize what exactly he's saying.

Oh god.

Oh my god.

Every single instinct inside wants me to push myself further into his hips, because fuck if I don't want to feel what thinking about me does to him.

I manage to restrain myself, though I'm still staring up at him with wide eyes, my mouth gaping slightly, while his own gaze burns into mine.

His breathing becomes labored, his chest rising against me, his nose flaring, his mouth set in a hard line. He's having a hard time controlling himself.

I want nothing more than to push him over the edge.

Here I go.

I swallow. "What if I want you to think about me?" I whisper. "What if it's all I've ever wanted?"

He blinks at me. Stops dancing. He can't believe what I've said.

And neither can I.

I try and think of the words to double back. I try and think of something to say that will shove all of that under the rug.

But there's nothing.

Those words still hang in the air.

What was I even thinking?

I wasn't.

I'm drunk and I'm horny and I think I'm falling for my boss.

My gorgeous, beautiful boss who is still staring at me like I've gone way too fucking far.

Not saying a word.

Oh god.

I have royally fucked everything up.

I read every signal wrong.

And that's all I had to go on.

Signals that probably only existed in my head.

"Jackie . . ." he finally says, his voice thick.

"I have to go to the bathroom," I say quickly, stepping away from him and hurrying off toward the bathrooms, dodging the couples who have started dancing to the next song.

I'm near tears. I don't want to cry. I don't like to cry. And I don't think my makeup artist used waterproof makeup. But damn if everything isn't rushing to surface.

I run down the dark corridor past the coat check room and a small room with a telephone, until I'm in the woman's washroom and finding an empty stall.

I close the lid and then sit down, my face in my hands, trying to breathe.

Holy fuck. That was so damn humiliating, I can't believe I said that.

He said he was thinking about baseball.

I assumed he meant he was trying not to get turned on as he danced with me.

Isn't that what that means when you're thinking about baseball?

It doesn't matter, it doesn't matter. Whether he meant baseball or the fact that he was trying not to get an erection, the fact is I said what I said and he said nothing in return.

Alyssa was wrong. It may have been in my hands but it doesn't mean that Will would go along with it. It doesn't mean for all his feelings and wants and needs and flirting and innuendos and jokes, it doesn't mean that this, us, would ever be more than boss and employee. It never did.

Oh fuck. I've screwed up so big.

What am I going to do now?

Go back out there and pretend that it never happened?

Knowing Will, he'd probably let that slide. He would do what's best for the both of us, for the company.

But fuck if that's not so humiliating.

I just told my boss that I all I ever wanted was for him to think about me.

I knead my forehead with my hands, wishing I could turn back time and erase that blunder. Just go back to the bedroom eyes and loaded looks and keep it all there, where it's safer for both of us.

I've been in the bathroom for at least five minutes, but I still don't feel ready to face him. I'll just have to tell him I'm drunk and I'm sorry. I don't have to bring it up, don't have to explain what I meant. Just tell him I had too much champagne and try and laugh it off. It's the best that I can do. It's all I can do.

I step out of the stall, relieved to see the bathroom still empty. I try and splash cold water on my face without ruining my makeup and take a good look at myself in the mirror.

My cheeks are pink, even more so than the coral blush Theresa used, and there's the distinct look of fear in my eyes. But other than that, I still look pretty good. Put together. Maybe there's a way to get out of this alive.

I straighten my shoulders, raise my chin, adjust my breasts in my dress.

Professional, professional, professional, I tell myself. *Go back out there and put things back to normal, back in their natural place.*

I take in a deep breath, steadying my nerves, then I turn on my Louboutins and head out the door.

I start walking down the dim hallway.

I see Will at the end of it.

He's walking toward me, his frame seeming to take up so much space, his stride commanding, the look in his eyes unlike anything I've seen yet.

"Will," I start to say, hoping the words come out right.

But he's not slowing down.

He's coming right for me.

And I'm stopped, frozen, while he strides toward me, his gaze burning into me, igniting a bonfire in my chest.

He's going to kiss me, the thought absently snakes through my head, my eyes locked to his.

And then he's leaning over slightly, both hands, large hands, warm hands, cupping my face. And I'm moving backward from his momentum until I'm pressed against the wall and his mouth is pressed against mine.

I whimper against his lips as he takes me, his mouth wet and hot, his tongue soft as it strokes against mine, building up with each movement. Will is kissing me. He's kissing me here, in this dark hallway, pressing me up against the wall. He's kissing me in such a way that he steals the air from my lungs, stokes the fire inside me, makes my heart pound rapidly in my head.

Oh fuck. Fuck.

I didn't think it could feel this good, this easy.

So easy.

His hands hold my face steady as he kisses me, and all I can do is kiss him back because it's now second nature, our mouths and lips and tongues moving against each other in this beautiful rhythm. I'm being devoured like fruit until everything inside me is bare, just seeds.

"Jackie," he says, breaking away for long enough to stare at me with heavy-lidded amazement, like he can't believe he's doing this, and I can't believe it either. He rests his forehead against mine and I feel his heat, the dampness of his skin, his nose as it brushes gently against mine, like a separate kiss, so terribly intimate.

I don't want him to stop.

Ever.

I find my breath for a moment as he finds his.

Then the hunger hits me, harder this time. I grab him by back of his neck and pull his mouth back to mine, a groan escaping from his lips and sending shockwaves through me.

Oh my god.

He makes the most beautiful sounds.

This is all I want to hear.

One of his hands drops to my waist, coasting over my hips, his fingers curling into the fabric of my dress.

This is all I want to feel.

I could kiss Will forever.

God, would that be too much to ask?

"Excuse me," someone says. It sounds like it's coming from somewhere in the distance, in some other world that doesn't apply to this one.

Then I feel the presence of someone else and Will is pulling away from me and my lips are throbbing at the absence of his.

I blink and see a man walking past us to the bathrooms, giving us a look like we need to get a room.

We do need to get a room.

Will agrees. He grabs my hand and pulls me around the corner into the tiny alcove with the telephone. For a silly moment I think maybe he's going to make a call but then he's pressing me back against the wall again, his mouth at my neck, his hands working down my back to my ass.

My eyes flutter closed as his lips suck at my skin. This is my kryptonite; doesn't he know that if he kisses along my neck I'm absolute putty in his hands?

But who am I kidding, I'm completely his. He can do whatever he wants to me, here, there, anywhere.

I can't believe this is happening.

"Neither can I," he groans against me.

Shit. Did I just say that out loud?

"You don't know how fucking badly I've wanted to do this," he says, his voice is so low, so hoarse, it's lust personified. He drags his lips down to my shoulder and back up to just beneath my ear. "I've dreamed of this. All this time. My fucking dream girl."

My mouth opens, wanting to tell him I've dreamed the same but only a moan comes out, breathless and throaty and nearly breaking with disbelief.

This is happening.

This is Will's mouth on my skin, sending shivers down my limbs, to my toes where they are curling in my shoes. A tight noise of want drives him harder against me, and now I feel him, all of him.

He's not thinking about baseball anymore.

Boldly I reach down and run my hand along his length where it's straining against his pants. I can feel the heat of him through the fabric, feel how long, thick, and hard he is. He seems unbreakable.

He could fucking break me. The thought scares me for a moment until I realize how badly I want him to try.

"Oh," he groans, biting my earlobe between his teeth, his words and hot breath in my ear. "You keep doing that and you're asking for trouble, Dream Girl."

"I wouldn't be your dream girl if I didn't," I manage to say.

"Fuck," he swears as I try and cup his length, his size already leaving me breathless. He brings his mouth back to mine and pulls me into a long, wet kiss, a kiss that rushes through me like waves, knocking me down again and again.

He's the best kiss I've ever had. I'll be ruined for anyone else after this.

That thought shouldn't stick around in my head but it does. Because it makes me think, *of course there will be others after this.*

This is Will. And despite how real this feels, how good and easy, he's still the man I can't really have. My boss. My father's friend. The same damn reasons I've repeated to myself over and over these last two months. Those reasons haven't gone away.

And so, then what?

What's going to happen?

We kiss? We fuck?

And things go back to normal.

Will slowly pulls back, as if sensing my thoughts. His breath is ragged, his gaze is lazy, focused on my lips. "I shouldn't be kissing you," he says roughly.

I can't say those words don't bite with disappointment. I stare at him for a moment. "Do you mean that?"

"Not a bit," he says, leaning in to kiss me again, sucking my lower lip into his mouth. "Jackie, Jackie, Jackie. What are you doing to me?"

"I'm not doing anything," I say against his mouth.

"You are, you are," he whispers. "You're being you. This impossibly beautiful wonderful you." He closes his eyes briefly, kissing at the corner of my mouth. "I want to take you back home. Let me take you home."

Oh god I want to go home with him. I really fucking do.

But I should say no. I don't want to say no, but I should say no.

It's getting late.

I should check on Ty.

I should not sleep with my boss.

"Come home with me," he says again, his hand running down to my hem, trying to bring it up but the dress is too tight. "There are things I want, I need, to do to you."

"What things?" I ask, unable to ignore it.

He brings his head back enough for me to catch his wicked smile. "You have no idea."

But from the raw, desperate look in his eyes, I have some idea.

Do it, I tell myself. Fuck it all. And fuck him.

"I should go home," I tell him.

I feel as disappointed that I said that as he looks.

But he doesn't protest. He just straightens up, putting some distance between us, his hand resting at my side. The distance is already fucking painful. It's wrong.

"I'll drive you home," he says, clearing his throat, trying to blink the desire away from his eyes, come back to this reality I just put us in.

"You've had too much to drink," I remind him. "I'll just get a cab."

He swallows uneasily, steps back even more. "Are you sure?"

I nod. I'm not sure. I'm not sure at all.

I just know the responsible thing to do is to get in the cab and go home and be a mother and his employee and forget this happened.

But that will never happen.

I'll never be able to pretend I don't know what Will McAlister tastes like—bourbon and cherries—or feels like—the hardest fucking cement—or looks like when he's deep in lust—like he's drowning in me.

I'll never be able to forget any of that, ever.

Change your mind. Go home with him. Let him fuck you senseless, you know that's what he wants, you know that's what you want. You want him.

Tell him!

But I'm not going to. My mouth is clamping shut and I'm stubbornly glued to my decision.

And Will looks fearful. Respectful, of course, because it's Will, but fearful nonetheless.

I grab his hand and squeeze it. "I just need to go home. It's nothing to do with you, with this."

He rubs at his jaw with his other hand and I can already see the walls going up around him, the detached look in his eyes. "I think it has to do a little with this," he says softly. "Hey, I get it. I'll walk you out."

And then he leads me out of the alcove, back into the hall, back into the ballroom and I'm regretting ever opening my mouth. He's not even back to being my boss, he's gone way back, to a man I don't know, a man I just rejected because I'm a stupid moron.

Before I even know it, I'm outside at the curb and a cab is pulling up and this is all happening so fast and I can't leave it like this.

But I am.

"Thanks for coming with me, Just Jackie," Will says as he opens the cab door for me. "I hope this doesn't change anything between us."

Oh god, but it already has. And it's my fault.

"Nothing has changed," I tell him. "And thank you for this. For all of this. I've never felt more like a princess in my entire life."

"I guess I don't make much of a Prince Charming, do I?" he says to me. "I'll see you Monday, kid. Have a good weekend." Then he shuts the door.

One minute we're kissing, lost to each other, the next I'm practically being pushed away.

I watch, shocked and saddened, as he turns and walks back up the stairs into the hotel.

The sound of him closing the door was like being shut into a tomb.

A tomb that takes me on a long journey back to my parent's house and the whole time I'm replaying what happened in my head. The whole time I am regretting my decision.

This wasn't the right choice at all.

And I'm not sure I'll have another chance to get it right.

CHAPTER TWELVE

Jackie

MONDAY.

I haven't dreaded a Monday this bad in a long time, and yet here it is. The day I never wanted to see coming.

The day when I have to go back into that office, back to working for Will, all while trying to forget what happened between us and how quickly I shut it down. How quickly he shut it down even further after that.

I've spent all weekend trying to make peace with it. I almost had myself convinced. I brought Ty to a local indoor ice rink to get him trying out for hockey, I took him to the park, we went riding. The weather was sunny and warm and I ended up even getting burned on my nose. It should have been a lovely weekend on the cusp of summer, had Will not occupied every single thought.

All the while I told myself I did the right thing. That I ended it before it could go too far. That I did what Will probably thought I would do. It wasn't out of character to scare, to back off like that. In a way, it was a classic Jackie maneuver.

But that didn't mean I didn't second guess myself every time I tried to convince myself otherwise.

That cab ride home in that dress and those shoes, the bruised feel of my lips, they were the only signs of Will that I had. The rest of me felt so damn empty and cold and alone.

It frightened me. I'd been used to being alone. I had started to embrace it.

But now that I had a taste of Will, now that I knew what it was to not only be doted on like that, treated like a queen, to be on his arm and envied, but to feel his desire, his desperate need...

Now I'm lonelier than I was before.

I had a touch of what could have been.

And I wasn't even expecting the world. Just a chance to connect with him on another level, to share my body and his bed. To really feel alive again, worshiped and desired like I'd only dreamed.

So yeah. Monday sucks. The office is the last place I want to be.

My chest is filled with barbed wire and hornets.

And when I walk inside the office, Alyssa and Tiffany are waiting at the door, practically squealing.

"How was it?" Alyssa asks, a little too loudly.

"What was the food like?" Tiffany asks.

"I looked for your picture in the Sun but I didn't see it."

"Did you see Ryan Reynolds?"

I give Tiffany a look. "Ryan Reynolds?"

"Jackie!" my father barks and all three of us straighten up, eyes wide, to see my father by the doorway. "I need to see you in my office. Now."

"Okay," I tell him, exchanging a worried glance with the others.

"You're in trouble with Dad," Tiffany jokes and then grows serious. "Only that joke isn't that funny because he really is your dad."

Alyssa pats my arm. "Tell me everything later," she says and scurries away.

I walk through the office, my heart galloping in my chest, wondering what my dad wants.

Then, as I put my stuff on my chair, about to head to his office, I see Will stepping out of his.

I freeze. My legs stop moving with just with one look from those lagoon eyes.

Eyes that are staring at me with apprehension.

"He call you into his office too?" Will asks.

Shit. My brows raised. Why is my father calling in both of us?

Oh my god!

What if someone saw us making out?

What if it was that man in the hallway who gave us the dirty look? What if he knows my father and he told?

Oh shit, what if Will loses his job? Would my father do that? Hell, he'd at least punch him in the face if not disown their entire friendship.

From the look on Will's face I know he's thinking the exact same thing.

Together we walk into my father's office.

He's sitting at his desk, sipping from his mug of coffee. "Shut the door," he tells us. Will does so and the click of the handle seems so finite.

"So," my father says, looking between the two of us. "How was the gala?"

I look up at Will as he stands beside me. His focus is

completely on my father.

"It was fine. Boring. Vancouver really is a no-fun city."

My father nods. "So you can see why I wasn't eager to go." He looks to me. "Did you at least have fun?"

I nod slowly. "It was nice."

"Nice? Well I guess I don't expect kids to be all that excited about a bunch of old farts standing around in tuxedos. Listen, the reason I called you in here is personal." He pauses, looking at Will, then at me. "There are some execs from Fox visiting this week. I need the both of you to make sure they're well taken care of. When our contract with Warner Brothers is up I don't want us to be left hanging."

I stare at him, my heart rate beginning to slow. Wait, that's it?

"Sure," Will tells him. "But why can't you do it?"

"Because I'm away this week."

"You're going back to LA again?" Will asks, folding his arms across his chest. And by doing so, now I'm drawn to the sight of the watch on his wrist, then his large hand—the very hand that grabbed me, held me. I'm practically melting in the memory.

"No, not LA," my father says, keeping his voice low. "I'm going on a golf trip to Bermuda with Badger Burke. Remember him? I just know Diane would kill me if she knew I was going to somewhere tropical without her." He looks to me. "Don't tell your mother or you're fired."

"So, I'm supposed to show the Fox guys around while you're in the Caribbean playing golf? Seems like maybe my title needs an upgrade and yours needs a downgrade."

My dad gives him a wry smile. "Seems like it's too early to start drinking, Will. Now get back to work you two. I'm taking off in an hour, but damn I want to see some work done around here before I go."

I get out of there without a moment to spare and I don't think I breathe again until I'm at my desk.

Will, meanwhile, goes into his office and shuts the door and then the blinds without even a glance in my direction. I'm pretty sure he was also having a mini heart attack in there.

I sigh and flop down in my seat, checking my emails. Part of me hopes I'll see something from him, asking to speak with me. Asking for anything, really. But there's nothing at all.

I do have some work to do—he had asked for me to look into a good group activity for the office, like a team-building exercise. For some reason when I think about shit like that, I think about something that would happen at Dundler Mifflin from *The Office*, but at least it's something to kill the time.

But my brain doesn't stop tripping over the could-haves and would-haves, something it does automatically. Always replaying my past, always going over my mistakes.

Two hours go by and Will doesn't once emerge from his office. Not even to get coffee. In fact, as much as I should give him space, I'm starting to get worried.

I email him. I have an idea for the team-building exercise.

There's no response for a good ten minutes. During that time Alyssa comes by, trying to get information from me until I wave her away, and Casey saunters past, giving me a look I'd rather forget.

Finally, my computer dings.

Can you come in here for a minute?

I get up and go to his door, knocking lightly. I can't pretend my heart isn't back to racing around again. I swear this morning is giving it quite the workout.

"Come in," Will's deep voice says from the other side.

I open the door and step inside. The main lights are off, with only one tall lamp on by the couch where a hardcover book has been propped open, as if he was reading before he asked me in.

Will is sitting at his desk, leaning back in his chair, his eyes on the computer, handsome face lit up by the glow.

"Do you want me to turn on the lights?" I ask him.

He shakes his head and then winces. "No," he says, waving his fingers at the door. "But get the door please."

"Are you okay?" I ask him, shutting the door and taking a step toward him. I don't want to get too close though. I feel like I might lose all nerve.

"I had a Sausage and Egg McMuffin for breakfast," he tells me with a frown.

"Oh, you're hungover?"

He nods carefully. "Yes. I met up with my friend last night and, well, old-fashioneds don't always treat you so well the next day."

"Maybe you should stop being so old-fashioned and have a beer for once," I tell him. Try as I might, I'm unable to take the flirty tone from my voice.

He manages to give me a smile. "Look, Jackie, there are two things I wanted to discuss with you. Well there was one. And now you have this team-building thing so let's hear that first."

"Oh. Well. Actually, you might think it's kind of funny but . . ."

"What are you doing hovering by the door?" he asks. "Sit down."

I take my seat, feeling on the spot. His eyes never leave me, as pained as his expression is.

I go on. "I thought maybe we could have a riding day

at my house. My mom can teach. Get everyone on board with horses."

Will cocks a sexy brow at me. "Team building with Diane Phillips?"

"Something like that. I know you've been saying recently that the company needs to tighten its purse strings. Maybe it was Bob in accounting. Anyway, my mom would do it for free. We wouldn't have to go far and it would be totally flexible."

"And what makes you think your mother would want to put up with us?"

"Other than the fact that she loves me, my father, and adores you?"

"Yeah."

"She's been putting up with this office for a long time. I honestly don't think she'd mind. She loves it when she plays teacher."

He steeples his fingers, resting his chin on them. Stares at me in silence for a few beats. Then says. "Okay. I'll ask Ted. When he returns from his secret trip."

"Does he always do that?" I ask.

"Executive lifestyle," Will says. "When you're the boss of the company you think you can get away with everything." Then he frowns, giving me an apologetic look. "Which is a segue into the next thing I wanted to talk to you about."

Here it comes.

"Will, you don't need to—"

He raises his palm. "Please. It has to be said. I'm very sorry for the way I behaved on Friday night. It was wrong of me and I apologize. Profusely."

"Profusely?"

"Jackie."

"You can't go back to calling me Dream Girl?"

He sighs, pinching the bridge of his nose between his fingers. "Look . . . "

"Will," I tell him, leaning forward, placing my hands on his desk. "I don't want your apology. You kissed me. And I wanted it."

There.

I said it.

It has been said.

He glances up at me. "It doesn't matter who wants it. It wasn't my place. I'm your boss."

"I know you are. But that doesn't change anything."

"It should."

"But it doesn't. Will, I have been . . . " Here comes the truth. "I have been working with you for two months now. And I'm happy here. Happy with my job. Happy with you as my boss. But I can't pretend that I haven't thought about us. In that way."

"I should know better," he says quietly, playing with his watch. "You're just twenty-five. You've been through so much and I'm just this old—"

"Will," I say sharply. "Don't even finish that sentence." I take in a deep breath. "It was a mistake for me to take the cab home. I should have gone home with you. I should have stayed with you. And I have regretted every single second since then."

His eyes meet mine. The pain he was feeling before is gone. Now I see a faint fire burning in their depths. "You don't know what you're saying."

"I know exactly what I'm saying. I may be just twenty-five. But as you've said, I've been through a lot. You say you know what you want and you go for it. So do I. You kissing me wasn't a mistake, Will. The mistake was not going back to your place and letting you fuck me sideways."

I can't believe I just said that. But damn if it hasn't gotten his attention.

He sucks in a breath, brows raised to the ceiling. The fire in his eyes building.

"God help me," he says gruffly, getting to his feet. "You have five seconds to get your gorgeous ass out of this office."

"Or what? You're going to fire me?"

"I'm going fuck you sideways," he says.

That phrase on his lips leaves me absolutely paralyzed. Glued to the chair. I couldn't get up and leave even if I wanted to. And I don't. I'm staying here. I'm not going anywhere.

He goes over to the door, twisting the lock, trapping us both inside.

When he turns around to face me the Will I know has been replaced by a carnal animal, zeroing in on its prey.

Still absolutely beautiful, though.

He stalks toward me.

"That wasn't five seconds," I tell him.

He's not listening.

He leans over me grabbing my face, tilting my head over the back of the chair. He brushes his lips against mine, teasing at first, and my eyes are still open staring in shock right at his. Then his tongue slides in and my eyes close, my body surrendering to his touch right here.

In his office.

This wasn't what I had planned this morning.

But I'm not going to stop it.

Not this time.

He moans quietly into my mouth, one hand making a fist in my hair, pulling lightly. I want more.

Then he stops himself, edging back, loosening his grip.

"What?" I whisper, the blood roaring in my head.

"I'm sorry," he says, his breath hitching as he speaks.

"Stop saying that."

"I was pulling your hair," he notes. Damn right he was. His brows come together, uneasy. "I didn't mean to hurt you. If that's something you don't like."

Oh. I get it now. He's worried that because of what Jeff did to me that hair pulling or anything else remotely painful might be a trigger. I can understand why he thinks that, but this is completely different. This is Will, a man I completely trust.

"No, I like it," I tell him imploringly. "Be rough with me. Pull my hair, choke me, spank me. It's you, Will, no one else. I want that side of you."

He's staring at me with wide, unblinking eyes. "Be careful what you wish for, Dream Girl," he says, then resumes kissing me, creating art with his lips and tongue, painting my heart with his name over and over again.

His fingers wrap tighter in my hair, giving it a tug, and it's like being pulled down beneath warm water. I could drown in his kiss and die happy.

"I should probably warn you," he says to me, placing quick kisses down my jaw, his stubble razing my skin, "that I can be bossy."

He then stands up and starts taking off his blazer, loosening his tie.

I sit back in the chair, trying to catch my breath as I stare up at him. His hair is barely out of place and I make a mental note to try and muss it all up. "Bossier than you are when you're actually my boss? Because that's not very bossy at all."

He narrows his eyes at me and throws his tie and

blazer on the computer, his long, nimble fingers undoing the buttons of his shirt. "I resemble that remark," he jokes.

"You're using puns from the Three Stooges. You really are old," I tease, biting my lip while I wait for his response.

"You want that spanking now or later?" he asks, shucking off his shirt.

I'm both in love with how easy and comfortable our banter is with each other—I guess that is one of the pluses of being around someone for nearly two months straight before you get intimate with them—and how god damn fantastic he looks. Even if he didn't have this current mood-lighting in his office shadowing the ridges of his abs and the lean curve of his chest, his rounded shoulders, his hard biceps, he would look breathtakingly beautiful.

"Now, later, I'll take what I can get."

He grins at me, devious and wicked and it has a direct effect between my legs. I can only guess at how wet I must be getting and he's barely done anything to me. I find myself gripping the edge of the chair in anticipation, squirming in my seat.

And of course, I can't help but marvel that my boss is getting naked in his office. With me.

He kicks off his shoes, bends down to take off his socks. Takes a step toward me. My eyes follow his hands as they undo his belt and then the zipper of his olive-green pants.

And then his pants drop to his ankles.

My boss is going commando, as usual.

My eyes go big and wide at the sight of something so big and, well, wide.

This isn't a stolen glance of him changing in his bedroom.

This is him in his office, with his dick, large and in

charge and jutting out right in front of me.

I manage to tear my eyes away from it and glance up at Will's face.

He looks awfully pleased with himself. I don't blame him. If I had a dick like that I'd probably be arrested for flashing it to everyone on the street.

"You're very naked," I tell him. My voice shakes a little.

"I am," he says. "You're not."

He steps toward me, his hand grasping his dick, sliding it on the long journey from base to tip. Oh, baby. Even his balls are fucking perfect, swinging slightly as he walks.

He stops a foot away and all my instincts are telling me to reach out and grab him, watch him moan from my touch.

But then he drops to his knees, his hands running up my bare legs and parting them.

I didn't see this coming.

He glances up at me as his thumbs slide over my inner thighs, brushing over the delicate skin, pushing my A-line skirt up higher and higher. His expression is both wild with desire and concerned, asking me silently if this is okay.

Of course this is okay. It's new and it's raw and it's mildly disconcerting to have Will totally naked and between my legs. But it doesn't feel the slightest bit wrong.

Still, I tense even though I tell him with my eyes to keep going, relieved that I took a good long shower this morning, that I'm wearing a new pair of silky red underwear I snagged at a Victoria's Secret sale.

Red underwear that Will is now raptly focused on.

I raise my hips slightly as he pushes the skirt up so it's bunched around my waist and he slowly runs his finger over the top of my underwear, from the lacy band all the way over the mound and down between my legs.

Hell. One touch and I'm already a bomb about to go off.

"I'm taking my time with you," he murmurs, sliding his finger back up, pressing in at my clit. "I don't give a fuck who is at my door."

Instinctively I look to the door, fully aware now that at any moment someone could try and see Will, try the locked door and interrupt the moment. Or be looking for me. And maybe putting two and two together.

But those thoughts fade away as his hands grip my hips, warm palms pressed against my skin. He lowers his head, pulls me toward his face, and I feel the hot outline of his wet mouth pressing against me, the thin barrier of my panties muffling the sensation just enough to drive me wild.

I suck in my breath, my fingers going into his hair, reveling in the silky smoothness of his strands while he runs his tongue over my clit, the pressure causing me to jerk my hips toward him.

"I've had enough teasing," he says, the vibrations spreading through me.

"I've had enough too." But the words barely make it past my lips. I'm trying to watch him with his soft dark hair between my legs, the way he keeps glancing up at me in this frenzied adoration, but I can't keep my head up. It goes back over the chair, my neck arching.

He pulls his face back for just a moment, long enough to slide my underwear down over my thighs until they're dangling off one leg, then he's pushing my legs wide again, his mouth going in for the kill.

Every worry, every tense cord inside me loosens with the wet sweep of his tongue. My mouth falls open, a groan rising out from my chest.

Damn. He knows what he's doing. My thighs are already quivering.

His mouth is so warm, so strong. He kisses me there like he kisses my lips, soft and gentle, then quick and wild, sliding up around my clit then down inside me with a grunt.

I can't contain my cry. It claws out of me, fueled by the need for him to be deeper.

But I probably should contain it.

Will pauses, staring up at me with a wet mouth, his brow raised.

For a moment I forgot where we are.

"Dream Girl, I'm taking you home later and you can scream as much as you fucking want."

"Sorry," I tell him, finding my breath. "It's just that you're very good."

He grins. "I can tell. It's hard not to be when you look the way that you do." His eyes drop and he's gazing between my legs. "I don't think you have any idea how beautiful you are, how amazing you taste."

I tighten my grip in his hair, giving it enough of a tug that his eyes pinch closed with pleasure. "Less talking," I tell him.

"And I was supposed to be the bossy one," he mutters to himself before shoving his face back between my legs.

It's immediate bliss and I bite down on my lip hard enough to draw blood to keep the cries inside my chest. He is so, so good. And he knows it.

Soon the office fills with the sound of his licking, his sucking, his groans and my breathless sighs. Then he's staring up at me, eyes burning with crazed lust and slowly pushing two large fingers inside me.

I'm gasping louder now, terribly close to coming.

"You have no idea how beautiful you look right now," he whispers into me.

"Please . . . keep . . . going." My skin is so flushed, I'm sweating, everything inside me is on fire, begging, needing to come.

With a throaty growl, he plunges his fingers back in, sucking my clit into his mouth, flicking it sharply with his tongue and I'm coiled in tight in waves of electricity, winding, winding, winding.

Then I'm exploding, wet, warm, pure fucking bliss. My hips jerk into his mouth as I spasm, my thighs gripping the side of his face, his stubble so beautifully rough. My fingers tug at his hair, holding on tight as though I might be thrown to the ground.

The world slowly shifts back, like sliding puzzle pieces. I'm staring up at the ceiling, open mouthed, glad I don't have fluorescent lights blinding me in the eyes.

"Up," he says gruffly, grabbing my hands and hauling me to my feet. I can barely stand; my legs are still shaking.

He leads me over to the couch, pushes the book off of it, and then turns me around, placing his hand between my shoulders and shoving me down so I'm on the couch on my knees.

"Hands up, against the wall," he says from behind me, his voice extra rough, borderline animalistic. Finally, bossy Will has come out to play and I'm ready to do whatever he asks of me.

I put my hands up so they're pressing against the wall, bracing me, just as one of his hands curls around the small of my waist. His touch is electric, hot, searing, especially over my hyper-sensitive skin.

"I'll go slow," he murmurs and I feel him position the

tip of his cock just below my ass. "I wanted you wet as possible. I know I'm a big boy."

I've never heard him sound less modest and I know he doesn't have a reason to. I brace myself, holding my breath as he slowly, very slowly, pushes himself in.

He sucks in air then groans it out as he squeezes into me. "Fuck. Fuck, Jackie. This is . . ."

He doesn't finish his sentence. His grip tightens around my waist and I bend a little more, trying to accommodate his size. I feel him everywhere, like he's filling me up in every way.

I'm barely breathing. I'm tense and I shouldn't be, but damn it's hard. It hurts just a little, even though I'm so wet I'm dripping down my thighs.

He leans over me, hands brushing the hair off the back of my neck, kissing me there. "Easy," he groans. "Easy. God, you feel like I thought you would. So warm, so tight."

I close my eyes, relishing his words, willing my body to relax.

He pushes in further. Inch by inch, until I'm so fucking full, spread wide, aching around him.

He brings his mouth to my shoulder and bites. Hard. A whimper erupts from him and I just want to listen to his noises all day long, every day. I want to feel him forever, just like this, inside me like he's always supposed to be. Two tectonic plates shifting in place against each other until there's one fiery fit.

"I swear I'll fuck you for hours, if you let me," he whispers, mouth now at my ear. His voice is rough with urgency. "I'll make you come until you can't walk, can't speak, can't see anything but stars. But for now, I just need to come inside you. And I'm going to do it fast and do it hard. You got that?"

I nod, trying to swallow, my nails digging into the wall. I fucking adore bossy Will.

"Good," he says, straightening up. "But just in case you don't..."

I feel a hard crack against my ass cheek as he slaps it with a strong, open palm, then slaps the other cheek, and then before the cries fall from my lips, he pulls his cock nearly all the way out and then slams himself back into me.

All the air is pushed from my lungs. His cock is in so deep I'm not sure where I end and he begins.

Then he starts working me, his fingers pressing so hard into my side that I think he's leaving bruises, holding me steady as he fucks me, hard.

There isn't anything in the world but this.

He grinds into me, over and over, his hips jerking, his balls tapping against my skin. I don't even know if he's in to the hilt, but it doesn't matter because the man is adept at control. His frantic thrusting is measured, his hips circling just enough to slide against every right spot. Faster, harder, deeper. He doesn't relent.

Then as he starts to tense, his breath becoming raspy and hard, a drop of sweat rolling off his face and onto my neck, he slides his hand over the front of my skirt and below, finding my clit.

Two slick rubs are all it takes before I'm coming, and I'm taking the fabric of my dress shirt between my teeth, biting on my sleeve to keep from screaming.

I feel like I've been electrocuted with stardust. A universe is being created somewhere in my chest, expanding with suns and moons and stars.

Holy fuck.

It's not just the intensity of the orgasm as it rips through me, causing my limbs to jerk and shake, it's the intensity of *us*.

Of Will, as he groans into my shoulder with one final thrust, his seed spilling into me, his cocking twitching.

Emotions I wasn't even aware existed are rushing through me, from my heart, up to my head, causing my eyes to burn with tears I desperately try to blink back. I'm so damn full of him, not just physically. This was never just physical.

And that's why it's so dangerous, I tell myself as my heartbeat slows and the feeling comes back into my heavy legs. My thoughts are rubbery at first, barely sticking in my brain before bounding off, but they're there.

That wasn't just a fuck with Will.

But it can't ever be more than that.

What have I done?

"Jackie," he whispers to me, kissing my neck. "Was that okay?"

I try and nod but I can barely move. My arms are locked against the wall, my skin red where my hands have bent back against my wrists.

He gently pulls himself out of me, his cum dripping down my thigh, and then pries my arms off the wall, holding me steady until I get to my feet.

There is no après-sex weirdness. I'd only slept with one guy, Lance, before I slept with Jeff, and with both of them it was always so cold and distant after we had sex. But Will is pulling toward me, cupping my face in his hands and staring at me with the same amount of adoration as he had before.

"How are you feeling?" he asks me, his forehead damp, his face flushed pink, both sexy and adorable.

"Fine," I say, licking my dry lips. "Better than fine."

His mouth quirks up into a half-smile. "I hoped you'd

be better than fine." Then his expression grows serious. He swallows, eyes searching my face. "I just want you to know, just in case you're thinking it, that what we just did, it wasn't wrong. It was the opposite of wrong. You, me. It's everything that's right."

I feel it too, burning in my chest.

But . . .

"Will," I say softly. "That needed to happen. For whatever reason."

"Because I want you," he says, running his thumb along my lip. "Because I need you. Because I'm falling for you."

Holy bejesus.

My heart feels like it's in free-fall.

No. No, this is so much, so fast.

"Jackie," he says to me, trying to keep his voice light. "It's okay. All of this. However you want to do it."

"You're my boss."

"I know that."

"I don't want that to change."

"It's not going to."

"We could get in a lot of trouble."

I mean, fuck, I'm only now realizing how much trouble we can get into. We just fucked in his office. He ate me out in his damn chair.

"I'm a big boy."

"Oh, I know that." God, I'm still aching a little from him.

"I mean, I know what I'm doing, what I'm getting into."

I sigh, trying to look away, but he keeps my face in place.

"We both could lose our jobs. We both could damage our relationships with my father."

"He'd understand."

I give him a hard look. "Do you really think that? Will, you might think he'd forgive you for fucking his daughter, and I highly doubt that. But I guarantee he won't look too kindly on me."

"Jackie . . . "

"No," I tell him, frustrated, I pull away and walk across the room to where his clothes are strewn about. I pick up his pants and throw them into his hands. "You don't understand. I was a problem child. I made his life, and my mother's life, a living hell in high school. Drinking, drugs, getting in trouble with the police. I was with the wrong crowd and I didn't care. And then I got knocked up by a piece of shit that they hated. I had Ty and then I immediately ruined everything, threw it all away, all their support and love, by moving up north with Jeff. I barely talked to them for seven years, and I was barely talking to them before that. Don't you see? I need to repair what I have with my father. I need to prove that I'm good, that I'm responsible, that I'm no longer the girl that they think I am."

He watches me steadily as he slips on his pants. "You're far from that girl."

"Yeah, well, you don't know that," I say, tossing him his dress shirt. "You weren't there to see it. And if you were, you weren't a part of it. Thank god." I rub at my forehead, trying to get my bearings. "Look, I know this is all okay to you. But it can't be more than this."

"Sex?"

I nod, biting my lip. "Yeah. Sex."

He slips on his shirt and raises his chin as he watches me. "That's all I get?" he asks quietly.

I gesture to the chair and the couch, giving him a small smile. "Honestly, I think if it's always like this, it's more than enough. You might just be too much for me to handle."

That brings a genuine grin to his face. "Okay," he says, coming over and doing up his shirt. "If that's all of Jackie Phillips that I get, I'd be a foolish man not to take it."

I stare at him for a moment, taking in his beautiful body, that gorgeous face, his damn big heart. "How can you even want more?" I ask him quietly. "After all you've gone through with Sasha. How can you put yourself out there again?"

He tilts his head thoughtfully. "Because being with Sasha taught me that life is short. And when you find what makes your heart beat, your soul sing, you have to hang on to it. That's you Jackie. I'm done doing things halfway. It's all or nothing now. And with you, I'm all in."

Damn. Damn his pretty mouth and those sweet, sweet words.

"So, can I take you on a date?" he asks.

I laugh. "I just said it was just sex."

"And I just said I'm all in. This is how I do just sex. Come on over to my place tonight. I'll show you what a date with me is like when it's just sex." He steps closer and runs his hand down my sleeve until he's holding my hand. "I respect your decision. But I'm still going to want to see you every single chance I get. Working with you is not enough. It's never been enough. We'll hide it and I won't expect much from you, but you're the only girl for me going forward, got that?"

"Got it," I tell him as he kisses me gently on the lips. "But my mom is teaching a class tonight. She can't watch Ty. What about tomorrow night?"

"It will be painful to wait that long. But sure." Then he reaches around and smacks my ass. "Now go back outside and finish those expense reports."

I grin at him. "I did those last week."

"Then go outside and look busy. And stop dreaming about me."

I shake my head and head to the door. "You're too much."

"I know."

I unlock the door and slowly pull it open, poking my head out.

Patty isn't at her desk. No one is looking in my direction.

I look over my shoulder at Will, give him a nod, and then I step out.

It's only a few feet to my desk.

I make it there without anyone noticing.

That is, until I turn around and see Alyssa standing in the corner, munching on an apple.

My eyes widen.

She winks at me and walks over. "You still have to tell me about the gala," she says, glancing at Will's closed door. "Something tells me it went really well." Then she leans in close and places her finger at her lips. "I've got your back," she whispers and then walks off to her office.

I sigh, long and hard, and sink back into my chair.

I can't believe that just happened.

And yet, somehow, I can.

CHAPTER THIRTEEN

Will

I THINK I MIGHT BE THE LUCKIEST GUY IN THE WHOLE damn world.

No. Scratch that.

I *know* I am.

And so far, I still can't quite believe it.

After what happened at the gala, I was certain I'd never get a shot with Jackie again. I had been putting it out there all night, trying to read her signals, trying to tell her how much I wanted her without coming across as the creepy harassing boss.

She was playing along. She was volleying back whatever I served.

And then she had to ask me that question while we were dancing.

I actually *was* thinking about hockey.

But I don't think she would have picked up on the analogy.

Then, when she told me she wanted me to think about

her, I was so stunned.

Just to hear her say it was like a fucking adrenaline injection straight to my heart.

I honestly didn't know what to do or say. I couldn't process it.

My body just wanted to devour her whole, right there on the dance floor.

But she took my silence to mean something else.

Watching her walk off, upset, was hard.

But it gave me something. It meant that what she said was true.

That's when I knew I had nothing left to lose.

We were finally on the same fucking page.

That kiss was unbelievable.

That kiss sealed my fate.

I knew at that moment I'd never be the same. That I was done for. That if I didn't end up with her, I'd spend my whole life searching for another kiss like that and I'd never find it.

When she freaked out and wanted to go home, I knew that might be the case.

Needless to say, I spent that weekend trying not to dwell on what had happened, trying to calm myself down and tell myself that Jackie wouldn't report me to her father or to anyone else. She's not like that.

But she could quit. She could decide she didn't want to work for me anymore and I wouldn't blame her.

It would rip my heart to shreds.

So Sunday night I decided I had to blow off some steam. I went out with Emmett to the L'Abbatoir bar in Gastown and proceeded to get very, very drunk. The Australian bartender seemed hell-bent on feeding us some of his own concoctions, along with my usual old-fashioneds. Pretty sure he poisoned us, but it felt good to talk with someone about it—after all, Emmett has been there for a lot of shit—but more than that, it felt good to drink it all away.

Until the next morning, of course, when Ted called both me and Jackie into his office. It wasn't really until then that I realized what I'd had with Jackie, even so briefly, could have cost the both of us everything.

The funny thing was, it didn't matter.

Just that one kiss was worth it.

Of course Ted didn't know a thing, so I retreated to my office to nurse my hangover in the dark and push the fact that Jackie was just outside out of my brain.

Then she emailed me.

I had to see her.

And whatever fears she had on Friday night, they had disappeared.

She put herself out there for me to see and I could only respond in return.

Damn. I never thought it could be *that* good. That someone could taste so addicting, feel so soft and sweet and pure. Being inside Jackie like that . . . it was a fucking religious experience, nirvana, anything fucking thing you want to call it, and now I'm left yearning for more.

A lot more.

I told her that I was falling for her.

She told me she just wanted sex.

I don't necessarily feel like I'm settling for less, only because I hope I can get under her skin in the process.

It just makes work more difficult.

Case in point: it's Tuesday. Tonight we have our date. In other words, she's coming over after work where I plan to fuck her in as many places as possible.

Usually Tuesdays are slow. The bustle of Monday and

the new week is over and people lose whatever enthusiasm they had, and the relief of Friday is too far away to even be considered.

I expect to spend the day on calls and in meetings, all while watching the clock tick past in excruciating slow motion.

But the Fox guys, Roger and Burt, are in town today.

I set up a meeting for them in the office, taking over the boardroom for a few hours. Jackie plays her role perfectly, ordering in lunch for them from the caterers, plus coffee and water and whatever else they need. Whatever materials I need to show them, Jackie is there on hand to present them with a smile.

In fact, by the time the guys are dragging me out the door to treat me to a drink, Roger wants to bring Jackie along.

"I could stare at her ass all day," he says to me with a sleazy wink.

I keep the smile plastered on my face, but inside I'm trying not to punch him right in his red-nosed face.

It's been a long time since I've felt a bit of jealousy, and how I'm feeling over Jackie is white hot and potent. I need to keep myself in check.

Luckily, Roger doesn't say anything else about my assistant. The meeting ends up going really well, no thanks to Ted, and I get back to the office just before the end of the work day.

Jackie, however, is starting to pack up when I stroll back inside.

"Where are you going?" I ask her.

She stares at me with big eyes. "Home?"

"Home?" I repeat. I look around. Patty acts like she's not listening as she types away at her computer but I know she is. I lean in closer to Jackie. "I need to see you in my office."

I head inside and she's right behind me. Like a good girl, she closes the door, though she doesn't lock it. Not that I would try anything with Patty just outside, having seen us both go in.

"Why are you going home?" I ask her, and before I know it I'm pulling her toward me, my mouth opening against hers in a long, wanting kiss.

My dick twitches in my pants, raring to go.

Okay, so maybe I would try *something*.

"Will," she says breathlessly, placing her hand at my chest and pushing back slightly. "Patty saw us come in together."

"I know," I tell her. I clear the lust from my throat and straighten up. "I know. Sorry. Instinct. You have no idea how hard it was today to keep my hands off you."

She looks down shyly and tucks a strand of hair behind her ears. "That makes two of us. How did the meeting go?"

"Fine. Thanks to you." I grab her around the waist, pulling her closer again.

"Will." She giggles and I kiss the top of her forehead since she's playing hard to get.

"You did amazing," I tell her, my hand sliding down over her ass and giving it a squeeze, relishing that I'm able to do this. This girl, my dream girl, is mine, no one else's. "I think they were more impressed by you than they were by the studio."

"Oh please," she says. "I just brought them food."

"You know how to win people over, that's all."

She frowns and I slide my finger over the line between her brows. "It's funny," she says. "I never really thought I'd turn out to be a people person."

"How can you not be? Everyone wants to talk to you, be by you. Myself included." I lean in and nibble on her earlobe, loving how delicate her skin feels between my teeth, her sweet, soapy smell. "You light up every room you're in."

"Stop," she protests, shivering under my touch. "You're trying to butter me up."

"I'm just being honest," I tell her, kissing a path down her neck, reveling in the taste of her warm skin. "You'll know when I'm buttering you up. In fact, I might just start here if you don't come home with me soon."

"I thought our date was tonight?" she asks.

I pull back and peer at her. "I meant after work. Do you have to go home?"

"I should see my son."

"Ty can wait."

"I should let my mom know I won't be there until later."

"So let her know." I watch her face as she mulls it over, worry lines appearing. "Jackie. Either you want to come over or you don't."

She blinks at me, surprised at my tone.

"I told you I'm all in," I explain, massaging the back of her neck. "An all or nothing guy. I want to see you tonight. I want to see you every night. If you don't want that, if you don't feel the same way, you have to tell me now. I don't have time for games."

She jerks her head back. "I'm not playing games."

"Not on purpose. But I need to know what you want."

With a sigh, her chin drops and she looks down at her feet. "I'm nervous."

"Nervous?" I place my fingers under her chin and lift it up until she's looking at me. "Why are you nervous?"

She rubs her lips together for a moment, staring at me

with soft eyes. "I don't know. Because this is all so new and, well, yesterday was yesterday and today is a new day. I'm just . . . I don't want to screw anything up between us."

Damn. She looks so fragile, it causes a few more cracks along my heart. I cup her face in my hand and lean in close so my forehead is against hers. "It's me. And it's you. And this works, the two of us, we work. Literally and figuratively. You wanted just sex and that's fine with me. I know how I feel about you, sex isn't going to change that. Are you scared it might change you?"

"I don't know," she says quietly after a few beats. "Maybe. I'm just . . . I'm shy, too."

I can't help my smile. "You didn't seem shy yesterday."

"But that was yesterday."

"And this is today. I get it. So what do you want to do, Dream Girl? You tell me."

"I don't want to go home. I want to be with you. I want to come over."

"Okay," I tell her. "We don't even have to have sex. We can walk the dogs. Watch a movie. Hang out. I'm one hundred percent okay with that."

"Really?"

"Ninety-seven percent okay with that. And I can jerk off that three percent later."

"I never knew percentages could be so sexy."

"You're learning a lot on this job. Including how to drive a man positively mad. Now come on." I smack her ass. "We should get out there before Patty suspects something."

Fortunately, Patty is no longer at her desk by the time we exit my office. Jackie quickly texts Diane, telling her she's working later and getting drinks with colleagues after, and we manage to leave the building together without raising suspicion. Not that Jackie and I don't often go off together like this, it's just I'm a bit paranoid now that we're actually fucking each other.

Good lord. I'm as horny and fucking stoked as a goddamn teenager by the time we get to my building. I've never really felt old before, but being around Jackie definitely makes me feel young. Young enough to throw caution to the wind and lose all sense of self. The elevator doors have barely closed before I'm pressing her up against the wall, my hands sliding over her hips, her breasts, clawing at her in desperation.

The moment we're in my apartment though, I know I have my work cut out for me. The dogs jump us when all I want to do is jump her. Without missing a beat, I grab some dog chew sticks from the pantry and throw them on the couch while grabbing Jackie by the arm and leading her straight to my bedroom, shutting the door.

"I thought this didn't have to be about sex," she says, stepping backward toward the bed and looking around the room.

"I changed my mind," I tell her. "Take off your clothes."

She raises her brows. "Back to being bossy."

"Take them off," I repeat, my tone firmer as I start taking off my shirt, pants, everything. "Take them off or I'll tear them off with my teeth."

Her eyes go so big I could die. "I'd rather you tear them off," she says.

Dangerous. She doesn't know what she's asking of me.

"Fine," I tell her, and once I'm completely naked, her eyes taking in my body with appreciation, I grab her dress shirt with both hands and rip it apart down the middle, the buttons flying across the room. A wine-colored lace bra is on display underneath.

"You owe me a new shirt," she says, trying to sound

annoyed. She's blushing, turning pink right up to her hair. Too fucking cute.

"How much was it, twenty dollars?" I ask mildly, knowing her penchant for cheap clothes.

She tries to glare at me but I just grin. I push her backward onto the bed and start pulling down the zipper at the side of her skirt, yanking the skirt down over her hips as she kicks off her shoes. Then I lean over and grab the lacy trim of her panties between my teeth. With a growl and a twist of my head, like I'm a wild dog, I tear into it, ripping her underwear right off of her hips.

"Okay, now you owe me new underwear," she says.

"I'll start a tab for you," I say gruffly, my eyes raking over her chest. "Now, you want to remove the bra yourself or let me do it?"

She quickly reaches behind her and undoes the clasp and I grab the front of it, pulling it and the rest of the dress shirt off of her, throwing it to the floor.

Fucking hell.

Fucking *hell*.

I've never seen her naked. I had a great look at her pussy the other day before I licked it inside out, but I hadn't seen the rest of her.

She's even more gorgeous than I imagined. Impossibly so. Lying beneath me with her large, round tits on display, she's just this creamy smooth dessert. Tempting. Decadent. I need to eat her, taste her all over, savor her on my tongue.

Her nipples are perfectly pink, hardened into little peaks, and I gently run my hands over them, feeling them grow even stiffer against my palm. Her skin is so soft, so pale, dotted with freckles here and there. I want to kiss each one of them.

"You're so fucking beautiful," I whisper to her, and I

know she doesn't believe me but it's true. "Every single inch of you is beyond perfection."

I run my hands over her stomach where she squirms. I know she's self-conscious about her weight, as if being a size ten and having ample tits and ass and hips is something to be ashamed of. She doesn't realize just how perfect she is to me.

"Trust me," I tell her, my hands now skirting over her hips, down to her full thighs and back up again over the dip of her waist. "The perfect hourglass."

"I don't know, my stomach and my arms are—"

"Jackie," I warn, my voice firm again. "Don't argue with me. That's rule number one."

She frowns but is still unable to hide her smile. "You have rules?"

"In this apartment, there are many rules. Number one is that you can't argue with me, especially when I know what I'm talking about."

"What's number two?" she asks.

I slip my hand between her legs, finding her already wet. "You have to do everything I say."

She closes her eyes, relaxing into the bed. "What's rule number three?"

I bring my fingers up softly over her clit, her legs spreading wider for me. "You can't come until I say so."

She opens her eyes in disbelief and lets out a laugh. "That's the worst rule I've ever heard."

"Hey, I don't make them up."

"Yes you do," she says, and then moans as I start rubbing my fingertip into her in hard circles.

"When you have me over at your place, you can make the rules."

"Yeah, like that will happen."

"As I said."

"And what happens if I break the rules?"

"You get punished."

"You'll spank me?"

"That I will."

"What if I want you to spank me?" she asks.

I decide to give her a taste of her own medicine. I pull my hand back and then lightly spank her, right on her pussy.

She jumps, staring at me. "What was that?"

I grin at her. "Did you like it?"

"I don't even know, I—"

I do it again with a quick flick of my wrist and then lick my fingers, gently soothing over the spot.

"Oh god," she moans, her eyes pinching shut, her mouth opening.

"As you can see, you might like the punishment more than the rules," I tell her, leaning down to squeeze her breast. I gently rub my lips over her nipple. "We'll have to play it by ear."

I take an obscene amount of pleasure in watching her writhe, listening to her breathy little moans as I suck her breast into my mouth, teasing, flicking. I have half a mind to just stroke myself off right here, I'm that ready for her.

But as much as coming all over her creamy skin would be a wish come true, there's something I want much more. To push deep inside her, her naked flesh pressed against mine. I was only inside her once and it wasn't nearly enough.

I hold her arms over her head, keeping her wrists together with one hand while I position my cock against her with the other. The anticipation is killing me but I want, need, to take this slow.

She stares up at me, cheeks pink, flushed, her eyes glowing. She's sex come to life lying beneath me.

Slowly, I rub the head of my cock against her pussy, my eyes closing as she gasps. "Look how wet you are," I murmur to her. "Have you been like this all day?"

She lets out a huff of air, something between a moan and a cry of desperation and starts moving her hips into me, wanting more. I don't think I've ever been harder, and the more I rub myself along her, the slicker she gets.

Finally, when I can't handle it anymore and her sounds are getting greedy, I ease myself inside.

She's tight. Jesus, she's tight, even tighter than she was the other day.

"You look so good, Dream Girl," I tell her, my voice hoarse and dry. "Feel so good." I take a moment to admire my hand, tanned and large against her pale skin as it works its way down to her hips, the smooth curves and hidden skin, places that no one else sees but me.

I rub my fingers along her clit in a V-shape and watch as I slowly disappear inside of her.

There's never been a more erotic sight than this, just seeing her take me in, inch by inch, until I'm completely feeling her from the inside.

"Fuck," I say, my words coming out in a burst of air as I start thrusting. "So fucking good."

She's looking now too, raising her head to watch as I press deeper and deeper, my cock thick and shiny with her as it goes in and out. My rhythm slowly picks up, making her tits jostle.

I reach down and slap one breast, enough to make her skin red.

"What was that for?" she asks, blinking in surprise.

"You were thinking about coming," I tell her. "Not yet."

I'm not really sure how long I can stretch out this game and that particular rule, but I'm going to have a fun time trying.

She doesn't even look annoyed. "You better stop with your fingers then."

I remove my hand.

Now she looks annoyed.

I let go of her hands above her head, telling her to keep them there, then I pick up her hips and start angling myself deeper, my pelvis rubbing against her clit as I fuck her.

She moans, her head rolling to the side, eyes pinched, mouth open.

"You like this, don't you?" I whisper to her. "You like that I'm in control. That you have my cock. That it's making you so fucking wet."

She nods, raring, lost to it all.

I'm close to losing it too.

But I have a reputation to think of.

I dig my fingers deeper into her hips as her own fingers curl around the sheets and I keep thrusting, adjusting the speed and depth to the expression on her face. I want her near the edge but not over it. Not without me.

By the time I'm sweating, working her again and again, and she's arching her head back, I lean down and suck at her neck.

"You want to come now?" I whisper in her ear.

She makes this moaning, pleading whimper that makes my balls tighten.

I fuck her harder, the bed inching across the floor, the walls shaking.

Then she's shaking.

Then I'm shaking, my neck corded as I shoot inside of her, nearly breaking her in half during those final moments.

Stars appear behind my eyes, ebbing and flowing like the tide, and I collapse on top of her, breathing hard, my heart trying to pound straight out of my chest.

I can feel her heart beneath me, trying to do the same.

Maybe they can meet in the middle.

A loud howl jerks me awake. It takes me a few seconds to realize I'm naked and lying beside Jackie, my arm draped over her chest.

"What is that?" Jackie asks groggily, blinking hard. "I think I fell asleep."

I glance at the alarm clock. It's already seven, and outside the windows the city is glowing in dusky gold, sunset approaching.

"Oh shit," I say, quickly getting up and grabbing my robe. "We did fall asleep."

I open the door expecting to see the worst, piles of shit and piss everywhere, but instead it's just Joanie and Sprocket, wagging their tails in a desperate way.

"I need to take them outside before they explode," I tell her, slipping my pants on and tying the robe around my waist.

"In your bathrobe?" she asks and I glance at her, momentarily dumbstruck.

There she is, lying across the white covers of my bed, the dying sunset coming in through the windows and lighting her up in swathes of gold.

"Jesus," I swear. "I need to remember this."

"What?" she asks, glancing down at her body on display. She reaches for the duvet to cover herself up.

"No," I say quickly. "Just let me look at you." I'd take a picture with my phone if she didn't think it was weird. Instead I hope it gets burned into the back of my head.

Sprocket barks again, followed by some whimpers that tell me I don't have much time.

"I'll be right back," I tell her. "Don't you dare get dressed."

I grab the leashes and the dogs and head down to the courtyard, taking them around a few times. Times like this I wish I smoked, I could use a clear head.

Then again, why would I want the clarity? Right now my whole world is whittled down to just one thing, and that's Jackie. The days can turn to night and back into day and it can keep doing that for a long time, but the only focus I have, the only thing I really care about and want, is her. Just her. Just Jackie.

Joan makes a pig-like noise, bringing my attention to her, as if she knows what I'm thinking.

"But of course I love you too," I reassure her and Sprocket.

The words coming out of my own mouth catch me by surprise. The dogs take no notice.

Love.

I knew I was falling for Jackie, that I've been falling for her hard and fast all this time. I knew that I was falling into love.

I just didn't think I'd already hit it.

But I have.

I've smashed into it, like falling from a building twenty-five stories up. They call it falling in love because eventually you hit the ground and that's where I am. On the pavement, blasted to smithereens.

I crane my neck back, staring past the balconies and

carved statues that protrude from the building like the bow of a ship, and I look straight up to my apartment, where Jackie is now.

I'm dizzy from the realization.

Reverse vertigo.

To see how far I've fallen.

I'm in love with her.

I'm. In. Love. With. Her.

Shit.

I sigh, giving a slight nod to someone in the building as they walk past. It's not unusual to see the dog-owners outside in their pajamas or half-naked sometimes.

I need to tuck this feeling away. Ignore it, no matter how hard it is. This is the last thing I need, and the last thing Jackie wants.

But, fuck if it isn't the best feeling in the world.

Like the sun rising in your chest.

And suddenly, just like that, everything is million times more complicated.

I take the dogs back upstairs and step into the apartment, heading straight to the fridge to get out a bottle of pinot gris. I pour us both a glass. I gulp mine down like it's water, then fill it up again.

There. That oughta help for now.

Taking both glasses, I head to the bedroom, hoping to find her where I left her.

But she's already dressed.

Well, she's standing in her bra and skirt, hands on her hips and looking at me, unamused.

"Why do you have clothes on?" I ask her, trying to hand her a glass of wine.

She waves it away. "I have to go home. Ty, my son, remember?"

"I remember, I just . . . stay for a drink."

"I really shouldn't. Look, I need a shirt to wear."

I raise my brows, slowly nodding, hiding the disappointment that's tumbling around my chest. Maybe it's my heart in there, trying to find a way out.

"Right," I say. "I might have something."

I put the glasses on the dresser and start rummaging around.

"Unless you have a store of women's clothes in here, I doubt you have anything that fits."

I pull a black dress shirt out of my closet and hand it to her. "It's too small. It will still be too big on you, maybe not at the chest, but everywhere else. But maybe you can knot it at the waist or something. Pretend it's the latest style."

"My mother will know it's your shirt."

"Then tell your mother I gave you my shirt."

"Will."

"Jackie."

"You know she'll be suspicious."

I have to fight to not roll my eyes. "Tell her you spilled something on your shirt and I had an extra one at work and I lent it to you."

"Fine," she says, slipping it on.

It does look oversized, even when she knots it, but damn if it's not the sexiest fucking sight to see her in my clothes.

"Are you sure you have to leave?" I ask her. "We were just getting started. I promised you hours of sex, and that was barely anything."

She grins at me. "Look at you, Mr. Cocky. That was enough for me. For now."

"How about lunch tomorrow? Instead of going to a café, why don't you come here and I'll eat you?"

She licks her lips, pink coming into her cheeks. God, she's beautiful. Why is she doing this to me? She's not even doing anything, she's just existing.

"Sounds good," she eventually says, like I had to twist her arm. She wants it just as badly as I do, why pretend otherwise?

She brushes past me as she heads into the living room, glancing at me over her shoulder. "Is there a bus that comes along Richards?"

"You are not taking the fucking bus," I tell her, going into the kitchen and grabbing my keys off the ring. "I'm driving you."

"Will, it's fine. I take the bus all the time. I don't need—"

"You say you don't *need*, and I believe you Jackie," I interrupt her. "But can you just let me take care of you for once? Don't you understand that this is what I want?"

She opens her mouth to say something then thinks better of it. Grows silent. Nods.

I grab her hand, kissing the back of it. "Sorry. I want to do things for you. I want to take care of you." I pause, staring at a freckle above her lip, the dimple on her chin, the streaks of green in her eyes. "I could be good for you. *Let me* be good for you."

My words fall around us like the dying light. I can't read her. I want to, but I can't. I don't know what she's thinking and I'm not even sure I want to know.

Finally she says, "I really need to go home."

"Okay," I tell her. "Come on."

Traffic is a pain at all hours of the day here, but even so it seems especially bad tonight leaving the city. On the plus side, it gives me extra time with her. On the negative side, she's not very talkative and locked inside her own head.

I don't push her to talk. I don't push her at all. If she needs space, I'll give her space. I can only hope that eventually she finds her way back to me.

I drop her off a block from her house since she wants to pretend she took the bus. It takes everything in me to not make a disparaging remark about it but I don't, because I can see just how serious she's taking it. It might be just sex to her, but the last thing she wants is for either of our lives to be turned upside down.

Although it looks like it's already too late for me.

CHAPTER FOURTEEN

Jackie

"Hey, are you finally free for lunch today?" Alyssa asks me, tapping her nails, now done up like rainbow unicorns, across the top of the cubicle. She shoots a smug glance down at Patty, so I know it's driving her crazy.

"Uh, yeah," I tell her, clearing my throat.

"Good. Because I'm buying," she says and then lowers her voice. "We still have a lot to talk about, and every time I've come by here this week you've already gone out to lunch."

"And gone for more than hour," Patty pipes up.

I fight the urge to stand up and look over the partition to glare at her.

"Sure," I say, giving Alyssa a measured smile. "Lunch is good."

And she's absolutely right.

The last two lunch hours this week I've been gone.

It's no surprise where I've been.

Where Will's been.

The only reason I'm sitting here now is because the Fox Studio executives are still in town and Will has taken them out somewhere for lunch. Otherwise I'd be back at his apartment for a quickie.

Fuck.

I'd give anything for that right now.

We'd only done this on Wednesday and Thursday, and now it's Friday and my body is craving him like a damn junkie needing her fix. And the fix is forever and always Will's cock.

Or his fingers. Or his tongue. Or his mouth.

God, he's *so* good.

"Earth to Jackie," Alyssa says and I snap my eyes open, forgetting that she's still standing here and staring at me. "Let's go now. Or are you busy napping?"

I hear Patty snort from the other side and I narrow my eyes in automatic response.

Soon Alyssa and I are walking past reception.

"Where are you bitches going?" Tiffany asks with a pleading look in her eyes, obviously wanting to come with us.

I'm about to invite her when Alyssa says, "We'll be back soon," shutting her down quickly.

I wait till we're out the door before turning to Alyssa. "That was harsh. I think she wanted to get lunch with us."

"Office politics," she says with a wave of her hand. "And I wanted to talk to you about the fact that you're sleeping with Will." She shoots me a loaded look before she slips on her sunglasses. "And I wasn't about to discuss that around anyone else but you."

"Sleeping with Will?" I repeat, wondering if I have enough nerve to lie to her. And also strangely touched that

Alyssa hasn't gossiped about this with anyone.

"Oh don't even think you can lie to me," she says to me. "I will sniff out your bullshit in a second. It's so obvious, Jackie."

Oh god.

"Shit. It is?"

"Ah, ha!" she says, jabbing her finger triumphantly in the air as we wait at a crosswalk. "No, it wasn't actually, but now I have the proof."

Fuck. "You're a sneaky bitch," I mumble.

She jabs her elbow into me, laughing. "Sneaky Bitch was my nickname in high school. That and Captain Jugs."

Now I'm laughing. I actually wish I had known Alyssa back in high school, she probably would have saved me from hanging out with a bunch of deadbeat losers.

"Captain Jugs, that's awesome," I tell her. "Mine was Jackie Pee Pee Pants." She gives me the most horrified look. "But that was elementary school," I add quickly.

"I'd hope so. Anyway, don't change the subject. You're sleeping with your boss and now you have to tell me all about it."

I look around as we cross at the lights. I don't even know where we're walking to. I lower my voice. "You might not want to say that too loud."

"So? Your dad isn't in town."

"Alyssa," I say testily. "It doesn't matter. No one can know."

"And they won't. For now."

"What does that mean?"

"Well, how long are you planning on doing this for?"

"Need I remind you that you were the one who said I could just fuck him and be done with it." I pause, thinking it through. "You know what? This is all your fault."

"My fault?" she cries out, as if I've dishonored her in some way. "How?"

I poke my finger into her shoulder. "You told me the ball was in my court. Remember?"

"And? Wasn't it?"

"Yes but..."

"Look, Jackie Pee Pee Pants. You're making this out to be far more complicated than it should be. You like him, he likes you. You're fucking. What's the problem?"

"There's no problem."

She wiggles her fingers at me. "Your face tells me there's a problem. Where should we eat?"

"I don't care. Somewhere with stiff drinks."

"You're really becoming one of us, aren't you?" She says this proudly.

We settle down at the Brix and Mortar, because every other patio is filled at this time of day. May can be wretched in Vancouver, or it can be glorious, and right now everyone is outside soaking up the sunshine like it might not appear for the rest of the summer.

In a way, it's like Will and me. I feel like this week I'm soaking up every second I get with him, preparing for when reality slaps us both in the face and we have to call the whole thing off.

Fuck. It's inevitable, really. This relationship can't be more than sex without one of us or both of us losing everything else we have. And yet in a perfect world, I wouldn't have to choose at all. It would be easy.

I find myself ordering a smoky old-fashioned, coming to like the strong sweet drink. Alyssa, of course, thinks I'm nuts.

"You're becoming one of us, and he's rubbing off on you," she notes, sipping her wine.

"You got that right."

"So tell me how it happened. Start from the beginning."

And I do. I tell her everything starting at last Friday from the moment I stepped into Will's apartment, getting ready for the gala, all the way to yesterday when he screwed me on the floor of his living room while the dog-walker was out with the dogs.

"I'm not sure I like you anymore," she says, though her eyes light up when the plate of nachos arrives at the table.

I shrug. "I wouldn't like me much either. I don't have to tell you he's incredibly good in bed. Sex should be his middle name."

"No you don't have to tell me, again, because you already have," she says with a roll of her eyes. "Plus, his middle name is Hung, isn't it? Will Hung? Get it?" She sighs. "I'm so jealous."

"Don't be jealous," I say, crunching on a chip and pondering the name Will Hung McAlister. "Okay, be a little jealous. But honestly, I don't know where this is going. Where it can go."

"Are you in love with him?"

The question is so point blank it catches me off-guard. The guac slips off the chip and lands with a splat on the plate. "What? No?"

"No, question mark?"

"No," I repeat, more forcefully this time. "I mean, I care about him. Of course I care about him. And I love spending time with him. I love fucking him. I love being around him and staring at him and I think he's one of the closest people to me, if not the closest but . . ."

"That's okay, say no more," she says. "You don't have to decide right now. Your heart is still working on it."

"My heart is working on it?"

"Working on being in love. With some people it doesn't happen easily. The heart isn't always a switch you can just turn on. But it does happen. And when it does, you won't hesitate, not even with me. The light will go on. And you'll know."

I watch her for a moment. "How are you still single?"

She gives me a wry smile and sighs. "I'm afraid I'm too philosophical for most men, believe it or not. I'm sure one day I'll meet someone who will take me for what I am, dare I say love me for what I am. But until then, I'm about having fun." She pauses. "I'd say you should do the same but . . . no. What you and Will have is different."

"We don't *have* anything," I remind her. "We're just fucking. Just screwing. And it's good. I want to keep it like that."

A ghost of smile appears on her lips and she nods. "I get it. Well, here's to that then. At least Will's blessed dick isn't going to waste."

"Hell no it's not," I say, raising my glass.

But even as the conversation turns to other things, my mind is still stuck on her words.

My heart is working on being in love with him.

What if I don't want that?

What if being in love is the last thing I need?

I don't think I could handle it. Jeff destroyed me in more ways than one and it's not even that he broke my heart. He ruined me, ruined my soul, my will to live, and ruined Ty. If I fell in love with Will and it didn't work out? Oh, Jesus. How could I survive that? And how could Ty? Ty's only been around him twice and he already adores the man. He'd be broken. I could never do that to him.

"Hey," Alyssa says to me as we wait for our check. "Everything is going to be all right, you know that?"

I try to smile.

"You're with the right guy," she adds. "If there's ever been a sure bet to stake your heart on, I'm pretty sure it's Will McAlister. You just have to give him a chance. And fuck everybody else."

When we get back to the office I'm sufficiently buzzed.

Luckily the office is half empty since everyone else seems to have had the same idea on this sunny Friday.

Unluckily, Will is back and in his office.

The moment I try and sit down at my desk, he's beckoning me inside with his finger.

I sigh and follow him in.

The truth is, I'd follow him anywhere, but the lunch with Alyssa has me in a mood and now the drinks have lowered my inhibitions.

He comes behind me and closes the door, then wraps his arm around my waist, pulling me up to him. "How's my dream girl doing?" he murmurs before he kisses me, long, deep and sweet.

And just like that, every worry I have is gone. I melt into his touch, into his arms, and I never want him to let me go.

"How is it that life can be so crazy, so chaotic, so scary," he says as he kisses the corner of my mouth, "and yet one kiss from you and all of that goes away?"

I swallow hard, feeling a rush of emotion washing over me. I'm really regretting those old-fashioneds now. The last thing I need is to be this in touch with my feelings.

"How was lunch?" I speak up after a few moments, his

hands getting lost in my hair. I've started wearing it down just because I crave this feeling, the way he brushes his fingers through, the way he pulls and tugs.

"It was good," he says, gazing at me. God, he has the most beautiful eyes I've ever seen. Whatever I need to know I just need to look at them and they tell me everything.

"Good," I say softly.

"You went for lunch with Alyssa," he notes. "And I can taste Luxardo cherries on your lips. You had an old-fashioned. Or two."

"What can I say, I guess I'm as old-fashioned as you are."

"Cute," he muses, kissing me again. "Since we both missed lunch, how about you come over now. Have dinner with me."

I hesitate. "I don't know."

"I'm calling your mother and telling her I'm taking you out for dinner. Then I'm telling her about the team-building exercise. I'm guessing you haven't run your brilliant idea past her yet?"

"Will, please, I can call her."

"Nope," he says, taking out his cell and jabbing the screen a few times until it's ringing.

"Will!" I cry out, trying to take it from him but he blocks me with his arm.

"Yes, hi Diane, how are you?" Will says smoothly into the phone.

I grumble like a child, folding my arms in a huff as I flop down in the chair.

"Yes, well I'm sure he'll call you when he gets a moment. You know how busy LA is," Will says, rolling his eyes because he has to cover for my dad and his stupid Bermuda golf trip. "Listen, your daughter was working extra hard this week and I wanted to take her out for dinner. Is that okay? Good. I agree. She deserves a break. So you'll take care of Ty? Perfect. I'll let her know. See you later."

I stare at him. "What happened to the team-building?"

"Something for another time," he says, sliding his phone back into his pocket. "By the way, your mother says to enjoy yourself and order the most expensive dish on the menu. Your father is paying."

Figures.

"Doesn't it bother you, having to lie to them?" I ask. "They're your friends."

He shrugs, looks at me with an open expression. "No. Not at all. It's none of their business what I do. Why, does it bother you?"

"No," I say. Though honestly? I kind of wish that one day I could tell them. It would be in a different universe, somewhere where I never made any mistakes, somewhere I didn't have so much to prove. Maybe a world where they don't know Will at all and I could bring him home with his nice suit and charming smile and they could see how good of a man he is for me.

"Hey," he whispers to me. "I don't like seeing you frown. So none of that now, you got it? I'm taking you home, then I'm taking you out for dinner and that's all you need to know."

The rest of the day flies by, and soon we're stepping into Will's apartment and I realize how much it's starting to feel like home to me, a feeling I quickly brush away.

The dogs are excited, as per usual, and they both fight for my attention, even Joanie who can hold back a bit. I like to think they genuinely like me now, not just as a human who gives cuddles and walks and treats, but as Jackie Phillips, Will Hung McAlister's secret lover.

I admit there is a huge fucking thrill in having to sneak around like this. As much as I hate having to hide it, I'm also revelling in the fact that it's forbidden romance at its finest. Aside from Alyssa, no one knows about our trysts together, no one else reads into our body language at work. No one knows that we play together just as well outside the office—or even better—than we do in it.

"I bought you something," Will says to me after he's come back up with the dogs, having walked them around the courtyard for their business.

"What?" I ask warily, perched on the bar stool, a glass of wine in my hand.

"You'll see," he says, disappearing into the bedroom.

I take a sip of the wine, waiting while Joanie and Sprocket start fighting over a dog treat I had tossed onto the floor while they were gone.

"It's actually a few things," Will says, coming back toward me. His hands are behind his back. He's looking fucking amazing today in his teal dress shirt, the way it fits each hard line of his muscles. Especially now with his arms held back, his shoulders are popping against the seams, the color of the shirt bringing out the depths of his eyes.

I find myself biting my lip, more in the Pavlovian way that I've been trained for sex with him than the fact that he got me a present.

But then he holds out two bags, one eggshell blue from Tiffany's and the other from Holt Renfrew. I want to grab both from him and peer inside, but at the same time I know I couldn't possibly deserve it.

"You deserve it," he says, reading me as he usually does. "You deserve everything, Jackie. I don't want you to argue with me. Remember the rules."

"I remember the punishment," I tell him cheekily as I

reach for the bags.

Knowing how much I've dreamed about having something from Tiffany's, I save that bag for last and open the Holts one.

I peek inside and pull out a dress. It's another Dolce and Gabbana.

I look up at him, feeling flustered. "Another D & G?"

His grin is nothing short of cocky. "Hey, I know they fit you now."

This midi-length dress is also black, but with three-quarter length sleeves that cover up my arms, a lace-trimmed V-neck, and flattering ties at the waist. Colorful cocktails are printed all over it. It's beautiful and fun and like nothing I currently own.

"Do you like it?" he asks, wincing because I haven't said anything yet.

"I love it," I tell him softly. "But . . ."

"No buts," he says. "As long as you like it. It should fit you like the other one. You can wear it out tonight, or another night, or not at all, but it's yours."

I exhale loudly, not wanting to seem ungrateful. He gets so annoyed when I put up a fuss over things like this, which makes me realize I should accept that Will is the type of man to buy me things and I should keep my stupid mouth shut.

"I'll wear it tonight," I tell him. "Whenever you like."

"It's for you, Jackie, not me. Remember, I like you naked and often."

I smile at him and start on the Tiffany's bag.

This one is smaller of course and I take the blue box out, carefully unwrapping the ribbon.

He stands there, rocking back on his heels, hands in his pockets, clearly enjoying my expression as I slowly open it.

My heart is starting to pound. I hope it's not what I fear it could be.

An engagement ring.

But that wouldn't make any sense.

He's told me he's falling for me, not that he loves me.

And I've never given him any sort of reason to think that I might feel the same.

Even so, I'm holding my breath while I flip back the hard box.

I gasp when I see what's inside.

A necklace. Simple, silver with a heart-shaped diamond pendant. But the diamonds are huge and the necklace is beautiful and I can't possibly accept this.

"Will," I tell him, shaking my head. "It's beautiful but I can't take this."

"Jackie," he says coming over to me and taking the box from my hands. "You know how I feel about you. You know I want to do this. So let me do it." He brings the necklace out and the way it catches the light of his kitchen, glimmering like a disco ball, nearly takes my breath away.

He spins the bar stool around and puts the necklace around my neck before spinning me back in place. He steps back and admires it. "It's not a pearl necklace, but it will do."

I let out a laugh. "I don't know, I think I want a pearl necklace too."

"After dinner, you hungry monster," he tells me, grabbing my hand and pulling me off the stool. "Go take a look. If you don't like it, I'll take it back."

I go into the bathroom, feeling unsteady on my feet after just one glass of wine. It doesn't help that I wore my Louboutins to the office today and I'm still not used to walking in them. Once I'm inside, leaning against his marble sink and staring at myself in the mirror, I feel like I'm looking at someone else.

This isn't the girl from up north living in fear, hoping that one day her life would make sense again.

This is the woman living here, whose life is finally coming together. It's no longer a fantasy. The security, the safety, the hope. This is all real. And I have a big fat diamond heart resting on my collarbone that proves it to me.

Will said he was falling for me, but I know what this necklace means. It means what he's been afraid to tell me. It means I have his heart.

And I realize now, staring at my reflection in his mirror, that his heart is all I've ever wanted. Even when I didn't know otherwise.

Easy now, I remind myself, taking in a deep breath through my nose. *You're controlling this ride. You can get off at any time.*

Pun not intended.

And I know . . . why, *why* would I want to?

I don't let myself finish that sentence.

I leave the bathroom and give Will my most reassuring smile when I come out.

I'm sorry, I want to say to him. *I'm sorry I'm kind of crazy. I'm sorry that I might break your heart. I'm sorry I have problems that might burn this all to the ground. I'm sorry that I don't think I'm ready for what your beautiful heart is giving me, and I don't mean the gifts.*

But I don't say any of that.

"It's beautiful," I tell him, trying to keep the tears from my eyes.

"Good," he says softly, pressing his lips together as he nods. "I'm glad."

Oh jeez. Those eyes of his. They pull me in. They make

me throw everything away and just give myself over, body, heart, and soul.

But I don't. Not even my body, not yet.

He takes me out for dinner instead. We go to Rodney's Oyster House just down the street from his building.

I wear the dress because it felt right. It looks right too (though I should probably size up to a twelve next time), hugging me in all the right places, making me feel like a million dollars. Probably because I am wearing a million dollars.

Will feeds me oysters which I slurp down gleefully in between dark draft beers. Every now and then I catch him looking at the necklace and smiling to himself. Every time that happens I feel my heart being pulled toward him.

He tells me stories about growing up on the west coast of Vancouver Island, how he basically grew up in a trailer in the woods, later upgraded to a yurt before yurts were even cool, and how his mother was a hippie.

"I can't believe that," I say to him. "You, who looks like he was swimming around the womb in a suit."

"Believe it," he says. "I was raised vegan. I attended many solstice ceremonies. I actually kind of liked that lifestyle. As a kid it was mysterious and fun."

"And when you escaped from that world you went the opposite?"

"Pretty much. I guess. I'm not even sure it was a conscious decision but it definitely looks that way now." He pauses, wiping his lips with a napkin. "To be honest, I never rebelled against it. It just happened. I have deep respect for my mother and her lifestyle. I guess it just wasn't me."

"But that's a creative lifestyle. And you're an artist. That came from somewhere."

"I suppose. My mother likes to make sculptures."

"And now you're sketching again."

He nods. "Something has me inspired."

His eyes trail over my lips and rest there. Then he looks away. "I hate to say it, but it was actually my father that encouraged me to draw."

"Your father? I thought he died when you were five."

"He did. But it was that year that he told me I was good at it. I had just done doodles before, like any other kid, but I guess he liked them. Or maybe he just felt guilty and had to say something. Either way, his encouragement stuck."

The muscle along his jaw is tensing and I get the feeling that this conversation is making him uncomfortable. I know it's horrible of me to want to see Will in this state instead of his usual calm and easy one. But I say, "Why do you say he felt guilty?"

He purses his lips for a moment, staring off into space before fixing his eyes on me. There's a world of pain in them. "Because he used to beat the shit out of me."

His admission nearly knocks me off the stool. Everything inside me sinks, like stones through water. "He beat you?"

"Yes," he says with a nod, staring down at the oysters now. "Most nights. I think my mother too, though she never talks about it."

"Oh my god," I cry out softly, reaching across the tiny table for his hand. "I'm so sorry."

He glances at me briefly. "It's okay. It's just life. It happens to a lot of people . . ."

"But you were so young."

"I was. But it happened and it's over. He died before he could do it for much longer. Drinking and driving accident."

I'm beside myself with his news. "Oh god." No wonder

he was so understanding about what happened with me and Jeff. "Will . . ."

"Please," he says, voice clipped as he fixes his gaze on me. "It's in the past and I've dealt with it. Counseling for both me and my mother. It's still there but it's also gone. That's the best you can hope for. It's made me a better person, made me realize I'll do anything to never become like my father."

"You could never be like that," I tell him, holding his hand tighter.

"I know," he says. "I wouldn't be here if I didn't know that."

"I feel like an idiot bringing up the cartoons now," I say to him.

"Jackie," he says imploringly. "First of all, the fact that my father encouraged me to draw means I have one good thing to latch onto when I think about him, and I think *everyone* deserves to have one good thing about them. And second of all, it's called fucking animation, kid."

I shake my head, punching him lightly on the arm. "You're becoming like the rest of them."

"You mean the stoners who spend their nights at the office, washing up in the bathrooms and living off the vending machines? No thank you."

"Guess you wouldn't have the money."

"No. And I wouldn't have you."

"You could have had me. Maybe not as an assistant . . ."

He tilts his head back, looking down at me. "You mean to tell me that if you were at this bar right now and you saw me here sitting alone, you would come up to me?"

"Oh hell no," I say, then grin at him. "You would have come up to *me*."

"Maybe," he says carefully. "You run a little hot and

cold, I hope you know that. I wouldn't know what signal to pick up on."

The thing is, I don't want to run hot and cold with him. I want to run hot for him all the time.

"So what signal am I putting out now?" I ask him, even though I'm afraid of the answer.

"Well," he says gently, reaching over to tuck a strand of hair behind my ear. "You love the necklace. You're happy with the dress. You want nothing more than to come back to my place after this and get thoroughly fucked. Show these oysters what they're good for. And then you want to go back to your home and think about the millions of reasons why you shouldn't be with me."

I stare at him with wide eyes. God how can he be so accurate?

"You're not the easiest woman to read," he goes on. "But I'm learning. And what I've learned the most from this week is that you feel most comfortable when I back off and leave things in your hands. The only problem I have with that is, if it's all in your hands, I might never see you again."

I chew on my lip, trying to protest, to say the right things. He pushes my chin up so I'm looking right at him.

"It's okay," he says. "I know this is all new. I'm in your hands. Every single part of me."

I believe him.

And that scares me too.

When we get back to his apartment after a few too many oysters and pints of beer, I'm just as amorous as I was earlier. If anything, the fact that he sat across from me for a few hours, in a public setting where I was too afraid to touch him, only made the desire more fervent.

Will shuts the dogs away in the spare room and by the

time he comes back to the living room, I'm attempting to get out of my dress.

"Let me help you," he says, coming behind me until he's grasping the zipper and pulling it down. He does this slowly, like he's enjoying the very tame show of my back being exposed.

Then he pulls it off all the way and I step out around the dress, totally naked except for my heels.

"Keep the shoes on," he says, a look of wonderment in his eyes.

"I will if you sit down on the couch. Take off your pants first."

"You're bossy."

"I'm bargaining," I tell him. Then I put my hands on my hips, waiting.

He tries to smile as he strips, his pants falling to the floor. No surprise at all, he's fully erect.

"Sit," I tell him.

He does so and then raises one hell of a sexy brow at me. He starts moving down the couch until he's halfway off, his back pressed against the edge. "Now you sit," he says. "I'm bargaining too."

Sitting on his face isn't that hard of a bargain though.

I climb on top of the couch, gripping the backrest while I straddle his head, slowly lowering myself onto his face.

The moment his tongue makes contact with me, I feel like I am spiraling out of control.

"Fuck," I swear, my fingers digging into the couch, my head going back. "You are way too good at this."

"Getting you wet?" he asks just before he dips his tongue inside me and back out. "Yes. Yes, I am."

I'd actually never done this before. The whole "sitting

on a guy's face" thing. I never thought guys actually wanted this.

But Will does.

I slowly grind my hips into his mouth, and his moans fill me from head to toe. When I glance over my shoulder at his body, I see his cock in his hand, slowly jerking himself off.

I want to watch this for as long as I can. There's nothing sexier than watching a man pleasure himself and Will is more than adept at it, giving me pointers of my own. He knows what he wants, knows how to handle himself.

But as his tongue works me deeper, his mouth and lips teasing my clit, sucking it in and out of his warm mouth, the smacking sounds filling the air, I can't focus on anything anymore other than chasing my own release.

I come fast, a rubber band inside that me snaps and snaps and I think I've ground myself so hard on Will's face that he's left me with rugburn.

I lean against the couch, breathing hard as Will sits up, with me on his lap.

"I never told you when to come," he says, kissing my neck, his hand gliding down my side to my waist.

"Guess you have to punish me," I tease him, still breathless.

"It's not as much fun when you want it." He presses his forehead against mine, both of us are damp with sweat.

"Is that so?"

"No, I'm lying," he says. Then he reaches around and spanks my ass.

I yelp, the sting bringing my head out of the clouds.

"You're a bastard," I tell him.

"Only when I need to be."

Then he grabs my waist with his other hand and

pushes me down over his cock.

"Fuck," I swear again as he fills me up, so impossibly full. This angle is plenty dangerous.

"I've got you," he whispers in my ear, "you ride me and I'll ride you. You want me deeper, you'll have me deeper. You want just a tease, you've got a tease."

I nod, adjusting to his size, to the rhythm of my hips against his, pushing down deeper and deeper on his cock until he's in almost to the hilt.

I've never been a fan of the woman on top position, only because I like the man to take control. I like to feel wanted, dominated. But Will is turning it around for me. He is in control and he is dominating, every single thrust he makes up into me, every little circle of his hips. His hands at my waist are firm, determined. He's working me, carefully, steadily, his eyes boring into mine and telling me just how much he wants me, how much he loves this.

I love it too.

Maybe too much.

I ride him on that couch for what feels like forever and no time at all. The slow, languid, sensual pace eventually turns to a frenzy, the slapping of skin, the splash of sweat as our bodies writhe and slam against each other.

And all this time he has a fist in my hair, holding my head in place, making me look at him. Even when I close my eyes for a moment in ecstasy, my mouth open and moaning, and I look back again, he's still staring at me. His gaze is crazed and adoring, feral and tender, and mirroring everything I'm feeling inside.

"You want to come, Dream Girl?" he whispers hoarsely in my ear and I can hear the need in his voice.

"Yes," I whisper back and he slides his fingers over my clit, setting me off like a bomb.

The orgasm radiates outward and I come with a choked-off cry, like the feeling is too much for my throat to handle. I buck and tremble and he's holding me, trembling too, his big, strong arms around me, keeping me in place until we both ride out the orgasms.

"Jackie," he says after a few moments of breathing heavily into my shoulder. "I don't want you to go."

Go? I hate that he's reminding me of it, even though it's the truth. I don't want to turn into a pumpkin.

"I know," I tell him, running my fingers down his gorgeous face. "I don't want to either."

"If you could just stay overnight. I want to wake up with you in my arms. I want to take my time and have breakfast with you."

"I'm sorry," I say softly.

Something passes over his brow, an idea.

"What?" I ask.

"Come with me," he says, sliding out from under me. He hauls me to my feet and leads me to the bedroom, pushing me on the bed and taking off my shoes.

"Not that I'm complaining that you think you can go again after that, but . . ." I say to him, wondering what he has in mind.

"Get under the covers. I hope you're hungry."

I frown. "What?"

"Just do it," he says and watches until I'm totally in his bed, sheets up to my chest. I have to admit, it's nice. And far too comfortable. "I might fall asleep," I tell him. "I have to get a cab home."

"We'll call you one in a bit," he says, leaving the room. "Just shut your eyes."

"But I'll fall asleep," I protest, but the words come out like whispers. My eyes drift shut. Sleep comes for me.

And then the smell of bacon tickles my nose.

Am I dreaming about bacon?

"Wakey wakey, eggs and bakey," Will says, standing at the foot of his bed, completely naked except for an apron, holding a plate of . . . breakfast?

"What is this?"

"Breakfast in bed."

I glance at the clock. "It's midnight."

Shit. My mother is going to kill me.

"Perfect. That means it's the morning." He comes around the side of the bed and hands it to me. "Here."

I look down at the plate. Hash browns, scrambled eggs, bacon, and a grilled tomato. It's the real deal.

"You just did this?" I ask.

He nods. "Yup. Quickly learned that I shouldn't fry bacon naked. You were out like a light for about ten minutes."

"Where's your plate?"

"It's coming," he says, disappearing out of the room again.

While he's gone, I poke the food with my fork. Strangely enough, even though it's the middle of the night I'm awfully hungry. All that sex makes you famished and oysters and beer aren't necessarily the most filling meal.

I take a tentative bite of the eggs. They're good. Really good. A spice that I can't even recognize.

"How is it?" he asks when he comes back, his own plate in hand.

"What is this spice?" I ask him. He gets in the bed beside me. "I can't place the flavor."

"It's a type of mild curry powder," he says proudly. "Told you I knew how to do a good breakfast. Now you just owe me a homecooked meal one day."

"Is Hamburger Helper okay?"

He grins broadly. "I'll take whatever you're dishing me, Dream Girl."

The two of us sit in bed and eat our breakfast. Maybe it's not the same as staying over and waking up in each other's arms, but it's a pretty good substitute.

CHAPTER FIFTEEN

Will

"So, tell me about the girl," Emmett says, between sips of his beer. "You've been awfully quiet all night."

I give him an easy grin. "I've had some stuff on my mind."

"I can tell," he says.

"Tell me about Heather," I ask, putting the question on him. "I haven't had an update in a while."

Emmett sighs, finishes the rest of his beer, and launches into it.

I force myself to be in the moment and listen to him, since he's been listening to me yammer on about Jackie for so long. The funny thing is, ever since Jackie and I really started seeing each other and sleeping with each other on the regular, I've been shutting up more and more.

It's been two weeks of us screwing around, two weeks of me realizing I've fallen in love with her, and I don't think I want to kiss and tell anymore. I'm in so deep and what I feel I have to keep for just me and her.

Of course I haven't told Jackie anything yet. In some foolish ways I hope that this will just go away, as if my feelings for her can be locked away in a box, the key tossed into the sea. That's not going to happen. It's too strong, too blinding, too *binding*.

I'm in over my head. There's no getting around it.

And I can't seem to stop.

I don't want to stop.

I haven't felt like this . . . ever.

Not even with Sasha, someone I grew with over the years.

With Jackie it's totally different. She might be young, but her soul speaks to mine. Her soul is bright yet weathered, having endured so much and come out of it still willing to shine. With her I can just be myself. I don't have to pretend. I don't have to guard myself. Maybe I should, but if I did then I couldn't feel half of what I'm feeling.

As soon as Sasha told me she was leaving me, that she was pregnant with another man's child, I made a vow inside, whether I knew it at first or not, to never love again. It wasn't worth the risk. The heartache. The self-loathing and humiliation. I spent so many years with a woman who only grew apart from me and in the end left me all alone.

But as much as I wanted my heart to turn to stone, it couldn't. It left me with this horrible optimism, like a disease. It made me believe that if I was lucky enough to fall in love again, that I needed to fall in head first and take the plunge. Because what are the odds of continuous heartache?

I know. That's ridiculous. People get their hearts broken over and over and over again.

But they keep on beating. They keep going. And each

time they get stronger. Not a heart made of armor, not a hardened shell. They get stronger because it's like any muscle. You keep using it and it will grow, and if shit gets rough it will bounce right back.

The heart is nothing if not resilient.

I realize that's what someone in love would say. That I'm being hopeless about our situation, that I believe that even being with Jackie now and getting my heart broken in the end is worth more than not being with her at all.

And so what if I believe it?

Because what if that's *not* how this ends up?

What if she falls in love with me just as I've fallen in love with her?

What if I get the chance to take care of her and Ty, and have the family I've always needed?

Is it worth throwing that all away on the risk that I might get hurt?

I don't think so.

Not all.

Even so, I know I have to tread with caution. Everything I'm feeling is not what Jackie is feeling, not even close. I have to tip-toe on eggshells around her because she's so afraid of this ever being more than what it is.

If it's because of the job, her parents, so what? I love Ted and Diane but I love Jackie more.

But if it's because she honestly doesn't feel anything for me other than the fact that I'm her boss and a good fuck, then . . .

Well, shit.

Worth it or not, I don't want to think about *that*.

I sigh internally and force myself to listen to Emmett, become involved in his world. I sip my drink, centering myself back in this bar, and catch up.

Emmett is single. Had a fiancé for a bit until he realized he wasn't in love with her. He's been on the market for a while, and while I know he meets lots of actresses and beautiful people because of his career as an actor and singer (musicals, mostly), he hasn't found The One.

I have no idea why. He's good-looking in that roguish, motorcycle-riding kind of way. Has money. Works out. Can sing. What woman doesn't want a man who sings? And yet he's stuck on dating apps like everyone else seems to be, searching for love. Why people can't just meet each other the old-fashioned way, I don't understand.

And Heather. She was one of his latest girlfriends, though from the sound of things they broke it off.

"So," Emmett goes on with a heavy sigh, palming his beer, "she said that she just couldn't commit right now. I mean, she's my age. She's thirty-seven. If she can't commit now, when can she?"

"I hate to tell you this but I think that means she just can't commit to you."

"I know."

"You know what the problem is?" I tell him, gesturing to the bar, which is quite busy for a Thursday night. "It's that right now everyone is on their phones. Everyone has that 'me, me, me instant gratification' shit going on and so when the going gets rough in a relationship, as it always does, they bail. They bail because they have a million other people on their phone, on those fucking apps, all waiting for a hook-up or a date. A million people around the corner, with their perfect filtered photos uploaded, their bios updated and edited so they all represent the perfect fake versions of themselves. So even when you're on a date with one person, you can look at your phone and go to the next person, have your fun, then go to the next. It's not fucking dating man, it's *shopping*."

"You're right." He looks me up and down. "And I guess your advice would be to meet a girl through work?"

I grin at him. "Yes. The old-fashioned way. Through work, on the street, hell even at a bar." I start looking around. "Maybe you'll find someone in here if you just opened your fucking eyes and put your damn phone away."

"Will," he says. "You're harsh."

"Telling it like it is. I can go on and on about what's wrong with society today if you let me."

"Please enlighten me," he says dryly.

"Maybe another time." I pause. "Listen, I need to ask you a favor."

"What?"

"I need to borrow your boat."

He stares at me for a beat before breaking into a grin. "Shit, man. You need to borrow my boat? What, are you becoming a pirate now or something? Getting that young pussy has changed you."

I stiffen, my smile fading. "First of all, she's not *young pussy*."

He edges back from me. "Just joking, man. Jesus Murphy, when did you get so fucking touchy, eh? Thought getting laid every day would help that."

"It's not every day," I tell him, my voice tense. "And she's a mother. She's not some young, I don't know, selfie-obsessed bimbo. And yes, she has a fucking nice pussy but that's for me to discuss, not you."

"All right then. You know, I don't think I've ever seen you so worked up over anything before."

I shrug, taking a gulp of my beer. "I'm a new man. A pirate, like you say. So can I borrow your boat or what?"

"Do you even know how to sail?"

"Look, I wouldn't ask to borrow it if I didn't know how. I took sailing lessons as a kid in Tofino. Now those are some real waves out there. Plus, Sasha was part of the Royal Vancouver Yacht Club when we started dating and I was on the boat with her father a lot. I learned the hard way with him, but I learned."

"You sure you don't want me to come along?"

"I want to bring Jackie."

"And I want to meet her."

"And her son, Ty."

"I see. Family outing."

I give him the side eye. "Something like that."

He sighs. "Fine. Yes. You can borrow it. Just please don't let anything happen to it. Sick Buoy might be old but he has a few years left in him. He's pretty nimble."

"You know you're supposed to name boats after a girl, right? And also, the term is *yar*."

"*Yar?*"

"You ever seen *The Philadelphia Story* with Cary Grant and Katherine Hepburn?"

"How fucking old are you, man?"

I ignore that. The funny thing is, Jackie would know exactly what I'm talking about. I just hope when I tell her tomorrow that I want to take her and Ty on a sailing trip that she'll think the boat is *yar* too.

"So whose boat is this again?" Jackie asks as she peers at it. I still can't tell if she's impressed or not.

It's not a new boat. The fact that Emmett actually has a boat makes him one of a rarified set in Vancouver, since owning a boat isn't cheap and affording moorage in the city is even worse. But it's a boat from the 80's, fifty feet long with a teak interior. According to Emmett they don't make boats like this anymore, and though all the newer versions are flashier, they don't have the same soul.

"It's Emmett's," I tell her. *You'll meet him some day*, I want to tell her but I don't want to scare her off. I practically had to twist her arm to get her to come, and it was only when I brought up how fun it would be for Ty that she finally relented.

So here we are, standing on the docks at the Royal Vancouver Yacht Club where Emmett keeps his boat, the sun just starting to break through the clouds.

"It's awesome," Ty says, staring at it in awe as he holds onto Jackie's hand. "Sick Buoy," he says slowly, reading the words on the side.

Jackie gives me a look. "Is this boat named after a Social Distortion song?"

I shrug. "I don't know. Want to come on board?"

Ty nods excitedly.

"Want to become a pirate?"

Now he's practically dancing in anticipation. Meanwhile Jackie is giving me the death eyes for getting him so worked up.

"Not without a life jacket," she says sternly, pulling Ty back to her before he can attempt to board the ship on his own.

"Aw, mom," he moans.

"Don't worry, I'll be wearing one too," she says, looking the boat over. "I didn't know you could sail, Will."

"There's a lot of things you still don't know," I say to her.

"Yeah and he's Batman," Ty says, rolling his eyes. "Jeez,

mom. Don't you know that Batman has a Bat Boat?"

"Well, sorry," she says defensively while I quickly climb on the boat and fish two life jackets out of the cockpit locker. Luckily Emmett has both children's and adult's lifejackets on board and I toss them both on the dock.

I watch as Jackie puts the jackets on both of them. The way Ty looks at her while she slips the jacket over his head, scrunched up and annoyed at first and then becoming something softer, more adoring. It's a fucking kick to my heart.

I want this. I want them.

Why can't this be my life?

Not for this moment. For all moments. Something real, something solid, something that will last.

Jackie then squeezes his cheek, saying something to him with a bright smile, something I can't hear, and I feel the hot burn of tears behind my eyes. She's such a good mom, whether she tries to be or not. She's absolutely everything.

I take in a deep breath and try and push it all away. These emotions aren't wanted here.

"Need a hand?" I ask them, holding mine out for them.

She hands me Ty first and I haul him on deck with ease before I grab her hands and do the same.

I move in to give her a kiss but she jerks her head back and gives me a look.

Oh. Right. Ty.

I look behind me but he's not paying attention. He's making his way over to the wheel like he's a captain at heart.

"Sorry," I tell her. "I'll be on my best behavior."

"Thank you," she says. I know the last thing she wants is for Ty to get the wrong idea about us, although I have to say it already feels wrong that we have to hide it from him. Her parents, yes. But her son? It doesn't sit right with me.

But she's his mother. I'm not his father. It's not up to me to make these choices. I have no doubt Jackie is doing what she thinks is right.

Jackie smiles at Ty, who tries to turn the giant wheel in the cockpit back and forth while making revving noises, then looks up and down the length of the ship.

"Is she *yar*?" she asks me, in a perfect Katherine Hepburn impression.

Fuck if I could kiss her right now.

"She's definitely *yar*," I tell her. "You really are my dream girl, you know that?"

"I think you've told me once. Figured you might have seen the film."

"One of the best."

"Who did you want her to end up with? Jimmy Stewart or Cary Grant?"

"Grant, of course. Stewart's character, what was his name? He was a bit of a louse. I remember Grant's name. C.K. Dexter Haven."

"The alcoholic husband trying to get his ex-wife back?"

"Don't worry, I don't relate to it."

"You better not."

"Can we please go?" Ty pleads impatiently. He shakes the wheel.

"Careful Ty," Jackie warns him, coming over and pulling him away from the wheel. "How can we help?" she asks me.

I think about what we need to get done with only the two of us, and how I can get Ty out of the way so he's not in any danger.

"Well Ty can help by sitting right there in the middle

and holding on to this rope." I grab a piece of rope from one of the winches, something we probably won't be needing today, and hand it to him. "Hey Ty-Rex, can you handle a very big, very important job?" I ask.

He nods, staring at the rope.

"This rope is what's holding the entire boat together. As we push off and get under wind, I want you to hold onto this with all your might. Don't let go. You got it?"

He nods more enthusiastically. "Got it," he says.

"Good. I'm trusting you because I think you can handle it." I pause, pretending to reconsider him. "You know it's not true what they all say about you."

"What?" he asks, alarmed.

"Will," Jackie admonishes me. "He's just being a joker, Ty. Ignore him."

"He can't be the Joker if he's Batman," Ty tells her, rolling his eyes.

"Yeah, *mom*," I add in exasperation before coming over to her.

"You're a cheeky fucker today," she says under her breath, trying not to smile.

I shrug. "Must be all the salt air. Makes me feel twenty-five again."

"Come off it." She gives me a playful shove and then looks at Ty. "Is that rope actually something important?"

"Of course," I say with a wink. "Now for you, you have two choices. Either get behind the wheel and steer the boat out of here, or throw the ropes up from the dock and then jump on board."

"As the ship is moving?"

"It's not so hard. It will be drifting slowly."

"Have you seen how short my legs are?"

A smile spreads across my face. "I have seen your legs.

And they are lovely."

"Will, I will fall in the water. That is a fact."

"Well then you have to steer."

"Why is this so stressful?"

"Because your father was an idiot who never took you sailing," I tell her. "All rich Vancouver kids grow up around boats. Or horses. So I guess you got one of them. Now come on, let's pick one before Ty figures out the rope is bullshit."

"You know, when we do the team-building exercise next week, I'm going to take great pleasure in making you do things you don't want to do."

"Why do you think I don't know how to ride a horse?"

She narrows her eyes at me. A real spitfire. "You would, wouldn't you. Perfect Will with your perfect everything."

"I don't know if everything is perfect. My girlfriend is being kind of annoying right now."

"You jerk," she says, pounding her fist into my chest.

But while she's smiling and pretending to be annoyed (and annoying), I'm smiling because I just called her my girlfriend and completely got away with it.

For now, anyway.

Because she fears her short (perfect) legs will land her in the water, I leave the steering to her. I turn on the boat, put it in neutral, and tell her to hold the wheel straight. Then I quickly jump off, grab the ropes, throw them on board and jump back on just as the gap between the boat and the dock starts to widen.

"You see," she points as I come and take over the wheel from her, shifting the gears so we're going forward and out of the marina. "If I made that jump, I would have drowned. You have long legs."

"I sure do," I tell her, glancing at her life vest which

pops over her chest, showcasing a hard line of cleavage. "Could that be any tighter? Not that I'm complaining."

"I want to see how *yar* this boat is when you're steering it before I relax."

I nod at Ty. "He doesn't look worried."

Actually he's got a look of utmost determination on his face as he holds that rope. I've seen that expression on men stationed outside army barracks.

"You're doing a good job, Ty," I tell him. "Just a few more minutes until we're set."

I just want to get the sail up and for the boat to be heading on a straight course. The area around English Bay can be tricky because of all the boats and the dozen tankers waiting around.

Once it's all under the control, a light chop on the seas, the main sail up and the boat heeling slightly, I tell Ty to let go of the rope and come sit by his mother.

It's a gorgeous day. I'm smiling into the wind and sun, the city of Vancouver—tall spires of glass rising from the water—looks extra bright under my aviator sunglasses.

"You can't get much better than this," I say, almost to myself.

"No, you can't," Jackie says in a small voice.

I look down at her sitting just to the left of the wheel, Ty beside her, watching the water rush past. She's staring up at me in such a way I feel it in my bones. Adoration. Want. Need.

I give her a quiet smile. This is everything I've ever wanted, right here, right now.

Is she finally realizing that this is what she wants too?

"You look like you belong on a boat," she finally says. As if that's what she was trying to figure out all this time.

I ignore the deflation in my heart. "Do I now?"

"Yeah. It suits you. Your khakis and your navy polo shirt and your sunglasses, your hair. Your tan, your white teeth. You look like an ad for Nautica." She glances down at my feet. "At least you're in Vans and not Sperry Topsiders."

"You know, Just Jackie, it almost sounds like you're mocking me."

"Oh, I would never do that."

I give her a look and continue to sail along. We make it around the bay once before Ty starts asking me questions about sailing. And dinosaurs. And Batman. And hockey. But mainly sailing.

I make Jackie handle the helm and go about showing Ty the proverbial ropes of the ship, the dynamics of sailing and the wind.

He's actually pretty keen, and he's quick to figure out my bullshit.

Just like his mother.

"So the rope I was holding, what did it do then?"

I glance over at Jackie who is covering her mouth with a beer, trying not to laugh.

"It was magic."

"I don't think I believe in magic anymore. I rode Taffy the other day and fell off when I repeatedly told the pony to hold on to me."

"No magic? That's a real shame," I tell him. "Well, perhaps I just wanted to test you."

"Test me? Like in school?"

"Yes. To see if you could handle the job. And you did. Hey, are you excited about school ending in a few weeks?"

He thinks this over, pursing his lips. Then he nods. "Yes. Although I really like the kids in my class so I'm going to miss them."

"Maybe your mom will put you in summer day camp,

so you can make more friends."

"Maybe his mother hasn't discussed that with him yet," Jackie speaks up.

I ignore her.

Ty grins. "Summer day camp would be cool. I want to go to hockey camp."

Jackie groans. "My little boy is going to grow up to be hockey player."

"Yes," Ty says excitedly. "The biggest, fastest, bestest guy on the ice."

"Well I'm sure whatever you do over the summer, you'll have a great time. And you'll see your friends when you go back to school in the fall."

"I'll see you all summer, right?" he asks, looking up at me with big eyes.

Damn this kid. "As much as I can," I tell him. "It all depends on your mother. Sometimes I think she doesn't like me very much."

Ty scrunches up his nose in shock and then looks over at Jackie. "Mom. How can you not like Will? Will is the best."

I'm grinning like an idiot. I reach over and tousle his hair because it seems like the thing to do. "I am the best. Thank you Ty-Rex, sometimes it's nice to hear that."

"Oh brother," Jackie mutters.

Then Ty's face falls slightly. "Will. I like you. Can you become my father? I don't really have one anymore."

Shit.

My heart is absolutely breaking.

I look over my shoulder at Jackie who is staring at me like she's both apologizing for it and fearful for what I'm going to say.

I sigh and give Ty a waning smile. "I don't know if

that's in the cards, Ty. But you know what I would love? I don't really have many friends in the city. I was hoping maybe you could become my best one."

"Really?" Ty asks hopefully.

"If you'll have me."

"Yes, of course we can be best friends," he says. "That would be so cool. Best friends with Batman."

"That's the spirit," I tell him.

I look behind me at Jackie.

Is she . . . *crying*?

Her eyes are watering, her nose is red and she's looking off toward the mountains, her lower lip trembling.

I come over to her, resting my hands on top of hers on the wheel.

"Hey," I say softly. "Jackie. Look at me."

She does, sniffing, her eyes shimmering with a pain I don't recognize.

"I'm sorry," I say, lowering my voice. "I didn't know what to say."

"It's not that," she says, wiping away a tear.

"What is it?"

She takes in a deep breath, looking at him over her shoulder before looking back to me. "I never realized how much you really mean to him."

I frown. "Do I mean that much to you?"

She stares at me for a moment, and in that moment I feel like I might as well be drowning in the waves. Then she says, "Of course you do, Will. You mean everything to me."

"Do you promise?" I ask, leaning in close.

I want, need, to kiss her so badly.

I'm willing to risk it.

"Yes," she says and then I'm pressing my lips against hers, tasting the salt of the ocean and her tears.

She kisses me back, sinking into the wheel, into my mouth.

Fuck, I need this. I need this so much.

But I remember we have an audience. I can't get carried away.

I pull back and tuck her hair behind her ear, my eyes searching her face. "Let's head back," I tell her. "Think you can handle it?"

"I can handle it."

And she does. She keeps the boat going straight (no need for autopilot), even lets Ty steer for a bit while I take out my sketch pad from my leather bag and start drawing Ty at the helm.

"What do you want to be Ty? Batman's Robin? A dinosaur? A pirate?" I ask him after I've done his outline.

"Are you becoming a caricature artist?" Jackie asks.

"Depends if I ever need another job one day."

It's good to start looking for other careers in case Ted finds out about us.

"I want to be a *Stegosaurus*," Ty says.

"It's a known fact that *Stegosauruses* aren't good sailors. The sails get caught on their spikes. What about Ty-Rex?"

"Fine," he says.

Good, because that's pretty much what my outline looks like. I just add the tiny T-Rex arms and a few fanged teeth protruding from his smile.

By the time I take over the wheel and get the boat back to the dock, Jackie deciding to be Lara Croft this time and leaping off the boat with the ropes, I've finished up sketches of both Ty and Jackie.

"Here," I say as we stand on the dock, placing the drawing in Ty's hand and hoping he likes it. "This is for you."

"Oh my god," Jackie cries out softly, peering around

my shoulder. "Will, this is amazing."

"So cool!" Ty says. "I love it! Raaaaar," he roars, pretending to be a dinosaur, coming at me with his tiny T-Rex arms.

"Jackie, he's attacking me," I plead before picking him up and tickling him until he squeals.

"Don't ruin the picture!" Jackie plucks it from Ty's hands before he can let go of it.

Laughing, I put Ty back down and tear out her portrait from the sketch pad. "Here, this is you."

In the same line as Ty, it's a borderline caricature. But instead of drawing her as a T-Rex, I've made her up as Cinderella, albeit a curvy version with a huge rack and exaggerated ass.

"I'm Cinderella?" she asks.

"Yes," I tell her, gesturing to the crown on her head. "But at this part of the story, she's already a queen. Something she was all along and never knew it."

"Until Prince Charming shows up."

I shrug. "Nah. She never really needed that guy, did she?"

She studies me for a moment before looking back at the drawing.

"Anyway, now that I've shown you what I can do, it's time you show me what you can do?"

"Is this innuendo?" she asks quietly, brow raised.

"No," I tell her. "I know what you can do, Dream Girl, and you do it very, very well. I meant your writing. Your scripts. Remember? Back in the day? I said I would show you what my passion is if you show me yours. You said screenplays. Why don't you find the ones you've locked away somewhere and send them my way? I would love to read them."

She shakes her head, looking scared. "That's not really fair," she says. "You *just* drew this. What I have I wrote when I was a teenager. It's all shit."

"Mom," Ty reminds her about the swearing.

"Sorry. But it's true."

"So write something now."

"When would I have the time to do that?"

I think about that for a moment. She's not spending every day with me outside of work, but I know I do take up a lot of her time and the last thing I want is for that to stop.

"Monday," I tell her. "All day Monday at work, that's your job. You write me a story, the first ten pages of a script. I don't care what it's about but that's what you'll be doing."

"You are the *worst* boss," she tells me.

"I know."

It's funny how interchangeable being the worst and being the best can be.

CHAPTER SIXTEEN

Jackie

I PICK UP MY KINDLE AND START FLIPPING THROUGH the carousel again, trying to find the perfect screenplay book. I've already read *Save the Cat* by Blake Snyder, *Story* by Robert McKee, and *The Screenwriters Bible* by David Trottier. I probably don't need to read anymore since this is now just borderline procrastination.

In fact, yesterday was Monday and I was supposed to write Will something, but instead I spent the whole day reading and learning. Which was actually really nice and I was quick to remember all that I'd learned in the past. Every now and then Patty would look over the divider at me, wondering what the hell I was doing since I wasn't typing, and I would just smile at her and read on.

Then Will would walk past and he wouldn't say anything either, just give me the eye that either says, "keep it up" or "I want you naked right now in my office." It's hard to tell with him sometimes.

Either way, that look always made Patty grumble since

my boss obviously approved of my reading and her boss—my father—had her working extra hard, maybe to make up for all that time he took off when he went to Bermuda a few weeks ago.

That said, I can't be too annoyed with Patty since the entire office is packing up and leaving in about thirty minutes to make their way down to my house to do the team-building exercise with my mother.

Honestly, I'm regretting this idea of mine. Now that I've got a ton of stuff to read, now that I have a project and a goal that entices me, the last thing I want to do is hang out at the riding ring with my co-workers. I actually just want to work. And how the hell does a team-building exercise even work with horses?

It doesn't help that by the time we're ready to go, I'm torn between going on the chartered bus with Alyssa and Tiffany and everyone else, going in Will's car, or going in my father's. It's like Sophie's Choice.

But even though I'd love to ride with Will—or ride Will—I end up going with my father. I don't think anyone would be suspicious of Will and I in the same car, but someone has to figure out by now that we spend an awful lot of time together.

Besides, I haven't spent a lot of time alone with my father, and Patty has been delegated to ride with Will now.

"So Jackie-O," my father says as we slowly creep along the traffic on Granville Street. "Feels like I haven't seen you all that much. You're home for dinner some nights, gone other nights. It's not my business what you're doing. I just want to make sure everything's fine."

"Everything is fine. I've been hanging out with Alyssa a lot." A lie, but I know Alyssa will cover for me if need be.

"Good. She's good people. And how are you and Will

working out?"

"Great."

"He speaks very highly of you, you know."

"Good. He should. I'm an awesome assistant."

He chuckles. "I have no doubt, cupcake." He pauses. "You're not getting bored or anything?"

"Bored? No way."

"He keeps you busy?"

I'm trying to detect if there's another layer to these questions, but it's hard to tell with my dad. He's the kind of guy that rarely smiles, and yet always seems to be joking. "It's just the right amount of workload." Damn. Am I diplomatic or what? "Enough to keep me challenged but not too much that I'm flustered and overwhelmed."

"Good, good, good," he says. "That's what I want to hear. Sorry I haven't been much of a help since you started. I've been traveling to LA so much with Will being up here." He glances at me through the side of his glasses. "You know I was worried for him for a bit."

"Will?"

"He didn't want to come back to Vancouver. Of course when he first moved to LA, he didn't want to leave Vancouver, but you know how it is. He had a life there, one outside of his marriage, and I think it was hard for him to leave it behind."

"I bet," I say and my mind is immediately drawn to what Will's life was like before. Until I saw him on his friend's boat this Saturday, I had a hard time seeing him outside in the sunshine, driving around LA. But now I know it suits him, just as his suits do. The man seems to fit in everywhere.

"That can ruin a man, you know? Divorce. Sasha put him through hell. I was worried he wouldn't snap out of it.

But he did. And fast. I was surprised. It was almost like you showed up in his life and all the cobwebs blew away."

I swallow hard and give my father a tight smile.

"Just let me know if you get tired of the position," he goes on to say. "I can easily move you elsewhere."

I sit up straighter. "Why would you do that?"

"Maybe there's a job you're better suited for at the company."

"But I love my job, I love working for him."

He studies me for so long that I fear he's going to rear-end the car in front of him. "I know you do." He clears his throat. "So, let's talk about this damn team-building exercise. I heard this was all your idea. You know the last thing I want to do is bring work home with me, and this is literally bringing the whole office home with me."

I'm barely listening to him though. I keep tripping over what he said, the way he said it. He knows I love my job, love working for him.

But how much does he know?

Certainly if he knew what Will and I were doing it, he wouldn't be so calm. And I'm pretty sure I'd see Will with a black eye.

He might just be testing the waters. I'm going to have to be extra careful around Will for the next while. Maybe even stay home a bit more, cancel our date for tonight, though the idea of having less sex, less Will, makes my chest ache.

"You know I'm proud of you, Jackie," my father says to me when we pull down our street as he gives wide berth to a pair of horseback riders on the side of the road.

I have to admit, the sincerity touches me. "Thank you."

"I mean it. I don't say it enough. But you're doing good. You've done a great job with Ty and you've got your mind in the right place at work. I think if you keep working forward with no distractions, if you have a goal in sight, you can really get somewhere." He pats my leg. "Just don't fuck it all up or you'll be living with us for the rest of your life."

He's smiling at me like it's a joke.

But I know he's not joking.

At all.

Fortunately, when we pull up to the house, the charter bus is already there and the entire office has gathered in the front yard.

Automatically my eyes go to Will and his go to mine.

It doesn't matter where we are, how big the crowd, I'm always looking for him and he's always looking for me.

And I can feel my father watching the whole thing.

I promptly look away and go and join Alyssa, the conversation having shaken me up. I suppose that was my father's point. The fact is, I've been saving up like a madwoman so I can eventually afford a place of my own with Ty, it's just hard right now because I need to live in the same area because of Ty's school, and this area isn't cheap. On top of it, my mother takes care of Ty when I'm at work. I'm not sure how that arrangement would work if I lived somewhere else.

And it's not really about living at home or not. It's about that other warning. That my dad is proud of me, that I have something good going on, and he's afraid it won't last, just as much as I'm afraid of the same.

There isn't much time to dwell on it though because my mother comes out of the house dressed in her riding gear, along with two other people that I recognize as instructors at the riding club down the street.

There's thirty of us here. Some are still back at the office, mainly the animators, and a few others who cited a horse allergy as a reason to back out. It's too bad I couldn't have pulled that same shit.

My mother divides us into three groups of ten. I'm not surprised when I don't end up with Will. Nor do I end up with Alyssa and Tiffany. Instead I'm with Casey and Patty. Oh joy.

Even though I pulled the idea for team-building out of my ass, it turns out the concept with horses isn't a new thing and Francesca, the instructor we get, tells us that working with horses can teach us about each other and make us a stronger office.

"There are always co-workers that have problems with communicating, right?" she asks, leading us into the stable. She comes to a stop in front of my mother's horse, Jeopardy, in the cross-ties. "They might not be able to pick up on the signals from other co-workers or may come into situations with their own ego and baggage. Just like people, you have to approach a horse a certain way. Approach with stress and anxiety and that horse is going to back off."

One by one she gets us to approach Jeopardy. Now with me it's not really fair since I'm used to horses and this horse in particular. But it's interesting when both Casey and Patty approach him. Jeopardy's ears go back, the whites of his eyes showing. Patty has too much negative energy and Casey is just . . . Casey. Whatever it is he has, the horse knows all. Probably thinks he'll hit on him.

Still, as it goes on and Francesca gets everyone discussing their behaviors and ways to bring good energy into the office, my attention is focused outside, in the ring.

Will is standing beside my mother's other horse, Duke, staring up at it, completely perplexed. My father is holding onto the reins and laughing. I have no idea what's going on with their group but I want to be a part of it.

I watch as my mother appears and encourages Will to get on.

And low and behold, I'm discovering that Will McAlister is a big fat liar. He might know how to sail, but he definitely doesn't know how to ride a horse. In fact, he's putting his foot in the stirrup the wrong way.

I can't wait to bug him about this later. He probably thinks I'm not watching the whole fiasco but I totally am. I just wish he was wearing riding pants instead of jeans, so I could ogle him freely. Then again, the whole office would have the same show. Then again, they often do.

But even though Will is now sitting on top of Duke and has no clue what he's doing, he doesn't look it. He's laughing as he tries to hold the reins properly, that infectious smile of his lighting up the space around him. So beautiful, so devastatingly handsome. Everyone, my father, my mother, my co-workers, everyone is staring at him with that same kind of smile because that's the kind of man he is.

And he's mine, completely. I'm the only woman he comes inside of, the only woman he spends his time with, the only woman he's giving his heart to.

So why can't I tell him this?

And why can't I give myself to him as easily as he gives himself to me?

My father's words ring through my head. A warning. And it shouldn't matter, yet it does.

I don't want to fuck up my job. I don't want to make things horribly awkward between Will and my father. I don't want to lose any respect that I've worked so hard to gain. I really don't want to get hurt. And I know that if the truth came out, that if I told the world that Will and I were together, all of those things would come crashing down.

So where does that leave us?

It leaves us with secret trysts and endless lies and the fact that every moment I am with this gorgeous man, I am trying so desperately to not fall in love with him.

I'm not sure how much longer I can last.

It's not long before the groups rotate and my group goes from communication issues to something else, and as they head outside the stable, I linger back in one of the tack rooms at the end of the aisle. The moment I see Will enter with his group, gathering around the cross-ties, I wave him over.

He looks behind him to see if anyone is watching—they aren't—and quickly makes his way over to me.

I grab his shirt and yank him into the tack room with me.

"What are you doing?" he asks, but his mouth is already ticking up into a devious smile, so he at least has some idea.

But not yet. I kiss him quickly and then place my hand at his chest, holding him back. His heart is already beating hard beneath my palm, his eyes heavy-lidded with lust.

"Hey, so I think I need to cancel tonight."

He looks crushed. Crushed and horny. "Why?"

"I think my dad suspects something."

"About us?"

I nod.

"Why do you say that?"

"I don't know, just the way he was talking in the car." I replay the conversation to him pretty much verbatim.

Will puts his hand at my waist, tugs at the end of my tank top. "I've known your father a long time. He's always had that way about him. Cryptic, you know? Like everything is both a joke and not a joke at once. I wouldn't read too much into it, Jackie. We might not talk as much as we used to, we're just so busy these days, and I'm definitely not as close with him as I was when I was with Sasha, but I do know that if he knew something, even thought something, and had a problem with me, he would say it."

"I just want to put some distance between us for a bit. That's all."

"I really don't like this idea."

"I don't either," I admit as Will steps closer, the warmth of his sun-soaked skin radiating toward me.

"It doesn't exactly help that your father is out there in the stable."

I give him a tiny smile. "I guess that means you'll have to hide out with me until the coast is clear."

"Yeah," he says, putting his fingers through my hair until I moan softly from the sensation. "We better not waste any time then." He brings his lips to my neck, sucking gently. "Oh, fucking Dream Girl. This is what I love about you," he says.

My breath hitches. My eyes open, focusing on the bridles hanging from the wall. He didn't say he loved me but it was damn close.

"What do you love about me?" I whisper.

"How quickly you turn to clay in my hands," he says. "I kiss your neck, pull your hair, and it's like I feel you melting into me, becoming me. You'll do anything I want."

"And what do you want right now?" I ask softly, my eyes closing again as his hands cup my breasts, his thumb brushing over my nipple until everything inside me sings, my thin bra providing no protection.

"Aside from you, from all of you?" he murmurs into my neck. "I want to fucking nail you to the wall." He pauses. "And I'm a bit angry that you're wearing pants."

I laugh softly. "I wasn't about to ride side saddle."

"You should have known you'd be riding me," he says as his hands go to my jeans, unzipping them. "Especially when you're about to withhold sex for an undisclosed amount of time."

"Just until the end of the week," I tell him as he pulls my jeans and underwear down to my ankles, bends down to take off my boots. I glance down at the ground. There is hay and sawdust and either dirt or horseshit everywhere.

"Don't want to get dirty?" he asks, and with one swift movement he picks me up, my legs wrapping around his waist as he pushes me back into the wall, in between a row of dressage saddles. "A little too late for that." He reaches down and starts unzipping his jeans. "You're coming away with me this weekend," he informs me, like I don't have a choice.

"What?" I ask but I'm distracted by the sight of his hard, long cock as he takes it out of his pants, positioning the tip against me. Good lord, how can he be so perfect?

"This weekend. If you're going to withhold sex, then we're going to make up for it." He slowly rubs the tip over my clit, determination and lust fighting on his brow. "I won't give you what you want until you agree."

"We'll talk about it later," I tell him, trying to pull him toward me with my calves, but he's got a strong stance and doesn't budge.

Damn it.

He runs his tongue down the length of my neck, making me shiver. He knows what he's doing. He knows I'm powerless, that I'm clay in his hands, that he can do whatever he wants. He knows and he's about to exploit it.

The smug bastard.

"Get a sitter or ask your mother," he says, his voice

growing huskier with lust. "Tell her you're going away with Alyssa. She'll cover for you. I know she knows what's going on."

I shoot him a reprimanded look.

"It's okay," he says, gnawing on his lip for a moment as he continues to slide the tip of his cock over my clit and back again as I get wetter and wetter. "You should have someone to talk to about me. As long as it's only good things."

I let out a moan as he slowly starts to push himself in, then open my eyes in frustration as he stops.

"Please," I tell him, aware of how desperate I sound. My nails dig into his shoulders.

His grin is wholly amused. "We don't even have to leave the city. I just want you for a whole weekend. No leaving me after sex. I want you day in and day out and all night long. Breakfast in bed, lunch, dinner, I want it all."

I grumble with impatience.

"Tell me you're up for this and I'll give you what you want."

"You're a dick."

"No, *this* is my dick." He pushes in another excruciating inch. "And it could all be yours . . ."

"Ugh," I say through a groan. "Fine. Yes. I'll spend the weekend with you. Or I'll at least try. Now will you please just fuck me?"

"I thought you would never ask."

His eyes turn to fire and with a hard thrust he pushes himself into the hilt.

I practically yelp, my eyes rolling into the back of my head and then the pain turns to pleasure as it always does, dissipating in waves of warmth throughout my body. In a second I've gone from greedy and desperate to getting what I need, and yet I'm still insatiable. I want more of him somehow, more of this, more of everything.

I don't know if it's the setting or the fact that the whole office is around the corner but this is so incredibly hot. Will wastes no time in fucking me hard against the wall, enough so the stirrups are rattling in their saddles. I can barely hold on, my nails digging into him through his shirt, my heels pressing against his firm ass as he flexes, pounding, thrusting. He really is trying to nail me to the damn wall.

My eyes close as the orgasm starts to build, a knot of fire and flames that twists and twists inside me, ready to unfurl.

When it hits, I open my mouth to cry out and Will is quick to shove his palm over my mouth, muffling my scream. I moan helplessly against his hand and he comes with a grunt, a few final pushes until we're both completely spent.

My legs are shaking from the strain as he gently pulls out and lowers me to the ground. I have to prop myself up against the saddles as he slips my underwear and jeans back on, practically dressing me.

Then he zips up his pants, giving me a lazy grin. A dark lock of his hair has swooped down, sticking to his damp forehead, making him look positively boyish.

"Remember your promise about this weekend," he tells me, kissing the tip of my nose.

I sigh. I can't say no to him.

"I'll remember," I tell him as he removes a piece of hay that somehow got in my hair. The both of us wait a few minutes until the groups rotate again before we sneak out and pretend that nothing had happened.

CHAPTER SEVENTEEN

Jackie

It's not every day that you wake up with someone's head between your legs.

But god, how sweet life would be if it was.

That's at least the case this morning.

Saturday.

I'm lying on my back on the world's most comfortable bed in a luxurious hotel room downtown, the window open, the sun streaming in.

And Will's thick head of hair is between my legs, his tongue gently sliding up and down over me.

"Good morning," I groan, my fingers reaching for his hair, relishing the feel of his silky strands between them.

He mumbles something that sounds like 'good morning' back to me, the vibrations of his mouth causing my hips to buck toward him, wanting more. I'm already jelly lying here, boneless and pliable, relaxed from sleep and spent from the night before.

Yesterday we checked into the Sutton Place Hotel right

after work, having dinner downstairs in their oyster bar before retiring back to the room for a few rounds of hot, loud, sweaty sex.

It's been long overdue. This whole week we've managed to play it safe and not see each other outside of work, not even see each other in his office in case temptation struck us.

And believe me, it would have struck us. By the time Friday rolled around I was practically squirming at my desk, waiting for the chance to be alone with him.

One thing I noticed was it wasn't just my body that was craving his. It was like a vital part of me was missing, something I never knew I needed. Being around Will isn't just good for a few (mind-blowing) orgasms. Being around Will is good for everything. My heart, my nerves, my soul. When I'm with him, he makes me feel powerful, unstoppable. Not at all the girl who threw everything away. He makes me feel like a new woman, Cinderella turned queen, the woman who has everything she needs and then some.

And really, who doesn't need being woken up by this man's effortlessly talented mouth?

It doesn't take long before I'm coming, my body pushed over the edge, drowning in everything beautiful.

I sigh, happily, everything inside me beating fast, throbbing, feeling ridiculously alive.

He gets off the bed and leans over to kiss me on the mouth. I don't even mind the way I taste on his lips. "Morning, Dream Girl. How did you sleep?"

"Sleep?" I ask. "How did I wake up is the better question."

He grins at me. "I'm going to order room service," he says, picking up the menu and tossing it to me. "Tell me what you want."

"I want some of Will's famous scrambled eggs."

"Well we can't do that, but I think they do a wonderful crab eggs benedict."

"Sold," I tell him without even opening it. "And coffee. Lots of coffee. Oh, and a Caesar too."

"Why not?" he asks. "I think I'll get one too."

We don't really have any plans for the day so we take our time being naked and eating breakfast and getting tipsy from the Caesars. In the past I would have never sat around naked with a guy, including Jeff, and especially in the harsh light of morning. But with Will I don't even think twice. It feels as natural as anything and from the way he's always looking at my body, in pure desire and amazement, I feel like the fucking queen he thinks I am.

It's nice.

It's really nice.

Not to be Ty's mother, not to be Will's assistant, not to be wild-child Jackie Phillips. It's nice to just be me, here with Will, and nothing else.

It's nice enough that it gets me thinking about the what ifs and the if onlys and the shoulds and the coulds and woulds. To think about the maybes . . .

Maybe this could be something good, something big. Something most people only dream about.

And maybe it would be that, if only everything else was different.

"It's not fair," I say softly as he slips on his dress shirt, the sky outside fading to purple. We're both too tired and spent to leave the hotel for dinner, so we're just going to the bar downstairs to have some drinks and share plates.

"What's not?" he asks, eyeing me briefly before adjusting his hair in the mirror, making sure not a strand is out of place. I love that he's particularly anal about his hair, and every time we make love I make a point of messing it up as much as possible.

"Us," I say, slipping on my Louboutins. "How we can't be together. I mean, really together."

He freezes in place, eyes darting to mine. "What are you talking about?"

"You know what I'm talking about. How we are. How . . . this is it."

He blinks at me in disbelief and turns to face me. "I don't understand. This is it?"

I wish I hadn't said anything. I'm going to blame it on too much sex and just move on.

But from the look in Will's eyes, the strange hardness, I'm not sure it will be that easy.

"Forget I said a thing," I tell him. "Let's just get a drink."

I go to move past him but he steps in front of me, blocking me. "Jackie," he says. "I need to know what you meant. This is what you wanted, isn't it? Just sex? Sneaking around, keeping it all a secret. This was your choice, not mine. You know how I stand."

"Do I?" I ask him. "Because I don't think I've ever heard you say it."

"Say what?"

I look away, shaking my head. The moment is becoming too much for me. "It doesn't matter. Let's just go downstairs and—"

"Forget about it?" he asks, grabbing my arm. Maybe a bit harder than he meant to.

I flinch and rip my arm away from his grasp. "Don't grab me like that."

His face crumbles, and in his eyes I see how much this bothers him. "I'm so sorry. I didn't mean to . . ."

I quickly put my hand on his arm. "I know. I'm sorry

too. I'm just . . . I'm frustrated. That's all. And I'm sorry that I'm ruining our weekend."

"Ruining our weekend?" he asks with a tiny smile. "Jackie, you're not ruining anything. This is the first I've seen you be real with me about us. I want more of this."

"Of me being frustrated?"

"Yes. Because it's real. This is real. It's normal. The two of us, you know we can't do this forever. You know that eventually things are going to change."

I have trouble swallowing. I look away. "I don't want to talk about it."

"Change isn't always bad," he says, tipping my chin up so that I'm forced to meet his eyes. Why does he do this? He knows how beautiful I find them.

"Yeah, well in this case it is bad. It's either this or it's . . ."

"Or it's more," he says. "Jackie, from day one I have always wanted more, and you know this. You need to stop . . ."

"Stop what?" And suddenly I'm defensive.

His expression softens, his hand running through my hair, over my shoulder, down my arm. "Stop pretending I'm not what you need."

He knows how to get me. He knows I hate that word. He knows I hate to need anything.

"Hey," he says, before I start festering on it. "It's okay to need me. I need you. I need you more than I can possibly tell you, Jackie. There's no shame in it. It's part of loving someone. You need their heart to help complete yours."

"You love me?" I whisper, the emotions rising up my throat, choking me.

The room seems to pause with my breath.

"Of course I love you. I've always loved you. There was no before or in between for me," he says softly as he holds onto my hand. "All in. I've always been all in with you."

Warmth. I'm drowning in beautiful, blissful warmth. For a split second, I feel completely whole-hearted. Heart full.

"But . . ." Oh god. Oh god, I can't handle this. I close my eyes. "How can you love me? I've got too much baggage, it's too hard, I . . ."

"You are so easy to love, Jackie." He squeezes my hand until I'm forced to look at him, his voice raspy and full and brimming in my bones. "You are so easy to love."

Why can't I let myself believe him? Why can't I let myself need him?

"You don't need to say a word," he goes on. "But just know this is how I feel. And while loving you is easy, I know love isn't easy. I get that. And I get that it's scary, believe me I do."

"Love should be easy though." I can barely hear my own voice. I stare at the patterns in the carpet, my eyes looping around them aimlessly.

"No," he says, stepping closer and giving my hand another squeeze. "That's not reality. Love just makes everything else in life easier to bear. It's like having an army on your side. But love itself isn't easy. Most people have to fight for it, they fight to keep it. Love is a war, and half the time you're battling your own fucking self."

Fuck. Don't I know it.

He clears his throat. "It doesn't always fall in your lap either. And if you're lucky enough to have love show up at your office one day in a grey pencil skirt and a nervous smile, you still have to work for it. I've been working for it ever since. And I'll keep working for it. Until you tell me not to."

There are three things for certain right now.

One, is that my knees are weak and if he wasn't holding onto me, I'm sure I'd be sliding to the floor in a puddle of goo.

Two, is that I don't deserve this man whatsoever and I know it.

Three, is that I need a few drinks and I need them now. Anything to yank my heart from this blender.

And Will. God bless him. He holds his arm out for me, gives me an easy smile as if his words didn't just shake up my entire world, as if they didn't mean the world to him.

After all he's been through, he's still able to move on, to love, to give every inch of himself.

And it's all for me.

The realization cuts so deep and hurts so good.

When we get to the Gerard Lounge downstairs though, I'm immediately at ease. The room is dark and elegant in an old English way, with wood walls and old paintings, with puckered leather chesterfields adorned with brass rivets. It feels like a place I can hide.

But there is no hiding from Will. We get a seat by the tinted windows that give only a hint between the heavy curtains as to what's going out on the street, but it's enough to steal my attention if I need it to.

Will doesn't dwell on what happened in the room. He immediately orders two old-fashioneds for us from the cute waitress and starts perusing the appetizers for something to eat.

Honestly, I'm not hungry. I don't think I could ever eat again.

Will told me he loves me. And he wants more of me.

And I just don't know if I'm ready to give him what he wants and needs.

Not right now anyway.

"Jackie," he says to me softly after he orders us some chicken wings.

I glance up at him, wondering what else he's going to say.

"I wanted to tell you yesterday but I got . . . distracted. I had a chance to read over your project."

Oh. *Oh.*

I wrinkle my forehead in dismay. "And?"

He flashes me his winning smile. "I loved it."

I give him a suspect look. "What do you mean?"

"I mean I read the first act of your screenplay and I thought it was great. I want more. Honestly, I'm surprised you were able to write that much so fast. Twenty-five pages, that's no easy feat."

I shrug, feeling uncomfortable with the praise. "I struggled a bit at first with the plotting, but then after page ten it just kind of filled itself in."

"I think you need to finish it."

I sigh and sit back in the booth. "That was just for you, Will. No one else."

"So finish it for me. As your boss, I order you to."

"I hate that you still have that over me."

"You love it," he tells me. "It keeps you on your toes."

"Anyway, I don't know how long it will take me to finish it. And believe it or not, you do have work for me."

"So finish it on the side," he says, giving the waitress an easy smile as she hands us another round of drinks. "I just think you really have something going on there."

"You don't think it reads too much like a kid's version of *Game of Thrones*?"

"That's exactly what I think it's like, and that's why I think you have something here. It's at least an idea you can sell. The professionals can take over the rest." He pauses at my face, rebuked by that last comment. "You know what I mean. It's a good thing Jackie, so finish it."

"I'll think about it," I tell him. I don't want to think about it right now. With Will's confession and now this, there's just too many things to get my hopes up over.

I push it aside. I push it all aside. I decide to live in the moment, this very moment here in the hotel bar with him, sipping smoky sweet drinks with a man who adores me. Who *loves* me. There's a future in front of me and I can't see what it is and it doesn't matter.

Right now, I don't need anything else.

Right now is enough.

For now.

A week has gone by since Will and I had our romantic rendezvous at the hotel. Despite that, I've still managed to put some distance between us, at least when it comes to our out-of-office activities.

I'm still stuck in this limbo over my feelings for him, which in turn puts more space between us. I know that I'm shutting down a bit, going inward, that I've stopped being open and communicating with him. I know it's wrong.

It's just there's this great, dark fear that wasn't there before. Or maybe it was, but it was lurking in the shadows where it should have stayed. As long as Will and I were just screwing around the fear was kept at the bay. The sex did an excellent job of masking it. It made me believe that it was harmless fun that we could call off at any time.

But with Will telling me he's in love with me, that he wants more from me, the fear has crawled out into plain view. It tells me that I could have all that, could have him and all he's offering. But it will cost me. It might cost me far more than I bargained for.

In a crazy, deluded way, I wish I could go back and never start up with Will at all. That things would have been easier for me and Ty if I just did what my dad told me to. Keep focused on a goal, on the future, keep working hard with no distractions.

Will has been the sweetest distraction.

And now I feel like the fear of what could happen is overshadowing the hope of what could be.

It doesn't help when Friday rolls around and I get a call from my mother.

"Will's line is busy," she says to me. "Can you tell him he's to come over tonight at seven instead of six-thirty? I don't think the roast will be ready in time."

"Will is coming over for dinner?" This is news to me.

"Yes. You'll be here, right? I made enough. It's just hard to know if you're going out with your girlfriends or not."

"Yeah," I say slowly. "I'll be there."

I hang up.

Shit.

Will is coming over to my parents for dinner?

This can't be good. This can't be good at all.

This is the danger zone of all danger zones.

I immediately get to my feet and go to Will's office, rapping on the door.

"Who is it?" I hear him call out.

"Just Jackie," I tell him.

He laughs. "Come on in, weirdo."

I open the door and step inside. He is on the phone but looking bored. "I'm on hold," he says, leaning back in his chair, his feet up on the table. I catch a hint of mustard- and blue-striped socks peeking out between his loafers and his brown pants. His blazer is hung up on the wall and he's wearing a navy dress shirt, silk and rolled up at the sleeves.

As usual, he looks perfect.

"Why are you on hold?" I ask him.

"My iPhone is on the fritz," he says. "Calling Apple Care. They're in no hurry to serve you, I'll tell you that much."

"I should be calling them," I tell him. "That's my job. I assist you in these kinds of things."

"Your job right now is to write that screenplay."

"And I told you I'll work on it on the side."

"My god, you're stubborn."

"And you're a liar."

He looks at me sharply. "What's that supposed to mean?"

"It means you're coming over for dinner tonight and you never told me."

"Oh. Well that doesn't mean I'm a liar. Just means I withheld some facts, that's all."

"Will," I say sternly, crossing my arms. "This is a big deal. Why didn't you tell me?"

"Because I didn't want you to worry. You're worried, aren't you? See? I didn't want that."

"Of course I'm worried . . ." I look out the open door and see someone walk past. I lower my voice. "It's going to be weird."

"Probably. But your mother does do a good roast."

"*Will*. I'm serious."

"So am I. Look, they're your parents but they're also my friends and your father is my partner, and I can't say no when they invite me. It wouldn't be right. Besides, I miss them and I miss you and Ty. This way I get to see you all."

I pause for a moment. "You miss me?" I whisper.

He raises his brows. "You just think it's easy for me to go from seeing you all the time to never seeing you at all?"

"But we had the weekend . . ."

"And a weekend is not enough. Nothing will be enough with you, Dream Girl. You should know this by now."

"All or nothing."

"Damn fucking right." He sighs, switching the phone around to the other ear.

"When were you going to tell me?" I ask.

"Maybe when I showed up at your door? Look, it's going to be fine. I promise. Go back to your script and I'll see you later. That's an order."

Yeah right it's going to be fine. My father will probably sniff it out of us. And Ty. God, I hope Ty doesn't say anything. Will did kiss me that once on the boat and if that ever came out . . .

Needless to say, I am a wreck once seven rolls around. Even though I had just said goodbye to Will at work a few hours earlier, fighting the urge to kiss him, I've had just enough time to stew over it on the bus ride over and while getting ready.

Part of me wants to wear the D&G cocktail dress again, but that's too risky. Instead I put on a simple black sheath dress that hides the fact that I'll eat too much, and adorn it with his silver Tiffany necklace. I know my mother might ask about it, but I'll just lie and I say I got it from Blue Ruby or something. She's not going to be nosy enough to search for the Tiffany inscription.

I'm in the kitchen helping her when the doorbell rings.

I jump a mile, the wine sloshing out of my glass and spilling onto the floor.

My mother gives me a funny look. "You're a jumpy one today."

"I just got my period," I blurt out. A lie that also makes no sense at all, but at least it throws my mother off for a moment.

While I'm bending over to clean up the spill, Will steps in, glancing down at me.

"Accident?" he asks me, placing a bottle of wine on the table.

"Ignore her, she has her period," my mother says.

Will laughs. "Good to know."

"Mom," I say tersely, standing back up and throwing the rag in the sink. "Way to share."

"Oh Will doesn't care. You're like a younger sister to him," she adds, bustling into the kitchen, leaving Will and I to exchange a glance, eyebrows raised in unison. "Why don't you two go relax and have a drink. And tell your father and Ty that dinner will be ready soon. Only one rule though: no talking about work."

"Promise," Will says, eyeing my necklace and jerking his head over to the living room.

I follow him, taking a moment to look him over.

He's not in a suit, but he's not all that casual either. Tan pants, black dress shirt. Everything fitting him just so.

I sigh internally. It's been far too long since I've felt those taut muscles underneath my hands, since I've tasted his skin.

By the time I'm sitting down across from him and he's handing me a glass of scotch, I'm already flustered.

"You're flushed," he says quietly, elbows on his thighs and leaning in close to me. "Don't tell me I had something to do with that."

I slowly sip my drink, not breaking eye contact. I've

missed being able to stare at him like that, so open, no shame. Fuck. Why did he have to come here for dinner? Why couldn't I have gone back to his place?

"I think you know what you do to me," I tell him.

"Funny, you're able to handle it at work," he says.

"Guess it just doesn't seem right that you're not naked right now."

"I don't think your parents would approve of me having dinner in the nude. This isn't a frat house." He swirls the amber liquid around the glass. "You've been awfully quiet all week."

I nod. "I know."

He licks his lips as he studies me thoughtfully. "I'm doing what you asked, Jackie. I'm keeping my distance. Physically. But I didn't sign up for this." He gestures to the space between us, his brow furrowed. "I don't like being cut off from you emotionally. I don't like it at all. You need to communicate with me. You need to tell me what's on your mind."

I don't need to do anything, I think, surprised at how defensive I'm feeling over this when all Will wants from me is just some reassurance.

But maybe Will just wants and needs too much right now.

"Hey," he says, reaching over to touch my knee. His touch is like a balm to me, soaking through my skin, making my eyes close briefly. "Was it what I said at the hotel? How I feel about you? You know I can't keep it to myself, but the last thing I want is to scare you off."

"I don't want to talk about it right now," I tell him just as Ty comes bounding into the room.

"Hey Batman!" he cries out, running straight to Will.

Will is on his feet just in time, putting down his

glass and scooping up Ty into his arms. "How you doing Ty-ger?"

"It's Ty-Rex," he tells Will matter-of-factly.

"Well whatever you are, you're an animal."

"Cute," my father says, appearing beside us with a drink in his hand. "Who knew you were such a child magnet, Will. You should have been a father."

I'm watching Will closely, as usual, so I'm not sure if my father notices just how that comment wounds him. But it hits him deep. I could kill my father for being so careless with his words.

Will plasters on a smile and puts Ty back down on the ground.

"Go help Grandma with dinner," my father says, practically pushing Ty out of the room.

I decide to go after Ty. "I guess I'll let the adults talk," I tell them, glancing quickly at Will before heading to the kitchen.

It's better in here. I can breathe. The last thing I want is to be alone with the two of them, so I busy myself by helping my mother and playing with Ty.

Finally, dinner is ready and we all take our places in the same seats as we did the last time.

Jeez. That feels like a lifetime ago. In a way, it was. It's late June now and that was back in late March. Spring has come and gone. Summer is here to stay a while. And I feel like a completely different person. The job, Will, going to a few therapy sessions and dealing with my past—each one is unveiling a new layer of myself.

Though one thing is still for certain. I'm still living with fear, only it's a different kind. The fear that everything I want is now in reach and it's up to me to screw it all up. Will was right when he said that love is war and we're often just battling ourselves.

Then again, he's right about most things.

"Ted," Will says after we've all had a few bites of the roast. "I forgot to tell you something about Jackie here."

My father and mother look at me.

"Oh?" my father says, cutting into his meat. "What? Is she stealing office supplies?"

"No. She's written a script. Or half of one."

I glare at him. "Will," I reprimand him.

"A script?" my mother asks. "You know, I remember back before Ty was born you were really into that."

"What kind of script?" my father asks suspiciously.

I open my mouth to speak but Will plows on through. "It would make a great project for Warner Brothers. Same line as the *DinoWars*, only it's fantasy with dragons."

"Sounds like *Game of Thrones*."

"Exactly."

My father waves the idea away. "They did it with *How to Train Your Dragon*. It's been done."

"Not like this. Jackie is quite adept at creating these characters you've never seen before. She's brilliant, really."

Damn. Will is certainly selling me. I'd be melting here at the table if it weren't for the fact that he's selling me a little too much.

"It's nothing," I say quickly. "Will is just talking me up because he caught me stealing office supplies."

"Figures," my father says and everyone laughs.

"Hey guess what, Grandpa Ted?" Ty says.

Oh no.

"What is it, Grandson Tyson?"

"Will is Batman."

"I've heard. You know we're not supposed to talk about that."

"And when we went sailing, he said that I was his best friend."

My father smiles, looking to Will. "Is that so? Well, you know Will is a very good friend. The best. Aren't you Will?"

I look over at my mother to see if she's picked up anything odd in my father's tone, but she's digging into her salad. My parents knew Will was taking us sailing, so that's nothing new, but even so I feel like my father is being a bit on the nose.

"If you say so," Will says to him, having a sip of his drink.

"And Will drew me a picture," Ty says. "He drew a picture of me as Ty-Rex."

"I know, I saw it on your wall," my father tells him.

"He drew a picture of Jackie too."

"Did he now?" he asks, looking between the two of us.

"Yeah," Ty goes on. "She's Cinderella. And he's Prince Charming."

"Actually," I interject as Will starts coughing on his drink, "there was no Prince Charming in the picture, Ty. It was just me. Just Cinderella."

"I see," my father says slowly. He looks to Will. "So you're back to drawing again?"

Will shrugs. "It's nothing."

"You're drawing and my daughter is writing. What is it exactly that you two do again at work, hmm?"

"I think it's wonderful," my mom says. "For both of you. Will, you're so good at it. And Jackie, this is a great thing to work on. I guess you bring out the best in each other."

"You know Will," my father says, leaning back in his chair. "I think it's about time we find you a woman."

Oh god.

"Ted," my mother admonishes him. "Don't embarrass Will at the table."

"I'm not embarrassing him. We're all adults here. Well, except for Jackie and Tyson. It's been a long time since Sasha left him and I think Will needs to move on. For his own sake."

"Ted," Will says, "I appreciate the offer . . ."

"But what? Look, I told you about Mona."

"Who is Mona?" my mother asks.

"Yeah who is Mona?" I can't help but ask too.

"Mona," my father says, "is a smart, beautiful, intelligent woman. Will's age. Old enough to have her past behind her, old enough to have learned from her mistakes. That's what Will needs. Someone with two legs to stand on, who has their own career carved out in front of them."

Does my dad know? His words seem far too deliberate.

And yet I can't even concentrate on that right now. All I can think about above the woosh of blood in my head is who the hell Mona is.

"I've talked to Will about Mona before," my father goes on. "She should have gone with him to the gala instead of you, Jackie."

Ouch. I try to smile, to show that it doesn't bug me.

It does.

"Will sounded open to it at the time," he adds. "About dating her."

I stare at Will for his reaction, trying to ignore the pang in my heart. Will's eyes turn cold, narrow ever so slightly. "I remember," he says carefully. "I believe I told you I wasn't interested."

"You did. But I can read between the lines. I know you, old boy. You're still single. You should at least be out there and dating, that's all. You're forty-one. Time to settle back down, with the right girl this time."

"Ted," my mother says again. "That was a bit of a low blow."

"Well Will needs to be blown, that's all I'm saying."

"Dad," I cry out, attempting to cover Ty's ears.

"Oh he doesn't know what it means."

"Ted, I appreciate your endless concern," Will says sternly, wearing a stiff smile. "But I think we need to drop it."

"Hey," Ty speaks up, "how come Will can go on a date with Mona but he can't go on a date with my mom?"

Oh my god, Ty.

I immediately look over at Will who looks just as shocked as I do.

My father puts his fork down, staring at Ty. "Now why would you even want that, Ty?"

"I told you," Ty says, exasperated. "Will is my best friend. Mom is also my best friend. I think it would be nice."

Jesus he's breaking my heart all over again.

My father laughs. "I'm sorry, kid. But Will needs to be with another grown-up. Not Jackie."

"Excuse me?" I say to him. "I'm a damn mother. I am a grown-up."

"Having children doesn't mean you're mature," my father says.

"Jackie is plenty mature," Will speaks up.

My father shoots him a look. "There's no need to defend her." He smiles at Ty. "Your mother needs to straighten up and fly right for a while. Will needs a woman his age who knows what she's doing. Besides, if Will ever laid on finger on your mother, I'm pretty sure Will would be moving back to LA with a few broken bones. He couldn't be your best friend anymore, could he?"

"You're being an asshole," I tell him, getting up.

"Why? Because I'm telling the truth?" He looks at Will who is focused solely on me, panic in his eyes. "Will, what has gotten into her? What is all this?"

"Oh I don't know," Will says slowly, eventually looking back at him. "Maybe she doesn't like being called a child. It's called respect Ted, you should give it to her sometimes."

"Bah," he says, shoving a piece of roast in his mouth and chewing thoughtfully. "She's flighty, always has been. She'll get over it."

"I'm standing *right here*," I remind him.

"I know, Jackie. We all see you." He looks at my mother. "Can you pass the salt?"

"You know what? I'm done," I say, throwing my napkin on the plate.

"Jackie, please, sit down," my mother says. "You know how your father gets."

"No. I guess I'd forgotten since I hadn't seen him much for seven whole years."

"Hey that was all on you, Jackie," my father says sharply, pointing his fork at me. "We tried to help you and you left us. You ran away. You went up to fucking nowhere and you lived like a damn animal, scraping to make ends meet, all because of some fucking loser. And all for what? What good did it get you? You cut us off like we never existed, you made it so we could never see our grandchild. You were so . . . stupid in love with Jeff that you did whatever he said."

"I wasn't in love with Jeff, I was afraid of him!" I yell. "You have no idea what hell I went through up there, no idea at all!"

"Jackie," my mom says calmly.

"No!" I yell. "No, I'm tired of you guys thinking that I'm just some hot mess. Okay, I made some mistakes, I made a lot. But Ty was never one of them. My mistake was staying with Jeff because I was afraid and I was too weak and scared to get out. I let the fear control me and in the end I paid for it. You want to know what really happened? What he did? He fucking beat me. Twice. Shoved me, kicked me, hit me on the head with a teapot. Those bruises I had were from him. I thought I was going to die. And I thought he was going to hurt my son."

The words hang in the air. Ty starts crying. I'm close to crying too, I just don't know for what reason yet. Every single emotion I've been trying to hide is rushing to the surface, ones that didn't even come up in therapy, and this is the last place I want to be when it happens.

"Come on Ty," I say, pulling him out of the chair and up into my arms. "We're going for a walk."

I take him into the hall and start putting on his shoes and my boots and I can hear my parents arguing in the dining room and then the sound of a chair being pushed back.

"Will," my mother calls out and then he's beside us, looking down at me like he's in pain.

"Jackie," he says, unsure how to proceed.

"I'm fine," I tell him, though I'm obviously not. "We're just going to get some fresh air. Maybe see the frogs in the pond at the end of the road. You'd like that, right Ty?"

He nods but I know he doesn't mean it.

"Let me come with you," Will says. "Please."

I give him a sad smile. "I don't need you," I tell him, and the words seem to slap him in the face. "I'll be fine."

He reaches out and grabs my hand and I flinch, even

though my parents can't see us. "Don't pull away from me, Dream Girl. Don't do it. Don't break my heart."

"If I break your heart, I'll have to break my own," I whisper. "I'll see you at work on Monday, okay?"

He's fighting. He's fighting to say something and he knows whatever he says, it won't have any effect on me right now. He saw what just happened and he heard what was said before.

"Nothing has changed, Will," I tell him as I grab Ty's hand and bring him to the door. "This is just what I do."

"Run away from those that love you?" he asks.

I don't answer.

I step outside with my son, shutting Will inside with my parents.

CHAPTER EIGHTEEN

Will

Fuck.

Fuck, fuck, *fuck*.

Watching Jackie and Ty head out that door was one of the most painful things I've ever had to witness. I understand why she doesn't want me to go with them, but to be shut out like that, especially when I know she needs me, it's nothing short of devastating. I can't help but think, no matter how much she told me things haven't changed, that they have changed for good.

And if being free of me means breaking her own heart in the process, I fear that's what she'll choose.

Because to Jackie, choice means everything.

And I'm starting to think solitude fits her like a glove.

I sigh, heavy-hearted, and turn back, heading into the dining room.

Ted and Diane are sitting there, silently sipping their drinks. No one is eating. Diane's face is red, Ted's showing me nothing.

Neither of them look up at me. You can feel the shame in the room.

"Will, she's not yours to worry about," Ted says before finishing his martini.

I just shake my head, leaning on the back of Jackie's empty chair. "I know that you're a family and you have a lot of catching up to do and issues to sort out," I say. "But you need to go easier on her."

"We didn't know," Diane says. "Jesus, Will. Had we known . . . did you know?"

I give her a tight-lipped smile. "Yes. I knew."

"You should have told us," Ted says.

"It wasn't my past to tell. That belonged to Jackie and it was up to her." I want to add in that she's been seeing a therapist every couple of weeks but that's up to her as well.

"So we kind of look like the horse's ass now, don't we?" Ted says.

I sigh, letting my head hang for a moment while I gather my thoughts. "Even if it wasn't an issue, you have to stop throwing the person she was back in her face. Maybe she acts like a child around you because you treat her like a child. And she's not. She might be young in a lot of ways, but her soul has gone through more than most do in a lifetime."

Diane gives me a funny look but doesn't say anything.

Ted clucks his tongue, pressing his fingers into the table. "I'll apologize when they get back." He gets up. "I can see you're ready to go, Will. I don't blame you. Thank you for coming anyway. We'll do lunch on Monday."

"You know where my office is," I tell him, watching as he grabs his drink and heads up the stairs.

I look back to Diane and give her an apologetic smile. "Thank you so much for the dinner. Family drama aside, it was wonderful as always."

She nods, giving me a small smile. Then she gets up and leans across the table. "I know what's going on," she says, keeping her voice low.

Well, shit.

I keep my face neutral. "I don't know what you mean."

She raises her brow. "You. And my daughter. I know there's something going on between you."

Damn it, I hate lying to her. But here it goes. I breathe in deep. "She's my assistant, Diane. That's all that's going on."

"You're lying to me," she says. "And that's okay. But I know, I *know* where she goes. I've seen her wearing your shirt. I've seen that necklace that I know is from Tiffany's, that I know she would never buy for herself. I've seen her Dolce & Gabbana dresses and her red-soled shoes. I know you drive her home a lot more than you should." She pauses. "And I know I've never seen her so happy. And the same goes for you."

I stare at her, not sure what to say. She's got me pegged all too well.

"Ted doesn't know," she goes on. "I think he suspects, but he doesn't know. Will, listen. I love you like a younger brother. You're a good man. And of course I love Jackie. In a way I think you're both perfect for each other. Never thought I would find myself thinking that, but it's true. But Ted isn't me . . ."

I nod. "I wish he were."

"But he's not. And I can't tell you what to do . . . hell, I don't even know what you should do. But you have to know that this isn't going to be easy. For any of us. Teddy is extra volatile these days, maybe it's all the travel, maybe it's getting older. I don't know. So I can't predict how he's going to act when he finds out, but it won't be good Will."

"What makes you think he'll find out?"

She cocks her head. "If I know, he'll figure it out eventually."

"Not if your daughter doesn't want to see me anymore."

She sighs and sits back down, putting her head in her hands. "See, this is exactly why shit like this should never happen. Someone is always going to get hurt."

"Maybe your daughter is smarter than everyone thinks," I tell her.

"Maybe," she says. "I'm sorry Will."

"Sorry?" I tell her, straightening up. "It's not over until it's over. It's not over yet."

"Where there's a Will there's a way," she mumbles, but gives me a warm smile. "All right. Just as long as you know what you're getting in to."

"I always did," I tell her. "And I still wouldn't change a thing."

Despite all of our dates, hookups, and yes, (one-sided) declarations of love, Jackie and I don't talk on the phone, and we rarely text each other.

This weekend though, I want to bombard her with texts.

I want to make sure she's okay.

That Ty's okay.

That we still have a shot at this.

That nothing has changed.

But of course with my iPhone not holding a charge anymore, I can't do any of that, and I'm not about to call her parent's house asking to speak to her.

So when Monday rolls around, the distance between us already feels insurmountable.

Every step I take toward my office feels like a funeral march. I barely smile at anyone as I pass them by, I can't seem to say hello back. My eyes are trained on Jackie's desk.

But Jackie isn't there.

I glance at my watch.

I'm actually ten minutes late.

I look down at Patty.

"Have you seen Jackie?" I ask her.

She barely glances up at me. "Nope."

"Okay. Can you tell her I want to speak with her when she gets in?"

"Yup."

Jeez. I thank my lucky stars I never ended up with Patty as my assistant. Then again if I had Patty, I wouldn't be in this damn mess right now, now would I?

I step inside my office, keeping the door partially open, and go through my emails. There's nothing from Jackie, but I fire one off to her anyway, asking if she's coming in today.

Then I do something I probably shouldn't. I email Michelle at Warner Brothers, one of the producers on *DinoWars,* and ask her if she wouldn't mind taking look at something for me. I attach Jackie's script and explain that it's only a partial, just a draft, and completely on spec, but if she wants to take a look and give me her thoughts, I'd appreciate it.

Of course I don't expect anything to happen, but it helps to have some extra eyes on it, especially from a studio like WB.

But Jackie doesn't come in, and it's nearly noon when Ted shows up knocking on my door. "Hey soldier," he says to me. "Remember we have lunch?"

"Right," I tell him, getting to my feet. "Where's Jackie?"

"Oh," he says and for one horrible moment I fear that she's quit on me. "She wasn't feeling well this morning. I'm not sure she'll be in today."

I try to look more annoyed than disappointed, but I'm not sure if it works because Ted adds, "See, this is the problem with having family work for you. She's mad at me because of what happened at dinner—she wouldn't even talk to me all weekend—and so now she's not coming in to work."

If that's the way Ted wants to see it, that's fine. I have no doubt Jackie is still smarting over it, but what I really think, really fear, is that she's not here because of me.

He pats me on the back as we leave my office. "As they say, don't shit where you eat."

I laugh. "I'm not sure that's the saying, Ted. I think it's don't mix business and friendship. Or family."

"Or pleasure," he adds and I swear he gives me the stink-eye for a moment. "Don't stick your dick where you lay your pen. Don't fuck where you get fucked. Don't have sex with your secretary."

I swallow thickly. "That last one wasn't as subtle," I point out, attempting to sound casual.

He gives me an easy smile. Those are the worst. You can't trust them.

This is going to be a long lunch.

But if Ted suspects anything, if Diane told him, he doesn't show it.

That is until we're being seated at Blue Water for lunch and he asks for a third setting.

"Who is joining us?" I ask him.

He doesn't say anything. Gives me that smile again.

For a moment I think it could be Jackie. That he's about to give the two of us the ultimatum. Call it all off or we're both out of jobs. Granted, I own half the company so it's not like Ted could get rid of me that easily, but he could definitely make my life hell for a while, enough so that the LA office would be a kinder version of it.

Then his eyes fix on someone behind me and I turn to see a beautiful woman coming my way.

I already know who this is.

Mona.

"Mona," Ted exclaims, getting up to give her a hug. "So glad you could make it. Mona, this is Will."

I get out of my chair to shake her hand, smiling at her because I'm a gentleman, but fuck I could murder Ted right now.

I have to admit, Mona is easy on the eyes. She's tall, thin, with a nice rack. Shoulder-length blonde hair and Scandinavian features. If I wasn't absolutely in love with Jackie, if I was single, if this was some other planet, I could see her being my type. She reminds me a Hitchcock blonde, not quite Grace Kelly, but Tippi Hendren.

But I have zero interest in this woman whatsoever, and I have no idea what Ted has told her about me. I just know whatever it is, it's given her the completely wrong idea.

And I can't say anything to throw her off. Make up that I'm seeing someone else? No. The lies have gone for far too long, I'm not about to add to them.

Despite Mona being there and Ted taking over most the conversation, neither of them take much of a hint. Especially when Ted invites her to come back to the office when we've finished paying the bill.

"Ted," I whisper to him as we walk down the street, "what are you doing?"

"Nothing, Will. Just showing Mona where we work. The empire we built. We need to take more pride in it from time to time, don't you think?" He gestures to my apartment building in the distance, the copper roof towering distinctively over the south end of downtown. "Look at that. That's yours Will. You earned that. I've earned what I have. We have done a great job of taking Mad Men to the next level and I hope we continue to keep doing it. In the meantime, let's be proud of what we accomplished. It could so easily be taken away."

Now, I have no clue if Ted is just drunk from his three martinis, or if he's hinting at something else, or if he's just trying to impress Mona for me, who no doubt can hear what he's saying. I just hope I can get back to the office before anything blows up. Today has been one ticking time bomb.

And it seems like I might just make it home free until I see the look on Alyssa's face as we pass by her and Tiffany at reception.

And then I see why.

Jackie is sitting at her desk. I can see her shadow through the partition at the top.

And Ted is taking both Mona and I toward her.

Oh, fuck.

"Jackie," her father says loudly, making Jackie slowly peer around the partition at us. "So nice of you to finally show up. This is Mona. Mona, this is Jackie. She's my daughter."

I can't even move. My eyes are locked on Jackie and she's doing her best to pretend I don't exist. She pastes a smile on her face and gives Mona a nod.

"Nice to meet you," Jackie says, and I catch the little tremble in her voice.

She's thinking the worst. The absolute worst.

"Likewise," Mona says. "I didn't know Ted had a daughter."

"He likes to pretend I don't exist," Jackie explains smoothly.

"We were just out for lunch," Ted says, not even paying attention to Jackie's slight. "I was trying to set these two up, as you know."

Holy fuck, Ted. I glare at him, not even caring that Mona can see it. For her sake, she looks embarrassed about it.

"That's nice," Jackie says. "I hope you'll like the office."

"Do you want to give her a tour?" Ted asks her. "I'm sure Mona would love that."

Jackie freezes, her smile faltering. "I think Alyssa would be better at that, I just got in and—"

"Nonsense," Ted says. "You've been here long enough. Go show her around." Ted looks at me and winks. "Hope you don't mind that I'm borrowing your assistant for a while."

"Actually I do mind," I say firmly, not smiling anymore.

And Ted isn't smiling either. "Too bad she has to answer to her father before she answers to her boss."

By now Mona doesn't look like she wants a tour either, but Jackie gets up and gives Mona a nervous smile, only glancing at me briefly as she passes me by.

Shit. I know that look. It's the look that says if this is me being all in, then Jackie is all *out*.

When Mona and Jackie are out of earshot I turn to Ted. "I could fucking murder you."

"Why?" he says with a wide shrug. "Who cares?"

"I told you I wasn't interested in Mona," I say to him, lowering my voice when I realize Patty is watching us.

"Now you're trying to set us up. It's not going to happen."

"Give me one good reason why. Hey, Will? Why? Tell me."

I look to Patty, who raises her brow at me. I have a feeling she knows why.

"She's beautiful and smart and you're single," he goes on, taking a step toward me. "You are single, aren't you?"

I raise my chin. I'm bigger than him, taller than him, younger than him, stronger than him. I don't want to have to kick his ass over his daughter but I will if I have to.

"I have work to do," I manage to say before my temper gets the best of me. It wants to. Oh, I can feel the red-hot rage working its way through my bones, wanting to get everything out in the open once and for all.

But I quickly turn and head into my office, slamming the door behind me.

And by work to do, I mean a relationship to mend.

If it's not too late.

CHAPTER NINETEEN

Jackie

I KNEW IT WAS A MISTAKE TO COME INTO WORK TODAY.
I knew that my stomach was feeling sick this morning because it was its way of telling me that leaving my bed was a bad idea.

A very bad idea.

I didn't want to see Will.

Even though I so badly wanted to see Will.

But I wasn't ready. I hadn't decided anything.

I spent the whole weekend trying to make peace with my feelings, trying to figure it out and I kept coming up empty handed.

I want to be with Will.

I don't want to lose everything else in my life, including my relationship with my parents, in order to have him.

Or do I?

The dinner on Friday showed just how fragile that relationship is, and how far we have to go before we're a fully functioning family again. Right now it's dysfunctional, and not even in the way that works for most families. Right now we're a bunch of strangers who are slowly coming to know and like each other—most of the time. Even my father, who can be a cold, superficial dick sometimes is still my father, still someone I need and want a better relationship with.

I don't want to throw that away and put me back to square one.

And I don't want that to happen to Will.

I know it's not my place at all to decide what is best for him, and frankly it pisses me off to no end when people do that for me. So I'm not going to end things with him because I think he'll be better off, even if it's true.

But it still matters. My father would probably think I'm being a hot mess again, the crazy wild-child still making bad mistakes. But when it comes to Will, he's going to think a lot worse. A forty-one year old man with his twenty-five year old daughter? He's going to think our relationship is based on sex when . . .

Well, maybe at first it was based on sex, from my point of view anyway, but that was never the case with Will.

Regardless, it won't go over well. And as much as it burns up my heart to think, to know, that Will would choose me over everything else, I don't want him to make that choice.

I'm just not worth it, not in the long run.

He wants me and Ty because we set off the protector and provider in him. His caveman instincts. Ty is the child he could never have, I'm the wife that he thinks he wants.

He knows this, deep down. He just doesn't know it yet.

And when he does, when he realizes it, it's going to blow up in his face and he's going find out he sacrificed everything for a relationship that never really existed.

Those were my thoughts this morning.

Then the guilt sets in.

Then my mother sets in.

She pulls me aside around ten a.m., just before she was going to head out to her horseback lesson.

"You're looking a bit better," she says, eying me closely. "Maybe it's a case of nerves."

I nod. "I guess it's tricky when you have to work with your father."

"I don't mean your father, I mean Will."

I try to shrug and open the fridge, looking for something to distract me. One of Ty's apple juice boxes should do. "I'm sure Will doesn't care about a family spat."

"He doesn't," she says. "But he does care about you."

I give her a quick smile and stab the straw into the top of the juice box. It's mildly cathartic. "That's because he's a good boss."

"Jackie," she says. "I had a good talk with Will on Friday night, before he left. You were off with Ty."

This isn't good.

"Oh?"

I suck back on the juice box until the sides cave in.

"He didn't go into any specifics but . . . look, honey. You deserve the best in life, you really do. You've gone through so much and it hurts my heart to know you had to go through it all without us. I realize that our relationship hasn't been that easy since you've come home, and I know that you've probably felt alone and Will has been the only person to lean on. It's only natural what happened . . ."

I glance at her sharply as I throw the juice box in recycling. "What happened?"

"I know you're together. That you're an item. Will confirmed it."

My nostrils flare. "He did what?!"

"To be fair, I brought it up," she says quickly. "I made him tell me. Because I know, Jackie. It's obvious."

I clamp my mouth shut, scared to death, angry as hell that Will told her.

She goes on. "The dresses, the shoes, the necklace, the late nights. I'm not an idiot. And you can't ignore the way he looks at you. Jackie that man is in love with you."

I nod. "I know," I whisper softly.

She tilts her head, examining me. "Are *you* in love with him?"

I try and swallow. I can't. "It doesn't matter," I say, my words barely audible.

"What do you mean it doesn't matter? I'm pretty sure it matters to Will."

"No," I tell her sharply. "It can't matter to him. It won't. I don't . . ."

I really don't want to have this conversation with my mom. I don't want to have it with anyone.

"Jackie, do you love him or not? It's a simple question."

I shake my head, tears threatening my eyes. "It's not simple at all. It's the hardest question of all." The tears spill over my cheeks. "I don't want to, don't you understand? I don't want to love him, not even a bit. God, this is so hard."

"Honey," she whispers, pulling me into a hug. "It doesn't have to be hard. That's all up to you."

"But I don't think I'm ready to just . . . give myself to him. How can I when we're always two seconds from falling apart?" I sniffle onto her shoulder, my eyes closing. I forgot how good it feels to have a hug from your mother.

"If it falls apart, you just put it back together," she says, rubbing my back. "That's what happens when you love someone, when you're in it for the long haul. Things will fall apart. They will get rough. But as long as you have someone who doesn't disappear when love gets tough, it doesn't matter."

"But there's just too much against us. Dad . . . the company . . . god, does Dad already know?"

"No, sweetie. He doesn't. But don't let that stop you." She pulls back, holding my shoulders. "He'll always be your dad, no matter what you do." She gives me a small smile. "And we both know you've done a lot."

"And Will?"

She exhales loudly. "Will is more complicated. But he knows what he's up against. He knew what he was getting into with you."

"Is Dad going to kill him?"

"Maybe."

"Mom."

"Your father is touchy, and the two of them aren't as close as they once were. So I don't know. But I do know that it's up to Will to make that choice, not you."

I close my eyes. My heart feels like it's being drained out of me.

"But you have a choice too," she adds. "And in the end, it's the one choice we all have to make. You can choose fear. Or you can choose love."

"I chose love once," I tell her, my words choked. "I thought I loved Jeff and I chose him and look what that did to me."

"I know. I know, sweetie. But the same choice will keep coming up in life, if you're lucky. And every time you're going to have to pick one or the other. You can choose fear over love, but then you won't have Will. I know that's not what you want."

I look away, take a step back. "I guess I should go to work."

"Are you sure?" she asks. "If you're only going because I'm asking the tough questions, then don't think you'll be able to avoid them when you're looking at Will. That man is madly in love with you, Jackie. But he's also not someone to be toyed with. He won't wait forever."

"I'm not toying with him," I say indignantly. "I would never do that to him."

"Whether you mean to or not, he deserves to have all of you. And if you think you're going to end up choosing fear over love in the end, then he deserves to know as soon as possible."

"And what if I don't know?" I ask, picking up the dishtowel and wiping away the rest of my tears. "What if I'll never know how I feel?"

"Jackie. You know already. If you didn't love him, this wouldn't be a choice at all." She glances at the clock on the wall. "I'm already late for the lesson. Get dressed, take the SUV and get yourself to work. He's still your boss," she adds.

How could I forget?

So I get ready, forgo makeup, and drive my ass down to the office, even though I nearly vomit into a leftover Starbucks cup when my nerves start getting the best of me. All the fucking yoga bullshit breathing exercises in the world aren't helping.

Luckily when I get inside the building, the first thing Tiffany says to me is: "Will went out for lunch." Followed by: "Are you feeling better? You look a bit pale."

"Yes," I tell her, giving her a small smile as I walk past. "I'm fine."

"Hey, you made it," Alyssa says to me as I pass her

office. "You could have just taken the whole day off you know."

I shrug and keep walking, my heart rate returning to normal knowing I don't have to face Will yet. Once I sit down at my desk and start putting things in their place—I swear the weekend cleaners like to rearrange my desk for fun—I've convinced myself that I might not even talk to him today at all. Maybe I can stretch it out the whole week. All work, nothing else.

I go through my emails and my pulse skyrockets when I see one from Will this morning, but he's just asking where I am and if I'm coming in. Nothing more, nothing less.

And yet his concern makes me happy. Happy, deep, deep, deep in my heart. I can feel his worry through those few typed words, I can see the expression on his face—his lips pressed together, his furrowed brow, lined forehead—as he writes them out. That's how tied this man is to me. Even a sentence-long email brings my heart this golden kind of joy, like the sun rising on a cold, dark morning.

How could I go on without him? How could I call it off and continue working here, knowing what he does to me?

How could I work anywhere, existing in a world without Will?

Why would I want to?

And while I'm pondering those questions, I feel the mood shift in the office. I feel it shift like a cloud covering the sun.

I hear people walking toward me, the shuffle of dress pants, the creak of leather shoes, and my father's voice.

And then I stand up.

See Will.

Beautiful, gorgeous Will in a grey suit, skinny black tie.

Standing beside a beautiful, gorgeous Kim Novak-type woman.

That my father promptly introduces as Mona.

As if he wanted me and only me to see her.

I couldn't feel more awkward, more on the spot, more disappointed and crushed. Not necessarily in Will. I know he probably didn't go out for lunch with this woman on purpose, the same woman my father blatantly said he's setting him up with, or at least trying to.

But even so, it's a reminder of how fucked up things are. This woman represents the person that I should be in order for everything to work the way it should.

If I was Mona, there would be no issues.

But I'm not Mona, I'm not even close.

She's a nice woman and all, but as I give her a quick, half-hearted tour of the office, all I can think of is how different this woman is to me. This is who my father thinks Will should be with. Over time, will this be who Will thinks he should be with?

I'm making this more complicated for myself.

I know this.

But I can't help myself. I'm a slow-motion car crash.

When I'm done and Mona leaves, going off to talk to my father about something, I head back to my desk.

"Mr. McAlister wants to see you," Patty says to me.

"Okay," I tell her, my knees wanting to buckle. I lean against the partition for a moment.

She reaches over and puts her hand over mine, looking me dead in the eye. "Go easy on him. He means well."

Then she takes her hand away and goes back to work, like nothing happened.

Hmmm. Maybe Patty is more astute than I thought.

I take in a deep breath, as deep as it will go, and turn around and knock on Will's door.

"Come in," he says.

Here it goes.

I open the door and step inside.

He's sitting at his desk, a paperback copy of *Meditations in an Emergency* beside him.

But he's not staring at the book. He's staring right at me. He expected me.

I close the door behind me.

"Lock it," he tells me.

"Will," I say, shaking my head *no*.

Fuck. What am I doing already?

I watch as he swallows. He nods. "Okay. Look. I didn't know I was having lunch with her. Your father never told me. When I got to the restaurant—"

I raise my hand to stop him. "It's fine. Honestly."

"How could it be fine?" he asks, frowning.

"Because I know you. And I know you would never do that to me."

"Oh," he says. "Well, good. Then . . . how come you look like you're going to give me some really bad news?"

I rub my lips together, trying to gather strength, trying to keep it all together.

"Because I do have bad news."

His face falls, his shoulders stiffen. "What?" he asks.

I blurt it out like it's one long word, "I don't think we should see each other anymore."

He stares at me. Right at me. Right through me.

And I can see through him.

See the pain building behind his eyes.

The pain I'm causing.

"Jackie," he says slowly.

"It's not about Mona," I tell him. "It's not about anything other than me. I'm just . . ." I quickly rub my fingers between my brows, as if that's going to bring clarity. "I can't do it. I just can't do it. I'm sorry."

He eases out of his chair. "Can't do what?"

"This. Us."

He walks over to me, so slowly. For some reason right now he seems taller and bigger than ever before. "What about this and us?"

Why does he keep asking questions?

"It's too hard!" I cry out. "All of this is."

He stops, brow furrowing in tight confusion. "Which part? I'm sorry, you're going to have to spell it out to me because I'm not a damn mind reader. I'm not letting you come in here and say this fucking bullshit to me without an explanation. Got it?"

And boss-man Will comes out. Bad fucking timing.

"I tried to tell you at the hotel."

"You tried to tell me? When? When I told you I loved you and you didn't say anything? You just acted like it was some nice gesture on my behalf, like it was what I was supposed to say? No. Fuck that. I didn't have to say shit. I said it because it's true. I love you, Jackie."

His words don't lose their effect. I feel them in every part of me, like an IV drip, slowly working its way through my veins, making me scared and numb and alive all at once.

He goes on. "I also told you that I would keep fighting for you, for us, until you told me not to."

"Maybe I'm telling you not to," I say quietly.

Fuck, I don't even think I mean it.

"You could have told me then instead of leading me on. Instead of pulling away."

"I wasn't leading you on. I didn't know."

"And you know for sure now?!"

"Don't yell at me," I warn him.

"Maybe you need to be yelled at!" he fires back at me. "Maybe it's the only way to knock some sense into your head. To get how fucking serious this is. This isn't us fucking around anymore. It's not a damn game. You just don't get to quit when you feel like it. This is my heart here. Okay? My heart and yours."

"Why are you getting so angry?"

"Why am I getting so angry?" he roars and I feel his fury all the way to my toes. My god, there's no way everyone in the office isn't hearing this right now. "I'm angry because after all the shit that could be thrown our way, you're giving up now. Now, just when it's getting really fucking good."

"Will, I can't be with you!" I yell back.

"Why the fuck not?"

"Because it's too hard! Can't you see that? This, us, the job, my father, your business, everything. It's too much, it's not going to stand, it's not going to be worth it."

"Says who?" he practically growls. "Says who? You or me? Because I can decide what's worth it to me. You need to decide what's worth it to you."

He grabs the ends of his hair, tugs at it, his face growing red. "Fuck, Jackie. If you don't love me, then you have to tell me that. Right now. Let's hear it. Tell me you don't love me and if that's the case I'll stop yelling and leave you the fuck alone."

He's angry. He's so angry.

I've never seen him like this.

It scares me. Not in the way you'd think, not like Jeff scared me.

It scares me because I think I'm finally realizing how much he fucking cares. The damage I'm doing because I'm too afraid and damaged myself.

"Will..."

"Tell me," he says, voice shaking. "Please."

I don't know what to say.

He runs his hands over his face, shaking his head. "Damn it, kid, you're breaking my heart."

I am.

And I'm breaking mine.

I've got both of our hearts in my hands and I don't know what to do with them except shred them up into smaller pieces. It seems easier somehow, to do this, instead of letting them grow. The bigger our hearts get, the harder they are to control.

I close my eyes, trying to breathe. The room seems to spin.

And then Will is at my side, holding me up by my arms. He smells like cedar and fresh air and everything I want my life to be.

"Jackie," he says, lowering his voice, though I can still hear the tremor in it. "Jackie. I know you're scared. I know you don't need me. I know that you don't trust what's in your heart because it's let you down before. But you're..." he exhales, leaning in closer to me, "you're the only one who fills me. My heart. Makes me whole. And I get that you want to throw it all away for a million reasons, but I only need you to stay for one: because you love me."

He reaches up, brushing my hair behind my ear, cupping my face. I open my eyes to see him staring at me with so much hope that everything I thought I knew, every resolve I had inside to choose fear over love... it crumbles to dust.

And we stand among the ruins.

I close my eyes and let myself feel it.

Really fucking feel it.

Him.

His heart.

Us.

This thing that's bigger than anything.

Too big for my own heart to understand.

Until now.

I open my eyes, a tear spilling down my cheek. He's searching me like he's always searched, always looking past my darkest, blackest spots, searching for the me deep inside that knows she deserves love.

"Dream girl," he whispers. "Tell me I have your heart. I won't let it go, not for any moment, not for any reason. Tell me I have your heart and I'll keep it next to my own."

Damn it, Will.

The floodgates open.

The tears fall.

My heart twists and swells with the truth, growing bigger than my body can contain.

"I love you," I whisper to him.

And the moment those words leave my lips, the world shifts back into place. The darkness and the fear inside are banished. The war against myself has been fought and been won.

Love won.

As it always should.

I chose right.

Will stares at me, tentative waves of hope coming across his brow. "You do?"

Now that I know the emotion, now that I've named it, owned it, it comes clawing up my throat like an untamed animal fighting to get out.

I grab the back of his neck, his shirt, holding on tight. "I love you, Will. I love you, I love you. I'm so in love with you."

He looks like he's melting before my eyes.

Then he's kissing me, hard, grasping my face in desperation, pushing me back against the door.

"Am I dreaming?" he whispers against my lips. "If I am, don't wake me up. Please don't wake me up."

"You're not," I manage to say, smiling against his mouth. I'm almost laughing with joy.

The happiness comes in waves. Big ones, a set of swells, one by one knocking me off my feet, crashing over everything I've ever known. It's like I'm starting over, all my truth has been replaced by one and that's that I love Will.

"So what does this mean?" he asks me, pulling back, his nose brushing against mine. "Are you still done with me?"

His words are a kick to the gut. "I would have never been done with you, Will. You said I'm easy to love. So are you."

"Are you sure about that?"

"Yes," I smile softly, running my fingers down his beautiful face. "Yes, you're easy to love, once you admit what love is. Something that's bigger than both of us. Something you can't control. Something you can only let loose and let fly free."

"That sounds about right." He places his hand at my heart. "As long as it always comes back." He smiles, looking so at peace, more than I'd ever seen him

And so I hate to bring this up . . .

"What are we going to do now?" I ask him. "Beyond this moment? Beyond this office?"

"You know I don't want to hide this anymore. If you're all in, then everyone is going to know about it."

"But my father . . ."

"Screw Ted," he says. "I'm sorry, but after that stunt he pulled today . . . sometimes I think your father is more of a child than you ever were. He's growing old and just projecting his shit on you."

"So what are we going to do?"

"I'll tell you what we're going to," he says. He straightens up and grabs my hand, pulling open the door.

CHAPTER TWENTY

Jackie

JUST AS I PREDICTED, EVERY SINGLE HEAD IN THE office swivels our way, including Alyssa and Tiffany who are hanging around my desk and eating popcorn.

Yes. Literally eating popcorn out of a microwavable bag.

Even Patty has a palm full, popping a piece in her mouth as she watches us go past.

I try and give them a disapproving look, but I'm not sure it works, since half of me is still giddy from my revelation and the other half is scared shitless over what Will is about to do.

He leads me right over to my father's office—*Ted Phillips, President* in big shiny letters on the door, reminding us who he is to both of us—and raps on it.

"Come in," my father says.

Will squeezes my hand but wastes no time in opening the door, ushering us both inside.

My father doesn't look up until the door closes shut,

and even then he seems disinterested.

"What's going on?' he asks, peering over his glasses. "Fighting over your workload?"

"Ted," Will says. "I have to speak to you about something."

My father leans back in his chair, a bemused smile on his lips as he looks between the two of us.

Shit. I don't know what that smile means.

"Oh really? Do I get three guesses?"

Will and I exchange a glance. "Uh," Will stammers.

"Is it about how they're popping popcorn out there and we have a 'no making popcorn, seafood, or hardboiled eggs' rule in the breakroom because the stink permeates the whole office?" he asks. "Or is it about Casey using the photocopier to make copies of his dick. I found a stack of them under Tiffany's desk."

"Ew," I say.

"Or," he goes on, "is it about the fact that you're screwing my daughter?"

I jolt. I never thought I'd hear those words coming out of my father's mouth.

"Ted," Will says.

"Look, Will," my father says, pressing on. "I don't know if you think I'm senile or what. Maybe I've been gone so often that you don't think I'm paying attention. But of course I'm paying attention. That's my fucking job, isn't it? And do you know what your fucking job is?"

"I'm not really sure I have a job at the moment," Will admits.

"That might be true," he says. He looks at me for a moment, like he's going to say something but doesn't. "Anyway. Did I guess right? I know the popcorn and the dick copies are right."

Will exhales heavily through his nose. "You're close. Ted, I know you don't want to think about this, let alone hear this but the truth is . . . I'm in love with Jackie."

I can't help the smile on my face, even when my dad looks to me for confirmation.

"Is this true Jackie?" he asks, gesturing to Will with his pen. "This old man here loves you and you're okay with that?"

I nod, trying to find the words. "I know you think this is something it's not, but it's true. We didn't . . . I didn't plan on it, it's just that . . ."

"That Will is a wonderful guy and you couldn't help yourself?" my father asks wryly. Then he sighs, tapping his pen along the desk. "To be honest with you, I admit it makes me feel a bit better to know that there's actually something real going on here."

"How long have you known?" Will asks.

He shrugs. "Probably from the start. You can tell a lot from body language you know, you learn to pick up on that shit when you get old."

"Then why the hell didn't you say anything? And why pull that shit today with Mona?"

"Well I had to know, Will, what your actual intentions were. You can't expect me to just be okay with the fact that you're screwing my little girl, who is sixteen years younger than you. Who was around, just a teenager, when you were with your wife."

"Dad, you're making it weird," I warn him.

"Because it is weird. Damn weird. Maybe not for you two lovebirds, but it is for me. Jesus. Talk about keeping the business in the family. Anyway, I couldn't quite figure it out, Will, if you were just trying to get over Sasha, if you were discovering the fountain of youth, or you actually cared about Jackie."

"And?" Will asks.

"Now I know the truth. You looked like you wanted to kill me today, Will. Hell, you were ready to murder me on Friday night. That's all I really needed to know, that you weren't just using my daughter to get laid, and I needed to know that Jackie wasn't using you."

"Why would I use him?"

"Because he's rich, young lady. Handsome and smart. And you two have been working awfully close together at a time when you're both lonely. I know how it goes."

"So . . ." Will says cautiously. "You're okay with this? Because I thought you were going to send me back to LA with broken bones."

"I was going to," he says. "I changed my mind."

A change of heart, just like that?

"Wait," I say slowly. "You talked to mom, didn't you?"

The corner of my father's mouth quirked up. "Maybe. The point is, I'm glad you both had the balls to finally tell me. And, when it comes down to it, now that I know it's genuine, well, I don't hate it. It's weird. But I don't hate it. Jackie, I at least know you're in good hands. And Will, well . . . I just feel sorry for you."

"Hey!" I cry out.

"But it's okay," my father goes on. "Because Will can be a little too perfect sometimes. It's good to know he's with someone who will give him a hard time, possibly for the rest of his life."

Will is trying not to get ahead of himself but I know that smile. "Let me get this straight. This is okay? Nothing else changes? Not her job, not my role? Not you and I?"

"Okay, well now you are getting ahead of yourself here," my father says. "Things will change. Jackie, you're free to stay his assistant if you want. I don't see a problem with it as long as you keep working. But, please . . . I don't want anyone here to feel pressured, but I'm not sure I like the idea of you living at home for much longer. If I have to keep seeing Will after work, that's really going to put a damper on things. I can only stand the guy so much."

"We'll figure something out," Will says.

"Oh, and you might want to tell the minions outside," he says, jerking his thumb at the door. "I'm pretty sure there have been office pools over this for the last few months."

Damn that Alyssa.

"On it," Will says, sounding strangely determined.

He opens the door and heads out of the office to the middle of main room where the picnic tables are.

I take a look at my father, giving him a grateful smile, and then step outside his office to figure out what Will has planned.

Will is climbing up onto the top of the picnic tables just as my father comes up, standing beside me.

"What is he doing?" my father asks under his breath.

"I have no idea," I tell him.

"Everyone! Can I have your attention please," Will calls out so that everyone is staring at him. Which was totally unnecessary because everyone already was staring at him. It's hard not to notice when a six foot two linebacker of a man in an Armani suit stands up on a table in your office. Good thing we have very high ceilings.

"This is your doing, Jackie-O," my father whispers to me. "He was normal before he ever met you."

I can only beam, the smile splitting my face as I watch him.

"Why do I stand up here?" Will projects, looking

around at everyone.

"Is he doing the scene from Dead Poets Society?" my father asks.

"I thought it was from Jerry McGuire."

"I stand up here," Will goes on, "because I have something to say. As many of you know I've had a pretty shitty go the last couple of years. My wife left me, pregnant with another man's baby. I still had to work with her as we figured out the divorce. You can imagine it wasn't easy. It was hell. Enough hell, for the both of us, that I eventually came up here."

"You think Sasha is going to hear about this?" I ask my dad.

"Probably," he says. Then a sneaky grin comes across his face. He's enjoying this way too much.

"Here to the land of rain and cloud and astronomical housing prices and endless yoga-pant attire. Where each and every one of you embraced me. Right from the start. You brought the sunshine I had so missed from LA back into my life."

A round of *awwww*s goes up from where Alyssa, Tiffany, and Patty are gathered.

"And it was with your kindness and Canadian hospitality and good old-fashioned passive aggressiveness that I really started to feel at home again." He pauses and waves his arm across the office to me. "And then I met my assistant. And she blew you all out of the water."

A few groans sound out from the room.

"Sorry, guys and gals, but just look at her. Look at this kind and beautiful Jackie Phillips as she stands there beside her father, a good man who is working far too hard for the better of everyone here. Those two are the most important people in the world to me, and I'm honored to not only still call Jackie my assistant but Ted my friend and partner," he pauses, "even now, especially now, after Ted found out that I'm sleeping with his daughter."

An audible gasp flows across the room.

I face palm.

Pretty sure my father is still grinning.

"Yes, that's right. Whether you thought you imagined it or not, I have been bossing Jackie around outside of work for a while now. And now, it's all out in the open. Where it belongs. The relationship part, not the . . . it doesn't matter. I just wanted to clear the air. Make sure there are no more secrets." He waves his hand at me. "Jackie, come up here."

"I would rather not," I mutter under my breath.

I look at my father who rolls his eyes. "Fucking crazy kids is what you are."

"Jack-ie! Jack-ie! Jack-ie!" Alyssa and Tiffany start chanting, banging their fists on the desk until the keyboards and pencil holders are jumping.

"You're dead to me," I yell at them as I do a strange walk of shame to the middle of the office, stopping at the base of the picnic tables.

Will holds his hand out for me. "Are you all in?" he asks.

This man, this man, this man.

What a stupid question.

"I'm all in," I tell him, grinning at him stupidly as I put my hand in his.

He hauls me up to the table, careful not to knock over the laptops and monitors, and then gives me a huge kiss in front of everyone. A kiss that takes my breath away, takes us away, just for a moment, to a place where we aren't on display in front of everyone we work with.

When Alyssa and Tiffany become my cheerleading

squad and start hooting and hollering though, everyone else starts to clap in support. Or even if they don't support it, it's at least a nice break from the doldrums of work.

"My, that was *yar*," I tell him as we break apart, placing my hand on his chest, staring up into his eyes.

"That's not how that word works," he tells me, looking extra smug.

"Then it was . . . magical."

"Ty says magic doesn't exist."

Ty. My son is going to be overjoyed at all of this. As if my heart couldn't feel any fuller. He's going to have a man in his life that he loves, that loves him.

"Ty might say that, but I know the truth," I tell him, grabbing his shirt collar. "You're magic, Will McAlister. My Prince Charming and Fairy Godmother all rolled into one."

"I'm just a man who knows what he wants," he says, cupping my face. "And Dream Girl, it's you."

He kisses me again, and if people are cheering I don't hear it.

I just hear my heartbeat.

Feel his lips.

And know the war is over.

EPILOGUE

A year later

Jackie

"Mom," Ty says, coming into the kitchen. "Is Will going to wear his Batman costume to the wedding?"

I close the dishwasher, hitting the *on* button. It starts so quietly I feel like I'm in an ad for Maytag or something. Everything about this place makes me feel like I'm in ad in a luxury magazine. I can never get quite over it.

"No, sweetie," I tell him, turning around. "He's going to wear a tuxedo."

"Batman is usually in a tuxedo. He wore one in The Dark Knight Rises."

I raise my brow. "Who let you watch that movie?"

"Will," he says. "Because he's Batman."

I roll my eyes. "Well Will shouldn't let you watch those movies, you know the rules."

"But Will is always breaking the rules."

I sigh. That he is.

I watch as Ty runs out to the terrace to play with the dogs, but now we've got extra high railings so that Ty can't get over them.

There's been a few changes to Will's place in the last while.

Especially now that it's *our* place.

About five months after Will and I officially got together, Ty and I moved into Will's lavish apartment. Originally I was looking to live in a basement suite somewhere, but even with my salary at Mad Men (I'm still Will's assistant believe it or not, but that's not all I do) and the option money from Warner Brothers (more on that later), making ends meet wasn't easy.

Naturally, both Will and my parents wanted to help out, but me being me, I wanted to do it on my own.

I'm a stubborn little bitch.

Until Will asked me to move in.

I knew he would eventually, but he was waiting until it felt right to me. I'm not sure how he could tell but he was right.

And living here felt more than right.

Then a month after that, he proposed.

Got down on one knee on Christmas morning at my parent's house where everyone was gathered and opened up that blue Tiffany's box with the most gorgeous ring you ever saw.

Underneath the band there were two words inscribed: "All in."

And we are all in.

The wedding is next month, which means I'm a barrel of nerves. Will, as usual, is cool as a cucumber. He's already been married before so he knows the ropes, plus he's the groom and he doesn't have to do much more than look pretty. And of course he's going to look pretty in that tux of his.

But for me? This is my fairy-tale come true. Will is the fairy-tale I never knew I needed to happen. When I was a teenager, the idea of Prince Charming was a pipe dream. When I was with Jeff, I learned the hard way that there were no happy endings. I thought that life was a straight-line, fixed on the path you chose and once you chose it, there were no detours, no turning back.

It's not that at all. You can change direction anytime you want. You can go forward, backward or stay still. You can do anything you want because you're in the driver's seat, controlling this ride. And yes, you have permission to grow.

What happened to me was awful. It was seven long years of abuse, not just physical but emotional. The emotional part is the one that really wears you down, gets under your skin, into your bones. It tells you you're not worth anything and that you're stuck in the life you chose for yourself. No way out.

But no one is stuck. Everyone can get out. It took me a long time to realize that, but I'm glad I did when I did.

And I'm glad that when I finally opened my eyes, not only in finding Will but finding myself, that I took that chance. I changed direction. I let myself be the person I knew I wanted to be, but was always too afraid to try.

Of course I can't take all the credit for my good fortune. It was Will who sent my half-finished script to Warner Brothers. I'm sure he would have encouraged me to do so at some point, but who knows if I would have followed through. It was just another thing I didn't think I needed or deserved.

But Michelle Thompson at Warner Brothers fell in love

with the script. Or at least the concept. They paid me a nice amount for the option rights to the completed screenplay. Now they've got other writers working on it, trying to make it as good as it can be. I still have a lot to learn about the craft, and even then it's not a guarantee that the movie will actually get off the ground.

It doesn't matter though. I feel like my life is off to a running start.

And that's not all.

Of course, the latest development is something I've been keeping very close to my chest. Very close.

It was a surprise. A shock, actually.

Where there's a will there's a way.

Will

"Hey Dream Girl," I say to Jackie as I walk into the apartment. "Hey guys."

It's funny how something so simple can become the best part of your day. For me, turning the key and coming inside is like being born all over again.

Not only do Sprocket and Joan of Bark come to greet me with their tails wagging, but Ty does too, flying up into my arms. And, as usual, behind them all, is Jackie.

Usually with a glass of wine in hand for her and an old-fashioned for me. The sweetest, sauciest smile on her face.

Jackie is still working at Mad Men of course, assisting me when she's not working on her screenplays, but she's only there a few days a week, and only in the mornings. What can I say? I don't really need that much extra help in the end, plus this means she gets to spend more time with Ty, picking him up from school, which is still all the way down by her parent's place. We could have put him in another school closer to us but he likes it there, and this way he gets to see his grandparents more often.

Which is extremely handy when I like to take Jackie away for date nights and weekends. It doesn't matter one bit that we live together or we're getting married next month, I know that you have to work to keep the love alive. I spend as much time as I can with Jackie, just the two of us, making sure we're getting all we need from each other. We might have Ty, especially as I'll be officially adopting him soon, but there's a world out there for just the two of us that's borderline sacred and I'll fight to keep it that way.

"How was work?" she asks me, handing me my drink.

I kiss Ty on the cheek and set him back down on the ground with an *oof*. The boy is getting heavier by the day.

He runs over to the couch and flops down on it, back to watching whatever show he's addicted to now on Netflix. I have been encouraging him to draw lately, but like most boys here he's more hung up on hockey. I still have my hopes though, that he might become an award-winning animator one day.

"Work was work," I tell her, kissing her softly on the lips, taking a moment to take her all in. I smile. "I think Patty has a boyfriend because she's getting all these mysterious phone calls."

"I know, Tiffany told me," she says. "I'm not sure it's much of a secret." A strange look comes across face, her lips twisting impishly.

"What is it?" I ask. "Don't tell me you have a secret boyfriend too."

"No," she says softly, glancing at Ty then back to me.

"But I do have a secret."

I cock my head, studying her. This woman surprises me more and more each day. "Can you tell me the secret?"

She nods. "I can. But you won't believe it."

"Okay..."

She hesitates then grabs my hand, leading me over to the bedroom. "You better sit down," she says, closing the door behind her halfway.

"Is this a bad secret or a sexy secret?"

"It's neither."

Now I'm really confused. And a bit worried. I put my drink on the dresser, sit down at the edge of the bed and fold my hands in my lap, looking up at her expectantly. "Okay. Lay it on me, kid."

She grins at that and takes in a deep breath. She's almost shaking but at least the news is good.

I think.

"Will..." she says slowly. "I went to the doctor's this morning. I haven't been feeling well the last three weeks and I wasn't sure why. It sure felt familiar but... anyway. Here it goes... and please don't freak out... but... I'm pregnant."

Oh no. Oh god. Oh fuck.

I'm going to fucking die.

"It's yours," she says quickly, putting her hand on my shoulder to make sure I don't keel over. My heart rate barely slows, even though I'm beyond relieved. "It's one hundred percent yours. I took a few pregnancy tests and they were all positive. I didn't think that was possible so I went to the doctors and they tested me twice. I explained that you had a vasectomy but they told me—"

"One in a thousand chance," I say absently, unable to absorb any of this.

"Yeah. Something like that. And I know you trust me because you damn well know I've been faithful to you, but just in case, we have a paternity test all ready to go."

I wave that away. I don't need that at all. I trust her completely.

It's just . . .

I slowly fall sideways onto the bed, my face pressed into the cool duvet.

This can't be happening.

It can't.

Life just isn't *that* good to you.

Or maybe it is, after it fucks around with you for a bit.

"Are you happy?" Jackie asks quietly.

"Am I happy? Jackie. I'm in shock. I am in . . . how is it possible?"

"Well you fuck me a lot and we don't use protection and apparently vasectomies aren't the answer to everything. That's how it's possible."

"Oh my god," I say softly as it all hits me. I straighten back up. "Jesus. Jackie, are *you* happy?"

She beams at me, her face absolutely glowing. "Of course I am. Obviously it wasn't planned but Will . . . this is us. This is our baby. This is . . . I never realized I wanted something so bad until I had it. I never even entertained the idea but now that it's happening . . . it's a dream."

I shake my head. I feel like it's going to explode.

The joy inside, the shock, the awe, it's indescribable.

"I'm going to be a father . . ."

"You're already a father to Ty. But now he's going to be a brother."

"Holy . . ." I stare at her, my woman, my beautiful dream girl who is now going to be the mother of my child. I'm unable to form words.

There's just love.

Love and gratefulness, so much gratefulness.

"Oh, come here," I tell her, grabbing her arm and pulling her into me. I run my hands through her hair, kiss her chin, her cheek, her lips. "You . . . Jackie. Me and you. And Ty. And now the baby. This is everything."

"We're all in."

I grin at her, a tear rolling down my cheek, my heart bursting again and again and again.

"We're all in."

THE END

ACKNOWLEDGEMENTS

This book came about in a number of ways. One is that I've always wanted to write a very gentlemanly hero that's full of manners, class and charm – but goes after what he wants with no games and definitely knows how to treat a woman in the bedroom.

My husband, Scott, definitely fits that bill. He's got an old soul in him and Will is based a LOT on him (hope he doesn't read this because it would embarrass the crap out of him ha ha).

He's also based on Jon Hamm. Well, at least he was the initial inspiration. I was flying to Kauai, supposed to be finishing up my last book (Dirty Souls), and my husband started watching a movie. I can't NOT watch a film that's playing beside me. It doesn't matter if I can't hear it, I will watch it (and, really, the best films don't require sound for you to understand it). And, well, it wasn't the best film (I watched it on the return flight with sound on), but damn did it reignite my love for Jon Hamm. The film was just a silly action comedy where Hamm plays a spy but it was enough for the bells to go off in my head and think I need to write a book about him.

Then came Jackie. Jackie is based loosely on a girl I knew back in high school and I thought it would be a lovely Cinderella story to combine her with the older, gentlemanly Will.

Plus, I decided to set Before I Ever Met You in my hometown of Vancouver, BC. Despite all my novels set all over the world, I had never set one in my beautiful city where I was born and raised. It was a lot of fun to show Vancouver love for once (okay apparently that's not true, Vancouver did have roles to play in Where Sea Meets Sky and Love, in English…but you get what I mean).

Enough about my inspiration. I need to thank some people, mainly my beta readers Nina Decker, Mary Ruth Baloy and Pavlina Michou for your encouragement and feedback. Sandra Cortez for talking me off ledges. All the anti-heroes for being so wonderfully gung-ho about this last minute book. Hang Le for her gorgeous cover and Laura Helseth for her edits that always make me laugh. Nina Bocci for making sure the book gets seen and all my author friends and readers who help me make my dreams possible every day.

Read on for a few of Will's drink recipes!

Will McAlister's Bar Cart

Will's Smokey Old-Fashioned

1 ½ ounces of smoked bourbon (or Makers Mark)
Dash of bitters
Luxardo cherries and orange slices
A sugar cube
An ounce of filtered water (or club soda)
Muddle the fruit and stir well to dissolve the sugar
Add ice cubes

Will's All-In Ceasar

2 ounces of premium pepper vodka (lemon vodka also works)
4-6 ounces of Mott's Clamato Juice
A dash of Frank's Red Hot sauce (adjust to your spicy levels)
A splash of olive or pickle juice (from the jar)
A teaspoon of Worcestershire sauce
A teaspoon of HP Sauce
Squeeze of lime
Salt and Pepper to taste
A stick of pickled asparagus and celery for garnish (add bacon if you're feeling adventurous)
Don't forget to put celery salt on the rim!

CPSIA information can be obtained
at www.ICGtesting.com
Printed in the USA
LVHW04s0902191018
594127LV00001B/52/P